Trouble at Zero Hour

The Complete Zero Hour Trilogy

Rob Lofthouse was born in Twickenham and joined his local county infantry regiment (1 PWRR) straight from school at the age of sixteen. After serving twenty years in locations such as Poland, Germany, Kenya, Canada, the Falkland Islands, Iraq, Northern Ireland and Kosovo, he retired in the rank of Sergeant. He now works as a defence consultant and lives in Portsmouth with his wife and three children.

Also by Rob Lofthouse

A Cold Night in June
Bazooka Town

Trouble at Zero Hour

The Complete Zero Hour Trilogy

Rob Lofthouse

Quercus

First published in Great Britain in 2016
This paperback edition published in 2017

Quercus Publishing Ltd
Carmelite House
50 Victoria Embankment
London EC4Y 0DZ

An Hachette UK company

A CIP catalogue record for this book is available from the British Library

PB ISBN 9781786482549
EBOOK ISBN 9781784299347

10 9 8 7 6 5 4 3 2 1

Typeset by Jouve (UK), Milton Keynes

Printed and bound in Great Britain by Clays Ltd, St Ives plc

CONTENTS

THIS TRILOGY IS DEDICATED TO THOSE WHOM,

REGARDLESS OF NATIONALITY,

ENDURED, SUFFERED, AND YET

PREVAILED DURING THOSE LONG

YEARS OF DARKNESS

1939-1945

Deep Trouble

PROLOGUE
Glider Landing

00.01 hrs, 6 June 1944, somewhere over the Normandy coastline

The flight so far had been uneventful, but I was slowly losing faith in the overloaded kite we were all crammed into. The Horsa glider bucked and jerked left and right, as if we were being dragged through the night sky by a large energetic child. My stomach heaved and I silently cursed the airsickness tablets they had given us that were no good to man or beast. The airframe creaked and moaned with all the forces imposed on it. With every creak of timber and aluminium, I waited for the glider to disintegrate. It looked great sat in the hangar back at RAF Tarrant Rushton in Dorset. It even looked a pretty awesome concept on the sketches we were shown, but it dodged and weaved so much as it was dragged through the sky by the Halifax bomber out front, I was worried when we released ourselves from its umbilical, we would plummet to the ground far below with the elegance and grace of a house brick.

Sleep seemed impossible, yet some of the boys managed it. How on earth could they sleep at a time like this? Never mind crashing at any moment, we still had the Germans to contend with. As I thought about our daring plan, the more absurd it became. We were to land our gliders next to a canal bridge and jump out and capture it in the vain hope Jerry would be scratching his arse in bed while we did it. Maybe the most absurd plans during war were the most successful. I glanced around the dim interior of the glider; most just sat there, eyes open, deep in their own thoughts. Boots tapping and knees bouncing – with nerves no doubt. I was not any better. I couldn't read their facial expressions. The camouflage cream was smeared on heavily, and I could just make out the moustaches on some of them.

Conversation was almost impossible. The glider may have been without an engine, but the air outside screamed past with a horrendous din. In the confined space it was rather warm. I was sweating like a beast in all my gear. Cam cream and sweat was causing my eyes to sting. I made a fruitless attempt to ease the stinging with my sleeve. My helmet was firmly in place, crude strips of green material attached to break up its outline. Heavy hobnailed combat boots were standard issue. Thick woollen socks made them as comfortable as they were going to be. Canvas gaiters were strapped around the tops of the boots, more for decoration than anything else, since I always ended up with wet feet. My combat trousers were rough, heavy and brown, held up with braces. My underwear was a basic affair, light shorts with an undershirt. I wore my heavy Denison smock over the top, which weighed a ton with everything crammed into the pockets. Equipment was basic, given the limited space we had in the glider. A canvas belt, shoulder straps, plus two large ammunition pouches on the front. Worn high on my back, I had a small canvas backpack, which only really had room for food but was filled with more equipment required for the mission, including wire cutters and raincoat. No luxuries, we just didn't have the room. Digging into the base of my back was my entrenching tool, a small lightweight shovel-cum-pickaxe. We all had one, so if we were static for a considerable period of time, we had the means of digging in to protect us from artillery fire and the like.

My personal weapon was a Bren light machine gun. A beast of a weapon. Its only real drawback was that it could be rather cumbersome, especially when moving around in confined spaces such as buildings. Its large curved thirty-round magazine protruded from the top, feeding it with .303 calibre rounds. The .303 could put an elephant down, no problem, let alone a man. I had an extra five magazines in my pouches, and every non-gunner in the platoon carried another four magazines for the gunners. The company commander, Major Anthony Hibbert, wanted maximum firepower, but we also had to be mindful of our weight for the glider. To top off our combat loads, each man had up to nine grenades, since they were excellent at dealing with houses and stubborn Jerries in trenches, really taking the fight out of them. Each platoon also had a two-inch mortar, which the serjeant controlled. For good measure, the riflemen in the platoon also had to carry two mortar bombs each. They carried all the extra ammunition in canvas sacks, enabling them to drop it off at positions when required. Despite my reservations, I was quietly confident we would give Jerry a proper good hiding, should they contest what we had in mind.

Strapped to a wall of the glider, I tried to adjust myself. I accidentally kicked a shin belonging to my platoon serjeant, Sean Wardle. In a faint glow of red torchlight I could make out his glare at me. It was a menacing, murderous glare, the red glow and his heavily cam-creamed face making him look all the more sinister. I smiled sheepishly and mouthed an apology, trying my hardest to break free of his gaze. Sean was a firm but fair man. His method of leadership was rather brash, but he would take time to show you how he wanted stuff done. If you put your hand up and admitted you didn't understand or had forgotten what he wanted you to do, that was fine; he would show you again. I never pretended to be the best soldier, since there were plenty of men more worthy of that title, but if I tried to cuff it, and everything then went tits up, he would be on my case like you wouldn't believe. Very rarely did he drink with me or the other lads in my section of the platoon. It wasn't because he didn't feel us worthy of his company, he just had enough on his plate. He wasn't on all the lads' Christmas-card lists either, but as far as I was concerned, it was a fair trade-off.

Sean returned his gaze to a torchlight-illuminated map in the hands of our platoon commander, Lieutenant Bertie Young, who was sitting next to him. Young was no clown; very intelligent, very fit and a good soldier. He was daring and reckless in equal measure. His devil-may-care attitude to life was rather fun but bloody tiring. He endeavoured to have his platoon doing the risky parts of any exercise, the toughest of the assignments dished out by Major Hibbert. Consequently, our level of physical fitness as a platoon was very high. Where Young got his energy from was anyone's guess. Sean spent most of his time keeping him out of trouble.

Sitting just out of the glow of Young's torch was my section commander, Corporal Terry Thomson. Terry was pretty much cut from the same cloth as Sean. They were long-term friends, but when it came to operations like this, you could see the professional boundary between corporal and serjeant. Like Sean, Terry was a family man, but had a more maverick streak. He had the same leadership style as Sean, but the rogue mindset of Young, a dangerous combination, some might say. But as far as I was concerned, Terry was a good guy to have in your corner.

Watching the three of them try and converse above the awesome din of the flight became a rather pleasant distraction. Young would shout like a madman, Sean and Terry nodding. Serjeant and corporal both knew what was required; Major Hibbert insisted we all did. Our rehearsals for tonight had been detailed, to say the least. Things could change in the blink of an eye, so even the newest private soldier had to understand clearly what the mission was, come what may.

My focus on their discussion was broken when the glider began to bob and weave heavily again. Another flicker of light caught my attention. In the glow of a match I could make out the heavily cam-smeared profile of Tony Winman. He was the same age as myself, twenty-three, and hailed from Southampton. How on earth he had managed to end up in the Oxfordshire and Buckinghamshire Light Infantry, God only knows. The story I heard was he moved up to St Albans at the start of the war, since Southampton was getting hammered by the Luftwaffe. St Albans was a safer bet for his mother and sister too. He had only joined the Ox and Bucks about a year ago, and was still very much one of the new boys.

Something thick and heavy clashed against the right side of my helmet, making me jump and feel rather agitated. The solid mass happened to be the dozing head of Frank Williams. This guy could sleep on a chicken's lip. A London boy, he was a bull of a man. But despite his intimidating frame, he was a wonderful guy, the platoon clown. His antics in and out of barracks would drive Sean to despair sometimes, which would do nothing more than fuel Frank's thirst for larking about. Without ceremony, I shoved Frank's head away from mine, and his bonce crashed into Dougie Chambers, on the other side of him. Even over the din, I could make out Dougie's curses. Frank emerged from his slumber. Sean slowly shook his head. Frank gave an exaggerated yawn and stretched his arms wide, pinning me and Dougie against the wall. Frank flinched as Dougie jabbed at his midsection. I just sat there, waiting for it all to subside, Frank's huge arm across my chest. Besides, I couldn't get a good jab in. Off to my left, towards the tail of the glider, I noticed Lance Corporal Bobby Carrol dozing away. Second-in-command of my section, he was also company fitness instructor. Frank lit a cigarette, and proceeded to blow smoke rings at those he knew were non-smokers. I noticed Sean and Young look at each other, shaking their heads and rolling their eyes.

A barely audible shout came from the cockpit: 'Action stations!' This was passed down the aircraft, and the professional in all of us came to the surface. Cigarettes were extinguished, torches put out, maps put away, dozing soldiers shoved awake. I got myself sorted, ensuring my helmet was correctly fitted, my seat harness secure, Bren stowed muzzle up between my knees. My stomach began doing somersaults; clammy hands gripped the gun. I couldn't help myself, but my left knee was bouncing up and down like crazy. I fought hard to prevent it, peering around at the other faces in the gloom. Some had bouncing knees too. We were really doing this. We were at the tip of the spear for the invasion of Europe. The Germans had had things their way for the last five years, and we were now back to tear things up and kick some arse. I found myself thinking of Mum and Daniel, my younger brother by two years. I knew Mum wasn't too pleased about me joining up. Daniel was now a cripple. He had been at Dunkirk and lost a leg in a Stuka attack while he was waiting on the beach to board a ship. Like him, I felt I had to do my part, like my dad had in a mud-smeared shit hole called Passchendaele all those years ago. I did not regret my decision; I just wanted to get on with it. Some of those around me had combat experience already, but for the majority this was about to become a whole new adventure.

My stomach lurched into my throat as the glider was released from its tow rope. The sudden drop in altitude caused us all to momentarily leave our seats. Good job we had harnesses on, since some of us would have got a face full of wood from the roof of the aircraft. We were coming down hard and fast. Through small portholes in the side of the glider, a rare glint of moonlight revealed a few features of the Normandy fields below. The aircraft bucked and swooped, left and right. I felt like I was on a fair-ground ride. Every time my stomach settled, we would drop suddenly again. I was not looking forward to the landing, if we were going to do it at this speed. As we got lower, I could just make out the tops of trees whipping past. They got thicker and darker as we descended further. This was going to be one rough landing. I caught a sudden glimpse of moonlight reflecting off what appeared to be water, before yet more trees whipped past. I glanced over at Sean. He didn't appear to be enjoying the experience either, but he did manage to give me the thumbs up.

'Brace!' came another shout from up front. We hit the ground big time. The impact of the landing took all my breath from me. My testicles felt like they were in my ammunition pouches. Aluminium buckled all around, screaming under the sheer velocity of the landing, timber creaking and splintering as the aircraft began to disintegrate. Amid the cacophony of our crash landing, the profanity coming from my fellow passengers was biblical to say the least. I had a few choice words for those who had dreamed up this absurd idea, and maybe a few more for the aircraft's inventors. A sudden rush of cold night air hit me as the tail of the glider gave up its fight to cling on, cartwheeling out of sight. We were going to die before it had even begun. Then the whole experience thundered to a complete stop, metal and wood groaning.

All was quiet in what was left of our glider. I was suddenly overwhelmed by fatigue, and as Mistress Sleep seduced me, I could faintly hear a foreign voice outside.

'*Fallschirmjäger! Fallschirmjäger!*'

A rough hand whizzed across my face in the darkness.

1
Ham and Jam

Fallschirmjäger. I had first heard the word a few hours earlier during Major Hibbert's mission briefing at RAF Tarrant Rushton. I tried to remember what it meant. Paratroopers, that was it. And that was us: D Company, 2nd Battalion, the Oxfordshire and Buckinghamshire Light Infantry. Although the battalion was a glider force, we were considered paratroopers, since it was intended that we work alongside parachute troops, a newish breed of soldier in Britain based on Hitler's very successful, almost legendary airborne forces.

I'd joined up at a recruiting point in High Wycombe train station. I had no clue how many battalions were in the regiment, but 2nd Battalion hadn't been my first inclination. However, I'd been impressed that, unusually, membership of the battalion was voluntary due to the rugged nature of its envisaged jobs. They'd wanted the fittest and toughest of the bunch. You couldn't join if you had ever suffered from malaria, which meant the battalion was a little short of boots on the ground as it had undertaken tours of the Far East and North Africa, sufferers being reallocated to non-airborne battalions in the regiment.

When people asked me why I'd enlisted I'd tell them about my brother Daniel losing a leg at Dunkirk and the injuries sustained by my father at Passchendaele during the Great War. But, in truth, I think it was a sense of adventure that prompted me to join up as much as anything. My job at the brewery had been fine, but my life had been little more than drinking and working. A beaming, very smart, clean-shaven but scarred recruiting serjeant loaded with medals had signed me up and told me that the first lesson of soldiering in the regiment was they spelt sergeant with a 'j'.

It was a different serjeant with a 'j' who led us into the hangar at RAF Tarrant Rushton one night almost two years later when our training was almost complete. The hangar was huge, stuffed with six Halifax bombers and six Horsa gliders. We were familiar with the machines having trained on them at Bulford in Wiltshire, on the edge of Salisbury Plain. As almost two hundred of us shuffled our way inside, skirting the tail of a Halifax, and saw Major Hibbert, Captain Brettle and Company Serjeant Major Jenkins, together with all the platoon commanders and other serjeants, it became clear that this was to be no ordinary operation. It was something big. The one we'd known was coming. The one we'd sensed in the tension around us. Getting the battalion down into Dorset had been a mission. The volume of military traffic on the roads between Bulford and Tarrant Rushton had been immense. And it hadn't just been British units caught up in the melee of convoys, we'd encountered American and Canadian traffic control parties at road junctions all the way down. We were on the cusp of one hell of a job, speculation was rife but facts had been scarce.

The officers stood in a three-sided square around an area of dirt and grass, the odd sketch and blown-up photographs taken from the air. Low whistles could be heard coming from people's lips as we surrounded the huge model on the hangar floor. 'Fuckin 'ell,' Frank Williams murmured, ever the diplomat. Level-headed Dougie Chambers looked at him in admonishment.

'Welcome, gentlemen,' Major Hibbert bellowed. 'Serjeant Major, please put them in their order of march. Thank you.'

It took a while for Jenkins to line us up in front of the model. The platoon commanders and other serjeants then joined us on the floor, leaving Hibbert and Brettle standing before everyone. A deathly silence descended. You could have heard a mouse fart in that hangar.

'Thank you, Serjeant Major,' Hibbert began. 'Gentlemen, we have all been training long and hard for this opportunity, and I intend not to keep you waiting any longer. Tonight we are bound for Normandy in northern France. We will be leading the way, the very first unit to kick in the door of Hitler's supposed Fortress Europe.' He smiled, seeming to enjoy releasing the bombshell. 'Before we go into the pleasantries, I must ensure housekeeping rules are in place. First of all, Serjeant Major, should anyone be seen or heard entering this hangar while my orders are in progress, would you be so kind as to remove the name cards from the model. Any such person is also to be held here until after our departure tonight. Understood?'

Jenkins nodded as Hibbert swivelled to face the model sideways on.

I'd taken a chance to study the details of the model for the first time. It was the biggest model I had ever seen. It was actually two models of equal size, set next to each other. The one on the left showed our primary target area, the other showed nearby geography. It was the Normandy coastline, that much was clear, and the clustering of name cards on the left-hand side gave away our target area. The towns of Caen and Ranville had been labelled, as had a beach called 'Sword', with an arrow indicating which way was north. The detail was very impressive; even the layout of fields was shown, the tiny hedgerows separating them looked just like the real thing. There was a single orange card – bright orange – which we took to be the main prize. It was located slightly inland to the south-east of Sword beach and it said 'Bénouville'. Just two of the cards puzzled me: 'Ham' and 'Jam'.

'Gentlemen,' Hibbert continued, 'you are about to receive orders for a deliberate glider raid onto two bridges in Normandy tonight.' Brettle reached down to the hangar floor and picked up a snooker cue. He used it to point at the 'Ham' and 'Jam' cards, which sat on two parallel bits of blue ribbon running from the coast to the city of Caen. Everyone from corporal upwards began to scribble furiously in notebooks. Hibbert suddenly looked very smug, like a child opening Christmas presents. It made my stomach turn a little. He went on to describe the model, as the flustered Brettle frantically tried to keep up with his cue: every card, every town, every village, every road, every stretch of water, every feature. Hibbert missed nothing. Nothing. To begin with, it felt like a father introducing his child to a model in his back garden, the child expected to run his toy cars about. But it quickly sank in that this was no game; the area the model represented would shortly turn into a very real battlefield.

He asked for questions. As one, everyone around me shook their heads. Hibbert wasn't happy with this, a sinister grin stretched across his face. So he picked people out, one by one, bombarding them with questions of his own. What had he called this? What did that represent? Why was the card orange? What were Ham and Jam?

He then briefed us on the general characteristics of the area: the type of farming, market days, population before and during the German occupation, condition of main roads and tracks, tide timings of rivers, their current average speed of flow, their width, barge traffic before and during the occupation. My head began to hurt: were we going to attack the place or build a replica of it in Dorset?

Unexpectedly, he then handed the floor over to a young captain from the troop of Royal Engineers attached to the company for this mission. The engineer clambered to his feet and hobbled forward, probably fighting off pins and needles from sitting on the hangar floor. He thanked Hibbert, then launched into detail, prompting Brettle to recommence darting the cue around.

'Gentlemen, as the major explained, our mission is to take and hold the two bridges on this road linking Bénouville to Ranville and to stop German reinforcements making it to the landing beaches, here. The Bénouville Bridge, which is named after the village behind it, will be known as objective Ham. Running over the Caen Canal, the bridge is one hundred and ninety feet long and twelve feet wide. There's a bridge-raising mechanism and control room on the east bank. The bridge is capable of holding the weight of any armoured vehicle currently fielded by both enemy and friendly forces.'

There was a horrible feeling in my gut at that moment. None of us wanted to hear about tanks that might give us trouble.

'And as the major explained,' he continued, 'there is another bridge nearby, Ranville Bridge, running over the River Orne, just a quarter of a mile to the south-east, which is known as objective Jam. It is three hundred and fifty feet long and twenty feet wide. It can take the weight of all known armour. Later on, my chief bomb maker, Staff Sergeant Bamsey –' he pointed at Bamsey in the crowd '– will talk about demolition.'

He nodded to Hibbert, then rejoined the rest of us. 'Any questions before we continue?' Hibbert asked deliberately.

'Will enemy armour be around, sir?' a nervous voice behind me asked.

'One thing to the Germans' credit is their battlefield discipline. We cannot deny them that. No matter what the vehicle, whether it be a motorbike and sidecar or their heavy armour, they will conceal it if stationary for more than ten minutes or so. Our sources cannot give us a firm picture as to the armoured threat in the immediate region. This is why I have insisted we take as much armour-defeating capability as our gliders will allow. Also remember our time on Salisbury Plain with enemy anti-tank weapons. Those weapons might be for the taking in Normandy, perhaps under repair or refitting. The German armoured forces in Russia have been badly mauled, and I would not be surprised if Normandy was being used as an area for rest and repairs.'

There were murmurs all round. The answer was ruthlessly comprehensive. I realized for the first time he wasn't referring to notes. He already knew every bit of fine detail relevant to the operation.

But I was also suspicious. If I'd been giving out orders, the last thing I'd have talked about was vast hordes of Tiger tanks, even if I'd known they were hiding in hedgerows around the target.

'Let me sum up the overall situation regarding enemy forces,' he concluded. 'The German Army has occupied this real estate since the summer of 1940. They have allocated a lot of time, money, resources and manpower in the form of slave labour to the area, so as to ensure we cannot return. Tonight, however, that all changes.'

There were nervous chuckles.

He continued: 'The lion's share of German forces is currently committed to their Russian and Italian areas of operation. Up to 80 per cent of them are committed to the Russian front. The German high command have taken their eye off the ball with regard to France. Convinced an Allied invasion force will eventually try to push across the Dover–Calais axis, the Germans have mustered their reserve panzer forces in the Pas-de-Calais region, leaving a very large proportion of the French coastline poorly defended.'

Heads bobbed all round me.

'We do have to take care of enemy forces in the immediate target area,' he continued. 'As of midday today, intelligence sources have indicated that fifty-plus enemy troops are guarding each of the bridge sites. But the troops are of low quality, tending to consist of wounded back from the Eastern Front, plus prisoners of war pressed into service: Polish, Russian, even French.'

Personally, I always had some sympathy for the prisoners of war, guessing they had joined the enemy to avoid a worse fate.

'Their headquarters and centre of mass are in Ranville,' Hibbert advised, prompting Brettle to wave the cue again. 'Their morale is mixed at best. Their weapons are in general a mixed bag, often outdated. There is however an anti-tank gun sited on the east bank of objective Ham. Regardless of age, it is a deadly weapon. We don't know its calibre, but we must quickly render it useless to the enemy. We don't necessarily want to destroy it, as it may be of some use to us. You never know, some of you may get on-the-job training with the gun. But if you should acquire the weapon, don't let your guard slip down through overconfidence. Regardless of the level of success you achieve at any time, you must always stay on your game. Understood?'

Everyone nodded again.

'Now let's talk about friendly forces. The first friendlies should be with us just before dawn, in the form of 7 Para. They will parachute into the drop zone nearest us, just as other elements of 6th Airborne Division arrive in a drop zone further away. Pathfinders will be in the area, but I doubt they will reveal their presence until the drops begin. As 7 Para make their way into our perimeter, coming through objective Jam, we will grow stronger as an overall force and should be able to hold the position until relieved by forces landing at Sword. The beach is just a few miles away, so if all goes well, it won't be too long after first light before landing forces are with us. Any questions?' There were none.

'Gentlemen, your mission is to seize and hold bridges Ham and Jam. Be prepared to defend against enemy counter-attack until relieved, in order to allow friendly forces to exploit out of the Sword bridgehead towards Caen.' Only the scraping of pencil lead on paper broke the brief silence. 'I repeat, your mission is to seize and hold bridges Ham and Jam. Be prepared to defend against enemy counter-attack until relieved, in order to allow friendly forces to exploit out of the Sword bridgehead towards Caen.' It was traditional to give the mission statement twice, so no one was in any doubt.

He went on to provide minute details as to how the mission should be achieved: who would do what within a preliminary movement plan. The entire glider force was to land on a narrow slip of land between the two bridges, he explained. It would be tight, especially given gliders have no brakes. I suddenly wondered why on earth anyone had come up with a plan involving gliders before realizing a silent glider landing would get a lot of people down at the same time with no parachute canopies for the enemy to spot; the landing should have the advantage of complete surprise. Once we were out of the gliders, Hibbert would take half the force, including me, to Ham. Brettle would take the remainder to assault Jam, engineers would be split equally between the two halves. Brettle and Hibbert explained how the enemy sentries would be overwhelmed with thunderclap surprise. The bridges would be captured before their dozing defenders could fall out of their bunks. It was possible for the distribution of forces to be revised at any time, he concluded.

It was my kind of plan: plain and simple, and easy to remember. Kill the bad guys, hold the bridge until relieved.

Serjeant Major Jenkins appeared before us. 'When we land, there can be no fucking about, dealing with the dead and wounded, especially if we crash-land or come immediately under fire. You get out of the bloody plane, and you deal with the enemy first, is that clear?'

A united chorus of 'Yes, sir' thundered through the hangar.

'You don't stop for no one. Clear and hold your objectives before you do anything else. When the situation allows, I will put men to the task, if we have to deal with casualties, both friendly and enemy. If I tell you to patch up a wounded enemy soldier, I want none of your fucking wisecracks; you just get it done. Fuck me off, and that enemy soldier will be patching you up. All casualties will be brought to the gliders.' I'd have bet money on no one risking his annoyance by disobeying him. 'Same with prisoners,' he advised. 'If the enemy drop their weapons, make the correct call. Clear them of any weapons and ammunition. Bring surrendered enemy to the gliders so I can take them off your hands. And when the situation allows, I want all enemy weapons and ammunition to my location, so we can distribute them around our perimeter. We may be there some time, with the enemy trying their bloody hardest to get them bridges back. Any questions?' There were none.

Hibbert introduced Staff Sergeant Bamsey. As Bamsey climbed to his feet, he hauled up a few sandbags. Once standing at the front, he slowly and methodically emptied them. There were different-sized blocks wrapped in black gaffer tape, wires of various colours hanging out. He arranged the blocks in two piles on the ground before clearing his throat. 'Gentlemen, these are demolition measures.' His accent was the thickest Welsh I had ever heard.

Almost as one, everyone leaned forward.

He lifted one of the contraptions. 'German explosive. Have a look, pass it round.'

There was a collective gasp as he'd tossed it in the air. We'd no experience with explosives, no idea how volatile they might be. But a lad in the crowd caught the contraption cleanly, and our confidence grew as it was passed among us.

'Now,' Bamsey began, 'if we don't quite achieve the level of surprise Major Hibbert, er . . . hopes for, then there's just a chance you might find enemy explosives on the bridges. Minimum of three sets of explosives to cut the main supports. Then a bridge comes down under its own weight. Now, if you could all convene around the model.'

As we surrounded it, he handed out British explosives and grainy photographs of Ham and Jam. Commandeering the cue from Brettle, he pointed at the model, explaining where and how charges could best be laid on the bridges to destroy them. It sounded straightforward, and there was some murmured discussion on how easy it would be to blow Jam and Ham up.

Hibbert asked us all to sit down again. 'Gentlemen,' he began again, 'a reminder that the bridges should be taken intact. But I'm afraid we'll have to sleep with the Devil. Armour coming out of Sword will need the bridges to break out and move on Caen. However, should there be enemy armour, we cannot allow it to cross the water and move towards the beaches. It may be tough, but until the last possible moment, we must ensure Ham and Jam remain up and intact, do you all understand?' Everyone nodded.

Hibbert took a whistle from his pocket, loudly blowing the Morse code for 'V' again and again. I wondered if the RAF Police outside were having kittens about the noise, but had a feeling they would never dare to enter. He further explained that he would whistle the code when our objectives had been achieved so everyone in earshot would know. Whistles would be distributed to everyone, and someone else should blow one if he couldn't. He missed nothing. Nothing. He organized a time check, and everyone set their watches. 'Gents,' he finally wound up, 'tonight we go. This mission has been almost two years in the making and finally conditions are right for us to make a move. The enemy in France is tired. His equipment has seen better days. Russia has really taken it out of him, but don't give him any time or room to react. Hit him hard first time. We are few in number, so we must be swift and bold. Does everyone understand?'

'Yes, sir,' everyone roared.

'Now, as you know, the Pegasus flying horse is the emblem of our airborne forces. When we are successful, there is some talk of renaming the bridge at Bénouville Pegasus Bridge, and renaming that at Ranville Horsa Bridge in honour of the gliders.

'You will be thrown into the lion's den. You will be outnumbered and outgunned, since that is the nature of airborne operations. But I make you this promise. You will not be outclassed, is that understood?'

'Yes, sir,' the roar came again. I knew it was true. Show time.

*

Back in our accommodation, we nervously packed in silence. Everyone had time with their own demons. I dragged my fighting gear out onto a veranda, then looked at my meagre personal possessions, spread before me on the bed. Shaving kit. Comb. Brylcreem. A couple of smutty magazines. Two grainy pictures of Mum, Dad and Daniel.

We followed Serjeant Wardle to the company offices, where our weapons for the mission had been laid out: rifles, sub-machine guns, light machine guns, grenades, two-inch mortars, a couple of shoulder-launched PIATs – projector, infantry, anti-tank.

Once outside, I cocked my newly acquired Bren gun to ensure it was clear of ammunition. It was a habit that had been drilled into us constantly: never assume a gun is empty until you have checked. We followed Sean back to the hangar. Major Hibbert and Captain Brettle had already applied camouflage cream to their faces. We were allocated ammunition and the hangar echoed with the sound of everyone clicking rounds into magazines. We applied cam cream to each other's faces in pairs, like native Indians applying warpaint.

Confined to the hangar, there was nothing else for it but to just sit and doze. The light outside began to fade as corned-beef hash was wheeled in for our final dinner before the off. I tried to get some sleep but found myself wondering about the other boys all over southern England waiting to invade Europe for what was undoubtedly going to be one hell of a fight. This was the one we'd been waiting for.

A clatter of chains woke me up with a start. The hangar doors opened, and revealed a ground crew wheeling in a large tractor contraption. It was hooked up to the nearest Halifax and towed the bomber out into the dusk. One by one, the gliders and bombers were pulled out. Ground crew used heavy tow ropes to attach the bombers to the gliders. My stomach started to turn as the reality of our situation dawned. For most of our training the war had felt a million miles away, but suddenly I was sat, heavily armed, smeared with cam cream, ready to fight. I looked at the men around me. By volunteering we'd missed the dreaded wait for call-up papers, and I think that drew us together as a unit. We'd opted for this, to take on the Nazis.

Major Hibbert and Captain Brettle toured the hangar, exchanging firm handshakes with everyone. Some got a slap on the shoulder or a mock jab at the jaw. Brettle and Hibbert helped some particularly weighed-down men to their feet. I could feel the fear building up. Brettle shook my hand firmly, pulled me to my feet and then gave me a light jab in the chest. 'Certainly different from a day at the brewery, eh, Stokes?'

'Yes, sir. See you in Normandy.'

His eyes glazed over. But with a broad grin he gave me an even firmer handshake. 'See you in Normandy, Stokes.'

I followed a line of men out into the darkness. Night had finally come. I had to increase my stride somewhat to keep up. All of a sudden, my gear felt like it weighed a ton. I had no idea how I was going to rush a bridge wearing all that. I was at the back of the queue for our glider. Sean was helping people inside, the ground crew were shaking everyone's hands. 'All the best, boys,' one said, extending his mitt to a boy in front of me. 'Give 'em hell. Wish we were coming with you.'

'No, you don't,' someone muttered.

Before long we were all set and fastened. I was just able to make out the murmur of our two pilots going through their checks. Outside in the warm night air I heard the propeller engines of the Halifaxes coughing, wheezing and spluttering to life. The aroma of burned aviation fuel drifted through our wooden cabin. The din outside, the roar of machinery, became horrendous. In the dimly lit interior we sat for what felt like an age, waiting for the inevitable. A change in engine pitch indicated our bomber was preparing to taxi. A creak and groan of timber signalled our first movement.

A scraping sound of rope unravelling came from beneath my feet. We suddenly shuddered to our left. The rattling and juddering made my arse ache. Heaven knows what condition we'd be in by the time we got to the other end, I thought. Then we started moving. The rope seemed to be made of elastic, lurching us along the runway in jerking movements and I had an awful vision of crashing into the back of a plane full of fuel before we even got off the ground. We rumbled around, meanderingly to the left. Then there was an increase in engine pitch as the bomber started its run.

'Get ready, boys,' a yell from the cockpit came. 'Here we go, then.'

We darted forward, suddenly gathering speed. The noise became ear-splitting, our airframe drifted left and right as it was dragged faster and faster by its master. Before long, the nose of the glider started to lift.

Then the rattling and juddering suddenly disappeared, and we were up, bobbing and weaving as we climbed. We were on our way to France and I began to wonder what the sixth of June would look like.

2
Bridge Assault

'Fallschirmjäger! Fallschirmjäger!'

I could still hear a foreign voice outside our dark, stationary, silent, wrecked glider.

The rough hand remained over my mouth, so I lashed out to grab my attacker. As my vision swam into focus, although not yet adjusted to the blackness, I made out the dark profile of Sean. With his free hand, he held his trigger finger to his lips, slowly shaking his head. The way the aircraft had settled, I was hanging from the wall behind me, which was now the roof. Sean rammed his shoulder into my crotch, releasing my harness, then stifled grunts of effort as he lowered me onto the other wall of the glider, which was now the floor. 'Find your weapon quickly,' he hissed.

I couldn't see much, but a small amount of ambient light was coming from the back of the glider, where the tail had been. I focused on the light, which slowly allowed my night vision to kick in. The aircraft was littered with weapons. I scrambled for my Bren as Sean moved to the next guy trapped in his harness. I realized there were a few guys hanging just like I had been. I found the Bren underneath satchels of PIAT rounds. As I picked it up, a hand grabbed my webbing strap and hustled me outside.

The light in the open air was an improvement. Some of the boys were in a very shallow ditch below a hedgerow. I was shoved into the ditch, landing on my arse. Sean was again my abuser. To his credit, he was trying to make sure all the guys were OK. Some had really taken a battering in the landing, vomiting while fighting hard to stifle coughs. Trying to gather my thoughts, trying to reflect on our hideous entry into the war, I acknowledged a thumbs up from Sean before he scampered away. But before I could even tune into my surroundings, a whisper came down the line: 'Gunners up front. Stay low.'

Three of us shuffled forward to Sean. As I got close to him, I had the fright of my life. In front of us were two enemy sentries sharing a cigarette on a road. Just beyond them was a small pillbox, the profile of a machine gun clearly visible. How the fuck had they not detected us? Where was the owner of the foreign voice I had heard? Maybe the glider had landed on him, or more likely Sean had quickly tackled him. Sean waved us down. I lay on my side to unclamp the bipod legs of the Bren carefully, ensuring they would not spring open with a clatter. I managed to get myself into a position where I could fire the thing. He pressed a rough cheek against my earlobe.

'Stay here. Concentrate on the pillbox. I'll deal with the sentries. We'll hit the pillbox with grenades. After that, switch your fire left and take care of anyone coming out of the buildings on the far bank.'

I tried not to nod, still unable to believe the sentries had not raised the alarm. I had just arrived in the war, but it was already too much to take in; I had only now registered Bénouville Bridge and the buildings across the canal.

He crawled away. I heard him click his fingers before he jumped up and rushed silently towards the sentries. He was almost on them when a few of our guys appeared from a hedgerow. My heartbeat sounded like a bass drum. It was all going to fucking kick right off. The right-hand sentry felt one of Sean's legendary right hooks and clattered to the ground. I was sure he had heard a noise but hadn't been able to spin round in time. From somewhere a Sten gun chattered a short concentrated burst, and the other sentry's head exploded like a tomato. He dropped to the ground; no theatrics, his life expiring before gravity took care of things. Sean and the guys from the hedgerow were almost at the pillbox when a third sentry on the bridge fired a flare gun.

As the flare zipped skywards, the sentry was cut down by rifle and Sten fire, and the machine gun burst into life. Its tracer fire snapped past to our left, slicing through the hedgerow behind us. I aimed at the muzzle flash, firing short sharp bursts. My own muzzle flash ruined my night vision. My ears popped into the familiar whine I had experienced countless times on the ranges of Salisbury Plain.

I knew my fall of shot was not always on target; I was in a panic, there was no doubt about it. But while much of my tracer was screaming off across the bridge, some rounds were splashing around the pillbox, a few chipping small chunks of concrete away from the firing slit protecting the enemy gun crew. Sean's group threw grenades at the pillbox, most landing behind it. I made out his profile as he dived for cover into a ditch with his assault group. As my hearing and vision became more accustomed to the flash and percussion of gunfire, I kept firing, my short-lived panic gone, my initial tension evaporating. There was no internal moral battle, the enemy in the pillbox just a target.

But as my confidence increased, the German machine gun directly engaged me, its muzzle flashing wildly. My position wasn't the best in the world, just a shallow dip in the ground. I might as well have been lying on a snooker table. Rounds snapped past my head, making the ringing in my ears worse. I was showered with grass and topsoil. But I didn't panic or feel the urge to seek shelter. I'd heard a bit about bullets during training on Salisbury Plain. If you could see the enemy muzzle flashes, those bullets weren't going to hit you. True or not, the thought made me even more determined to silence the threat or at least make the gun crew stop firing and take cover. Your instinct is to hide behind your weapon, so I continued to do just that, firing at the flashes. Beside me, my fellow gunners were also firing at the pillbox, but we couldn't subdue the bastard. More rounds flicked up the soil around me. *Fuck.* I wondered if it was only a matter of time for us.

But then a series of loud thuds sounded, and the gunfire from the pillbox stopped, dust and debris drifting from its firing slit. Sean's team had knocked it out. I stopped firing, only then properly realizing the German machine gun had engaged my position. I snapped my mind away from the memories the pillbox encounter had imprinted on me and noticed gunfire flying in all directions, accompanied by flares rising from the far bank. The enemy was now well and truly alert, our guys all engaged.

I adjusted my position to fire down the length of the bridge. Some of my rounds were a bit wayward, sparks flicking high off the metal structure. Profiles of people appeared, coming out of the buildings on the far bank. The gunner to my left jabbed my shoulder. 'Switch left,' he roared. 'Enemy in the houses.' Sean's group emerged from their ditch, dashing onto the bridge. We had to help them get across somehow, since there was fuck-all cover on the structure. I engaged the enemy profiles on the far bank but couldn't confirm any hits, the only real light being that from the flares.

A series of dome shapes bobbed through my line of sight at close range. My first instinct was to fire at them, but I silenced my gun. What the fuck were they? I pushed myself up a little. I was glad I hadn't fired. It was our guys moving along a nearby trench I hadn't noticed. It led to a pit for the German anti-tank gun Hibbert had said we were to capture or destroy. In my panic I hadn't even noticed the weapon but now wished we'd had it in play when the German machine gun was blazing away.

Beyond the far end of the bridge a lot of bullets began smashing into and around a particular building. I decided not to fire at it, as Sean's group had made the far bank so there was no way of knowing who I would be firing on. 'What's going on?' snapped the gunner to my left.

'Don't just lie there doing nothing,' rasped another voice next to me, although I could only see the shadow of his head in the corner of my eye. 'Those guys going for the anti-tank gun could do with some Bren support.'

I wasn't too sure if we were still operating on the original plan, but it seemed to make sense to move forward, so I leaped up and moved, although the gunners around me didn't follow into the trench, probably as confused as I was. I managed to latch onto the rear of the group heading for the anti-tank gun, and we quickly made it to the pit. The gun wasn't manned but faced away from the bridge, and it looked like a bastard to swing the gun round towards the enemy. One guy clambered out of the pit then began legging it across the bridge. We followed like sheep. The bridge had metal gantries right and left. We sprinted beside the left-hand gantry as fast as our kit allowed. My lungs burned with the effort, my heart thundering in my ears. More German troops dashed out of the buildings on the far bank, jumping into a line of trenches. The two front runners in our group threw grenades, then fired long Sten bursts.

The loud thuds of the grenades sounded from the trench in front of us. We sprinted off the bridge, following up with gunfire. Desperate for cover, we jumped in on top of the now-dead enemy, capturing the trench, at least temporarily. On either side of us, our lads were using grenades on the trenches and buildings. Crumpled grey and red heaps littered the area, some of them groaning loudly. We hadn't killed all the Germans, but it looked like our grenades were quickly taking the fight out of those who remained.

One of the guys in our new trench moved along it, stepping over the bodies, making sure they no longer posed a threat. It was only then I recognized him as Corporal Terry Thomson, my section commander. 'Stokes,' he barked, pointing at a two-storey house, 'cover the front door of the building there.'

I set up my Bren gun accordingly. He then shoved past me to check the other end of the trench, before scrambling out to approach a corner of the building. Most of the windows on the ground floor were already broken. He lobbed a couple of grenades in just to make sure, which blew out the remaining ground-floor windows. I braced myself for dazed and wounded enemies to stagger out, but none came. Dashing to the door, he put a foot over the threshold, looking inside. He waved us to join him. The more agile lads leaped out of the trench, but I wasn't far behind. He led me to the right-hand back corner of the building, siting me at a broken window there, which from my memory of the model faced back towards the centre of Bénouville and Sword Beach beyond. 'Keep your eyes peeled for a counter-attack,' he told me, 'while we search upstairs. Understand?' I nodded; it was straightforward enough.

While keeping a lookout, I had a chance to gather my thoughts. Over to my right I made out Sean and his group. They were still engaging the enemy, but resistance was sporadic at best. It had seemed to take an age to get from the glider to the house, but I realized it had only been a few minutes. I was soaked in sweat and had a throbbing headache from the landing, the gunfire and the grenades.

A grenade thudded in a room above me. Terry's group had either silenced the last opposition in the house or were just making sure. Sean's group pushed on, away from the canal, further into the village. From the limited light of the odd flare, I could see they were vaulting hedges and fences, making their way to a pair of small houses. I adjusted my fire position in case support was required, but the buildings turned out to be empty, which suited me fine.

I heard boots above me, heading down. The guys were coming

back down the stairs. I kept my eyes fixed outside. Before long, I felt a nudge on my left boot. Terry had silently crept up on me. He was all smiles, a cigarette hanging from his lips. 'This, young Stokes, is how we do things.' We had taken objective Ham, there was no denying it. Bénouville Bridge would become Pegasus Bridge. An amazing feeling washed over me for a brief moment. He noticed, his smile becoming a glare. 'We're good here now, but only until the bastards decide they want their bridges back.'

'Bridges?' I blurted.

'Don't you listen to anything, Stokes? Captain Brettle's group are at the other objective, Jam. The bloody Ranville Bridge, just over there.' He pointed down the road to the south-east. 'I haven't heard gunfire from that direction for a while, so things there are hopefully going well.'

Other lads joined us, some dishing out cigarettes. Pleased they had distracted Terry, I decided to stand up and have a stretch. I was aching all over. The landing had really roughed me up. Joints creaked and cracked as I loosened myself up. All the faces were unfamiliar. Obviously Terry had decided to follow them along the trench leading to the anti-tank gun, but where were our guys, the guys from my section of D Company? 'Where are the lads, Corporal?' I had to ask.

He let a smoke ring form and drift skywards before pointing back over the bridge. 'Probably sunbathing next to the bloody glider. They all took a bit of a battering in the landing, mate.'

I heard shouting from across the bridge. 'Ham and Jam! Ham and Jam! Ham and Jam!' The shouting started on our side of the water. Both bridges must have been secured. Good news.

The drone of hundreds of aircraft began to sound above us. Way east, beyond the Ranville Bridge, searchlights flickered into action, long white beams of light waving wildly, trying to find our aircraft. We watched the light show. At that moment the entire bloody German Army could have walked back onto the Bénouville Bridge and we wouldn't have noticed. A searchlight illuminated the belly of a plane. Enemy flak guns were creating an awful din. Tracer from anti-aircraft defences to the east streamed up, eventually burning out. The projectiles were still dangerous after that; you just couldn't see them any more. We noticed a plane engine on fire. Then more aircraft flamed up, falling from the sky without ceremony, their demise plain to see in the dark June night.

As the drone continued, the searchlights began to pick out clusters of parachutes, heavily armed men dangling below them: 7 Para had begun their drop. It wasn't long before almost every single parachute was illuminated as the lights converged on the paratroopers. Small-arms fire from the ground joined the anti-aircraft barrage, lead whizzing among the chutes as they drifted ever lower. It sounded close but it was still east beyond Ranville Bridge. The drone of aircraft began to fade, replaced by shouting and screaming, the sound of firing and the odd grenade going off. I didn't envy the boys jumping into the enemy's backyard; at least our descent had been quick and clean. But I also didn't envy the German flak gunners and infantry when our surviving pissed-off paratroopers reached them.

Searchlights continued blazing until just a few parachutes remained in the air. We began to hear the sound of fierce fire-fights on the ground, the action now hidden in the darkness of the drop zones. Our guys were taking care of business.

A whistle blast echoed. Three long blasts, then a short one. Repeated again and again. From somewhere Major Hibbert was confirming both bridges were secure. In the low light I noticed a figure approaching quickly. It was Sean. 'Good effort, lads,' he told us through my window. 'Stay alert. That's the OC's whistle. Be prepared to receive para lads in our perimeter shortly. Not too sure where the priority for manning will be right now. The fucking Germans are all around us. Terry, shake these boys out. I don't want anyone larking about. I want some guys upstairs, keeping an eye on the centre of Bénouville.' He waved an arm to the west. 'Not that I'm sure the enemy are there. Everyone is to remain awake. In a while I will make the call to begin resting troops.'

3
Counter-attack

Sean brought a couple of new guys over to join us, and in preparation for the expected counter-attack, Terry resited everybody. I took up a fighting position in the trench outside the house, along with the two new guys. They had Stens and a shoulder-launch PIAT anti-tank weapon. Before long I realized they were glider pilots.

Major Hibbert had made sure that all three units temporarily seconded to the battalion – pilots, engineers and signallers – knew how to operate both our weapons and the enemy's. We had all done lots of time on the Salisbury Plain gun training ranges, firing thousands of rounds of ammunition from our own platoon weapons: Lee-Enfield .303 rifles, Sten sub-machine guns, the Bren light machine gun, the Webley revolver and Colt automatic pistol. We also had to master the two-inch mortar until we could adjust our fall of shot to within two rounds, to ensure targets could be neutralized quickly if ammunition was in short supply. And I don't know if the Far East theatre was short of grenades, but there had been a huge amount on the ranges to play with.

The chance to fire German weapons had been unexpected. I don't know how he managed to acquire enemy weapons and ammunition, but Major Hibbert was full of surprises. He insisted we be as skilled with German weapons as we were with our own, since when it came to the crunch enemy weapons might be the only ones left in our operational area with any ammo. The Mauser rifle was a steady dependable rifle, along with their sub-machine gun, the MP 40. We put the Luger pistol through its paces, and the jewel in the crown, their machine guns; both the MG 34 and MG 42 were formidable beasts. They were weapons we'd learned to fear from reports earlier in the war telling of the enemy's devastating use of them. The MG 34 was the older-generation model, but still widely used.

The German stick grenade was also fun. The explosive was at one end of a thick wooden shaft, so you could really lob it some distance, its crude but effective design impressive. The Panzerfaust was great too, a lightweight disposable one-shot anti-tank weapon. The Panzershreck was however their main infantry tank-killing asset. Both anti-tank weapons were terrifyingly accurate, their killing power humbling. To the credit of their designers, they made a mockery of our PIAT.

We also got to try the German lightweight flamethrower. The concept of using such a weapon put a bad taste in our mouths, and flamethrowers were one thing we didn't have in abundance, since fuel was at a premium. Two men per platoon had a go at firing the enemy flamethrower at hay bales. The roaring licks of fire were impressive but horrifying too. Those who tried it were not fans, since the fuel tank on your back was not protected in any way, so if the enemy spotted you coming, you would without a shadow of a doubt be their prime target.

We were also trained in the use and maintenance of radios should, God forbid, something happen to our radio operator. Enemy vehicle recognition was also on the training programme, in case we had to call in air support or artillery. In the barracks theatre we endured hours of mind-numbing images from a projector: air and ground photos of enemy aircraft and the different types of German land vehicles – tanks, tank destroyers, self-propelled guns, halftracks, supply trucks, staff cars, motorbikes, you name it. Hibbert even insisted we were able to recognize the German machines from the appearance of their exhausts or gun barrels, should they be half-hidden. 'Knowledge is power, gentlemen,' he would chant with Brettle. 'Knowledge is power.'

The training had been intense. Hibbert left nothing to chance – nothing – and we'd been battle-ready for months before we finally got the off. I remembered on numerous occasions we had got all kitted up, ready to move out for action against the Germans. Sicily and Italy were rumoured more than once, but at the last moment we were always stood down. The weather wasn't right, it was too hot or windy or the best landing zones were too heavily occupied by the enemy. We were told about the carnage experienced by the German paratroopers dropped on the Greek island of Crete, back in '41. They won their objectives, but at a horrendous cost. After a time we became accustomed to missions being cancelled, until the day we were moved to RAF Tarrant Rushton. This cycle of stop and go meant company life on Salisbury Plain could be a very polar experience, where we switched from being in a very relaxed, informal state, where we could all be drunk and sing songs, to the sober formality of operation prep.

Terry shook me out of my training memories. Emerging from the building, he was carrying something large and heavy. I couldn't make it out until he got really close. With a familiar metallic clatter, he carefully placed it to the left of my Bren. Spare magazines in a sandbag. 'Thought you could do with these, mate,' he said, squatting down and patting them.

'Thanks, Corporal.'

There was a sudden whimper from the bottom of the trench, which made us all flinch. It was a wounded German. He had probably tried to keep quiet, fearing we'd kill him out of hand. The enemy might have done that to our wounded, had they held the bridge. Terry carefully lowered himself into the trench. There wasn't a lot of floor space, much of it taken up with the dead. He couldn't work out which German was alive so gave each of them a shove. One let out an almighty squeal, then sobbed uncontrollably.

Terry was gentle with him, almost apologetic, hardly the harsh NCO I had always taken him for. From his smock he produced a torch and lit it with a flick of its switch. Not the wisest move I had ever seen, what with so many Germans in the region, but he must have concluded needs must. He quickly checked over the wounded soldier. The German's trousers were dark with excrement or blood, or perhaps both. Terry extinguished the torch. He ordered one of the glider pilots to find a medic. The pilot scrambled out of the trench and jogged away over the bridge. Terry crouched down next to the German, relighting the torch. I was meant to be looking out for the enemy but couldn't help notice Terry was holding the German's hand, quietly chatting away. The German nodded every so often, still sobbing. I realized he was in a lot of pain. Terry fished out his cigarettes. He lit one, putting it between the German's bloodied lips. I wasn't sure if the German was a smoker, but he didn't cough and splutter much. As he took drags from the cigarette, he fought back sobs. The trench soon filled with cigarette smoke. I was a non-smoker, but I couldn't help inhaling the soothing aroma. I thought the German was dying. At least the cigarette gave him something to do, probably distracting him from the pain, rather than actually relieving it.

The metallic crunch of combat boots on sheet metal sounded. Our glider pilot was returning over the bridge with two other guys, who had a canvas stretcher between them. They placed it beside the trench. I was in a bit of a dilemma. Should I help them or keep my eyes peeled for the enemy? Terry made the decision for me. 'Stokes, two of ours are in the house, keeping an eye on the town. Help us, mate.' I hauled the Bren up out of the trench, putting it down beside the bag of spare mags. Terry and I lifted the German, who ground his teeth in agony. The guys with the pilot put him on the stretcher. The German was trying hard not to show his pain, probably out of pride. Terry gestured for me and the other pilot to follow him up out of the trench. 'Glider pilots will stay here to back up the boys in the building. Stokes, and you two other guys, grab a corner of the stretcher with me. We need to get this guy some medical attention.'

I had to take my Bren and spare mags with me, even on stretcher duty. As we organized ourselves around the stretcher it dawned on me that the guys the pilot had brought over the bridge were Dougie Chambers and Frank Williams. Even Terry hadn't recognized them at first. In the low light they both looked badly bashed up. Terry had already mentioned the landing had really battered us.

As one, we lifted the stretcher. The German yelped slightly as we carried him onto the bridge. We slowed the pace. 'Take it easy, mate,' Terry told him. 'We will get you sorted. Just hold on, mate, nearly there.'

Really feeling the effort, I was sweating buckets with the weight of the German and my own gear. Sweat stung my eyes, my helmet feeling like a tin pot coming to the boil. Halfway across, I made out three bodies lying in a road on the other side of the bridge. I had forgotten there was even a road there. It was the road on which two enemy sentries had shared a cigarette. As we drew closer, I saw one of the bodies was ours. Such a shame. I honestly thought we had got away with no casualties. Clearly not. Remembering one of the sentries had been floored by a punch from Sean, I wondered if one of the enemy lying there was alive, just unconscious. But the bodies were so close to the bridge, I assumed someone must have checked. I noticed smoke smouldering from the pillbox Sean's group had knocked out.

We continued to hear sporadic but obviously vicious firefights in the direction of the drop zones. They became a little louder as we stepped off the bridge: long scything bursts from MG 42s – an unmistakable sound – along with the tinny chatter of Sten guns and the dull thud of grenades. I wondered which side was throwing the grenades; probably both. It all went quiet for a few moments, then started up again. We made our way off the road. The glider landing site almost immediately appeared from the darkness. The gliders all seemed to be pretty much wrecked; no soft landings by the look of it. Beyond the gliders faint moonlight glinted off what appeared to be a large pond. I began to notice our guys, sitting or lying around the gliders. Occasionally torches momentarily flicked on. I guessed that many had been injured during the landings. There was only the odd enemy soldier being treated. We staggered on, Terry instructing us to put the stretcher down beside the pond. He darted off to find a medic. Suddenly there was a break in the cloud cover. Moonlight lit up the area. Still facing the gliders, I saw most of our injured guys were indeed not combat casualties.

A commotion sounded behind me. A group of our guys was rushing into the water, heading for an object in the pond. They began to drag it out. It had a bizarre shape. I thought it was equipment but soon realized it was a body. I didn't have the bottle to go over and be nosy. Terry arrived with a medic, who examined the German on our stretcher. 'Should have saved yourselves the trouble, guys,' quickly informed the medic. 'He's dead.' He moved away, looking for his next patient.

We just stood there, numb, looking down at the poor German lad who had perished in our care a long way from home. 'He was just a boy,' I said. In the brighter moonlight I saw his body had been smashed with grenades and a few bullets to boot. He had died a slow painful death, already fading away as we had started to try to help him. 'A boy, just like Daniel.'

'Daniel?' asked Dougie.

My thoughts drifted to Daniel. We were inseparable for most of our childhood, growing up next to the Thames just a hundred yards from Mortlake Brewery. Dad had worked there before the Great War, and after that was over his lifelong friend Colin Hennessy, a supervisor at the brewery, got him his old job back. It was a happy childhood, I think. Dad had a short temper, but most of the time we deserved it – like the beer raiders incident. That was back in '36.

Daniel and I reached our teens and had begun to show off to other kids with our knowledge of the security – or lack of it – inside the brewery. We'd known how lazy some of the guards were, where the best places were for climbing the walls, and where the street lamps left a particular stretch in shadow. This inevitably led to more and more daring sorties over the wall and eventually to targeting pub deliveries and making off with some free beer. Bernie Campbell-King was the old fella who ran the guard rota. Monday nights were his regular shift. He would sit high up on a walkway which had a grand view over the whole storage yard. But he would have his fat arse slumped in a chair, listening to whatever shit old people listened to on the wireless, probably supping a few bottles he had acquired from the shop floor.

The Monday-night beer raids were a success to begin with. They were carried out with military precision, using a human chain over the wall, as we passed up as many crates of the brown bottled booty as we dared. One particular Monday we managed to get one crate for everybody raiding. Twelve fat bottles per crate, each one about 4 per cent proof.

But it wasn't long before our antics were noted. I remember it was a Tuesday. Daniel and I returned home to find Bernie on our doorstep, talking to Dad.

'Get here now, you pair of shits,' he roared. We were dead. He lunged forward, grabbing Daniel by the shirt, giving him one almighty clout around the back of the head. Dad propelled him over the threshold with a shove and a swift kick up the arse. Daniel crashed to the floor in the hall, already sobbing, his fate sealed. Then Dad swung round, causing me to flinch, on the verge of heart failure. 'If I find out you was in there last night,' he warned, 'you'll be for it too – do you understand?'

I nodded. Bernie's pursed lips and raised eyebrow gave away the fact he suspected I'd been in on the raids but he couldn't quite be sure. Daniel got the hiding of a lifetime. Bernie was billed by the brewery for all the missing beer, a substantial amount of money. Dad didn't think it was fair for Bernie to pay but couldn't take on the debt himself and was worried the brewery might sack him if they found out about Daniel's involvement.

In the end Hennessy agreed that both Daniel and I should ride shotgun on Dad's pub delivery round. It wasn't unknown for people to steal the odd bottle on the streets of Richmond, Sheen and Mortlake. I was put on the payroll at a pound a week, but Daniel had to work for nothing until the debt was paid off, his only recompense being a crate of beer, if all deliveries in the week were made without a single loss. I felt a bit sorry for Dan, who kept his mouth shut regarding my involvement in what became known as the great beer robbery. So I paid him a share of my wages and gave Mum his housekeeping money every week.

Daniel paid off his debt, and the brewery took him on full time, but it wasn't long before Dad's Passchendaele injuries finally forced him to retire. Hennessy had been protecting him for some years, but even he was unable to convince the clipboard brigade that Dad should be kept on when it transpired a combination of injury and advancing years meant he couldn't lift barrels any more. It was a humiliating end for a proud man. He'd always tried to hide his injuries as best he could, shuffling on and cursing the Germans.

Cursing the Germans. I looked down at the dead boy at my feet trying not to well up, knowing I was beginning to lose it.

'Er . . . yeah, my brother Daniel,' I replied to Dougie. 'He's alive but lost a leg at Dunkirk.' I hesitated for a moment. 'Sorry. It isn't just this German lad.' I looked around at the guys among the gliders. 'This place . . . Medical places always remind me of Daniel.'

'Yeah, well, I'm sorry to hear about your brother,' said Terry, attempting to sound sympathetic but failing. 'We're here to avenge people like him, Robbie. We aren't training on Salisbury Plain any more; everything is for real now.'

News from the pond distracted him. The dead man dragged out was Lance Corporal Bobby Carrol, company fitness instructor as well as second in command of my section. He had somehow been thrown into the water from the glider. With all his kit on, he had no chance of staying afloat. I remembered he had been sitting near the tail. He must have been thrown out when it was ripped off, just before we landed. What a way to die. Of all the grim ways you could meet your end in battle, I bet no one ever considered drowning, certainly not on an airborne operation. I remembered he had run us ragged for Major Hibbert. Endless fitness runs, full-kit marches, navigation exercises. Bobby had been a git for that. He had a sadistic streak in him but had been a real nice guy. The company would feel the loss of one of its characters.

Up on the road I could just make out the profiles of men shuffling from the direction of objective Jam, the Ranville Bridge. Were the shuffling men bringing in more casualties? As they drew closer, I realized they were paratroopers from one of the drop zones, our reinforcements for the expected counter-attack. But there were only half a dozen of them or so, and it looked like they'd had a right time of it already. Their appearance came as a shock to me. Most were limping. Parachuting had its own hazards, without anyone on the ground bloody shooting at you as well. They were in smocks and armed, but all were dishevelled, and where the hell was their equipment? Maybe they had lost it during the drop or while battling Germans in the darkness of the drop zones. I waited for some clown to make a comment about the state of the paras. They found Major Hibbert, who I noticed was chatting to Company Serjeant Major Jenkins.

Hibbert waved in our direction. 'Corporal Thomson!'

Terry jogged over to him. After a brief chat, Terry led the

paratroopers away towards the bridge. He whistled, waving to us to join him. On the way over I took the opportunity offered by the brighter light to look at our dead guy on the road. I kind of wished I hadn't. It was Lieutenant Bertie Young, our platoon commander. Frank and Dougie, both more experienced than me, hadn't looked. I supposed the priority for now was consolidating the objective rather than dealing with the dead. I fell in column with Dougie, Frank and Terry behind the paratroopers. With Young dead, Serjeant Sean Wardle was our platoon commander now.

On the other side of the bridge we gathered in front of our trench. In the moonlight I saw German weapons scattered around – two MP 40s and a couple of Mauser rifles – and noticed there were spaces in the trench where enemy dead had previously lain. I looked sideways. The bodies were piled up at the end of the trench like firewood. One of the para lads asked Terry if he wanted him and his mates to occupy the building behind the trench. Terry shook his head. 'No, mate. I've some guys in there on look-out. I don't want all our fighting power pinned in one building. If the bastards have got armour, they could easily sit back and shoot the shit out of the place. My men and I will occupy this trench as well. The enemy will be in our killing area, no matter which direction they come from.'

A figure suddenly dashed over to us. It was Sean. 'All right, boys?' We all nodded and muttered. 'I've got a section of guys in the buildings forward right, with PIAT and section weapons. You lot don't fire until we have engaged any enemy first, understand?' We all nodded again. 'When you do fire at any remaining enemy, make sure it's accurate, since they'll be closer to you at that point, and we don't want to be lit up by your overshooting, OK?' We all nodded.

After Terry explained our defensive layout, Sean made to leave. I had to ask. 'Sarje, did anyone see Mr Young go down?'

Sean bit his lip. 'Part of the job, mate, just one of them things.'

'You never think it will be one of the main players though,' said Terry.

'Our casualties in the immediate area of the bridge seem to be light so far,' replied Sean, trying to switch the conversation away from Young. 'The operation is going to plan. More reinforcements can be expected from the drop zones.'

'Their casualties will be much heavier than ours,' Frank Williams said grimly, looking across at the para lads. Although a light-hearted gentle giant, the clown of the platoon, he was also known for being ruthlessly professional in combat situations.

'I can still hear the sound of firefights from the drop zones,' offered Dougie, calm and diplomatic as ever. 'The Germans were never going to make the war easy for us.'

'The peace wasn't easy, either,' Frank reflected. 'I knew years ago that Hitler was going to make life difficult for everyone. That's why I joined up.'

'My girl thought that all along,' lamented Dougie. 'Wonder what she'll think when she hears about this lot.' I didn't have a girlfriend to wonder about and for a moment I envied Dougie his sweetheart.

'Probably the same as all our families back home when they hear the good news,' Frank replied. I wondered if the invasion had made the news yet, picturing my family crowding around a wireless.

'We've got to hold these bridges first,' warned Sean. 'And our boys have to get off the beaches. Or there won't be any good news.'

Frank took a break on the floor of the trench. I followed suit with Dougie and the para lads. Neither Sean nor Terry seemed to have an issue with this. I guessed Terry had ordered the enemy bodies moved just before coming out of the house with the spare mags for me. He sent the glider pilots to relieve the watchers in the house. I put my Bren on the lip of the trench. The paras relaxed in their fighting gear, just dozing where they sat. They were even allowed to smoke, as long as they didn't make too much light with matches and lighters. The adrenaline of action began to fade from my body and I felt drowsy. As summer evenings go, it was rather warm with all my gear on. Little bugs buzzed around my head, trying their hardest to piss me off, and it was working. *Hold until relieved*, I reminded myself. That was our task now, nothing more. It was a waiting game. The odd grunt and stifled snore sounded around me, but I found I couldn't sleep.

Despite being two years my junior, Daniel had joined up first. I think it was only for the fun of it at first, rather than any concern about Hitler's ambitions in Europe, but he decided to join the Territorial Army, the 2/6th Battalion of the East Surrey Regiment. It was just once or twice a week at the local drill hall, but he loved it, bragging about it, thinking it gave him the moral high ground in any argument with Dad.

But then Hitler invaded Poland and we were at war with Germany. I remember the day we heard Daniel's regiment was to be sent to France. What had started as fun suddenly got very real. Mum was distraught and Dad wasn't much better about it. With no work at the brewery any more and Daniel gone he deteriorated fast, and it wasn't long before I had to help him get around the house.

At first we got regular updates from Daniel describing how little was happening in France – the so-called Phoney War – but then Hitler swept across Belgium, Luxembourg and the Netherlands. It sounded as though we were being outclassed. The letters abruptly stopped. Weeks passed until one day Mum and Dad called me into the living room. Mum had a telegram in her hand with Plymouth postmarks. Tears were streaming down her face. She had a hand over her mouth. My stomach flipped, knowing I wasn't going to enjoy the news. But then she revealed a tear-smeared smile. She kissed the telegram over and over, stroking her wet cheeks with it.

'He's alive, Robert. Daniel is alive.' She fought hard not to flinch with the sobs.

'Where is he?' I asked.

'Plymouth. A hospital just outside Plymouth.' She threw her arms around me. I pressed my nose into her tied-up hair. She always smelt of soap. She wiped her face on my shirt and looked up at me. 'We just need to let it sink in, and we can see about maybe going to see him. I haven't even read the thing through yet. When I knew it was him, I dived on your dad. Made him bloody jump.'

I chuckled with her, then we embraced again. I was so relieved Daniel was alive. A lot of the old boys at the brewery had their lads in the regiment, but they had yet to receive any news. 'He's lost a leg, your brother,' said Dad matter-of-factly.

The news was a jab in the gut. 'How?' I asked.

'His group were strafed by Stukas,' said Dad, simple and to the point as usual. 'Caught some in the right leg.' Mum welled up. Stukas were dive bombers which gave out a signature whine as they went into a dive prior to attacking targets. Horrible bloody planes.

'Surgeons in Plymouth thought they could save the leg,' he continued, 'but the infection was too great, so they had to remove it. The key thing here is that he is alive and just a train ride away.' He turned to Mum, offering his hand. She sobbed once more. Dad pulled his tiny wife into his lap, and they held each other like I had never seen them do before. They almost looked like young lovers having a cuddle on a park bench.

A shove brought me round with a start. 'Wake up, you lemon,' Terry said. 'We've got armour out front.' It took a while for my sleep-fogged brain to decode his message. I scrambled to my feet. *Armour. Fuck.* The glider pilots were back with me with their PIAT. I got myself into as decent a firing position as the trench would allow, Bren gun on my shoulder, ready for action. I wasn't too sure how I could deal with a tank, and if the Germans were anything near predictable, infantry would flank their precious panzers.

I peered left and right. Everyone was on full alert. 'Four panzers,' Terry whispered, 'types unknown, with fifty-plus infantry. Six hundred metres on the main road.'

'Tigers?' a worried query came from somewhere.

'Don't know, who cares?' Terry replied. 'They're fucking tanks.' But he should have cared. If they were Tigers, our PIAT wasn't up to the job. I strained my ears, trying to pick up engine noise, but all I could hear was my own racing heart. He clambered out of the trench and scampered at a crouch to the house facing it. I could hear engines now and the squealing of metal on metal. The panzers were coming. 'No Tigers,' he shouted across. 'Panzer IVs. Four hundred metres. Infantry behind, fifty metres.' I was relieved. The Panzer IV was an earlier generation, thinner armour, so our PIATs would be more effective. The mechanical rumbling grew louder, the ground vibrating slightly. 'Two hundred metres,' he hissed. I began sweating like a maniac, my palms slippery, quickly making sure my spare magazines were to hand, checking the Bren was cocked, ready for action. Beside me the glider pilot PIAT team had a projectile loaded, ready to go. The vibration stepped up. 'One hundred metres,' he sounded, sprinting back to our trench. 'I've told the boys in our building not to get involved unless the enemy make it upstairs.' We couldn't allow German infantry to get to an elevated position; it would cause real problems. The panzers were now directly behind the building. I just wished Sean's group would open fire and take care of them, so we could get on with fighting the enemy infantry. The waiting seemed worse than the fighting.

There was a loud thud in the direction of Sean's team, followed by a closer *crump*. In a flurry of sparks, the lead panzer emerged on the right-hand side of our building. My ears screamed as the glider pilots fired. Another *crump* accompanied a second flurry of sparks on the panzer. Two direct PIAT hits.

The buildings occupied by Sean's team were splashed all over by tracer rounds, many of which bounced off in all directions. A ground-floor window burst out with its brick surround, showering the garden with glass and masonry. The panzers were wasting no time in trying to eliminate threats. Muzzle flashes from Sean's team pierced the moonlit darkness.

From our trench we had yet to see enemy infantry. Our PIAT team had reloaded. 'Keep an eye on our left side, boys,' Terry ordered, 'should the bastards try to come round there to outflank Sean's group.' We heard Germans shouting. From behind our building they were engaging Sean's team. There was the odd ripple of MG 42 fire, along with a lot of smaller infantry weapons, but the roar of engines began to subside. Were the panzers we couldn't see falling back? The fire of the German infantry also began to fade. Were they regrouping, preparing to push around the left-hand side of our building? Its side would provide them with cover from Sean's group so I wasn't looking forward to the prospect.

The buildings occupied by Sean's men began to receive a right good hiding from the panzers. The tracer element of their tank fire thundered across, glass, tiles and bricks flying everywhere. His group couldn't stay in the buildings much longer, the panzers enjoying the advantages of range and firepower. Then I watched them dash out, heading for a nearby trench system. Some were hobbling, probably hit. We didn't know how many guys Sean currently had, so I couldn't be sure if they all got out. Even as they hunkered down, tank and MG 42 fire still hit the houses. But despite all the damage, the sturdy buildings held up, and after a while the enemy tired of redesigning them. As the echo of fire subsided, the rumbling cough of panzer engines could be heard moving away. Were the panzers out of ammo? It would be naive to think we had seen the last of them.

A sharp whistle sounded. I could just about make out Sean waving. 'Terry,' he roared, 'send me one of your gunners. Tony's Bren is shagged.' Although the squads had become mixed up, Tony Winman had managed to stick with Sean.

'OK,' shouted back Terry with a thumbs up. A rough heavy hand landed on my shoulder. 'Grab your gear, Stokes, and get over there.'

I grabbed my Bren by its carrying handle and picked up the sandbag of spare magazines. Sprinting across, I jumped down beside Sean. He put his Sten aside, taking the sandbag from me. 'Fucking panzer whacked Tony's Bren. Rang his bell for him, but he'll live.' Tony was slumped next to me, a bandage in place of his helmet. A dark patch of blood was seeping through, but he gave me two fingers – his way of saying hello. He seemed fine in principle. The other guys in Sean's trench were not familiar faces, probably a mixed bag of engineers and glider pilots. Some had Stens. It seemed each group was made up of a random mix of guys. Although someone seemed to be in charge of each, the type of order you would normally see in training appeared to be nonexistent. Sean slapped my shoulder. 'How you doing, kid?'

'I'm fine, Serjeant.' My mind drifted back to Hibbert's orders, delivered during the briefing in the hangar. *Gentlemen, your mission is to seize and hold bridges Ham and Jam. Be prepared to defend against enemy counter-attack until relieved* . . . I was feeling a little disorientated from lack of sleep but appreciated that Sean's current need for Bren support was greater than Terry's.

Sean slapped my shoulder again. 'Four panzers with infantry. We hit the lead tank; crew bailed out. We took a pop at the infantry. Can't confirm any hits, though.' I nodded. Smouldering badly, the lead panzer was still at the side of Terry's building, its hatches open. I guessed the crew had got out while I was watching Sean's buildings being hammered. Now and again the panzer would pop and fizz as its ammunition cooked off. I wondered if all the crew had escaped. I thought tank crews had a shit deal. Get smeared all over the inside by a shell screaming through or burn to death as you try to escape. Not good odds. Infantry had less range and protection, but you were smaller, more agile, less to shoot at.

The clatter of boots on metal caught our attention. Three men were at our end of the bridge, one with a large radio set on his back. A large column was behind them in single file. I recognized Major Hibbert as one of the radio group. The guy with the radio had to be his personal comms operator. The three of them got down on their bellies and crawled over to us. 'How's it going, Serjeant?' Hibbert beamed. 'I've been trying to get hold of you. I've just seen Mr Young. The serjeant major is recovering him back to the company aid post among the gliders.'

'Yes, sir,' said Sean. 'Our radio took some frag when we took on the panzers.'

'Good man.' Hibbert waved forward the man in his group without the radio. 'This is Captain Palmer, 7 Para. I'm pushing his boys forward into Bénouville town to the west, just so we can have some breathing space and get ourselves sorted. Please be prepared to reinforce, should he call for it.'

Sean nodded, followed by Palmer. Palmer shook Hibbert's hand, then headed back to the bridge, waving the column forward. During the hangar briefing Hibbert had mentioned that 7 Para would be the first to reinforce us in our defence of Bénouville Bridge, before forces from the beach landings arrived to relieve us. But 7 Para were about to advance and attack, not reinforce. They were heavily armed but, like the first six paratroopers I had seen, many looked in bad shape, some limping or adorned with bandages. Palmer joined them halfway down the column, as they gave a wide berth to the smouldering panzer. I watched him survey the darkness ahead. I wouldn't have fancied the trip across open country to Bénouville in that. There were at least three panzers out there somewhere, with infantry.

A wave of fatigue swept over me. I slumped back against the wall of the trench, allowing gravity to work its magic on my eyelids. It felt wonderful. The only sound I could hear was the now very sporadic exchange of fire from the drop zones and the odd crackle and pop from the wrecked panzer. A dog barked. The little bloody bugs began pestering my eyes and ears again, but I found them rather therapeutic. I could smell fresh cow shit, but even that didn't seem so bad. My knees buckled. I snapped out of it for a moment, knowing I couldn't fall asleep. It would be a while before I had the feel of a pillow on my face once more.

I stamped my feet to stay awake and looked down at my already grubby uniform. My gaze rested on the badge on my arm with the Oxfordshire and Buckinghamshire Light Infantry insignia I'd first seen outside the train station in High Wycombe. We'd moved there to my aunt's to escape from the Blitz. Mortlake had still been a mess. The brewery was gone, my job with it. Daniel's war pension and dad's brewery pension were OK, but we couldn't rely on them to support everybody. I had gone out to look for employment in High Wycombe and my eye had been caught by a glossy poster. 'Join your local county regiment, the Oxfordshire and Buckinghamshire Light Infantry,' it urged above an image of a group of soldiers in the thick of action, charging a German machine-gun post with berets on the backs of their heads, the bugle cap badge in pride of place.

But war hadn't turned out as glamorous as the poster, for me or for Daniel. After Daniel was injured at Dunkirk he was repatriated back to Roehampton with relative ease. On his release from hospital and arrival back in Mortlake, I insisted he come down the pub with me. He was rather reluctant, feeling somewhat of a fraud because only a handful of his unit, including the commanding officer, had made it back to England. We found out through various letters that Daniel's 2/6th Battalion of the East Surrey Regiment had surrendered to German forces at Saint-Valéry-en-Caux, most being marched to captivity in Poland, although there was no list of those who had survived the German advance.

In some ways maybe it was just as well that we had been forced to move from Mortlake to High Wycombe. Daniel's lost leg broke my parents' hearts, but sorrow soon became anger. Firstly towards the Germans. Then it turned to the authorities who had run the whole operation. The large majority of Daniel's fallen regiment were Mortlake, Sheen and Richmond boys. The entire area was numb. The politicians gave themselves a pat on the back for getting the army home; the Dunkirk chapter was over, never mind the boys left behind. The whole bloody British nation became gripped by invasion fever; local authorities issued gas masks, insisting we dig air-raid shelters in the gardens, dishing out instructions on how to deal with German paratroopers using brooms and garden rakes. The bombing started, blackout rules enforced, street lamps out. For a while Mortlake was entertained by the vapour trails of dogfights high above, the German bombers not targeting our area of west London, and I found refuge in the pubs. There was talk of beer rationing, which reduced my morale even more than walking home pissed in the pitch black. But it wasn't long before Daniel's regiment took the blame for the rationing, the bombing, the fear. It was their fault, their cowardice that had let the Germans come to our shores. It was the same everywhere in Mortlake. Conversations hushed as I arrived. Daniel was no longer welcome in the area and we began fighting among ourselves.

I opened my eyes. Off to the east I could just make out the flickering arrival of a summer's day. Little by little, minute by minute, our surroundings were unwrapped by the approaching daylight, the smouldering panzer becoming ever clearer. As I made out its wheels and tracks, I realized the crew had not escaped unscathed. Two dusty black piles of rags were slowly revealed as two bodies. Should I feel happy they hadn't escaped to man another panzer? Or sad their mothers would be informed of their deaths? I felt neither. I hadn't played a role in their deaths, but may well have, had a PIAT been in my hands. Other German dead were gradually revealed by the light: lone figures, crumpled heaps here and there. Unlike the panzer crewmen, they wore field-grey uniforms. Some appeared half-dressed, white blood-stained undershirts clear to see; they must have been shaken from slumber in their bunks, thrown straight into action. I wondered if one of the enemy dead had killed Mr Young. Or was his killer still at large? At large; it suddenly sounded absurd in my tired mind, like his killer was a bloody criminal rather than an enemy soldier.

Off to our left a series of dull thuds sounded. I wasn't concerned until the roof of one of the buildings exploded in a shower of brick and tiles. There was an explosion right next to the panzer, throwing tarmac and gravel into the air. The explosion made me flinch, but I couldn't move for some reason, fixated. 'Mortars!' Sean roared. 'Stay in your fucking holes.'

A second mortar round landed closer to us, another more distant strike hitting the canal bank. My ears rang, my balls ached; it felt like I'd been beaten up. Still I couldn't move, strangely fascinated by it all. It was only the sound of another round coming in that made me realize the danger I was in. I got my head down, finally appreciating it only takes one small fragment of shrapnel to ruin your good looks. All I could feel was the hard concussion of mortar rounds as they hit all around our positions. A round or two must have gone into the canal, splashing geysers of water skyward, since we were showered in a fine mist. 'If only it was beer!' some joker nearby shouted.

I was becoming used to the din, and my hearing slowly returned. I just about heard Sean bark, 'Get ready for German infantry.' My stomach flipped. The mortar fire continued. We got another dousing from the canal. I wondered how long it would be before the bridge was hit. What would we do if it was destroyed? Our objective was to hold it intact. I realized the sound of some of the mortar rounds was coming from the direction of Jam. I also felt for the guys among the gliders, hoping they could find some decent cover.

I slowly mustered the courage and stupidity to put my head up to look for enemy infantry. My head felt thick, but I could tell the sounds of battle were coming from the centre of Bénouville: machine-gun fire, the thud of grenades, rifle shots and the loud echo of tank rounds. I felt for the para guys. 'Serjeant!' barked a voice from behind us. It was Major Hibbert, scrambling forward with his radio operator. 'Captain Palmer reports a reinforced infantry company plus armour to his front. He plans to fix them in place so we can prepare demolition for both our bridges.'

'Yes, sir,' Sean replied.

'Not quite what I want to do,' reflected Hibbert, 'but we can't let them have the bridges. If enemy armour gets to the beaches, the poor bastards landing will be chopped up on the sand.'

'Do you want my engineers, sir?' Sean enquired.

A headset was shoved to Hibbert's ear by his radio operator. Hibbert's face became grim before he handed back the headset. 'Captain Palmer has lost sight of one of the enemy platoons. He's certain they are trying to bypass him. Get ready, Serjeant.' He scampered over towards Terry's position, his operator following.

'Get ready, boys,' barked Sean. 'Don't take 'em on until you know you can hit 'em! Stokes, I want short bursts. Not sure how much they are gonna throw at us, mate.'

I nodded, focusing on and across the buildings. The light was improving further as dawn approached, but not enough to spot the enemy at distance. I was suddenly overwhelmed by thirst. Without taking my eyes off my arc of fire, I felt my way around my belt kit for my water bottle. I removed the cap and enjoyed some long greedy gulps. It felt wonderful. On any other day it would have been the usual bland sensation, but on this occasion it was the finest pint I had ever tasted. I could have done with a few real pints, though, pints of beer. The harrowing soundtrack in Bénouville was getting worse. It sounded like hell. I hoped Palmer's men were dishing it out, but guessed they were feeling the brunt of the German attack. I wasn't looking forward to reinforcing the paras in Bénouville, should Major Hibbert give the order.

I flinched. Terry's group had opened fire, their tracer rounds screaming past the burning panzer and off into the gloom. Their fire ended as abruptly as it had begun. I could just make out Terry reprimanding those responsible. I glanced at Sean, who slowly shook his head. We were all scared, especially knowing that some of what was in Bénouville was coming towards us. Suddenly, even more thunderous tank fire erupted from the direction of the village, overwhelming the sound of small arms. We didn't have tanks. The biggest and best of the German machines had arrived to confront the paras. My stomach turned.

Tony, still sporting a bandage round his head, jabbed me in the shoulder. He pointed to the right of the buildings. I shook my head, shrugged my shoulders. He leaned in close and hissed in my left ear, 'Infantry, look.' Squinting in the early-June light, I could make out hedgerows and spindly trees slowly waving in what breeze there was, but I couldn't see any bloody German infantry.

The hedgerows suddenly erupted in muzzle flashes. Tracer snapped past our heads. 'Contact right!' Tony roared. I pulled the Bren into my shoulder and started firing short chugging bursts, my own muzzle flashes ruining my night vision. The din in the trench was horrendous. Like the others there, I knew what I had to do – just fire back.

I felt someone shove past behind me. A quick glance confirmed it was Sean. 'Short bursts, you idiots! Identify muzzle flashes and engage. Take cover on the mag changes.'

'Magazine,' roared a guy in the trench. He ducked down to change it.

Sean took his place in the line, firing short bursts. Once the new magazine was in place, Sean stepped back to continue controlling the firefight and abusing us. Just as I was getting into my rhythm, I too had to change magazine. He took my place while I dropped to deal with replacing it. His hot brass casings rained down on me, one getting into my collar, burning my fucking neck. I clambered back up into the fight. The targets had moved, but the task remained the same: destroy the German infantry. He screamed in my ear. 'Shout next time, you fucking clown. Let me know when you have to change mags. I didn't have much ammo in mine.'

'Sorry,' was all I could muster. The enemy out front kept moving left and right, changing their fire positions. I wished they would just stand still. Before too long I had to change my magazine again.

There was a burst of mud and turf just short of the hedgerows, followed immediately by two more explosions ripping into the foliage. Our mortars were having their turn. They continued to thump and shred the fragile cover. After a short while the number of enemy muzzle flashes reduced, then they stopped altogether. Had we killed them all? Had they withdrawn? Who knew? I liked to think we'd got some of them. 'Check fire, check fire!' Sean shouted. 'Watch and shoot!' Watch and shoot was a fire-control order used to control ammunition expenditure. You should only engage clearly identifiable targets, although this didn't quite always happen in practice. 'Ammo state,' barked Sean. I quickly inspected my magazines. I had emptied two and was about halfway through a third. To keep the maths simple, I would report I had used three magazines firing on the hedgerows, which looked in a sorry state.

I fished out two mags from the sandbag I had brought to the trench and refilled my ammunition pouches.

'Good work there, guys,' Sean said once everyone in the trench had reported their ammunition status. 'Keep your eyes peeled. Them fuckers might try it again.'

All hell suddenly erupted. Tracer screamed in all over Terry's position, pinning them down. It was the unmistakably rippling sound of MG 42 fire. Some German infantry had made it behind and into a battered building Sean's group had once occupied. We couldn't fire on the enemy because we couldn't see them.

'Stokes,' roared Sean. He put his arm around my shoulders. 'Stay here. Make sure none of them fuckers get across the road, understand?' I nodded. We couldn't let them make the bridge or outflank Terry's position. But I wondered what Sean had in mind. 'Follow me,' he shouted to the others, scrambling out of the trench. Tony and the rest of the group followed, leaving me on my own.

Realizing they were going to take care of the MG 42s, I chose to focus my aim on the area of the burning panzer, allowing me to switch left and right at will, towards Terry's trench or any of the nearby buildings. The panzer was well alight now, licked with flames, the air shimmering above it. I watched Sean line his group up along a chest-high garden wall, fearing I was missing enemy rushing past the panzer towards Terry's trench. One at a time, Sean and his group clambered over the wall into the grounds of the enemy-occupied building. Amid the continuing sound of MG 42 fire, I began to hear other rounds and grenades exploding inside. There was shouting and swearing, most of it in English.

Suddenly figures appeared below the shimmer of flames coming from the panzer. During the darkness enemy infantry had hidden behind the tank, using it for cover. I fired a burst, then another. More enemy appeared around it. Did I hit any of them? I couldn't bloody tell, but I had obviously drawn them out, because Terry's group began to mow them down.

The gunfight in the building assaulted by Sean's group ceased. A head bobbed above the garden wall. It was Tony. 'Rob, get in here, quick,' he shouted.

I fought my way out of the trench, Bren gun in one hand, the bloody sandbag in the other, and legged it as fast as I could across open ground towards him. He extended his arms. I chucked the sandbag and Bren at him, before almost diving over the wall, ending up in a sweaty heap on the other side. As I slowly straightened up, he handed me the Bren but kept hold of the spare mags.

He chuckled at my equipment-throwing and diving antics. 'There were a dozen enemy, mate. Scared the daylights out of them. We've got their MG 42s now. Most legged it, leaving their guns behind, with loads of ammo too.' A wave of relief washed over me as I followed him through the garden. We entered what was left of the kitchen. Grenades and gunfire had really ruined the decor, crockery scattered all over the place. The windows were blown out, bullet holes in the doors. But bizarrely on a table was a pot of tea, untouched amid the carnage. I wondered if the Germans drank tea before realizing Sean's group must have made the pot before being forced out into the trench.

Tony led me through the house, which had looked quite big from the trench, but I was surprised how small it actually was. The whole place had been redecorated by British and German grenade manufacturers. Through a heavily splintered doorway, Sean stood at a living-room window, two MG 42s with belt ammunition at his feet, their muzzles still smoking, belt ammunition still attached, two extra tins of ammo beside them to boot. 'Help yourself to an MG 42, Stokes. Good shooting earlier.'

Good shooting? Had I hit some enemy infantry then? He pointed through the blown-out window frame. Three field-grey clad bodies lay just outside. I didn't feel anything about them, good or bad. It just felt like I had done my job, the best I could. 'Winman,' Sean ordered, 'go and tell Corporal Thomson to get back into his building. We'll reoccupy this place. We can't have them German bastards sneaking up on us again.'

Tony handed me back the sandbag and hurried off on his new errand. I placed the Bren and sandbag underneath the window frame, taking great satisfaction from acquiring a fearsome MG 42 along with two tins of ammo. I had really enjoyed using one on the ranges on Salisbury Plain. That felt like such a long time ago. But this time yesterday we had been in bed. 'Serjeant,' I asked, 'are there any Germans in the house? Dead, I mean.'

Sean shook his head, then wandered away. I eyeballed the three dead Germans again. Still no feeling about them, just business. I got myself set up at the window. Outside a large area of grass led back to the hedgerows. Behind them, in the pre-dawn light, I could now see the chimneys and rooftops of Bénouville in the distance. Only sporadic shots now sounded from the village, but the occasional roar of tank fire reminded me that we still had to defend the bridge. I felt confident, though. We had already defeated one German counter-attack.

Tony skidded back into the room, sweating like a maniac. He paused to catch his breath. 'Corporal Thomson is back in the building in front of his trench. No casualties among his guys. Our boys are out in the garden. They'll be coming in here soon. Major Hibbert wants the engineers to take care of the bridge.' He left again. I heard him talking, probably thanking the engineers who had fought with us.

Sean made his way back in with his group, including Tony. 'Listen up, guys,' he began. 'We've now been reinforced, but not yet relieved. We've got just over platoon strength on this side of the canal. It's taken us a while to get a proper hold on this position, but that's war for you, I suppose. I will make up a sentry list, since I want some of you to rest. It's getting light out there really fast. Who knows what the bastards will try next.'

We settled down into defensive positions. With my MG 42,

I couldn't help feeling optimistic, despite the ongoing danger. But sobering thoughts entered my tired brain. Bobby Carrol had drowned, and Mr Young was dead. Sean's radio was broken. We had wounded men, and my platoon was scattered all over the place. What a situation, but no one had said it would be easy. However, only the clanking of tank tracks now sounded from Bénouville. A peculiar peace descended.

4
Rescue Mission

The odd shot echoed out of Bénouville. Pretty much running on empty, I fought hard not to fall asleep on my watch. Although I wasn't hungry, I slowly nibbled away at some hard-tack biscuits I had in my smock. Munching kept me awake. It was a miracle Sean managed to keep going. I didn't recall him taking a rest. He was always moving about, checking on us all. He wasn't harsh on those who struggled to stay alert, just handing out chores to keep them active: move ammo, get a message to Terry, anything to keep his battered, fragmented team operational.

'Friendly coming in,' came a shout through the building. Slightly out of breath, Terry came in, asking for Sean. Someone pointed along a corridor. Terry disappeared.

After a couple of minutes, he appeared in the corridor again, on his way back outside. 'My lot will lead first, OK?' he shouted over his shoulder.

Sean assembled his group in my room, except two guys he left on watch. 'The para lads in Bénouville are in a bad way.' He paused to allow this to sink into our tired, numb brains. 'They are low on ammunition and have a lot of walking wounded. From what Captain Palmer has deduced, the Germans have been continually reinforcing two infantry companies. Their armour is fresh with every new contact. He hasn't seen the same panzers twice. They operate no less than three at a time.'

'What does that mean, please?' said a tired voice behind me. Sean rolled his eyes.

'It means whoever Palmer's fighting knows what the fuck they are doing. They aren't showing all their cards at once. They know airborne troops can only fight with what they carry and are therefore drip-feeding men into the fight to wear us down. Captain Palmer has now asked for our help. If the Germans keep hitting his company, he's going to struggle to stay in Bénouville. We are to reinforce Palmer's men, right now. It's quiet there at the moment, just sniper activity and lone enemy soldiers trapped in houses. So Palmer wants us with him in his positions before the enemy has another go. Questions?'

Heads shook all round.

'Corporal Thomson's group will take the lead, to give us advance warning of any trouble. I want the MG 42s to stay here. Take our weapons. Be sure of your targets. I don't want Palmer's boys shooting us up. Bren gunners, I want you one bound behind me, so if things kick off, I can direct you, understood?' I nodded, not knowing which of the others had acquired Brens. 'Kenny,' Sean continued, 'yours is lead section. If it all goes fucking wrong out on the open ground, get your arses back here, OK?' It turned out Kenny Thomas was the section commander of the guys that had joined Sean in the assault on the pillbox. The first buildings at the centre of the village were beyond the hedgerows, three hundred metres at most, but it would be a long way back if we were ambushed.

'Terry's group is on the move,' shouted one of the watchers.

'OK, get your shit ready, boys,' Sean commanded. I got my Bren ready for action, loading a fresh magazine. Emptying the few mags remaining in the sandbag, I shoved them into my smock, giving me two hands available to deal with the gun. 'Let's go,' bellowed Sean. We made our way through the kitchen and out into the garden. Two at a time, we made a comedy act of getting over the garden wall, before shaking out into formation on the open ground. Terry's group appeared forward left of us. Terry now had enough guys to make up a section, but insufficient to constitute a platoon. The magazines stuffed into my smock made me feel clumsy. I made a mental note to rearrange the mags once we got into town. It was as good as full daylight now. I could hear birdsong, the odd cow and the annoying buzz of little bugs loitering about my ears. I was already starting to perspire. My smock was heavy, and the extra mags made me even hotter.

Off to my right there was a sound like thunder. Nothing above us indicated the weather was about to turn. The rumble remained constant. We all looked at each other, not too sure what to make of it. Underneath us the ground was shaking. There was an almighty crash. Almost as one, we dropped to one knee. The rumbling started again. I'd never heard anything like it. Sean stood, waving us on. 'That's naval gunfire, boys. The beach landings have started.' I stayed on one knee for a moment, watching the skyline beyond Bénouville. Biblical columns of smoke began rising. The navy was really dishing it out. I tried to picture the model from the hangar and those five flags on the landing beaches just a few miles away to the north-west. I got to my feet, taking comfort in the enormity of our new fire support. Regardless of what happened in Bénouville, the cavalry were on their way.

Our pace increased as we approached the village, Terry's group still off to one side. Close to the first outbuildings, we took cover, kneeling in a hedgerow. Above the outbuildings, and the houses they belonged to, I could only see the village's distinctive church tower. Terry came over to talk to Sean. They agreed Terry would take a small team to link up with Palmer and the paras. Then Terry would come back to escort the rest of us in. It quickly dawned on me that I didn't know the layout of the village. I couldn't remember the details on the model back in England. Terry ran back to his group, quickly moving through the buildings with some of them.

There was a sudden vicious exchange of gunfire from the

village. All around us, birds took to the air from the trees. The guys around me stood up, trying to see what was going on. The gunfire resumed, staying constant. I recognized the sharp static-like bursts of Sten guns. Then a sudden huge thud from a tank gun raised the stakes. I listened to the Stens for a while.

'Friendly coming in,' came a shout. Terry skidded into the hedgerow, sweating and breathing like a maniac. He held up a hand as he tried to control his breathing. Sean waited patiently.

'German armour and infantry,' Terry gasped. 'Lots of fucking infantry.' He took a deep breath. 'Palmer's boys have really taken a hammering. We managed to link up with his reserve platoon. He's with his forward platoons. I'll lead you in.'

Sean gave him a heavy slap on the back. 'Good man. Right, boys, let's go.'

Terry led off at a crouch, Sean right behind him, the rest of us following in single file. Ahead of us, I was relieved to see the members of Terry's scout patrol still in one piece. They were spread across prominent junctions in the maze of the village's outbuildings, and gestured towards Palmer's positions. Without Terry's guides, we could become lost, ending up in crossfire between the paras and the Germans.

Gardens with chicken coops divided the outbuildings. The gardens had wire-strand fences. The firefight in the village grew louder, accompanied by shouting. Chickens were clucking away like mad, their feathers shedding onto the grass. Tank fire sounded again. Terry halted us just short of a cobbled road. He whistled to get the attention of some paras in a two-storey structure, obviously Palmer's reserve platoon. They waved us in. We made our way into the back of the building, linking up with them.

Surprisingly, the place didn't look in too bad nick, even given the door and windows had been kicked in. But the troops there were in a terrible state. Their appearance shocked me, as had the look of those few paras arriving at the bridge from the landing zones. All were either limping from rough landings in the drop zones or sporting a bandage or two. Some couldn't wear helmets because of head injuries. Every one of them had a cigarette hanging from his lips, though, so life wasn't too bad. They were heavily armed, but I had no idea of their ammunition status. A bloody and battered corporal came forward, offering his hand to Sean. Wiping his sweaty brow with the cuff of his smock, the corporal looked shattered. 'Thank you for the assistance, Sergeant. The boss said for you guys to sit tight. He's on his way back.'

Sean shook his hand with enthusiasm. 'How you boys holding up?'

'The tanks are not the problem, believe it or not. We've kept out of their line of sight, so they haven't come into town. It's just their fucking infantry. It's like trying to plug a leak; they just keep coming.'

Palmer entered, offering his hand to Sean. 'Thank you for coming to us, Sergeant. We are starting to feel the pinch a bit here. Follow me, and I will show you what we are up against.' He led Sean upstairs. Kenny told us to find a corner and make sure our gear was ready to go. I took the opportunity to sort out the bloody magazines that had been jabbing me in the ribs. There was no room in my ammunition pouches, so I took out the poxy empty sandbag, which I had carried with me, and put the mags back in.

Sean came clattering back down the stairs, calling us to gather round. 'We are going to join Palmer's lead platoons. They are just across the street, scattered in four buildings. We have to keep the panzers interested in us. If they disengage from the town and make their way to the beaches, it could prove disastrous for the landings.' The continued rolling thunder of naval gunfire rammed his point home. 'How many PIAT have we got?'

'Two.' An instant answer came from someone. 'Eight rounds between us.'

'OK,' continued Sean, 'our task is to hold the right flank. The cobbled road we crossed goes all the way out to the right, and swings out to where the panzers are moving about. If they realize where we are, we could have them screaming around behind us.'

Palmer reappeared beside Sean. 'Their infantry are also constantly trying to get around our right side.'

'So what are we to do, sir?' Terry asked. He had a menacing glare about him. I wasn't sure if he was relishing the idea of taking on tanks or was worried about becoming bait.

Palmer took a rough sketch from his pocket and laid it on the floor. I craned my neck to look at it. 'Each square on this sketch is a building,' he explained. 'The number in each square indicates how many floors there are. The lines are the roads.' It looked as though the buildings near the outskirts of the village were predominantly single-storey, those closer to the centre being two- or three-storey. He pointed at an area of the sketch. 'I want you guys to quietly occupy this building.' From the position of the three-storey building, which lay on a central road, it looked like he wanted an ambush rather than a holding position. I sensed he was about to announce a desperate gamble designed to draw their tanks into the open, any post-engagement escape from the building being fraught with risk and danger.

'I will get my front-right platoon to make a big show of abandoning its current position,' he continued. 'They will fall back across the road and establish themselves directly behind you. The German armour will see them retreat, so should make a bold move forward, going for our right flank. You guys will be able to hit their tanks with your PIATs. Everyone else, including my withdrawing platoon, will take care of the enemy infantry. Understand?' A few people nodded. His eyes narrowed. 'Don't let the panzers get past, or we're screwed. They would have us trapped, any movement across that bloody road being a turkey shoot for them.'

'Two minutes, boys,' Sean commanded. 'Get ready to move.'

'I will lead you and your men, Sergeant,' said Palmer. 'After all, it's my silly idea.'

Sean nodded. 'Won't be the last silly idea an officer will put to the boys before this is all done.'

Palmer nodded back, grinning.

Once we were ready to go, he led us out the front door onto the road. I was behind Kenny and Tony from Sean's platoon. A couple of PIAT teams accompanied us. There were also a few glider pilots with Brens. Flanked by Sean and Terry, Palmer quietly led us up the street, hugging the buildings. This was a main road heading towards the centre of the village, the taller village houses towering over us. I realized some of the three-storey buildings on Palmer's sketch were actually two storeys with windowed attics built into the roofs.

My heart was in my mouth. I couldn't help repeatedly looking over my shoulder, thinking the enemy might ambush us from behind. I cursed them for not showing their hand, opening fire to enable us to get it over with. The anticipation was the worst bit. Adrenaline killed fear, but in the moments before combat I found my hands sweating and my pulse racing out of control. At least I wasn't the only stupid idiot walking up the road. One thing that struck me was the lack of civilians. Where the hell were they? Hiding? Moved away? Despite the heavy fighting, Bénouville was still in decent condition.

I heard a violent exchange of gunfire. We all went firm, going down onto one knee. The firefight sounded horrendous. I could hear British swearing. The odd German screamed, probably similar obscenities. Grenades echoed loudly. There was no tank fire, just the sounds of close combat.

The exchange gradually reduced to shots here and there. Palmer dashed across a gap between buildings. We all rushed after him. I rattled like a tin pot during my dash. Terry confronted me, looking rather pissed off. 'How much more fucking noise do you wanna make?' I nodded sheepishly, quickly opening my smock and wedging the fucking rattling sandbag tight under my left armpit. It would have to do for now. Palmer led on. We carefully picked our way through some small gardens, trying our hardest not to get caught up on chicken mesh and wire fences. Off the main road, within the outhouses that seemed to encircle the village, I guessed Palmer would look for a safer way to reach the building we were to occupy.

We entered a maze of single-storey structures, all still in good condition. A message came down the line to sit tight. Palmer and Sean moved ahead to check out what lay ahead. The thunder of naval gunfire suddenly ceased, but was replaced by the gunning of engines. I could just make out people shouting, but couldn't tell which side they were on. It was probably the panzer teams getting ready to deploy, since although I could hear the enemy machines, I couldn't hear the clatter of tracks.

Sean and Palmer returned. 'PIATs and gunners up front,' Palmer ordered. I made my way forward with our two PIAT teams and the glider pilots. Sean took us across the main road at a crouch and through an open door into a house, then up wide wooden stairs into a kitchen. It was neat and tidy, but the decor would soon be ruined. He led us into a hall and up another flight of stairs to the top floor. I stayed put while he positioned the PIAT guys.

Eventually he emerged from a room, calling me forward. He took me into the room, a child's, judging by all the toys and dolls. I hoped the family was somewhere safe. One of the PIAT teams was hunkered beneath the window frame, the window above open. 'The cobbled road is directly below us,' Sean quietly explained to me. 'When these guys hit the tank, your job is to kill the crew as it bails out. If we don't get the crew, they just become more infantry we have to fight. Most of our guys will be downstairs. They'll take care of any infantry supporting the tanks. When you hear "Break clean" shouted, you are to get downstairs like shit-hot lightning, and back into the gardens. We will not be staying here, understand?'

I nodded.

'Remember,' he continued, 'the captain plans to make a show of moving his platoon out of its current position. They'll move into a building across the street, so should help stop enemy infantry getting in here.' My stomach flipped and tightened. I was terrified at the idea of Germans downstairs while I was stuck upstairs. He gave me a slap on the shoulder, then made his way downstairs.

I took a seat on the floor, leaning against a wall. The grubby, tired faces of the PIAT guys seemed familiar, but for the life of me I couldn't remember where I'd seen them.

My mind drifted back to training with the PIAT on Salisbury Plain. It was a bitch of a weapon, spring-loaded and shoulder-fired, a very primitive variation of the American bazooka or German Panzershreck. The spring in the bastard thing was industrial-strength and thick. Unless you had the arms of Goliath, there was very little play in it. It wasn't a challenge to fire the PIAT – we were hitting tank hulks up to 300 metres away – the real problem was re-cocking the bloody launcher for a second shot without exposing yourself to the enemy. It was almost comical watching slighter guys trying their damnedest to reset the spring. The only guy that came close to taming the beast with his brute strength was Frank Williams, but even he couldn't make a living out of it. Inverting the PIAT was the only way to get it back into action for a second shot, literally standing on the cocking handle as if you were trying to start a motorbike. My only advice was to find somewhere suitable to invert it, since I very much doubted young Fritz would politely sit still in his panzer and allow you another go.

'Sorry, guys, I'm shit with names. I'm Robbie, Robbie Stokes.'

'Donny Grant.'

'Tommy Mason.'

This broke the ice and we nattered for a while, mostly about my glider's horrible landing. They were horrified to hear the tail had broken off, causing Bobby Carrol to drown in the pond. We chatted about horrible fitness sessions on Salisbury Plain with Bobby, having a giggle that those up at the Pearly Gates would now be doing press-ups for him. We jabbered on about the usual stuff – home, the war, when it would end.

Boots clattered up the stairs. Sean entered, taking a knee at the threshold. 'Palmer's platoon are moving out of their position. They plan to be behind us in the next five minutes. Everyone OK?'

We all nodded.

'We've got a two-storey building just in front of us. The panzers won't be able to sit back and shell us. If they want to get their infantry in here, they'll have to come in close. Make sure them shutters are open fully. Don't want any delays.' He moved into the next room, where the other PIAT team was situated. The street was quiet, but I could hear distant fighting to the north and I wondered if it was the lads on Sword Beach. I bloody hoped they'd got ashore all right.

'Panzers moving about,' came a shout from downstairs. I could indeed now hear multiple engines, not idling any more. More than one panzer was definitely coming towards us. Donny and Tommy checked their PIAT over.

'Twenty-plus infantry on the right –' another shout from downstairs '– running alongside the leading tank. Three hundred metres.' I took a deep breath. The clattering tracks and rumbling engine of a single panzer were growing ever louder. I could hear their infantry shouting above the din. My heart was beating like a bass drum. I clenched my fists, trying to prepare myself. Rubbing my sweaty palms over my smock, I made sure I had my spare magazines ready. I squatted over the sandbag. The PIAT boys kept looking at each other, shaking their heads. They had a lot of pressure on them: they had to stop the panzer.

'Two hundred.' Another roar from downstairs. I began bouncing on my haunches, wanting to get it over with. Although my combat career had been very short, I was learning once again that waiting was the worst part.

The house began to vibrate. Trinkets and ornaments fell from their perches around the room. Framed pictures crashed to the floor. The PIAT guys didn't reveal themselves; to do so would be suicidal, although with the limited resources we had, fighting panzers and infantry was suicidal enough.

'Now!' someone screamed downstairs. The PIAT guys sprang up and with an ear-popping thud fired their projectile. There was an almighty *crump* outside. As I stepped forward, they jumped away from the window. Fighting to get my Bren onto the window ledge, I was greeted by a shower of sparks from below. It had come from the back engine deck of the lead panzer, the only one I could see, but the tank was continuing to move forward under our window.

Movement opposite caught my attention. A mass of grey-clad infantry was rushing up some steps into the building across the street, not our house as expected. I fired a long burst at them. Some of the enemy sprayed out a red mist as my bullets splintered the doorway behind them. Those men I hit crumpled, moving more like liquid than solid bodies. A few remained partially propped up by their equipment, before more bullets hastened their journey to the ground. One slid down the steps, face up. There was no Hollywood gloss to mowing them down. I didn't feel anything for them, certainly not sorry. The survivors smashed their way through the door, the last of my burst following them in.

The panzer stopped moving, stricken after all. I ducked away from the window, shocked to find my magazine already empty.

The advantages of firing successive short bursts were constantly drummed into us during training – for greater accuracy while preserving ammunition and preventing the weapon from overheating – but that had all gone out of the window as soon as I sighted the throng of enemy infantry opposite. I had felt I needed to be quick on the draw, blazing away to get as many of them as possible, to stop them from killing me and my mates.

The PIAT guys stepped forward and fired another projectile. Between them they had obviously managed to reset the spring. A loud thump confirmed a second hit on the panzer. As I scrambled to change my magazine, random voices revealed hell unfolding downstairs. 'Germans in the house!' someone screamed above the racket. A warning of grenades sounded.

The concussion of grenades going off downstairs caused the floorboards in the room to flex up, the wood snapping in places. My ankles, shins and knees felt like they'd been hit with a hammer, the pain intense.

'Break clean!' sounded from the stairwell. I only just heard it over the ringing in my ears. But despite our disorientation, we immediately responded to the call, moving at a crouch as we made our way onto the landing. Sean was at the bottom of the first flight of stairs, waving us down. 'Let's go. We've got Germans all over us. Follow me.' He dashed through the kitchen.

We sprinted after him, passing scattered bodies before making it outside. He darted across the street into an alleyway, past the German bodies on the steps. The alley would surely lead back to the gardens. I struggled to keep up with the PIAT team, but there was no way I was going to be left behind. Other running boots sounded behind. A tank round hit the building occupied by Palmer's platoon, glass, bricks and tiles flying skyward.

Sean broke out into a garden yard. Running for our lives, we watched him drop to one knee and spin. He fired a couple of short bursts with his Sten. 'Contact left!' Suddenly finding the adrenaline-fuelled strength to sprint past the PIAT team, I was first to reach him, taking up a position at his side. He fired again, his rounds smashing into wooden outbuildings standing in front of a larger brick house fifty metres away. Catching a glimpse of an enemy muzzle flash, I fired short bursts at the windows of the brick building. Rounds snapped past me, others kicking up turf and gravel around us. The PIAT team arrived with some of our other guys, quickly forming a firing line with us. I could just about hear excited German voices.

Sean began hurling grenade after grenade over the outbuildings. Some of the grenades bounced back off the brick house, but one rolled through its front door. The Germans shouted as one just before the grenade went off. The explosion must have hit them hard; they stopped firing. 'Right, let's fucking go!' Sean shouted, giving me a clip on the shoulder as he clambered to his feet and ran. I led the group sprinting after him.

Sean ran towards the front door of a house. 'In here!' he yelled. He crashed into it with a shoulder charge, but bounced back, crumpling to the ground. I thought he'd knocked himself out, but he was just gasping to get his breath back, slumped. His eyes narrowed to a glare. 'Stokes,' he wheezed, 'open that fucking door.' He wasn't happy. I put the muzzle of my Bren against the lock and squeezed the trigger. The frame around the lock splintered, and after a couple of kicks with my size tens, we were in.

Sean's only wound was to his pride as he began ushering the other guys through the door. I was more concerned to establish if they had all escaped after the ambush. Most had cuts and bruises but nothing major. Only Terry seemed to be missing. Palmer rushed through last with his radio operator, trying to catch his breath. 'Fucking hell,' he gasped. 'I thought we'd bitten off more than we could chew back there.'

Sean didn't look too pleased about the venture either. 'Did we stop that bloody tank?'

Palmer nodded. 'The crew managed to bail out though. It's chaos back there. Those Germans not engaged with our nearby friendly call signs are shooting at each other. There's no way anyone can go back to that building. It would be suicide.' I could certainly still hear a lot of firing coming from the direction of the ambush.

Sean looked around. 'Bloody Terry got himself trapped in the basement before I gave the order to break clean.'

Palmer stared at him, the awful truth unsaid. Terry was on his own now.

Some guys took water on board. Sean ordered us all to check our ammunition status. I realized I had dropped the sandbag in the yard. I had a magazine fitted to the Bren and four more in my ammunition pouches. They would have to do for now. Everyone was low on ammo after the ambush. I hoped Sean wouldn't ask me about the bag and wondered absently if he'd be more annoyed if I said I'd lost it or used it all.

I suddenly decided to go back for it. My mind made up, I quietly slipped out the door as most of the guys around me sparked up cigarettes. I slipped across the garden, worried about being seen. But Palmer hadn't quite gotten around to organizing sentries or spotters in the windows. I saw the sandbag immediately and scurried towards it, then stopped as the sound of gunfire ahead became ever louder. I thought of Terry. My platoon commander, Bertie Young, had already been lost that day. I didn't want to lose my section commander too. Terry might find a way out, but he might not. I took a look round the side of the house and couldn't see anyone. We obviously hadn't been followed through the alley after the ambush, so there was just a chance I might be able to help him escape. But to go back would be to disobey what might as well have been a direct order from Captain Palmer.

Before I knew what I was doing I broke into a run along the alleyway. Stopping at the end, I once again encountered the sprawling German bodies on the now-crimson steps. And there was Terry, framed in the doorway of the building opposite, just visible through the smoke drifting up from the panzer we had taken out. All around the doorway the wall was severely pockmarked, bullets still striking the area. Terry took half a step forward, still using the shattered doorframe for cover. He fired a short Sten burst in one direction along the street, followed by a burst of equal length in the opposite direction.

I leaned out slightly, quickly looking left and right, before snapping my head back into cover. There were two small groups of enemy infantrymen in the street, one group to the left, the other to the right, both firing at the doorway. I supposed they had no way of knowing Terry was on his own. Behind him the building was obviously clear. And he wasn't being fired on from the building above me; perhaps the enemy there had moved on, perhaps they couldn't see Terry through the smoke, or perhaps the Bren-wielding glider pilots had got them. In any case, the problem was that Terry couldn't make it across the street to the alley without becoming caught in a lethal crossfire.

I decided surprise was my best weapon. Hauling the Bren in front of me, I stepped out of the alleyway, firing a burst towards the group to my right, followed by a similar burst at the group on my left. No hits, but I'd chewed up the cobblestones around them, and they dispersed as they dived for whatever cover they could. As I stepped back into the alley, the firing stopped as they tried to re-evaluate their position.

The momentary lull was all Terry needed. He jumped out, scrambling behind the panzer, which gave him cover from one direction. But the stunned Germans didn't fire, so he remained standing, carefully scanning either side of the stricken smouldering tank, before running into the alleyway. 'Thanks, Robbie,' he said, passing me at a jog.

'I wasn't supposed to come . . .' I breathlessly replied, following him.

'Don't worry,' he replied knowingly. 'I won't let on.'

But back in the house beyond the garden Sean was the first person we encountered. He glanced at Terry, then stared at me. Palmer was busy with his radio operator. I thought Sean almost cracked a little smile as he looked at me.

Muffled chat on the radio caught my attention. Palmer listened for a while, his face deadpan. Was it good or bad news? He finally spoke: 'The Germans are falling back, at least for now. My guys have seen the remaining panzers around the town begin to move north, probably towards Sword. They have bigger fish to fry now.' He looked disappointed, obviously fearing for the guys on the beach, but I was chuffed to bits the tanks had moved on. My reasons were selfish, I knew. 'We got three of the bastards anyway,' he confirmed before shrugging his shoulders.

Sean assumed the role of sergeant major for Palmer's company, siting everyone in defensive positions in our new house and the ones immediately surrounding it. Palmer's CSM had broken his back landing on their drop zone. Palmer explained that a lot of his command structure was gone. His OC had shattered his femur on a stone wall when landing. Many of Palmer's men had landed badly or had been hit by ground fire during the drop. Some hadn't even made it out of planes downed by flak.

The only sounds of real fighting were now coming from the north and seemed to be getting louder. It sounded horrendous on the beaches. I began to hear distant tank fire and hoped it was our guys. A few mortar shells hit the village, bursting roofs. The odd round landed quite close to us, one exploding in a garden. Sean told everyone to stay clear of the upper floors, explaining that some enemy mortar rounds had delayed fuses, allowing them to penetrate buildings before exploding. But Palmer didn't get any reports of further casualties on the radio.

5
The Diver

In my exhausted state of fitful rest, amid the short but now more frequent mortar attacks, the morning in the house dragged on. Terry came over and thanked me again for rescuing him from the scene of the ambush. As he sat smoking he started to talk about home, but I only listened with half an ear. Most of my attention was on the noise coming from the direction of Sword Beach, which seemed to be growing even louder. I sat with my eyes closed, picturing our boys storming German positions on Sword, Juno and Gold. I hoped they were giving them hell, though it occurred to me that we might be getting some retreating enemy coming our way if that was the case. I tried to bring to mind the model in the hangar again but found I couldn't remember it clearly any more. Nothing on the ground was quite how it had appeared.

During lulls in the mortar fire Sean and Captain Palmer had taken their chances, visiting our guys in the nearby houses. On their return they gave me and Terry the same chat I imagine everyone else had. 'My battalion will very shortly reinforce us,' Palmer began. 'We need to provide guides for the commanders coming in.'

'The panzers are gone,' elaborated Sean, 'and as far as we can see there's no immediate threat to the bridge from the village, so we can spare a few lads to act as guides.'

'We've also ascertained that the Germans must have had a spotter somewhere in the town –' Palmer took over '– because an increase in the rate of mortar fire followed the arrival of our reinforcements. The reinforcements decided to stay on the outskirts until the mortars stopped and I've sent people in to find the bastard.'

'The mortar fire has now stopped,' continued Sean, 'so we reckon the spotter's either dead or scared off, but the reinforcements have still decided to push only one company into town.'

'Some of the reinforcement will relieve my lead platoon,' Palmer concluded, 'which still occupies a key building. Hence the need to guide it in.'

Sean assigned me back to Terry's group, which had been tasked with the guiding role. It took an age for Palmer's lead platoon to fall back through their replacements. They looked in no better shape than the men who originally arrived in Bénouville so the Germans were still giving us a rough time in the drop zones. We guided the new commanders around the place. I was horrified to see the condition of the buildings facing each other across the ambush site. They were now smashed to shit: caved-in roofs, partially collapsed walls, fires. The panzers, infantry firefight and recent mortar fire had taken their toll. I realized that while I had been resting Palmer's lead platoon had really earned its money, keeping the Germans at bay. Intending to assign defensive positions to the reinforcements, Terry went into the building originally occupied by Palmer's lead platoon. But I guessed the paras would reorganize their defences once Terry had gone.

There was an almighty bang. 'Mortars! Get out of the street!' screamed a voice. I dashed into the house Terry was in, crashing my way into a kitchen. Mortar fire seemed to concentrate around the building, the concussions spilling crockery from the cupboards. My ears popped painfully, leaving me hearing a dull whine. The enemy spotter was obviously still about. I got underneath a heavy oak table.

After a fair while the mortar fire stopped. My hearing quickly returned. Muffled garbles in the house became voices. I walked out of the kitchen and looked around. Whoever owned the place was going to be fucking pissed off with the German Army, assuming the owners had escaped rather than perished. The building was completely trashed, a lost cause. In the hall a staircase had completely collapsed, its remnants lying in a deep hole in the floor.

I wandered outside. There were plenty of 7 Para guys around, brushing dust and grime off their shoulders and gear. Someone's dinner was scattered across the middle of the debris-littered road. I couldn't find Terry or any of his guys. 'Mate, your section commander is getting treated by our medic,' one of the paras offered.

I went looking for Terry, fearing the worst. Eventually I found him on a street corner. A medic and another guy stood over him. Terry put two fingers up as I approached. The medic had given him a nice new bandage around his head. I smiled at Terry but couldn't help noticing the medic and his mate were chuckling away, coughing and spluttering, both struggling to hold cigarettes between their lips. Terry gave me a murderous glance, which reduced them to hysterics. 'Don't you fucking start, Stokes,' snapped Terry, 'cos it's bad enough being treated by these comedians.' The medic and his friend laughed so hard, they struggled to breathe. Terry clearly didn't get the joke, shaking his head at them. 'Should have asked them to take me to a fucking chalet.' Their laughter redoubled, reducing them to tears. Up and down the street, paras were grinning. Medic and mate did their best to compose themselves.

I had to ask. 'What happened?'

They were now screaming with laughter. Terry clambered to his feet, irate. 'Go on, then, fucking tell him.'

It took a while, but the medic managed to pull himself together. 'When the mortars started, the corporal was in the building there, upstairs with us.' He cracked up again, but managed to continue the story. 'He shouted to take cover, and as far as I'm aware went for the stairs. But the first round landed so close, a wall and the stairs collapsed. It was like he took a swimming-pool dive into the space where the stairs had been, and just went down and down into a hole. All we could hear throughout the shelling was "Oh, fuck!"' He completely lost it, giggling uncontrollably. His mate doubled over, a dribbling mess.

Terry was red-faced. I imagine he was feeling a right wally, his pride in tatters. He looked at me sternly and then pointed at the building, like I was a child being sent to my room. 'Cheers, boys. I'll buy the beer in Paris.'

'No problem!' screamed the medic. 'You might feel a little sick later, but that'll be due to your concussion. Just stick to fighting in chalets!' The medic and his mate became ruined with laughter.

I walked away with Terry. A few guys from our platoon made an appearance, Frank Williams and Dougie Chambers among them. Apart from a few more cuts and bruises, they all seemed OK. I just hoped they wouldn't ask about Terry's bandage. I wasn't sure I could keep a straight face much longer. Big Frank clocked the bandage straight away. I gave him a subtle shake of my head and a wink, letting him know the explanation should wait for later.

The 7 Para deployment was in full swing, so we made our way back to Sean and Palmer, hoping we could leave the village soon. Sean was poring over a map with the para platoon sergeants, jabbing away at it with a filthy finger. He saw Terry, did a double take and glared at us, demanding an explanation for Terry's head injury. Frank sidestepped, making me the focus of Sean's stare. I merely shrugged my shoulders. Sean went back to his map, but I knew that sooner or later I was going to be asked about Terry's misfortune.

Frank and Dougie collared me, taking me off to one side. 'What happened, then?' Frank asked. I had no reason to lie to them. They had really helped me out during training in England when things got tough. I kept my voice down as I related the tale, continually looking over my shoulder, thinking Terry might be behind me. Dougie and Frank struggled to keep grins from their filthy smug faces.

Once I'd finished the story, they found a spot to relax, struggling to stifle their chuckles. It was funny, no doubt about it, but in a way I felt sorry for Terry. He was a good leader, like one of the tough ones you saw in comic books, and it could have been worse. He had just been unfortunate. I resigned myself to the fact Frank and Dougie weren't going to keep the tale to themselves. It was just a matter of time before I would face the high jump.

6
The Piper

'Right, my guys, get ready to move,' hollered Sean. 'We're finally getting out of Bénouville.'

I looked around. Like some of the paras, a few of our guys nursed head wounds that meant they could no longer wear their helmets, so they had attached them to their fighting gear. Including Terry. He led our platoon out. I brought up the rear with Frank and Dougie, happy to be going back to the bridge and not envying the 7 Para boys we were leaving behind to hold the village. Lord only knows how long they would be expected to hold their positions. Sean's group marched about a hundred metres behind us. As we reached open ground, a column of 7 Para stragglers began to pass us, going towards the outskirts of the village. We exchanged professional nods with them. As was the case with the other para groups we had encountered, they looked battered and knackered; many limping, bloody bandages on them. The invasion of Europe was not even a day old, and everyone already looked shattered. There were some grizzled veterans among our ranks, but the lion's share of our guys were as green as they came, including me.

Mortar fire began sounding again from Bénouville, and we copied the 7 Para column, taking a knee or getting down on our bellies in the long grass. It was force of habit; grass was no cover against high-velocity shrapnel. Although the mortar fire wasn't as intense as when we were in Bénouville, the thin treeline in front of the outbuildings was shredded, tree debris raining down on us. The odd mortar round made it into the open ground, showering us with dirt and turf. Sean slid up to Terry. 'I thought they'd taken care of that fucking spotter.'

'They probably have,' Terry replied. 'The mortar crews can still shoot on their recent target information.' Perhaps the enemy were just chucking what they had in our general direction. I wondered if the bastards knew they were not being quite as effective as previously. With any luck, 7 Para patrols might catch up with the fucking crews and their spotter. Or they might piss off soon, if they ran out of ammunition.

'During the last few hours I could have sworn that some of the firing was coming from the direction of the bridges,' piped up Dougie. 'I wonder what's been happening there.'

Sean gazed across the open ground. A line of trees and foliage prevented a clear view of Bénouville Bridge and the buildings around it. 'We're about to find out. But Major Hibbert's still pushing 7 Para past us into Bénouville, so the bridges must be OK. The firing you heard might have been from the drop zones.'

'It's obvious the para boys haven't had it their own way on the drop zones,' Terry added, 'but we're well dug in at the bridges, and knocking the first German counter-attack back has clearly given the OC the confidence to push the paras through.'

'He pushed them through to stop enemy tanks and infantry in Bénouville from advancing on the bridges,' surmised Sean, 'as well as stopping the tanks from moving on Sword Beach.'

'But it's a big shout to hold those bridges all night and all day,' Frank chipped in, 'all the while surrounded by enemy. I wonder how the beach landings are going, how long it will take those boys to get to us. It's been a lot more intense than I expected.'

Dougie and I both nodded in agreement. I'd thought I'd experienced war through Dad and Daniel, but nothing could have prepared me for the reality: mind-numbing, terrifying, nothing like the glamour portrayed on the recruiting posters. I couldn't quite believe how much had already happened in a day. I seemed to be acting on instinct with only my training getting me through.

'Robbie, I heard you were really on your game back there,' teased Frank. 'I bet you couldn't keep your finger off the trigger when push came to shove.' I wonder how he could have possibly known that I'd abandoned short bursts when firing from the window in Bénouville. Perhaps he had done it himself when first confronted with a large number of moving enemy. Not that it mattered. I knew that he was the very best to have in your corner, if you got into a tight spot.

'Leave him alone,' Terry responded. 'He did good. Took down most of a platoon trying to find cover in a building at the ambush site. Some of the glider boys had Brens, but my money is on the fact that almost all of the bullets were his.'

The shelling from Bénouville became sporadic. Sean ordered us to our feet, and we continued to head towards the bridge. The para column chose to stay in the long grass, waiting to see if the mortar fire would die out altogether, which was understandable.

We reached the house from which we had deployed to Bénouville. Like the bridge the building faced, it was technically part of the village but separated from the main settlement by open ground. Even though the bridge was therefore only five hundred metres or so from the centre of the village, it had seemed much further than that, a measure of how long the day had been. The building had friendly new tenants, some of whom waved to us as we headed on towards the bank of the canal. Most jokingly gave us a finger, though.

Company Serjeant Major Jenkins was directing some troops as they pulled German dead out of a trench system. They were being careful. A few of our guys were retching, but none stopped working. Some of the dead had already been laid on a poor excuse of a wooden cart, all face down. I supposed whichever guys got the job of hauling the cart wouldn't want dead faces staring at them. But then a lad came out of the building with bed sheets and covered the macabre cargo.

A detail was chosen to haul the cart away. Terry told us to rest as the dead were wheeled away over the bridge. I noticed the area around the bridge had already been cleared of dead, including Mr Young. A CSM would oversee many grim duties. Our primary task was to hold the bridge until relieved, and the clearance would stop the area from becoming a fly-blown hell hole. The guys with the cart were already flicking their ears and slapping their necks. Unless the bodies were cleared, it would only get worse on a hot June day.

We followed onto the bridge as soon as the cart had cleared it. Jenkins ran to catch us up. To our left, on the canal, I noticed a burning boat with German markings. 'What the hell is that?' I said instinctively. The words just slipped out.

'While you lot were away,' explained Jenkins, 'they even threw bloody gunboats at us. Two of the bastards decided to come and have a go. We managed to whack that one with a couple of PIATs, and then the other one pissed off.'

While in Bénouville I hadn't heard any battle noise coming from the area of the bridges. Maybe Dougie's position had not been subject to the gentle breeze heading inland from Sword. Maybe the naval gunfire had blocked the sounds out for me. Or maybe he had placed the sources of the noises better, because he was more experienced than me. But no one had talked about gunboats during our training in England. Where had they come from? How many were there? What information did we have on them?

'They even sent one of their fighters to have a go at the bridge,' Jenkins continued, nodding enthusiastically. 'Just the one bomb. It clipped the right side of the bridge but exploded in the water. Lucky or what? Without the bridge, we would have no way to get across the canal.'

An almighty thud set my ears screaming. In the area of the gliders a plume of smoke drifted skywards. We dropped to one knee, fearing a mortar attack, but Jenkins remained standing, his cart rumbling along in the near distance. He smirked. 'Don't worry, that's outgoing. Got a couple of the boys on that gun over there, helping the boys in Bénouville with a sniper problem.' I noticed a gun just in front of the gliders. A few of our boys milled around it, some rather clumsily loading another shell. Before long another round headed off in the direction of the town.

I didn't recognize the weapon, until it suddenly dawned on me it was the anti-tank gun we had moved past the night before. We hadn't trained on it back in England so I didn't envy the group of our guys sitting off to the right. Its crew were still trying to figure the contraption out. I just hoped they had some kind of clue how to take on any panzers that might present themselves on the far bank. There were more injured around the gliders than before, more dead too, but it still seemed our casualties were amazingly light considering everything. The company aid post seemed much better organized now. Plenty of medics were attending to our wounded, sending the odd one past us back into the fight. Jenkins had even got the wounded into a trench system around the gliders as shelter against mortar or other forms of bombardment. Only now, in the full light of day, did I realize the trenches formed part of the original German defence system around the bridge. I suddenly found myself swelling with pride for the tough bunch of idiots I was with, especially my D Company colleagues.

All hell broke loose again in Bénouville: mortars, grenades, long bursts of MG 42 fire, the static-like chatter of Sten guns, the works. The Germans were back in town. But the paras were there in strength now, and as long as they weren't routed, I would remain quietly content. My thoughts were with them, although I was glad I wasn't. It would be a very long day at the office for them.

Major Hibbert appeared beside us from God knows where. He looked shattered. His radio operator looked like he could do with a kip as well. 'Bloody well done in Bénouville, boys,' said Hibbert. 'Captain Palmer has nothing but praise for what you guys did while his battalion got its act together.'

We all smiled and nodded, some passing around lit cigarettes. 'How is Captain Brettle's group getting on, sir?' Sean enquired.

'Fortunately he only faced a limited counter-attack. Most of his potential opposition had already withdrawn to the drop zones to deal with the parachute landings. Many of Brettle's guys are a bit battered and bruised, but no more than a Saturday night downtown.' Grins appeared, chuckles sounded. 'But we have just received word there are panzers prowling the drop zones and beginning to push towards Jam. Much of our radio chatter talks of SS panzers in the area, but no one can confirm it.'

Jam was Ranville Bridge, which Captain Brettle's group was assigned to defend. I'd heard about the SS, Hitler's best troops. Vicious bastards not famous for giving any quarter, or asking for any. If there were SS units on the drop zones when the paras landed, the fighting would have been savage. Had Hibbert known about panzers in the area before we came? Would he have told us? I wouldn't have.

'Captain Brettle has enough PIAT in his position,' he continued, 'so he can take care of armour threats. You boys grab some rest. You are now in reserve. The serjeant major has spare ammunition, plus a few enemy weapons that could well be put to good use.' Sean nodded as Hibbert began to head off towards Jam with his radio operator while Jenkins went back to his grim trench duties.

But then Hibbert did an abrupt about-turn, returning to squint at Terry. 'What happened to your head?' I held my breath.

Terry kept his composure. 'Fell down some stairs, sir, while doing the relief for 7 Para.' He could have easily lied, but to his credit he – kind of – hadn't.

'Take it easy for a while, Corporal. I'm a bit short-staffed right now.' He gave him a wink. Terry smiled. 'The battalion is to rendezvous in Ranville,' Hibbert continued. 'We will join them once we hand over here, so I'm afraid it will be another long night.'

'Who will we hand over to, sir?' asked Sean.

Hibbert shrugged his shoulders. 'Not entirely sure at the moment. The 2nd Battalion of the Royal Warwickshire Regiment is assigned to the relief, but I will happily take any offers that come our way.' He led his radio operator away again.

It felt bitter-sweet, being in reserve. We deserved a break, though, having been on the go for a while. Up until then only the Germans had dictated when we could take a breather. We made our way over to the gliders. I found the one I had flown in and peered inside. Everything of use had been cleared out. I took off my fighting gear. Without it, the feeling of being able to stretch out properly on the grass was wonderful. Then I heard some god-awful screeching coming up the road. It soon became so loud, it was enough to make Hibbert and his radio operator rejoin us once again. But what the bloody hell was the racket?

We followed Hibbert onto the road. Jenkins joined us. Two columns of troops were approaching at a pretty fast march, a lone soldier at the front. Playing bagpipes. They looked like they were fresh from action; soaked in sweat, many lightly wounded, a bandage almost a badge of rank. I guessed they were the first arrivals from Sword. 'What the bloody hell is this all about?' muttered Sean.

Hibbert shrugged his shoulders again. 'Damned if I know. Wait here.'

They began clattering their way onto the bridge as he reached them, the piper's tune reaching a crescendo, even blocking out the soundtrack from Bénouville. Lads on the far bank emerged from trenches and buildings to take a look. I wasn't sure if the whole thing was marvellous or just plain weird. Had the piper played as they came ashore? The columns stopped on the bridge, the bagpipes ceasing, as a guy I assumed to be their OC stepped forward. Hibbert courteously shook hands with him, and they began conversing softly. Was this our relief?

'What the fuck is going on here?' Jenkins whispered. 'A bloody piper on the middle of a bridge during an invasion. Bonkers.' He decided to join Hibbert, who introduced him to the officer.

After a while, Hibbert and Jenkins stood off to one side and the piper got back into action. He led the columns back off the bridge towards us, like the march onto the bridge had been symbolic. They started to pass us, heading towards Jam. Strutting just behind the piper, their OC gave us a thumbs up and a casual wave, as did a couple of guys behind him. A few others even broke rank, racing into our company aid post, shaking hands with our wounded, before racing to catch up with the columns. As they marched away, Jenkins and Hibbert rejoined us. 'Gentlemen –' Hibbert smiled '– you have been in the presence of Lord Lovat and his commandos.'

'Not our relief, then, sir?' Sean snorted.

'No,' replied Hibbert, raising his eyebrows, 'but he apologized for being delayed. He had a prior engagement with some ghastly German fellows down the road.' His demeanour became defensive. 'His words, not mine.' He wandered away, his radio operator following. The whole experience had been truly bizarre.

A mortar round landed nearby, then a second, even closer. The gun crew was forced to take refuge with the rest of us in the trench system, medics hurriedly moving the wounded to cover. My trench was close to the now-abandoned German gun. The fighting in the town seemed to reduce to a mixed bag of machine-gun bursts and the odd rifle shot. Listening to aircraft high above but not bothering to look up, I noticed for the first time that you could see the town's church tower from the aid post. We sat tight, hopefully staying out of trouble, waiting for our relief to finally arrive.

Hunkered down at the bottom of my trench, my head resting against the side, I tried to get some sleep. I knew if I took my helmet off, I would probably be more comfortable, but I just couldn't be bothered. I was exhausted; what food I had was gone, and I needed to refill my water bottle. I looked at my Bren, hanging over the top of the trench. The gun needed cleaning, but it could wait a little longer. I was just a tired soldier in a hole, much like the rest of my unit. Suddenly thinking of the sandbag of spare magazines I had left in Bénouville, I hoped the para boys had found it and put it to good use. Lord knows they would need ammunition.

A mortar round fell close, snapping me out of my slumber with a start. We were showered in wooden splinters from the glider wrecks. Dougie, Frank, Terry and Tony were with me in the trench. They brushed the splinters away and got on with the vital task of resting. They hadn't even bothered to open their eyes. Why worry about a mortar shell that missed? If there was a direct hit, you wouldn't be around long enough to worry. A round splashed up water from the canal. I risked a look over the top. Another round threw up dirt from the far bank. The Germans seemed to have become more interested in Bénouville again. Fragments of what could only be roof tiles and timber were cartwheeling skyward before showering back down. Behind the town, in the distance towards Sword, coal-black and grey smoke columns were rising.

'It's all a bit surreal, wouldn't you agree?' a voice above and behind me suddenly said, making me jump. It was Major Hibbert.

'Yes, sir,' was all I could muster.

'Sir, get in the bloody trench,' Terry barked.

As if on cue, another couple of rounds landed close to the aid post. Not even flinching, Hibbert actually waited for the spiralling debris to come to rest before casually lowering himself into the trench. I thought he was mad. He got comfortable next to me. 'Nice little spot you've got yourself here, Stokes.'

'Thank you, sir.'

'Anything going on?' he asked.

'Nothing here, sir,' I replied. 'Bénouville is still getting a hammering, though.'

Nodding, he put his head over the top, pointing to the right of the bridge. 'After landing in their gliders, the remainder of our battalion will arrive on the far bank. They will march through us, and on east to Ranville. We can't leave here until our relief arrives, after which we'll follow the battalion.' It was about time someone else guarded these bloody bridges from the Germans. He glanced at his watch, looking a little worried. 'I'm not sure the overall invasion is going quite to plan. I would have expected more than just Lord Lovat's commandos to have come through here by now.'

'Any news from Sword, sir?' I wondered.

'No real detail. The Germans are not giving up ground easily. The grand plan was for lead elements of our infantry and armour to be in Caen by the end of today, but that plan has gone out of the window, it would seem. I think this is all going to take a while.' By the sound of things, we weren't going to be in Paris any time soon, let alone Berlin. For now it was a case of sitting tight and waiting for the cavalry to rescue us, Bénouville and its bridges.

7
Jam Reinforcement

Afternoon slowly became early evening. The mortaring of our position became occasional, then stopped. Even the fighting in Bénouville appeared to calm down. But then the shelling of our position was replaced by mortar fire coming from the area of Ranville and second bridge objective, Jam. I saw geysers of water shooting skyward in the near distance. Eventually, in the light breeze, a fine mist drifted across us.

Sean went over the bridge to chat to the serjeant major, before jogging back with two satchels of PIAT rounds. 'We are to reinforce Brettle's position near Jam,' he said sternly, 'now.' During the mortar bombardment I hadn't quite managed to drift off to sleep. What I would have given for just five minutes of proper shut-eye. But it would obviously have to wait. I wasted no time in getting my gear back on, even though I was terrified at the thought of heading towards the panzers Hibbert had talked about.

Sean set off at a trot along the road. We all fell into single file behind him, Tony Winman from Sean's platoon close to Frank, Dougie and Terry. At the front the PIAT guys were nearest to Sean, since they might be needed first at Jam. We were all soon puffing and panting. Some of the guys were fit as fiddles, but even they were getting knackered.

German mortar rounds hit the open ground to our right. I wondered why they were targeting it. Were they firing blind, their spotter dead? Sean led us left off the high camber of the road. Partially obscured by a high bank beside the road, a large wooded area came into view to the right. On our side of the road the bank was lower, the treeline sparser. There was no sign of Brettle's men. The column clattered to a stop. Sean clambered up the lower bank, peering around. A mortar round fell a little too close for his liking, making him flinch then lie down. He mimed some carefully chosen words, probably for the culprit.

Getting to his feet, Sean waved us to follow him to a ditch on the side of the road beneath the taller bank. As we followed the ditch, the woods came ever closer. When the distance to the trees became short enough, he led us across the open ground towards them. As the pace slackened over the last hundred metres, I spotted profiles of men moving about in the shadows. We had found some of Brettle's sentries. Making our way into their position, we exchanged nods with them. They looked in no better shape than us. We jogged past them into the woods.

Before long, I heard the crackle and static of radio sets. Sean told us all to go firm and prepare for deployment. Captain Brettle came into view, chatting to Major Hibbert. Their radio operators were slumped at their feet, leaning back on their radio sets, enjoying cigarettes, blowing smoke rings in the air. I didn't envy them, having to lug them bloody sets about, chasing after two over-energetic masters. As we pulled up, Frank didn't need a second invitation. A cigarette was between his lips before his arse touched the ground. Through the trees, Jam was visible over the River Orne, Brettle's men entrenched in defensive positions. I watched mortar fire continuing to come down on open farmland. But the rate of fire had slowed markedly, the explosions not creeping our way.

I earwigged the conversation between Sean and the officers. The word 'panzers' featured a lot. Were we going to find some? He waved us over. No one bothered to put their cigarettes out as we made our way to him. Brettle took a knee and spread a map out on the ground. He held a pencil in one hand. 'Crowd round, boys.

I'll explain everything for you. Saves Serjeant Wardle repeating it all later.' Some of us lay around the map, Brettle joining us on our bellies. Others had to crouch to get a proper view. Hibbert stayed on his feet, overlooking us all. Brettle became all smiles under his fading tired-looking cam cream.

'Firstly, boys, fucking well done with what you did around the other bridge. Cracking job. And top marks for your efforts in Bénouville – 7 Para are full of praise for your efforts to help them occupy it, so thank you very much.' It felt good, like we were making a difference. I could sense the motivation come flooding back. His expression became more businesslike.

'Now I need your help, guys. Two things need to happen. Division have reported panzers just to the east of the drop zones. Some are mobile, but most were undergoing repairs under camouflage netting, the repair crews making a run for it when the paras landed.' That last piece of news was good, but you just knew there would be a sting in the tail. He pointed to the map with his pencil. 'The mobile panzers are obviously a threat to everyone. Their crews don't appear to be amateur. They are cautious about pushing onto the drop zones, probably not sure of our tank-killing capability. Sources indicate one panzer unit in particular has recently been relocated from Russia.' That didn't sound good.

'Our guys around the drop zones are scattered everywhere,' continued Brettle. 'Firefights have broken out without warning, especially in the dark hours. Probably because of the difficulty of establishing who is where, people haven't always known who they're shooting at.' The drop zones sounded a nightmare, everyone shooting at his own shadow.

'The original plan was to have my PIAT teams stalk the panzers,' he explained, 'along with any para anti-tank guys out there. But sending my PIAT teams in would have made a confusing situation worse, and still would, perhaps resulting in more friendly-fire incidents. Therefore I intend us to have a PIAT screen situated where we are here on the east side of the river. Should panzers come out from Bénouville and occupy the far riverbank to the west, we won't reveal ourselves, since they could just sit back and shoot the shit out of us at their leisure. If they were to attempt a crossing, I've already got the bridge ready for demolition. But that is my final card to play, if it all goes wrong.' Hibbert had hinted at that last resort during his mission briefing at RAF Tarrant Rushton. 'We would engage any tanks that remain after blowing the bridge,' went on Brettle. 'Does everyone see what I'm getting at?' There were nods all round. 'In conclusion, we are to sit tight for now and allow the bastards to come to us. Questions?'

Terry raised his hand. 'You said there were two things, sir?'

Brettle clambered to his feet. We all copied him. 'I need you to leave your PIAT teams with me to complete the screen. The second thing concerns those fellows over there.' He pointed through the woods to the east behind us. After a while squinting, I realized there was a group of about a dozen camouflaged paras in the near distance. They looked to be a shattered, sorry sight. Almost all were wrapped in blood-soaked bandages, two strapped to stretchers. Smoke drifted above a few of them, and I could see the guys on the stretchers were sharing a cigarette.

'What the fuck happened to them?' whispered Tony.

Brettle heard him, suddenly looking sad. 'The stretcher cases have broken backs. The remainder have busted ankles, broken arms, gunshot wounds, shrapnel wounds. All what you would expect from a wild day in Normandy, I'm afraid.' I guessed his group had done what they could for them, but their priority had obviously been to deal with the Germans. 'In the morning would your non-PIAT guys be so kind as to get them back to our company aid post? Given the situation, I think you guys should all stay with us until first light. They'll be all right until then.'

I heard the drone of aeroplane engines. I squinted up between the trees, just making out a cluster of dark shapes in the sky. They were too small to be bombers or transport planes, but could well be fighters. They began to lose height. Then they flipped over, diving. As I lost sight of the planes behind the bank of the road, a series of loud *crumps* sounded.

'RAF Typhoons on task,' Hibbert confirmed, 'taking care of the panzers close to the drop zones.' Typhoons were menacing beasts, fighter-bombers especially good at tank-busting. The news made me feel better, although it sounded as though carnage still raged in Bénouville. The odd shell made me flinch as it crashed into the village. But as the Typhoons continued to swoop down, I found the sound of their engines very soothing. As they climbed out of each dive, their noise would fade a little, the reassuring sound of hits on panzers making me feel all the more confident. Eventually, the engine noise and *crumps* subsided. I felt my eyes beginning to close.

There was the drone of mass aeroplane engines. The light was fading fast. I propped myself up on my elbows. Hibbert wasn't anywhere to be seen. A large number of black dots appeared in the sky. The dots split into two, forming two groups. One group began to lose height, getting larger. Eventually it became clear they were gliders: our battalion reinforcements consisting of A, B and C Companies.

Suddenly the sky was lit up with flashes all around them. Flak! Where the hell was that coming from? I watched appalled as the defenceless wooden aircraft got hammered, small-arms fire joining in for their final descent. Even from a distance, I could see a few were shredded, coming down faster than the others. One burst apart in a shower of splinters. We were too far away to assist, and thankfully too far away to hear the terrible din of crippled gliders crashing onto French fields at speed. The last glider dipped out of view. I just hoped the majority of the boys were OK and would quickly start dealing with the bastards that had already reduced their numbers.

I felt a wave of tiredness pass over me and slumped back but couldn't help thinking about those poor buggers landing in a hail of flak and bullets. That had been me just a few hours earlier. Felt a lifetime ago. I wondered if we were making any difference. Did our victories at Ham and Jam mean anything to the men landing on Sword or those gliders coming in now? I didn't know and I wondered if anyone did. So far, war was nothing like the clear-cut narrative the newspapers back home made it out to be. I sat like that, lost in a daze, until the first flicker of light appeared on the horizon.

Most of the guys were moving around. There was still no sign of Hibbert as I watched Brettle lead Sean through the trees to the group of injured soldiers. Sean shook hands with someone who was presumably the most senior para. Sean and Brettle briefly talked to him before Sean waved us over. As we made our way across, Brettle passed us, heading for our PIAT guys.

Without them, I wondered if we'd have the manpower to get the two stretchers and the rest of the paras back to the medical area among the gliders at Ham, especially since we had to lug their gear too. Sean assigned me to the corner of a stretcher. I checked my Bren was set to safe, its bipod legs stowed properly in the raised position, and slung it across my back. Any walking wounded with a good arm helped out with the stretchers. The others would just hobble along. Even Sean took a stretcher corner.

The trudge out of the woods was difficult, as was the short trek across open grass to the road. I was already sweating my bollocks off. The tarmac of the road made the going easier, but all of a sudden I felt terribly exposed, cannon fodder for any bastard snipers knocking about. Hopefully there were none, or they were asleep in the trees. There was no way we could make our way along the roadside ditch using it for cover. We tried to keep the pace slow, smooth and consistent since Brettle had no pain relief for the injured, even the stretcher cases. But despite our best efforts, they often flinched, yelped or groaned, prompting us to apologize. The walking paras often fell behind, prompting Sean to stop so the stragglers could catch up. It took a while to get just two hundred metres along the road.

We heard a terrible racket coming towards us. It was Company Serjeant Major Jenkins with his wooden cart. Brettle had obviously radioed ahead of us. I was overjoyed. Jenkins and his cart sure were a sight for sore eyes. But my joy was short-lived. He decided the walking wounded would be taken on the cart. I couldn't help but curse the bastard under my breath. We struggled on, Jenkins' party pushing the cart. He chatted away with Sean while I helped heave my stretcher along, sweating and cursing under the strain. Out on the open ground the mortar fire had long since ceased, but in the distance I could still hear chaos reigning in Bénouville. 'Why don't the Germans just fuck off and get some rest,' I moaned. 'That's all I've got in mind now.' My stretcher-side shoulder was killing me. Sean massaged his awkwardly.

Eventually, the welcome sight of the glider wrecks beside Bénouville Bridge came into view. Medics jogged to us, then took the stretchers the rest of the way to the company aid post. I suddenly felt light as a feather. We followed the cart in. I wasted no time getting my gear off and stretching out on the grass. I was going to enjoy whatever precious time I had there, come what may.

Things at the post were a little less busy. A lot of our wounded had been patched up and sent back to their units. Of those remaining, the paras we brought back from Captain Brettle's position were in the worst state. The medics gave them a lot of attention. I just hoped the two boys on stretchers would be given something for their pain quickly. I couldn't even begin to imagine how painful a broken back could be. The fact they hadn't already been given pain relief made me wonder if the supply was exhausted here too. I hoped we would soon be able to get the badly wounded to a field hospital.

Beside one glider a pile of British equipment was growing ever bigger. Most was probably from wounded who couldn't return to the fight. There was also a stack of German weapons, mostly rifles and grenades; I couldn't see any MG 42s. They were far too valuable to leave lying around. All of the dead were now out of sight. I felt secretly relieved. It seemed Jenkins had everything in order, but I was too inexperienced to make a proper judgement.

But then it dawned on me that the people around the bridge and in the trench network had changed. Jenkins was wandering about; as ever, Hibbert was touring positions with his radio operator, but the rest of my D Company had gone. Looking at the uniforms, I realized we had been relieved overnight by the 2nd Battalion of the Royal Warwickshire Regiment. I guessed Brettle's boys had also been relieved at Jam.

Hibbert did a double-take at us and made his way over. Surely he didn't have another lugging job in mind for us. Out of courtesy, we began to get to our feet, but he waved us down. 'Relax, boys, relax. Since our communications are still not that great, what with damaged equipment and all that, I've done a lot of walking of late, so I know what it is to be on your feet.' We all smiled. He was a good field officer, working us hard but leading by example. 'As you can see, we have been relieved by 2 Warks. The rest of our battalion have already been through here, after arriving by glider last night. Despite our Typhoons taking the panzers to task, I'm afraid they were given a hell of a reception by the Germans. The CO didn't hang around on the drop zones.' I wondered if the whole glider idea had been a good one. Perhaps the planners should come and try it for themselves.

'Are all the panzers taken care of, sir?' Sean asked.

'Quite a few. Some have managed to make their way back east past Ranville, to join up with larger formations. Hopefully, they won't interfere today. Reports from Sword are that a number of units are now ashore, after having to deal with some stiff opposition in the landing areas. The fighting we can still hear to the west of us in Bénouville is due to Germans retreating from the beaches running into 7 Para. In a way, the Germans coming back from the landing areas are trapped between the landing forces and us. The fighting in town is now very heavy because they've got no easy withdrawal route, no real option other than to engage.' He gave a tired smile. 'But we are nevertheless in a bit of a fix here. There are many panzers to the east, and with the mass of German infantry retreating south from the coast, we are kind of stuck in the middle.'

I was even more relieved we had left the town. It sounded as though things had turned really nasty there, and could only get worse.

'Nothing we can't handle, sir,' said Terry proudly. 'Nothing we can't handle.'

'Overnight,' Hibbert explained, 'our battalion settled in Ranville. The Germans were no longer there.' I hoped our advance units had kept the pressure on withdrawing enemy units, not giving them time to catch their breath and consider a counter-attack. 'But the battalion has now been tasked with pushing on beyond Ranville to the south-east and clearing Hérouvillette and Escoville. Our men are preparing to make their way through fields and hedgerows towards Hérouvillette. Company Sergeant Major Jenkins will resupply you with food, water and ammunition, and then we'll leave together to join up with them.'

8
Assault on Escoville

I kept the Bren slung across my front as we moved off along the road. Apart from wanting to keep it ready for any enemy contact we might encounter, I didn't want 2 Warks to think we were a rabble. Hibbert led the column with his radio operator. CSM Jenkins followed with his men, leaving Sean to lead my group at the rear. As we marched quickly along, only sporadic gunfire in the distance interrupted the crunching of our boots on the tarmac.

It was about a mile and a half along the road to Ranville, then maybe a mile across country to Hérouvillette. Just before reaching Ranville Bridge, we found Brettle's group sitting in roadside ditches. Hibbert took a moment to catch up with Brettle. We began to pass through Brettle's group, smiles and mild insults thrown back and forth between the ranks, the usual pleasantries soldiers extend to each other. Brettle's group rose, tagging onto the back of our column, Hibbert racing to the front.

We marched proudly across the bridge, through positions now occupied by 2 Warks. They nodded or waved, some congratulating us on a cracking job. We accepted their promises of drinking competitions in Paris and Berlin. I must admit I did feel rather proud of what we had achieved. We had managed to seize two key bridges and keep them open. I had hoped to see some of our tanks, but there were none.

We moved south-east into unfamiliar country. Our battalion was already in Ranville and perhaps beyond, but we were told to remain vigilant, looking out for both enemies and friendlies.

Hibbert slowed the column to patrol pace then ordered us off the road, platoons marching on either side to avoid being caught in an ambush. It wasn't long before I saw the outer limits of Ranville. We moved in as close as was comfortable before he told us to go firm.

My section was given the task of moving forward alone, establishing the link-up with the battalion. Terry led us off towards the village. We were spaced out on either side of the road. He had ditched his head bandage a while back, his helmet back on. I wondered if in years to come he would entertain his grandchildren with his little diving mishap in Bénouville. Hopefully, we would all tell stories about the invasion to our grandchildren.

Before long we entered the outskirts of the village. At a road junction he ordered us to stop. We listened for a while. Nothing. We moved further into the village, very slowly, very steadily, keeping noise to a minimum. But all we heard was the light breeze, the occasional barking dog and the distant sounds of battle. The quietness made for intense tension. I hadn't been this nervous before. It was a creepy, dark feeling. Terry clicked his fingers. Had he spotted a German ambush? He waved us down into kneeling positions. 'Wait here,' he commanded in a hushed tone.

He made his way forward, arms out in a cruciform posture. Then he slowly took a knee. An arm slowly extended from behind a wall. I made out a handshake. Relief washed over me. We had found our battalion. Terry and his new friend made their way back towards us, three more men emerging behind them. Terry clicked for us to come out of our positions, and we joined his group of five. 'These boys were told to expect us,' he explained. 'We'll take them back to our guys, and then we'll all move forward together. Keep it nice and quiet, lads. I want no fucking around.'

It wasn't long before we rejoined the rest of our battalion in the outskirts on the other side of the village, all four companies back together, over six hundred men in total, but as a force we looked as bashed up as 7 Para. I thought back to the glider landing I had witnessed from Jam the night before. Glider pilots, engineers and signallers were no longer with us; the additional units assigned for the bridge operation had gone back to their parent outfits.

It seemed like we were ready to move out. Sean gathered my platoon around a map on the grass. His grubby finger wandered across the map. 'We are here, in Ranville. The recce platoon deployed out towards Hérouvillette, not long ago. They will try to get eyes on any Germans there.' I had no room in my life for Germans at the moment, just sleep, but he continued anyway. 'C Company will then patrol aggressively into the village, in an attempt to get any enemy units there to give away their positions. If enemy are flushed out, C Company will keep them engaged, which will then allow A Company to be deployed, hopefully clearing the place.'

'So what about us and B Company?' Terry enquired.

'The rest of us will hold here in reserve. The CO is fully aware we're feeling a bit rough right now and doesn't want to commit us to anything, as of yet. But don't be surprised if the Germans make the call for him, if you get my drift, so be ready to move.' There were slow, tired nods of acknowledgment. 'C Company should be making their way out any time now. Any questions?' There were shakes of heads all round. 'Good.'

It was quickly decided that we needed to be closer to C Company, in case they encountered any trouble, so we slowly filed out. Mindful of German observers, we kept ourselves tucked in behind outbuildings. Behind us, observers on the upper floors of houses monitored C Company's progress in the distance. At any moment I expected all hell to break loose, but all I heard was birdsong.

'Prepare to move!' came a shout down the line. Maybe there were no Germans in Hérouvillette. D Company filed out into the fields, my platoon bringing up the rear. As described by Hibbert, hedgerows separated the fields. After fighting our way through a couple of these bastard things, never easy in full fighting gear, we broke out onto a large piece of open ground. I was already glazed in sweat, flies buzzing around my ears, the overwhelming aroma of cow shit thrown in for good measure. Spread across the field, our platoons moved forward in single file. Way off to our right, I noticed men from another company doing the same. Maybe B Company was also moving forward. Progress became easier, the approach to Hérouvillette being slightly downhill. On the outskirts of the village we encountered some of our guys in hedgerows. They must have been recce boys, since I could see C Company moving into the village.

As we made our way through outbuildings and gardens, word quickly spread that the village was unoccupied. It was the best news I had received that day. We were warned about booby traps, so took our time in confirming the buildings were unoccupied. There weren't many locals about; the place was more or less deserted. Eventually the village was confirmed clear, so we went upstairs in one of the houses to get eyes on Escoville, a little further to the south-east. I had no binoculars, but from what I could see, it was about as sedate as Hérouvillette.

'A and B Companies are going to patrol into Escoville,' Sean advised. 'We're in reserve again, so sit tight. Any questions?' There were none.

There was a thud in the distance, which made me flinch. There was a louder *crump* nearby. The familiar clatter of brick, tiles and glass confirmed a direct hit on someone's home. A second shell smashed into Hérouvillette, then another. We quickly made our way downstairs, not wanting to be on the top floor when the Germans really got their eye in. We sat on the floor, keeping away from the windows.

Sean disappeared briefly, but then reappeared, crouching in

the doorway. 'Everyone OK?' We nodded, just tired. 'C Company has spotted German troops legging it into Escoville. Our fighting patrols are still going ahead. There is every chance an enemy artillery observer is in Escoville. So I don't think we'll be staying here long. Be ready for a quick move on Escoville, understood?' He scrambled away as another shell exploded somewhere close by.

After a little while, the shelling shifted away, becoming distant, and Terry went upstairs to see what was going on in Escoville. Frank and Dougie took the opportunity to get comfortable and before long began to snore. Tony was more interested in the contents of the kitchen cupboards. Nothing took his fancy, so he returned empty-handed. 'They're trying to shell our patrols,' shouted Terry down the stairs. But most of the other guys in the platoon were dozing too. 'They're in contact,' Terry advised. The Germans were definitely in Escoville.

'Prepare to move!', a voice echoed through the house. The dozing were shoved awake. Sean appeared again. 'A and B are moving on Escoville, sharpish. Their lead patrols are in contact with German infantry. There's no estimate on enemy strength, but there is armour in the area. All PIAT crews are to stand by for tasking.'

Company Serjeant Major Jenkins called everyone outside. We were going into Escoville. In the absence of full knowledge of the enemy strength, we would go in mob-handed, our company bringing up the rear. There could be an enemy platoon there, or there could be a whole fucking regiment.

We fell into single file, the pace very brisk across the fields. 'Keep spaced out,' a voice shouted; 'their artillery is active.' I was soaked with sweat within a couple of minutes, fighting through more hedgerows. It was a good job Hibbert had really put us through the mill on Salisbury Plain. We were all exhausted, but our fitness levels were paying dividends. A heavy battle started in Escoville – infantry weapons, no signature sounds of armour entering the fray. My heart began to pound, my breathing laboured. The odd shell crashed into the fields around us, but none found its mark. There were so many hedges, it didn't feel like Escoville was getting any closer.

Eventually we came to a halt on the outskirts of the village, seeking refuge behind mud banks and yet more hedgerows. The sound of A and B Companies fighting their way in was louder. I scanned the rooftops but couldn't see much. Hibbert was hunched over his radio set, listening.

It wasn't long before the Germans raised the stakes. The now-familiar thunder of tank rounds roared. There was some commotion in the hedges around me, people wondering where our PIAT teams were. The teams soon appeared, and Hibbert called them over. Brettle joined them. The volume of tank fire suddenly increased, sounding closer, concussions rippling through the ground. It sounded as though our boys were taking a hiding. I could hear the sound of houses collapsing, the shouts of fighting men quickly becoming hysterical over the horrific din of German firepower. We were going to pay for taking Escoville, by the sound of it.

I looked down the length of my hedgerow and caught the eye of Frank Williams. His face told a story. As big and brash as he was, he didn't look like he wanted to go into the village. I think all of us were wearing that same facial expression, but his seemed most prominent. I suddenly felt overcome with tiredness. Hibbert and Brettle gathered their platoon commanders around them. It was a sure sign we were about to go in. My stomach turned over with every thud of tank fire. The whole soundtrack seemed pretty much one-sided, the pathetic signatures of our weapons almost drowned out by the unmistakable sounds of MG 42 and panzer fire. 'Prepare to move!' hollered Brettle. My stomach took another nosedive.

My platoon brought up the rear, with the rest of D Company taking the lead. We began forcing our way through the hedges.

The first cluster of single- and two-storey buildings was untouched by the fighting. We shuffled between the buildings at a crouch, reaching an area of gravel. Off to the right, I noticed another platoon moving in a similar manner along a raised bank. I peered over towards them again, noting they were dressed in grey. Not giving them a second thought, I kept on forward. When I glanced over for a third time, I saw they had stopped and were nudging each other, pointing in our direction and talking in strange accents. There was no one off to our left. Up ahead our column was still shuffling forward, but a few were pointing towards the bank.

Time seemed to stop. We all stood up. The enemy platoon looked at us, and we looked back. I don't know who started shooting first, but all of a sudden it erupted into a hurricane of chaos. 'Oh shit, Germans!' roared Frank as our salvos splashed all over the bank. Bursts of red mist indicated we had hit a few of them, but some of their shots also found their mark, signalled by the distinctive *thwack* of high-velocity projectiles hitting canvas, meat and bone.

'Contact right!' I swung towards the enemy, dropping to one knee, firing the Bren in short controlled bursts. My rounds buzzed among field-grey uniforms, flicking up turf, mud and dust as the soldiers dived for cover behind the bank. I couldn't confirm any hits. As I kept up my fire, some of our guys took the initiative, charging towards the bank. I couldn't lie down, since the bipod legs of the Bren wouldn't give me the elevation required to shoot at the Germans. My magazine expired at the critical moment, just when our guys reached the base of the bank, lobbing grenades as they went. My magazine change was quick, but not quick enough to support them. As I got the gun back into my right shoulder, a series of thuds sounded behind the bank. Dirt and turf sprayed up. Before the dust had cleared our guys dashed over the top. All I could hear was the din of men shouting in English and German, and the horrific cluttered rippling of infantry weapons.

It was over in just a few seconds. I looked left and right. Other Bren gunners were also trying to make sense of what had unfolded. A few of our guys were in crumpled heaps, some groaning, some face down in the gravel. Large dark pools of sweet coppery blood were growing wider beneath some of them. 'You lot,' shouted a voice. It was Jenkins. He carried a radio. 'Get back. They're reorganizing themselves behind the bank.' I hope he meant our guys, not any surviving Germans.

I clambered to my feet with the other gunners. We wasted no time getting out of sight. On a nearby narrow street I slumped against the relative cover of a wall, frantically scrambling for my water bottle. Water never tasted so good. I looked up. Jenkins was peering down at me. 'You OK, boy?' All I could manage was a nod. I got a thumbs up from him in return. He checked the other lads. They were too stunned by the short fierce action to find any words. He surveyed us, giving an approving fatherly nod. 'Just waiting for Serjeant Wardle to call me into his position, once he's got his act together.' It wasn't a sergeant major's place to get involved in fighting. Jenkins' job was to deal with the aftermath – ammo resupply, casualties and prisoners. It looked as though he would soon be ticking all those boxes, once we had secured our new position.

I heard a crunch of boots on gravel. Dougie slid round a corner, sweating like a beast. He composed himself before reporting to Jenkins. 'Position clear, sir. Three enemy dead, as well as ours. The remainder of the enemy platoon pissed off before we could get 'em.'

'Why didn't you lot use the radio?' wondered Jenkins. 'I would have come to you, lad.'

'Our radio got smashed on the first night,' Dougie explained. 'Haven't had one since, sir.'

'Fuck's sake. Get the rest of your platoon back here. We'll find hard cover, then we can take care of wounded and ammo.'

'What about the dead, sir?' Dougie asked.

'Leave 'em. I'll take care of them later. Move your arse.'

'Yes, sir,' acknowledged Dougie, before dashing away. I got myself together, then stood. My numbness from the escapade had faded. I was back in the game. I was about to ask the serjeant major if he was OK, but he raised a hand as chatter crackled through his radio. 'Yeah, roger that,' he quickly acknowledged. 'I've got our assault call signs on their way back in with casualties.' He listened for a few moments. 'No sign of armour this side,' he continued. 'We will be with you shortly. We can sort new positions for ourselves further in, once we know where the enemy are. Over.' There was more static chatter. He nodded through it. 'Roger, out,' he concluded.

A few more of our guys arrived. He stood away from the group. 'Listen up, guys. Stay on your game. More enemy fuckers are trying to sneak into town. Their armour is on high ground just south of the village, and will try to pick us off. A and B Companies are really getting what for. We will be the rear-centre Company. We're just waiting for Serjeant Wardle's platoon to get back in. Then we can move on, understand?'

'What about our dead, sir?' asked a young lad.

Jenkins kept his sergeant major face on. 'I want two sections to collect wounded. Don't waste energy carrying the dead, just take what kit is of use to us, OK?'

Without waiting to be asked, a group of about twelve lads splintered away to deal with the grim task. One shouted back, letting us know Sean's platoon had arrived. They came round the corner with Terry, looking like they all just had one hell of a fight. Tony and Terry were sporting fresh field dressings. Sean had one around his neck, blood already starting to seep through. He looked pissed off. They all looked really done in. He watched as our casualties were brought through from the area of the bank. Medics applied bandages to some. The dead were stripped of any kit that could still serve: water, ammunition, rations, and so on. It was grim.

The tank fire stopped, MG 42 and other infantry fire subsiding. But mortar rounds suddenly rocked us, crashing into nearby rooftops and gardens. Concussion from the explosions punched me square in the chest, winding me. 'Find better fucking cover,' the serjeant major roared.

We scrambled. I ended up in a shallow stairwell which led down to an external cellar door. Sean, Terry and a few others quickly joined me. A round landed in the middle of a cobbled road, shrapnel fragments whizzing past my head, chipping brickwork behind me. I wished the steps went down a little deeper. I could see many wounded hadn't been able to take cover, medics choosing to stay with them. 'Get them casualties inside, now!' I heard the serjeant major yell above the din of shellfire. A nearby rooftop burst, hit by a mortar round. The medics half-threw their bodies over the wounded as bricks, timber shards and tiles rained down. I thought some of those in the open were finished, but the medics all got back up, shrugging house debris off themselves. They slowly but surely escorted or dragged the wounded into buildings.

The shelling ended, dust drifting away. The area was coated in debris, which also covered our dead. 'Serjeant Major, Serjeant Major!' called the familiar voice of Brettle.

'Sir?' came the gruff response.

'Gather the men. We have found what we need to occupy.'

'Sir.'

We were all rather reluctant to emerge from cover but soon found the motivation when we heard all hell break loose again deeper inside the village. We gathered in the road, debris cracking and crunching under our boots. Buildings were quickly allocated. Sean led a group of us to one of them, wincing with the pain of his neck injury. I realized the fighting was slowly creeping towards us, the echo of tank rounds becoming louder.

Sean sited me upstairs with Frank, Tony and Dougie. I was paired up with Dougie. Frank and Tony occupied a neighbouring room. The remainder of the group stayed downstairs. Sean and Terry settled on the stairs so they could relay information. I looked out of a window. It wasn't a house I would have chosen. There was no real clear field of fire; we were surrounded by single- and two-storey structures. But it suddenly dawned on me that it wasn't dissimilar to the ambush site in Bénouville. Tanks had no view of us unless they got in very close. Enemy infantry would also have to come in close to be effective. Here the chances were we would only have infantry to contend with, so I concluded we had a chance of holding the place. The tank fire stopped again. Mortar rounds soon replaced it, more sporadic now. I could still hear fighting. Panzer engines were gunned, the squeal of tracks and moving metal echoing all around. What made me nervous was that we didn't know the exact location of their fucking armour.

'Listen up, lads!' Sean bellowed from the stairs. 'The Germans are sending in small groups of infantry to detect us and draw us into a fight. The fighting you can hear is not a huge assault. It's fucking enemy patrols, making A and B give away their current positions so the panzers can come in to shoot them. You are to ensure the enemy get in real close before you shoot, so we can kill them before they have an opportunity to report back. Understand?' All round the house acknowledgements were muttered.

'Contact!' shouted a voice from downstairs. The entire place erupted with gunfire. With my heart going nineteen to the dozen I carefully looked out of the window, but I couldn't see shit.

'Grenade!' came another shout, followed by an almighty thud downstairs. The floorboards beneath my feet flexed and cracked, causing my feet to throb. My ears rang. The weight of fire downstairs became biblical.

'Robbie, Robbie,' screamed Frank. I scampered onto the landing and into the next room. He was standing beside a bed, Tony squatting below a window.

'Infantry,' Frank said with an exaggerated jab towards the street. Bren in both hands, I crept forward, skirting the bed. I peered over the window ledge. A platoon of field-grey troops was below, spread out all over the rubble and gardens. I lumbered the Bren onto the ledge and began firing, but the gun wasn't correctly in my shoulder, so my rounds splashed over and wide of the German troops. Two of them engaged me, shots splintering the ledge before whizzing past me, deafening me once more. I dropped to my belly. Incoming fire became intense, fittings in the room splintering all over us.

Tony dropped to the ground like a sack of potatoes, slumping over the back of my legs. He held his left hand hard against the side of his head, blood oozing through his fingers. 'Fuck!' he growled. He rolled off my legs, then slumped against a smashed bedroom unit.

The dull thud of grenades outside caused the enemy fire to lift, so I clambered back into a fighting position at the window. The Germans were moving back, some providing covering fire for their comrades. A couple of their number lay dead, two less to shoot at me. I put the Bren back on the ledge, taking aim at the dusty grey figures sprinting away. As I began to fire, they sought cover. Remembering to keep my bursts short, I engaged one particular enemy soldier. A burst of red mist indicated a hit, and as he fell my next burst kicked up masonry and brick dust. I couldn't be sure if I had got him twice. As the dust drifted, I just made him out, crawling into more solid cover, where I couldn't hit the fucker any more.

The German platoon managed to break contact with us,

leaving the street and three dead behind. 'Watch and shoot, boys!' shouted Terry. 'Watch and shoot!' Downstairs there were lots of shouts for medics.

I glanced at Tony. Frank crawled over to him, then carefully prised Tony's hand away from his head. A bullet had clipped his ear. 'Lucky bastard!' Frank bawled. 'How many lives you got, Tony? You've been hit three times since we arrived in Normandy!'

Tony glared at his bloody hand. I wasn't sure if our medics had any more field dressings. He looked up at me. 'Tell me you got the fuckers!'

'I got one, but he got behind hard cover.'

Frank clipped Tony's bad ear. Tony winced, then dished out a right hook to the side of Frank's head. 'Get off, you prick.'

Frank chuckled. 'It's a scratch, you big girl. The medics will sort you out. Stop crying.' I stifled my amusement since I could tell Tony was shaken up. I peered back out at the street. Nothing but three dead Germans and loads of bloody debris.

There was movement on the landing. Sean crouched low as he peered through the doorway. 'Everyone OK?'

Frank and I nodded. Tony wasn't so enthusiastic. Sean could see his ear was a mess. 'He fractured an eyelash,' Frank joked.

Tony glared at him. 'You are such a cock.'

Sean kept low as he approached Tony. The bandage around Sean's neck was redder, and caked with dust and grime. The wound needed tending again, by the look of it. 'I've got medics downstairs,' Sean told him. 'German fuckers got a grenade in on us, the shifty bastards. Didn't see it till it rolled against my bloody foot. I managed to kick it away and the furniture absorbed most of it. Lucky fuckers downstairs have got cuts, bruises and a head-ache.' He was less heavy-handed than Frank with Tony's ear, but Tony winced all the same.

Boots clattered up the stairs. A medic arrived with a canvas bag of goodies. He stood in front of the window, looking down at Tony, then suddenly flinched, realizing how exposed he was. He lay across the bed and had a look at Tony's ear, fishing out a bandage from the bag. Deeper in the village the fighting calmed down, just potshots and the odd tank round. A shout came from downstairs that movement had been sighted in a building opposite, but the medic didn't hurry his work. Sean scrambled out onto the landing. 'Make sure the guys across the street aren't ours,' he hissed. 'Don't want us shooting up stragglers.' Sean had a point. By the look of things, we had guys strung out all over the damn village. We'd managed to keep the Germans at bay for now, but we all knew they would be back. It was just a matter of time.

9
Last Stand

Downstairs I could make out Major Hibbert's voice. He must have arrived from the building opposite with whatever command group he'd been able to assemble. Good job he didn't come blundering in before, or who knows what might have happened. I felt the tension lift.

Boots sounded on the staircase. Sean reappeared in the doorway. Keeping low, he spread a map over the bed. Tony and I joined him, Frank keeping an eye on the street from the window. Sean called Dougie in. 'Hibbert is doing the rounds of our positions. Silly sod almost got himself shot up by us.' There was tittering and shaking of heads. 'We are here in Escoville.' He pointed on the map with a grubby finger. 'We appear to be on the line of march of a rather substantial enemy force comprising infantry and self-propelled guns. The tank rounds we thought we heard weren't tanks. It was their artillery, firing directly at A and B Companies. We're preventing the Germans from getting to the bridges we secured. I've just heard that 7 Para are getting the shit kicked out of them in Bénouville, since they're blocking the path of another German formation, trying to get to the bridges from the west. The Germans want them bridges badly. So 2 Warks are digging in deep around both bridges, just in case the Germans get through. The enemy we're facing here are believed to be forward elements of a large panzer reserve.'

Hibbert had been right. We were indeed in a bit of a fix regarding the bridges. Frank had been right too. We couldn't hold the bridges indefinitely without heavy support from our landing forces. It was a race against time.

'Our forces are still gathering at Sword,' Sean went on. 'C Company have been back at Hérouvillette for some time, holding the fort. Our anti-tank guns have now arrived with them, but the fields are too exposed to try to move the guns here. They have reported German infantry reinforcements trying to move around to our north. Shortly things around here are going to get even crazier.'

Looking at the map, it seemed to me that we were in danger of being surrounded as the Germans tried to retake the bridges from both sides. I thought Tony and Frank had picked up on this too, but I still felt it wasn't my place to raise the issue. By the look of things, we weren't going anywhere soon, forward or backwards, so would just have to soak up whatever the Germans threw at us.

Over the next few hours the fighting in the village continued sporadically, interspersed with periods of inertia. German fighting patrols occasionally continued to cause trouble. Hibbert decided not to mount any patrols of our own, since radio communications were now hit and miss at best, and, not knowing where everyone was, he didn't want to risk our guys getting shot up by our own side. But we did manage to get some updates over the radio. Apparently the recce platoon, which was on the outskirts of Ranville, had seen the Germans trying to move tanks around us and got word to our anti-tank presence in Hérouvillette, who scored a few kills. We later heard the Germans had lost their enthusiasm about moving their armour.

But instead the Germans decided to hammer Hérouvillette and Escoville with mortar fire. Rounds rained down in such numbers, we were confined to the downstairs rooms, squashed in. Discovery of a cellar relieved the squeeze a little. In between salvos Hibbert resited some guys in houses that had better fields of fire for us, but still no direct line of fire from German armour and artillery.

As the afternoon wore on, German infantry began re-engaging A and B Companies deeper in the village. The German attacks became stronger and more savage, making both companies feel the pressure. But time after time the enemy were beaten back. Although information was limited, drip-fed via the radio, we guessed our casualties were mounting. I was left with the soldier's dilemma: on the one hand I was quietly pleased it wasn't us holding the line against ever-growing odds, but in equal measure I wanted to go and help our guys. But Hibbert decided to keep us in reserve. He eventually informed us that we would be withdrawing. Escoville wasn't an ideal position to hold and he felt the higher ground of Hérouvillette would be easier to defend. But the continuing German assaults on A and B made starting the withdrawal difficult, and Hibbert was wary of turning his back while fighting.

The shelling began to relent. Sean ordered sentries to occupy the upper floors once more. I ended up in the kitchen with Frank under a big oak table. I tried to make myself comfortable, but the big oaf took up most of the room, so I just had to slum it as best I could. We all had to remain ready for action; Escoville was far too dangerous a place to relax. But the space under the table was rather cosy, the afternoon air warm, and I began to doze.

'Infantry!' roared a voice. Automatic weapons began going off around the house. Frank and I almost comically attempted to get out from under the table at the same time. He had more horsepower than me, so was up firing his Sten first, through swinging, splintered wooden window shutters. The back garden was full of German troops. By the time I joined the chaos, and my Bren was ready for action, several enemy soldiers already lay dead or dying among sheds and wire fences. My head was still ringing as Frank dropped to the floor to change his magazine. This gave me more room to assume a better fire position, placing the Bren on the window frame. But as I pulled the gun into my right shoulder, a projectile clipped the inside of a shutter, which now hung from its bottom hinge, and smashed into my cheek. I reeled back against a draining board. The projectile was a stick grenade. My time had come.

The huge mass of Frank pushed my face into my Bren magazine. He grabbed the grenade and chucked it through the window. As it vanished from sight, he grabbed me by the scruff of my neck, dragging me down with him. My head crashed against the table as an enormous dull thud blew in what was left of the window shutters and frame, sending it all flying across the table. Before the debris and dust had a chance to begin settling, Frank tossed me to one side and was back on his feet, firing again. I clambered shakily to my knees. The Bren was on the table amid the remains of the shutters. German rounds snapped through the open window, splintering and smashing what was left of the kitchen fittings. Without standing, I managed to stretch up and grab one of the Bren's bipod legs. The gun fell on me, accompanied by the shutter remains.

'Keep your fucking head down, you idiot,' Frank screamed as more rounds smashed crockery. I discarded the shattered shutters and quickly gave the Bren the once-over. Nothing appeared to be damaged. I looked up. He pulled the pin on a grenade, lobbed it into the garden and then ducked down. Excited foreign voices indicated the bastards had noticed it. As it detonated, he stood back up, firing again. Emboldened by his example, I got to my feet and got my Bren back on what was left of the window ledge, scanning the garden for targets. Mud-smeared field-grey helmets bobbed about, taking shots at us and anything that moved. We splashed them with tracer, the sheds splintering. Grenades arced towards them from somewhere else, exploding around the garden.

Having recovered from the initial violence of the contact, we were giving it back to the enemy and seemed to be getting the upper hand. How wrong I was. 'German troops in the house!' came a hysterical scream from behind us.

The sheer concussion and noise of close combat was overwhelming. I could hear Germans screaming at each other. Frank spun round, firing a short burst from the shoulder. A grey-clad soldier collapsed in a fine red mist, slumping in the doorway leading to the living room. As I heaved the Bren onto the kitchen table, another fucking stick grenade spun into the room, bouncing off the table into a corner. What the fuck were we to do? We couldn't dive into the garden. Like the living room, it was full of German troops. We were fucked. The seconds ticked away. But the grenade didn't go off. The fucking thing didn't go off. What were the odds?

A terrible scream sounded from the living room as some of our boys got in there. Gunfire in the room quickly subsided, but I could hear the unmistakable cracks and thumps of a full-on brawl to the death. The impacts sounded dull. Before long some had the wet smack of blood to them.

'Friendly coming in,' a desperate rasp eventually sounded.

'OK,' called Frank.

Sean appeared in the doorway minus his helmet, bathed in sweat and breathing heavily, the filthy bloody bandage still around his neck. His hands and smock were covered in blood. He glanced down at the dead German in the doorway, the one Frank had shot, and took a deep breath to regain his composure. 'Grab your shit, you two,' he barked. 'We're getting the fuck out of here. They're all over us. Let's go!'

As we departed what was left of the kitchen, Frank felt it only fair to give the Germans back their property. I flinched as he grabbed the unexploded grenade, tossing it into the garden. 'Here you go, you fuckers,' he shouted. 'Pick the bones out of that!'

I wasn't sure if the thing would go off, but excited shouts indicated enemy soldiers were running from it.

I scrambled out into the street. Sean was ahead of me, Frank behind me. Opposite, a cottage had partially collapsed. Aiming fire off to my left, our guys were spread out among large chunks of rubble. Sean scurried to the cottage, putting a knee inside the front door. He moved just inside, waving us down behind him in the hall. Long rippling licks of MG 42 fire could be heard between shouting English and German voices. Exploding grenades echoed in the street, throwing up plumes of brick dust and shards of masonry.

Sean flinched. The doorframe had splintered just inches from his head. 'Fuck!' he roared, holding a hand over his right eye.

He winced as Frank quickly checked him over. Sean appeared to be OK, just minor facial cuts. 'You're fine,' Frank told him. 'But fucking hell, they nearly took your head off.' He let out a nervous chuckle.

'Bastards!' Sean composed himself, ready to get back into the fight.

'Sean! Sean!' came from across the road. I only just made it out through the din. Terry was trying to tell us something.

'What?' bellowed Sean.

Terry roared something back at us, but I couldn't make it out. Sean looked at Frank and me, but we were no wiser than him. The penny dropped when a PIAT team scampered in beside Terry. He gave us the thumbs-down sign for enemy, then pointed off to our right. I thought I glimpsed a panzer down the street. German fire splashed all around Terry and the boys trying to find cover among the rubble. The PIAT boys raced across the road and set up among them.

Suddenly a grenade shattered a room just behind us. Rounds started flicking and screaming through our position. We heard German voices loud and clear. They were coming through the cottage towards us. My stomach turned. I didn't think I could go through it all again. All I could do was point the Bren in the direction of a closed internal door and fire.

The Bren chugged and thundered like a bass drum. The huge .303 rounds shattered the door, smashing through into a kitchen. Two Germans slumped, already dead, kitchen cupboards bursting into a fine red misty pulp of splintered shards. Two further enemy soldiers appeared in the doorway, trying to rush us, but my withering fire destroyed them, dropping them like liquid as they leaped over their dead colleagues. The lead one ploughed face first into the floor, his knee high into his chest, his backside in the air. The second smashed face first into the remains of his freshly fallen colleague.

I ripped out my empty magazine, fighting like a maniac to attach a fresh one. Sean and Frank covered my magazine change with tinny bursts of Sten fire. Four dead Germans now blocked the doorway, making it difficult for the assault group behind them. Their cries were hysterical as they tried to find a way to get to us. A stick grenade clipped the doorframe, dropping behind the pile of dead men. The pile jerked as the grenade detonated with an almighty thud, rendering me virtually deaf. I thought I was screaming but I could hear nothing but a solid whine. Another grenade settled a foot away from me. In a flash, Frank scrambled for it, tossing it back towards the kitchen. A German soldier appeared in the doorway, his gun in his shoulder, ready to fire. The grenade clipped his weapon before spinning up and away behind him. He dashed off, out of sight. For a few seconds the sound of battle returned to my ears, until the grenade went off behind a wall. Sean scrambled to the doorway, using the smashed German bodies for cover, firing controlled bursts through the kitchen into a garden. His magazine expended, he turned with a thumbs up.

We headed back to the front door. I was nervous about taking my eyes off the kitchen, but watched our boys lying among the rubble, taking MG 42 fire. Clouds of brick dust flicked up all around them. I couldn't tell which of them were lying low, which were dead, and which were wounded. Terry and the PIAT team raced into view. I guessed they had been very wary about exposing themselves to the panzer, waiting for the right time to engage. The PIAT guys fired their projectile, then instantly scrambled for cover.

I didn't know the outcome for the panzer, but Terry waved us over. A few of our guys sprang up from the rubble and put down a heavy weight of fire. 'Come on, come on!' he hollered to us. Sean accepted the invitation, racing towards him, with Frank and me in tow. I was happy in a way, not fancying another gunfight inside the cottage, but my lungs were burning something fierce as I gave it everything I had in the dash. I turned both ankles as I ran through the debris.

Once we reached decent cover, I fought to get my breath back. I peered along the street, just making out German troops moving seventy-odd metres away, around a smouldering vehicle. It wasn't a panzer; it was a knocked-out halftrack with an MG 42 still mounted behind a ballistics shield above the crew cab. Its crew nowhere to be seen. 'Smoke now!' roared Terry, making me jump. Our guys threw smoke grenades, which landed short of the halftrack. We all stayed put until the thick white phosphorus smoke built up. The guys among the rubble began to help the wounded to their feet. Terry enquired if we were OK before leading us down another narrow cobbled street, where we encountered other members of our company. They looked exhausted but still in the fight. Off to our left, we heard fighting break out again.

Terry decided to try and find Hibbert, and we made our way back to the smashed cottage. The major was kneeling in a living room with Jenkins, both accompanied by their trusty radio operators. Hibbert was frowning, radio headset firmly against his ear. 'Roger that,' he said. 'Are you in contact? Over.' As he listened, his frown increased. 'Roger that,' he acknowledged. 'We will hold our position until all of your call signs have broken clean of the village. Let us know when you are all out. Over.'

There was a muffled response. Apparently content, Hibbert handed the headset to his operator.

'The CO has ordered A Company to withdraw through here. They are really taking a beating. All across their frontage there are fresh German troops and armour. A Company never sees the same armour twice. It leads me to believe we are seriously outgunned right now, and the enemy bastards have been throwing fresh men at us all bloody afternoon.' He turned to Jenkins. 'Please tell our forward-left platoons to be wary of friendlies moving right to left in front of them. Thank you.' With a grunt, Jenkins got to his feet and headed towards the door, his radio operator following.

'Where do you want my guys, sir?' Sean enquired.

'In reserve. Captain Brettle is checking our positions. He will be back shortly and will site you. We've got a two-platoon frontage, with PIATs on the flanks. Enemy armour keep trying to push into the village, but they soon lose enthusiasm for it. It's their bloody infantry. Fighting patrols keep turning up – about platoon strength. It keeps us fixed. Our left flank is going to feel the pressure very soon, once the Germans realize one of our forward companies has given up its position. B Company are forward right, but they are in no better shape than A. If B Company withdraws, we become the lead company.'

The sounds of battle got louder and I slumped down behind a broken piece of masonry. My head ached, my shoulder hurt and I didn't like the sound of being lead company when the Germans were coming hard. I wondered again if they knew airborne troops could only carry so much ammunition.

The sound of boots approached. It was Brettle and his radio operator, a PIAT team in tow. Brettle knelt with us, the PIAT crew and his operator sitting off to one side. Brettle looked like he could do with a decent kip, just like the rest of us. He cleared his throat. 'Our forward-right platoon is all set. B Company are not too far in front of them. The Germans keep us fixed, with little if no room to move except backwards. Makes you wonder what their officers put in the coffee in the mornings. The patrols keep engaging us with almost no break. They just keep coming. It's worrying when you can tell fresh units are continually coming in to fight us.'

My ignorance got the better of me. 'How can we tell they're fresh units, sir?' I expected a reprimand for such a poxy question, but nothing came my way. Perhaps Sean and Terry wanted to know his secret too.

Brettle looked at me. 'Troops that have previously been in action have, shall we say, a way about them. Their look, their smell. The manner in which they fight is almost fatalistic. Their urgency is exhausted. Fresh troops are cleaner, energetic and more afraid of getting hit, but their shooting tends to be way off to begin with. If they're seasoned troops, their marksmanship tends to be a lot better from the outset.'

I wondered vaguely if the Germans were saying the same about us.

A shout came from outside: 'Friendlies on the left!' We all scrambled out, taking in the sight of A Company. They were too far away to identify individuals, but as their column crossed a road junction, you could tell that they were absolutely shattered. They moved the wounded any way they could – stretchers, arms round a limping buddy, a couple even mustering the strength to fireman-carry. Most were limping or being assisted. They had really taken a lot from the Germans. And I feared that as the enemy grew bolder, they would turn their attention to us.

Hell suddenly erupted around A Company. I watched in horror as tracer flicked among them from houses to their left. Many of them fell. Amid the din of MG 42 fire, I could see and hear the company begin to fight back: the chugging of Brens, the snap of Lee-Enfield rifles, the chatter of Stens.

Grenade thuds echoed through the streets and narrow alleyways. Rounds snapped through the rubble, many hitting the cottage. Masonry splinters stung my face. Sean fell against Hibbert. 'Contact front!' Brettle roared. My ears rang, my face smarted like hell. I had put my precious Bren down somewhere while watching A Company, so I fell onto my belly, frantically searching for it.

I found it in front of a pair of blood-speckled boots. Their owner had his Sten in his shoulder, his face like thunder, firing short bursts. I guessed the blood on the boots wasn't his. Rounds snapped past just inches from him, but he was not distracted, keeping his bursts professional – short and sharp. His magazine expired, he dropped to one knee to change it. It was one of the quickest, slickest changes I had ever seen in my short career. 'Don't fucking watch me, boy,' he screamed. 'Fight, you clown.'

I spun on my belly, heaving the Bren around. The cover among the rubble, and indeed that offered by the cottage, was slowly but surely disintegrating. I got the gun into some kind of suitable firing position, quickly realizing the Germans had somehow sneaked into the buildings around us. I tried to spot enemy figures, but only saw muzzle flashes coming from windows. They were keeping well back from the windows, so as not to offer easy targets. I engaged the first muzzle flash. Bullets smashed into the rubble all around me. It felt like all the enemy fire was concentrated on me.

I knew to stay there would be suicide, so I shuffled back on my elbows, dragging the Bren with me into the cottage. Its bipod legs gave way, the muzzle clattering to the floor. I heard firing behind me. Glancing round, I saw Hibbert, Brettle and Hibbert's radio operator kneeling in what was left of the living room, firing short bursts through large holes in the wall. Terry appeared at the front door, kneeling over what I could only guess was Sean. Terry fished out a field dressing from a pocket, frantically ripped its wrappings open and then fought to open Sean's smock. He roared for a medic.

Behind me, a medic raced from a doorway to a room I hadn't noticed before, a few rounds of tracer following him. As he jumped over me, I slid back into the living room and saw Frank lying dead on the floor. After taking a deep breath, I knelt with Hibbert's firing line, even though Frank's body made it difficult. Through the holes in the wall, I noticed movement behind the windows of another house, so joined the others in firing at it, splintering and smashing shutters. Dull muzzle flashes appeared behind the remains of the shutters. Brick dust, wood splinters and masonry flicked up all around us. The German infantry weren't backing off, and it dawned on me that we were now making our last stand. Hibbert and Brettle dropped to their bellies to carry out magazine changes. I kept firing with the radio operator.

Brettle was back up amazingly quickly, but jogged my shoulder, causing a few of my rounds to go astray. He fired a couple of bursts. 'Follow me! Let's go!' he shouted, heading for the kitchen. Crouching, I took a few steps towards him, still firing despite slipping and tripping on the debris. He slapped me on the shoulder as I clambered over the pile of enemy dead in the kitchen doorway. The kitchen was in a sorry state, a heavy wooden table on its side among scattered smashed crockery. Rounds whizzed through as we dashed towards the door leading to the back garden. I wondered if the cottage would completely collapse before we could get out.

He led me into the walled garden. I was shocked to see medics and wounded everywhere. The wounded were on their backs, some on stretchers, the medics on their bellies tending them. Some of the wounded were in a bad way. My ears had been reduced to hearing only dull thuds and screaming ricochets. I saw Terry and a medic beside Sean, who was bathed in sweat, gasping for breath, looking very pale and totally out of it. Judging from the position of his roughly applied dressings, he had taken rounds to the chest and gut. A second medic crawled over to help. I thought about Frank, already dead.

As my hearing improved, I began to hear voices all around shouting in English and German. Grenades thundered in the houses around us. Hibbert and his radio operator slid on their bellies into the garden. Static sounded from Hibbert's radio set. He grabbed the headset, pushing it to his ear. His operator began trying to roll a cigarette, but his hands were shaking. Brettle placed a hand on his, taking the tobacco and papers from him. He slowly and methodically constructed and rolled a cigarette, then placed it between the operator's lips, lighting it for him.

'Roger,' barked Hibbert into the radio. 'Do not, I repeat do not, engage to your north. We have enemy forces between our call signs. Keep your men in hard cover, and we will take care of the threat here. We don't want to be shooting each other up. Over.' Inaudible chatter crackled. He began to lose his cool. 'Stay put! Do not move anywhere. The enemy are to your north. Do not move! Stay put! Over.' He shook his head in exasperation, probably forgetting people were watching him. But then again, in the circumstances, maybe he didn't give a toss. He listened again and suddenly looked content, passing the headset to his operator. 'Fucking B Company are really feeling the pinch from the south but can't move because the enemy bastards have got between us and them. Captain Brettle, remain here while I try to see how our platoons are getting on. A Company must have broken clean by now, so we must hold firm on our left side.'

As Brettle nodded, Hibbert was already crawling into the

smashed cottage, his poor operator following him, cigarette hanging from his lips. Just as the major disappeared from sight, mortars started to scream in around us, smashing more roofs, sending tiles sky high. Before long tiles were raining down on us. The medics tending to Sean immediately leaned their bodies over him, absorbing the falling debris with groans and gasps. A fragment almost hit me, a complete tile just missing my Bren magazine. We were spoilt for choice now. Death by debris, death by bullets, or going back inside to die when the cottage finally collapsed. The mortar fire became sporadic, but I knew what would happen if any rounds landed in the garden or struck the cottage.

After a time, the firing around us began to lessen, mortars reducing to the odd round. I could hear B Company's fight in the near distance. It sounded as though the Germans had rounded on them, really pressing home their attack, their self-propelled guns giving it some. I wondered when more enemy infantry would arrive.

'Friendlies coming through!' came a shout from the cottage.

Hibbert reappeared with his radio operator. The remnants of platoons started to file into the garden, the area becoming crowded. Some of the guys looked really beaten up, some helping mates who were limping. Medics rushed forward to tidy up or replace crude field dressings applied during combat. Jenkins was the last man through. He began to allocate defensive positions around the garden to those who were fit to fight, but 'fit to fight' had become a loose term now.

Tony and Dougie appeared in the garden. They looked like they had really gone through the mill, slumping down without ceremony, looking immune to the continuing sounds of fighting. I think we had all got that way now. I made eye contact with Tony, who winked at me with a thumbs up. Dougie didn't look quite as sociable. His eyes were glazed, tear streaks running down his filthy face. I looked back at Tony. 'Frank,' he mouthed. I guessed

Dougie must have seen Frank, or whatever remained of him. They had been good friends.

The serjeant major emptied a very sorry-looking sandbag at our feet. Items clattered out: a few water bottles, Bren magazines, a couple of Lee-Enfield bayonets, grenades. It was all glazed with the red sticky tinge of blood. 'This is off our dead. More use to us than them. Dish it out between you.' He made his way to Sean, taking a firm grip of his hands. I couldn't hear what Jenkins said, but imagined the words were gentle, almost fatherly. It always amazed me that, however rough and gruff they appeared on the drill square, when their boys were in a bad way, our senior NCOs had time for them.

I looked away, focusing on the bloody booty at our feet. It was only right to take the Bren magazines. I wiped them one at a time on the coarse grass. It took some of the blood off, but thicker clots remained. I persisted until the mags were at least semi-clean, before stowing them in my pouches and smock. I then tried to remove the blood from my hands but couldn't get it all off and gave up. I thought about giving the Bren the once-over, knowing she could do with a damn good clean, but then changed my mind. I couldn't find the energy. Later, perhaps. I got my water bottle out. Dougie and Tony followed suit, and we had a little sip. Terry came over for the water bottles Jenkins had left with us and gave them to the medics for the wounded.

'D Company, listen up,' Brettle hollered, B Company's battle still sounding in the background. Brettle had come up through the ranks. A former sergeant major, he had joined as a boy many moons ago but still had it in him to match Jenkins in the shouting stakes. On Salisbury Plain he had known every trick in the book; they were nothing he hadn't done as a young soldier, I was sure and I realized what a welcome addition he had become to our company. 'The commanding officer has ordered us to withdraw to Hérouvillette,' he announced, and I could immediately sense the relief in the men around me.

'This village is untenable at this time. Enemy strength continues to grow, fresh units on their way here. We are running low on ammunition and water.' He wasn't wrong there. 'Airborne troops we may be,' he continued. 'Tough we may be. But we can only fight with what we carry. A Company have managed to break clean, and are heading for Hérouvillette. B Company are keeping the enemy interested, to enable us to withdraw. I want 10 Platoon to lead our withdrawal, and as you have the greatest numbers you'll take care of getting our casualties back.' It sounded as though 10 Platoon had drawn the short straw. '11 Platoon,' he went on, 'you will be at the rear of our column, since you have sufficient men to turn and face any enemy forces pursuing us. Corporal Thomson, you will take 12 Platoon and join the company command group in the middle. I will be just behind you, as link man for 11 Platoon. Any questions?'

There were none. I don't think anyone wanted to say anything that might delay our exit. I sat with the rest of 12 Platoon as Terry immediately got to grips with his battlefield promotion and got us ready to travel. Despite what some people felt about Terry, he was a good leader. Hibbert continued talking on the radio as we all picked our way through the cottage and out onto the street, where 11 Platoon got into line. The shattered and bloody men of 10 Platoon gathered up the wounded – walking and stretcher-bound – and they led the way out of that bastard place called Escoville.

We slipped through streets and gardens with Hibbert's command group, B Company still getting the good news from the Germans. You could be forgiven for thinking the heavier noises were tank fire, but they were probably artillery. The *crump* of grenades sounded pathetic in comparison. Occasionally I heard what sounded like buildings crashing to the ground, probably collapsing under their own weight. I hoped B Company wasn't underneath them. The afternoon was warm and sticky, and before long I was a sweaty mess once again, but as we broke out of the village back into fields, a cool breeze wrapped around my face and the back of my neck. It felt wonderful. But Escoville had been a pressure cooker of intense fighting, and the warm June day helped to still make things feel oppressive.

A Company hadn't quite made it to Hérouvillette. They were spread out in the distance, forward right. I wondered why they were all lying down in a field. Then plumes of dirt and turf shot up around them. They were getting mortared. The familiar dull thuds took a little while to reach our ears. Not much we could do for them. Our pace became painfully slow, not helped by again having to negotiate hedgerows. And the lads of 10 Platoon were starting to run out of steam as they lumbered along with the wounded. We were having to stop and start so as not to bunch up with them. During one stop in the middle of a field I suddenly realized if the Germans managed to get through B Company, we would have no cover. I prayed they would hold on long enough for us to get back to Hérouvillette, a position we could defend with a fighting chance, if need be. The guys with the wounded knew this too, the pace picking up as they got their act together.

The rooftops of Hérouvillette gradually got closer. The village still felt a lifetime away, but I knew we would soon find sanctuary in its cool cellars and cottages. I was sweating buckets now and jumping at my own shadow, snapping glances behind me every few steps, convinced the German infantry would race out onto the fields behind us.

We made the outskirts and they couldn't have come soon enough. C Company guys came out of the cottages and houses to help 10 Platoon. Having returned to Hérouvillette after the initial exchanges in Escoville, C Company looked pretty fresh, and I felt an irrational animosity towards them. But, as always, professional nods were exchanged. I supposed if we hadn't maintained a presence in Hérouvillette, there was a very real chance the Germans could have moved into the place, cutting off our retreat.

But the Germans had seen us arrive. The mortar barrage moved across the fields, following both us and A Company in. Company Serjeant Major Jenkins came down the line, allocating us to new fighting positions. Terry led my section through cobbled streets and alleys until we saw Major Hibbert and Captain Brettle ahead, already poring over a map. On seeing us, Brettle pointed towards a two-storey house. Its window shutters had once been white, but the paint was now flaking away. The building was completely intact, although I wondered for how much longer. There were children's wooden toys in the garden, which were also losing paint. A monster chicken coop dominated the right side of the garden. The coop had old household doors held together with chicken wire. No sign of the chickens, though. Perhaps, I mused, they had been taken away by the family, or eaten by the Germans a while ago.

'Corporal Thomson,' Brettle said, 'this is all for you. Don't play your music too loud on Sundays, please.' Even through his fatigue he managed to crack a laugh at his own joke.

'Great,' replied Terry. 'Now you're my fucking landlord.' There were chuckles all round. Even Hibbert grinned.

We made our way up the garden path in single file. I heard Brettle laughing. I didn't know what he found funny, but it spread among us. 'Shells are falling nearby,' he pointed out, 'and you're keeping off the grass. Unbelievable.'

He had a point, but to me it felt wrong to abuse a lawn that wasn't ours. It always felt a bit sad to occupy someone's home. Whoever had lived there had kept the place looking as nice as they could, and I felt some responsibility to them, even though I couldn't guarantee the Germans would feel the same. The front door was unlocked. As we piled inside, mortar rounds landed a little closer. The kitchen was immaculate, as was the living room. I knew it was unlikely to remain so for long. We were probably going to have to fight from the place; death or destruction, whichever came first. Upstairs was pristine too, except the family hadn't made the beds before leaving, empty cupboards and chests of drawers hanging open. Terry sited me with Tony in the largest bedroom. It had a grand view of the cobbled street outside and the houses opposite. A handful of our guys were milling around in fighting gear, cups of tea in their hands, cigarettes hanging from their lips.

'Sit tight, guys,' said Terry. 'I'm going back to see Hibbert, to get briefed up on what's going to happen next.' He made his way downstairs.

Strolling around, the troops across the street looked confident, but we kept away from the windows nonetheless, making sure they were fully open, shutters splayed out wide. You never knew what might happen next. I sat beside the doorway, my back against the wall. I peeled my helmet off but kept the Bren beside me. I couldn't remember when I'd last shaken my hair around. The sweat on my brow began to chill immediately. It felt rather nice. Tony got a roll-up on the go, and soon enough smoke rings were drifting through the warm, still air. 'And now we wait,' I said, stating the obvious.

'Yep,' replied Tony. A comforting near silence descended, B Company's fight in Escoville only just audible. I could also just hear battle noise from the direction of Bénouville.

I enjoyed the feeling of my eyelids closing. Just for a little while I was past giving a toss about the war. My slumbering thoughts wandered to home. Surely what we were up to in Normandy would now be front-page news. My war was only two days old, but I was already exhausted. Was this what war was: a battle for sleep as much as against the enemy? I wasn't sure I could make Berlin if it was going to go on like this. How long would it take us to get all the way to Berlin anyway? Here we were, back with a toe in Europe, back where we were four years earlier, back where Daniel had been.

I smiled to myself wryly; we had something else in common

now. I had never pretended to be the first in the queue to go and fight, but here I was in the arse end of Normandy, doing my bit. Just like he had back in 1940. I cursed myself for being a prick and mocking him. He had wanted to serve, was proud to have done so, and at the time I had cared about nothing more than opening time at the Jolly Gardeners. I didn't remember him ever complaining about his injuries, his lot in life. I wondered if he'd have acted any differently in my shoes. I hoped I was doing him proud.

A rough shove snapped me out of my slumber. Terry was back. At a crouch, he made his way towards the open window. Tony and I squatted behind him. Behind the houses opposite, dark columns of smoke drifted up in the still June evening, marking burning buildings in Escoville. The odd mortar round hit a rooftop there. Why hadn't B Company withdrawn?

Terry cleared his throat. 'B Company is holding the Germans in place while we establish a defensive area here. The troops in the houses opposite are C Company. Their anti-tank guns are on the right flank. The enemy is continuing to try and get between the villages, but B Company will hopefully be able to withdraw here after dark. The Germans, it seems, are not fans of night fighting. The battalion is sitting on the main German axis of advance towards Sword. Our units landing on the beaches are breaking out, making slow progress inland. German forces are all over the fucking show. We are to hold them here. How the fuckers haven't already overrun us is anyone's guess.'

The fighting in Escoville died away as the light began to fade. We heard our wounded, Sean included, had been taken to the regimental aid post at Bénouville Bridge. Tony and I settled down for the night but agreed not to sleep in case it all went wrong.

There was a crash of furniture and crockery downstairs. I feared the worst – German infantry. Tony scrambled out onto the landing, then came back smiling. 'Noisy fuckers downstairs, preparing the house for defence.' I was relieved but wondered why defence preparations had become urgent enough to rush. Had B Company been overrun? I couldn't hear any noise outside. Cautiously I made my way to the window. Opposite, nothing looked out of the ordinary. Some C Company guys were just visible at the windows, quite a few spaced around outside. They seemed to be maintaining excellent battlefield discipline. Those few smoking were making every effort to keep light to an absolute minimum. Night-time routine seemed to be in operation: no noise or light, twice as many sentries, all alert.

I heard a creak of floorboards behind me. In the poor light of dusk I just made out Terry in the doorway. 'B Company are now preparing to withdraw,' he told us. 'Patrols from the recce platoon will guide them back here. So just be mindful of who and what you are looking at. To be honest, I'm not getting any shut-eye until I know them poor bastards are behind us in reserve.' We nodded in the gloom before he left.

And so began one of the longest nights of my life, worrying if B Company would make it back. If the Germans noticed their withdrawal, would they pursue them to Hérouvillette, or would the enemy wait until morning before launching an all-out assault on us? We dragged the bed over to the window, just to have something to sit on while on watch. I could no longer make out Escoville. The lights were out there too. Pangs of hunger ripped through my stomach. But cooking or making a brew was out of the question until morning because of the light it would generate. Ignoring strict night-time battlefield discipline could attract enemy attention and mean you didn't live very long. Noise travels further at night, and the slightest noise or light could get you killed.

The warm June night wore on and on, sleep nothing more than a fool's fantasy. We occasionally heard distant noises of battle, but Escoville remained quiet. At that time of year I knew darkness was only a brief friend. There had been just a very few short hours of darkness the night before in the forest.

Terry appeared again. 'B Company are coming through on the right flank. Don't fire, whatever happens, OK?' We both nodded. I took a chance, craning my neck to look down at the street. It was true: B Company were coming past us. In the gloom I could see the shadows of them struggling with their wounded, maybe even their dead. Figures appeared from nowhere to help them. B Company's time in reserve would be well earned. Being the only company in Escoville had been the shortest straw of all.

I relaxed on the bed again, thinking about the dead we had left behind. What would happen to them? Would the Germans clear them? Would they just leave them? Would they loot the bodies? I shouldn't have let it bother me, but it really did. I thought of Frank. Would he still be where we had left him? I knew that after Escoville I had become more nervous, more paranoid. I didn't know whether it was tiredness or battle-weariness, but I knew I had to get a grip on myself or I'd never make Berlin. And I wanted to get there – for Frank, for Sean, for Daniel, for my dad and for a bloody sleep. I looked across at Tony, Dougie and Terry and thought how far we'd come and how far we had to go. And then, finally, I fell into a deep sleep. The sleep of the living.

Double Trouble

PROLOGUE
Final Confirmation

'Gentlemen, it's on,' General Urquhart reassured us for the second time that day. 'We are going to Holland.'

We'd been ushered through the main doors of a headquarters building and led into a huge room with a high ceiling. A massive map of Holland was mounted on the far wall, a sergeant major standing on a stage just beneath it. He waved his swagger stick about, positioning us all. Most sat on the floor, the chairs to the rear being occupied by senior officers, their sergeant majors and senior NCOs already standing behind them.

MARKET GARDEN was printed bold black letters in the top right corner of the map. All across the chart, a series of American and British flags were stuck next to towns and cities. American flags dominated, but near the top of the map a cluster of Union Jacks surrounded a town, again picked out in bold: ARNHEM.

I stared up and remembered the last such map I'd seen almost four months before. Four months! I could hardly believe it had been so short a time. I felt as though I'd lived a lifetime since Major Hibbert had stood in the hangar at RAF Tarrant Rushton and outlined the plan for Operation Overlord. If I closed my eyes I could still feel the shuddering jolt of the glider landing and breaking apart, hear the thud of bullets striking flesh and smell the churned-up earth and blood. They didn't show you that on a map. Flags and arrows were all very well, but in my brief experience of fighting I'd already learned that war was confusion, shouting, tiredness and a lot of waiting.

1
All Quiet on the Western Front

I'd returned from France along with a few blokes from the 2nd Battalion, the Oxfordshire and Buckinghamshire Light Infantry in August 1944. As always we'd no real idea why we'd been moved. One minute we were busy trying to help hold the line in Hérouvillette, Normandy; the next minute we were ordered home – jumping on a truck for Gold Beach, witnessing the destruction that 40,000 heavily armed men had wrought in a day there. I got another reminder of the cost of the operation just before embarking on a boat for England, when word came through that my platoon serjeant, Terry Thomson, was missing in action. I'd been through a lot with Terry. His disappearance was a blow, an unpleasant reminder that I was leaving friends and unfinished business behind. It made for a bittersweet homecoming as we disembarked at Gosport, Hampshire in the early hours. A grim place. All along the jetty ambulances were lined up to take our broken boys away.

An army truck unglamorously took us to RAF Tarrant Rushton, people in villages going about their business oblivious to the carnage going on across the Channel. I did notice one smartly dressed old gentleman, who nodded to me as we passed as though he knew where we had come from. Perhaps he was a First World War veteran; soldiers, no matter what generation, always remain soldiers.

Back on home soil the chat turned to family, and as soon as the truck dropped us at the airbase there was a scramble to grab kitbags, travel warrants and backdated pay as quickly as possible. We were told we had two days' leave, after which we were to use the travel warrants to get to Fulbeck Hall in Lincolnshire, headquarters of 1st Airborne Division. Two days wasn't much time, especially with the country's transport up the spout. Last I'd heard, my family were staying with my aunt in High Wycombe, having moved there from London to escape the Blitz, and I knew it would take me many precious hours to get there. Fortunately I decided to ring ahead, and my aunt told me they were back in Mortlake, collecting some stuff from our house.

I got the train to London, hoping there was sufficient rail infrastructure left to get me to Mortlake. My carriage was full of Americans who felt the need to shout at each other. There seemed to be more Yanks in the country now than before D-Day, or maybe they were just making more noise. Some were giving it the big 'I am', saying what they would do to the first Nazis they came across. I smiled to myself, wondering if we were ever that arrogant when I was a rookie. And what was I now – a veteran? I certainly felt different, and I wondered if it showed. Would my family see it?

One of the two lines running through Mortlake was in service, and the place didn't look too roughed up, all things considered. The brewery had reopened, and it looked like business as usual as I made my way across a green which had a couple of weatherworn bomb craters, grass now evident in them. Off to the left the houses were a mess. Where the front gardens met the green, a group of kids wearing caps were throwing vinyl records and crockery found in the ruins at each other. A couple of them noticed me. Sprinting towards me, they waved their friends to join them. I knew what they were after: food. Kids knew soldiers always had at least chocolate on them. The biggest lad, knees scuffed and bloodied below his short trousers, found the confidence to ask, 'Got any grub, please, sir?'

I pulled my kitbag from my shoulder. 'Have you been fighting, sir?' a squeaky little voice from the group piped up. I nodded. They gazed open-mouthed at each other, clearly impressed.

'Where?' another lad enquired.

'Normandy.' Their eyes opened even wider as though I was a movie star. I smiled to myself, aware that I was enjoying their adulation.

The biggest lad grinned. 'Killed any Jerries?'

I laughed. 'One or two.' I rummaged through my kitbag and fished out some biscuits, a small tin of jam and some chocolate. They ran off with it all; it was almost all eaten before they made their way back to the ruined houses.

I headed to the Jolly Gardeners pub. Pushing my way through the double doors, I was greeted by a thick haze of cigarette smoke. It hung from the ceiling to about waist height throughout the place. Nothing new there. Some of the windows had been boarded up, though, and the remainder had grimy white tape strips across them, forming crosses of sorts. The place wasn't exactly brimming with life. No one was manning the bar, but I could hear the crashing and rattling of bottles and crates out the back, the racket probably made by Kirby Green, the landlord. Over in the corner a couple of old fellas sat quietly playing dominoes, pint glasses almost empty, their dogs dozing under their table.

Most of the regulars would still be behind the brewery walls, humping casks until the whistle, before streaming into the pub, shouting their usual orders to Kirby. He was built like an ox, just like my father. Kirby had served in the Middlesex Regiment during the Great War, and I had heard he had been decorated for evacuating his platoon commander under fire. He had apparently won the Military Medal. When I was a kid, I remember thinking the two Ms behind his name on the plaque above the pub doors were the initials of his middle names.

I realized one of the blokes in the corner was Bernie Campbell-King, a nightwatchman at the brewery. He was no spring chicken when I was a kid, stealing beer from under his nose. But now he looked really old. 'Blimey,' he began, 'Robert Stokes, as I live and breathe. How are you doing, lad?'

'Not bad, Bernie, not bad.'

The other fella turned. I realized he was another of the old brewery guard force, Wally Bath. 'Hey, Bobby boy,' he said. 'Looking good, son.'

'Hey, Wally,' I replied. 'What are you two drinking?'

They quickly snapped childish grins at each other. Swiftly they finished their dregs and handed me their warm pint glasses. 'Two milds, please, Bobby lad,' said Wally.

I left my kitbag with them, before leaning over the bar, craning my neck to look out the back. A female voice called out, 'Be right with you.' I knew the voice but couldn't picture the owner. I heard a feminine clip-clop of heels, then a beautiful blast from the past appeared behind the bar. Molly Gardner was never the tallest of girls, but her heels made up for it. She had a fresh face of make-up on. Her brunette hair was up in a bun, held in place by numerous clips. She was looking rather trim, which was hardly surprising given the rationing situation. When we were kids, I remembered her being tubbier. It felt like a long time since I'd seen a woman, and my eyes were drawn to the sizeable knockers trying to fight their way out of her dress. She bent slightly to get my attention. 'Blink, Robert, they're just boobs.'

I snapped out of my trance, feeling myself blushing. Behind me, Bernie and Wally chuckled away like a pair of kids. 'Oh. Hello, Molly,' I managed to get out. 'Wow, you look great.' At least the words weren't as clumsy as my gaze.

'Thank you, Robbie,' she cooed. 'You look quite dapper yourself. What can I get for you?'

A few things sprang to mind, but they would probably get me a slap across the chops and kicked out of the pub. I had to focus, get a grip on myself. 'Three pints of mild, please, and have something yourself.' Her little pale hands and her scarlet fingernails worked the draught pump. As she filled the glasses, her boobs bounced lightly with the effort. I found them mesmerizing.

She lined the glasses up on the bar, my cheap thrill over. I paid her and took the giggling schoolboys their pints, before composing myself to go back to the bar. 'How long have you worked here?' I enquired as I took my first sip of the dark, sweet, malty liquid, which tasted good.

'Couple of months now, since Kate went to work the bar at the American base over in Bushy Park.'

Kate was Kirby Green's wife. I took another long pull at my ale and smiled ruefully. 'Mr Green can't be too happy about that.'

'You can say that again. But then they pay handsomely, and God knows we all need the money these days. She'd have been a fool to turn it down, and Mr Green saw that in the end.' She paused to stack some glasses before turning back with a wink. 'And the pay's not all that's handsome either.'

I looked aghast. 'You don't mean Mrs Green and some American serviceman . . .'

'No, silly. Me. I've got myself a lovely Yankee sweetheart.'

'Oh,' I said, feeling slightly crestfallen. 'Is he from the base and all?'

'He is. They know how to have a good time, those boys. Some of us are going over for a dance tomorrow night, if you fancy it.'

I shrugged, feigning nonchalance. 'Yeah, maybe.'

'Come on, Robbie. Must have been a good while since you had a night out, and you've the look of a man in need of one. Not all the girls are spoken for.'

I smiled. 'You're not an easy person to say no to, Molly.'

'So you'll come.'

'Well, let's see how I go. I haven't even seen my folks yet.'

'They're over at your old place in Alder Road,' she said. 'It's a bit of a mess, I'm afraid. The fuckers have stripped everything.'

'What do you mean?' I asked.

'When you moved out to High Wycombe, your dad asked Mr Green to secure the place. The street was a mess from the bombing, but apart from some blown-in windows and missing roof tiles, your place didn't seem so bad. Mr Green found the house key under a stone pigeon by the doorstep and managed to board up the broken windows, draw all the curtains. He fitted an extra lock and clasp to the front door, but the looting bastards still got in and stripped the place. I'm sorry, Robbie.'

I felt anger begin to boil inside me. I found my fists clenching as I thought of the bastards stealing our belongings. People who'd never worked or fought for anything stealing from those who were busy fighting to protect them. I wanted to wring their bloody necks. The shrill whistle from the brewery signalled the end of the day shift, piercing my thoughts. Soon workers began pouring into the bar, and Kirby Green appeared behind the bar, rapidly serving drinks with Molly.

I looked around for some familiar faces and found Mum's. She was just coming through the door. My stomach flipped, excitement building up inside me. I got to my feet and waved. She didn't notice, but someone pointed her in my direction. Her eyes lit up. She began to shove her way through the mass of drinking bodies, letting go of the door. It flew back, whacking my brother Daniel in the chops as he struggled forward on his crutches. He had lost a leg to a Stuka attack at Dunkirk. Dad shuffled his way in after him. It wasn't long before Mum's arms were around my neck, her eyes full of tears. I instantly recognized the soap she still used. She planted kisses all over my cheeks. 'How long have you been back?' she asked.

'Not long.'

A firm hand grabbed my shoulder. I looked up. Daniel had a huge grin on his face. 'How you doing, bruv?' he asked.

I almost had to fight Mum off me, just so I could shake his

hand. Dad waded in and put his big arms around Daniel and me. 'Good to see you, boy,' he enthused. 'Still in one piece, I see.'

He flinched as Mum gave him a mock clip around the back of the head. 'Don't say things like that, you silly man.'

It was good to be home. We nattered, catching up on things, the pub thinning out as the evening progressed. Kirby made sure we didn't pay for a single drink. I don't think I had ever seen my mother drunk before, yet she tried her hardest to appear sober. 'When do you go back, Rob?' Daniel asked eventually.

'Day after tomorrow. I plan to get the train late morning.'

'So why have you been sent back to England?' enquired Dad. 'You been reassigned?'

'I don't really know, to be honest. They've not told me much . . .'

'No change there,' chipped in my brother.

'All I know is that me and some other lads from 2nd Battalion are joining the 1st Airborne Division in Lincolnshire. I don't know why or for how long. Apparently they have something big coming up, and they're pulling some boys out of Normandy to help.'

'Berlin,' Daniel announced. 'My money is on Berlin.'

Dad shook his head. 'No, no, you silly boy. It's too far. Our lot are still in France. It's got to be somewhere closer. Paris maybe?'

After a guessing game involving French and German cities, Mum tottered her way through the bar, on her way upstairs to the guest rooms. I had learned they were staying at the pub, so Dad and Daniel soon followed, but I lingered briefly with Kirby. 'Thank you, Mr Green,' I said, 'for all that you've done for my family.'

He gave me a warm smile. 'No problem, Robbie lad, but call me Kirby, please. And just remember, don't try and be a hero. All the ones I know are dead.'

The next day I woke early, trying to remember where I was. I couldn't think of the last time I'd slept two nights in the same bed.

Breakfast for guests at the Jolly Gardeners was a very basic affair, but it sure beat army rations: lovely sweet tea and plenty of jam on toast. I felt born again as I took a bath, the first in a very long time. Then Dad and Daniel took me back to Alder Road. Some kids were kicking a ball around. The houses didn't look too bad, although close to the railway line some roofs had partially collapsed. I couldn't see any broken roof tiles on the ground, so the remaining residents must have made an effort to clear up.

Dad led us to our front door. The stone pigeon was still in pride of place, standing guard. The dark blue paint on the door was beginning to flake, and it was clear to see where it had been forced open, despite the fresh-looking clasp and lock. Dad undid the lock, and we made our way in. You could instantly smell the damp that had seeped into the carpets, certainly in the hallway and on the stairs. He flicked a light switch. We had power, which was unexpected. The bastards who had stripped the place hadn't left enough of anything to make a mess; they had pretty much taken everything except the carpets. But I could smell soap and polish. Dad explained that, despite everything, Mum had insisted on scrubbing the place from top to bottom.

I felt sad, then anger began to build up inside me. The injuries suffered by my father at Passchendaele during the First World War had eventually forced him to give up his job at the brewery. Daniel had lost a leg in France. And now the Germans had put paid to our home life with their bombing, and that had led to our house being ransacked. I knew the robbers were just trying to make a living amid the chaos in London, but I wasn't in the mood to see reason. I decided not to bother going upstairs.

'Are we coming back here, once this whole shitty war is over?' I asked as we made our way out.

'That's the plan,' replied Dad as he secured the front door.

I stared back at the narrow two-storey frontage and felt relief at my father's words. It wasn't much, but it was home and something worth fighting for.

Back in the pub, I couldn't help but feel rather deflated. It was clear nothing was sacred, not even our home. Dad and Daniel made their way upstairs. Dad's feet hurt, and I knew Daniel's hands and armpits would be raw from his crutches.

Molly appeared to sense my mood and brought me a pint of mild. 'Tell you what, Robbie: we don't have to go all the way to the American airbase tonight, if you don't fancy it. You can treat a girl to a bag of chips, if you like.'

Staying closer to home had far more appeal. I wasn't in the mood for Yanks showboating. A bag of chips sounded just the ticket. 'That's a great idea, and thanks for the beer.'

As she placed it down on the table, there was a sting in the tail. 'No funny business, Robert Stokes. We're just talking dinner. Figured you could do with a friend.'

She had a point, not knowing yet that I only had the weekend in Mortlake, which was going far too quickly. I smiled up at her. 'No problem, Molly. No funny business.'

2
First Date

It was a nice evening, so Molly and I slowly wandered through Sheen to Richmond. The town centre was heaving with Yanks looking to spend their money on all manner of British skirt. Neither of us was hungry, so we grabbed a drink from a pub, sitting outside on the riverbank by the bridge. Molly looked out across the river, fingering the top of her glass with her scarlet nails. 'So, what will you do?'

'When?' I enquired after a mouthful of beer.

'When this war is over?'

'Not sure, to be honest. I think it will either be going back to the brewery or staying in the army.'

She looked up, rather surprised. 'The army, really? Even after all that you've been through?'

'Sure. Can't be at war for ever, surely.'

She took a polite sip of her drink. It was my turn to ask questions. 'So tell me about this American.'

Her relaxed demeanour changed to a frown, her eyes burning into mine. 'Don't start taking the piss, Rob.'

I leaned back, hands held up submissively. 'Calm down. I'm only being nosey.'

Her frown relaxed. She looked up beyond me, once more stroking the top of her glass with her fingers. 'He's a nice lad. Met him in Putney a while back. He's in the airborne. The 101st, I think. Haven't seen him since just before the invasion.'

I was starting to worry. From what I had seen of our airborne blokes in Normandy, none of them looked in very good shape. 'Have you had any letters since?'

She shook her head. 'Not for a while. Last letter said he was in a place called Carentan, wherever that is.'

I took a long pull at my pint, hoping she wouldn't ask if I thought he was safe. I wasn't sure I would be able to bring myself to tell her the truth – that it had been hell, and if he'd stopped sending letters then he was either, dead injured, or had bigger things on his mind, none of which she wanted to hear. 'What's his name?' I asked instead.

'Captain Carwood Jackson.'

An officer. Blimey, she sure knew how to pick them. 'City boy?' I asked.

'Manhattan. I've seen pictures of the place – it looks huge.'

My knowledge of the United States was not that great, but I knew of New York City and its huge high-rise buildings. 'Sounds like quite a guy.'

'You're just taking the mick now.'

'Molly, what does it take to pay you a bloody compliment these days? He really sounds great. I'm sure you'll be very happy . . .'

She focused intently on me. I'd set myself up for a fall, I could feel it. 'If he comes back,' she finished, eyebrows raised.

I had painted myself into a corner with my stupid mouth. 'Look, he'll be in touch soon, I'm sure. Can we please change the subject? I'm like a worm on a hook here.' My vulnerability encouraged a wicked grin from behind her blood-red lips. She had a hell of a pretty smile. If he was still alive, this Jackson bloke had better realize it.

We chewed the fat about anything and everything as the drinks flowed and the night got cooler. Inside the pub, British and Yank servicemen vied to outsing, outdrink and outfight each other. It was like watching a film when you knew the ending.

'It's been like this every weekend since they arrived over here,' said Molly, nodding to a group of America soldiers trying to carry a friend along the towpath. 'They're spending money like it's going out of fashion.'

'They came, they spent, they conquered, eh?' I said more bitterly than I meant.

Molly smiled ruefully. 'How about those chips, Robbie?'

I nodded, and we walked arm in arm through town. It was a romantic moment, and might have been more so if I hadn't been bursting for a pee. Molly just laughed as I excused myself and disappeared down an alleyway between the terraces. I let the dam break, and a wave of euphoria washed over me, but as the flow lessened I could hear the sound of movement and scraping further into the darkness. I peered along the alleyway and could just make out a woman sobbing, followed by a muffled squeal. I zipped up and moved towards her.

'Shut yer fucking mouth and don't snap your cap,' hissed a male voice in an American accent.

The girl's sobbing became more spasmodic, but then another squeal sounded. 'Who's that?' I demanded of the voice. 'What's going on?'

'Not a fucking sound, bitch, do you hear me?'

As I advanced, my night vision was instantly destroyed by a torch shone straight in my face. 'Keep on moving, pal,' the voice demanded. 'Go get your own broad to fuck.'

'Help me, please,' the woman gasped.

With my forearm shielding my eyes, I moved towards the light. It faded instantly, leaving my vision nothing more than large red blobs drifting down towards the ground. Whatever connected with the left side of my head made my ears pop, and I saw stars, pain exploding through the numbness of beer.

I reached out with both hands and grabbed my attacker. Keeping my arms locked, I managed to shove him against the alley wall. He let out a loud grunt and dropped the torch. With my left hand I felt for his throat, and then as my night vision improved, I tried to get a look at him. I just had time to make out an unpleasant angular face pockmarked with acne scars before he kicked me square in the balls and pain erupted in my stomach.

I dropped like liquid, my assailant falling on top of me. The dropped torch was digging into my lower back. It was too dark to establish where the punches were coming from; all I could do was try and find his throat once more. It was then I was aware of the rapid clip-clop of heels coming down the alley.

My sparring partner let out an almighty roar and instantly bucked back. 'Fuck you, fucking bitch,' he gasped, then made a jerking movement. I heard Molly yelp and thud to the ground. Instantly, the American was up, sprinting up the alley, back out onto the street. With my balls and lower gut on fire, there was no way I was going after him. I just lay there for a few minutes, waiting for the burning to stop.

As my strength returned, I became aware of groaning coming from one direction and sobbing from another. 'Thank you, thank you, thank you,' the unidentified woman further down the alley sobbed. Coming to my senses, I was suddenly aware of what I might have stumbled across. The torch was still digging into my back, but I managed to get to my feet.

The very low light in the alley allowed me to see Molly's groaning profile moving about, before she too clambered up. 'You OK, Molly?' I asked.

'Yeah,' she replied, somewhat shaken. 'Bastard punched me in the face. Wanker.' I helped her steady herself and then scrambled around for the torch. It clattered as I swept the concrete surface with my boot. I picked it up and checked Molly over. Her lip was split, and I was certain she would have a black eye in the morning, but other than that she was fit to fight. I swung the torch round on the other woman and Molly cried out, 'Kate! Oh my God, oh my God.'

In the glare, I was horrified at what I saw. The woman's blouse was ripped, one breast exposed and bleeding. Her face was bruised and bloody, her underwear hanging off one ankle, stockings ripped, legs bleeding, dark fluid pooling between her legs. Stunned, I thought I was going to be sick. Molly on the other hand dashed to the woman, knelt over her, wasted no time covering her modesty, before helping her to sit up. I felt as good as useless, not knowing what to do or say. Molly shielded her eyes from the torch as she waved me forward. 'Help me please, Rob.'

I turned off the torch, which made everything go black once more. I carefully stepped forward, fearing I might tread on the seated girl. But Molly grabbed my wrists and put my hands where they were needed to lift the girl. On Molly's count, we lifted her together. Once on her feet, the girl let out a gasp and sobbed, thanking us over and over again as we slowly and carefully walked her to the street.

Molly led us over to a low brick wall that separated a front garden from the pavement. Carefully, she and I lowered the girl down. She yelped and tried to lift herself up once more. 'It's OK. Kate, it's OK,' Molly said in a breaking voice. 'No one is going to hurt you any more. We need to get you to hospital, then home to Kirby.'

My stomach turned. Kirby? Kirby Green? The penny suddenly dropped: this was his wife, Kate. I stood there, useless with shock while Molly put her coat over Kate's shoulders. She turned to me. 'Rob, start banging on doors. We need to get her to Roehampton Hospital. She can't walk like this.'

Daylight was just touching the high chimney of the brewery when we got back to Mortlake. Molly hadn't spoken the whole way, and as we sat in the car outside the Gardeners I couldn't think of the words to break the silence. Suddenly she just collapsed into her hands and began to sob. I reached over and put an arm around her, and she leaned in closer.

'Poor Kate,' she sobbed gently. 'She looked so small and alone in that hospital bed. God, how do I tell Kirby?'

I shook my head, not really listening. I wasn't thinking of Kirby but of the man's angular face inches from mine. Why hadn't I just headbutted him while I had the chance? I ground my teeth in frustration as I thought of him maybe getting away scot-free. 'The bastard,' I said aloud.

Molly looked up at me, confused. 'Kirby?'

'No, no,' I said quickly. 'I was thinking of the fucker that did it. I should have done more to stop him. I hesitated and messed up.'

'Robbie!' Molly said incredulously, pulling out of my embrace. 'This isn't about you. It's about Kate and Kirby. You realize what this is going to do to them?' She pulled out a handkerchief and dabbed at her eyes.

I looked back at her blankly, shocked by her outburst.

'Men!' she said in disgust. Then she opened the car door and disappeared into the pub.

I thought about going after her but felt numb. I knew she was right – it was about Kate and Kirby – but I couldn't get over the sense of guilt I felt. I should have done more. I looked up at the pub and knew I couldn't face Kirby. Instead, I headed south and found myself walking along the river. I was angry at myself, at the rapist, at the fucking awful world we had created. Suddenly I wanted to be back on the front more than anything else. I wanted to be in a world I knew, a simpler world where there was right and wrong and you could do something about it. I wanted to be back doing what I did best, back to being a soldier.

3
The Plan

Crammed into the corner of a compartment on a train to Lincolnshire, it felt good to be back with comrades again. It took my mind off my anger and the images that had been flashing through my brain of what I'd seen in the alleyway. I'd left early in the morning, creeping out like a thief with just the briefest of farewells to my folks and Daniel. I knew I should have seen Molly and Kirby, but I felt utterly unable to deal with it. I was running away like a coward, and yet already it felt better. The banter of the boys was distracting, and as soon as they discovered I'd seen action in Normandy they were all over me for details. And I wanted to tell them because those memories were so much better than the more recent ones. So I told them about landing in gliders the night before the D-Day landings, about how we'd captured and subsequently held two key bridges near Bénouville and how the Germans had counter-attacked, causing significant casualties. And finally how, against all the odds, we'd held out until relieved.

I felt a familiar swell of pride as I told the stories and they kept asking questions long after I'd finished, eager for any details they could glean about life at the front. It reminded me how unusual it still was for a British soldier to have seen action in this war.

Life at Fulbeck Hall, headquarters of 1st Airborne Division, was far from luxurious, but there was a definite buzz of excitement about the place. A town of canvas tents populated the vast woods and grounds surrounding the main building, all camouflaged to conceal them from the air. I was assigned to the Defence Platoon, which consisted of a number of Vickers machine gun crews, tasked with defending divisional headquarters in the field against attack.

Each gun team had a controller, normally holding the rank of corporal. Simon Walton was our controller. A gunner and ammunition loader completed each team, me being the gunner on our team, Ernie Pullen supporting me as loader. The Vickers was a beast: a thirty-pound lump capable of firing around 500 rounds per minute. Firing the machine gun out on the ranges was exciting, but hauling it there and back took the fun out of everything, as did cleaning it afterwards. I was also tasked with carrying our jerrycan of water, while Si and Ernie each hauled a box of belted ammunition. In addition, as loader, Ernie also had to carry the tripod for the gun. The three of us also had our personal weapons, which were Sten sub-machine guns and grenades, as well as binoculars to observe the fall of shot of the Vickers.

We had to speed-march to the ranges, fitness being the priority in all airborne units. Once there, all of us soaked in sweat, Si would decide on a site for the gun, Ernie slamming down the tripod and its mounting cradle. I would then slide the gun into place, attaching it to the cradle by knocking securing pins into place. The barrel was surrounded by a cooling water jacket with a filler cap, the jacket being filled from the jerrycan, before the can was stowed between the tripod legs. A hose was then run between the can and the jacket, to enable steam to drain off while firing. As it cooled and condensed, the steam replenished the jacket with water.

To begin with on the ranges we were like chimps fighting over a deckchair, getting nowhere fast. But Vickers had been proved in the wastelands of Flanders during the Great War, so we were soon whipped into shape by our platoon commander, Lieutenant Dan Simmons, and our platoon sergeant, Bob Hilton.

Before we knew it, getting the gun in and out of action became really slick. Our targets were nothing spectacular: clusters of empty oil drums at various ranges, plus wooden man-shaped targets. We often practised 'grazing fire', which involved mounting the tripod lower, enabling us to lie on our bellies to fire long streams of bullets, grazing the grass. The lower position was ideal for dealing with enemies trying to rush your position, and combining multiple Vickers in a crossfire had devastating results. 'Point fire' involved mounting the tripod higher, ideal for saturating a single target area with fire, for example a road junction or a gap in perimeter wire. It was also possible to fire at distant 'map predicted targets', the fall of shot being observed and reported by a radio operator instead of using our own binoculars.

But the endless marches to the ranges eventually began to lose their shine. The division became restless, feeling rather left out, particularly because it had not been called on to participate in the original D-Day landings. Because of our involvement in Normandy, everyone from 2nd Battalion, the Oxfordshire and Buckinghamshire Light Infantry was treated like a minor celebrity, as were our colleagues in 6th Airborne Division. We were bombarded with all manner of questions regarding Normandy warfare and logistics. We were open and honest about it all, but one day senior officers from 1st Airborne asked us not to be too frank about landing in bullet-ridden wooden gliders.

This was fair enough, as the majority of 1st Airborne were untested, unlike most of the boys immediately surrounding me in the Defence Platoon. Sergeant Hilton had fought at Dunkirk with his local county regiment, managing to wade out to a fishing boat with panzer shell fragments in his back. After making a full recovery, he volunteered for airborne forces, seeing action in North Africa, Sicily and Italy. Si Walton had been one of the survivors of the Merville Gun Battery drop on D-Day.

Most of the rest of the Defence Platoon were from companies in my battalion: lads like Corporal Johnny Braithwaite, Mark Lavelle and a huge bloke called Eddie Karlow, the three of them making up another Vickers gun team. With a reputation for being rather blunt, Eddie boxed for the battalion. He was undefeated in all fights, with a shattering right hook, long arms perfect for destroying opponents at distance, and nothing on his face to indicate he had taken any real punishment in the ring. Ernie Pullen was also from 2 Ox and Bucks. He may have looked nine stone, but he could march with the best of them; fit as a butcher's dog, he could really pack away the grub. Tommy Kettles and Elliot Kemp were exceptions: not from my battalion, they had a Royal Signals background.

Sunday was normally a day off. You could catch up on your laundry, nip into town and have a pint or two. September 10 was different, though. We were confined to the tented area and ordered to convene in front of Fulbeck Hall at noon. Briefings were nothing new; the 1st Airborne had lost count of the number of times they had been stood ready for a drop into enemy territory, then stood down. Tough marches through the Lincolnshire countryside designed to lift morale were always scheduled after such disappointments, but they never did. However, as we lined up waiting for General Urquhart, this noon parade felt different. One of the many sergeant majors called for quiet as Urquhart walked down the steps leading from the building to address us. Urquhart was a well-built fellow with a harmless-looking demeanour, but today he had a stern look about him. From what I had heard, he had seen his fair share of action.

'Gentlemen,' he began, 'it's on. We are going to Holland. This is one drop that will not be called off. Officers, prepare your men and their equipment. Detailed orders will follow. Arrangements for a move to Barkston Heath are under way. We will not be returning to Fulbeck Hall once committed. Good day.' And with that he turned away, ascending the steps into the building.

That brief speech changed everything. We didn't go to the ranges any more; new kit arrived; senior offices became more edgy, and tempers frayed as the whole camp felt like it was on the verge of something. There were more questions than answers. Johnny and Si were both given Jeeps with trailers, which we were told would travel to Holland with us, but we didn't get any more information about the target or how we would drop.

We ferried our kit down to RAF Barkston Heath in dribs and drabs. I shuddered when I saw the gliders waiting around the runway. The memory of my last landing was still fresh in my mind. One of the pilots told us that hardly any of the gliders that went into Normandy had come out, so these were the last of a precious commodity. The pilots claimed not to know any more than we did about our mission, but most of us found that hard to believe. Then more confusion was heaped on when a truck arrived full of dinner jackets, suit covers and golf clubs, and a few boys got tasked with loading it all onto an aircraft. We stood around, hands on hips, shaking our heads and wondering what the hell we had signed up for.

It was on the morning of Thursday 14 September, after we'd formed up for parade in front of Fulbeck Hall, that we'd filed into the large ballroom and found ourselves confronted by the vast map of Holland. Some of the senior officers were having a smoke while drinking tea from bone-china cups and saucers; they looked exhausted, their eyes bloodshot, like they hadn't slept in ages. Lieutenant Simmons gave me a friendly nod when he caught my gaze.

There was more of a light-hearted atmosphere in the room, in stark contrast to the stomach-flipping briefing given by Major Hibbert for the Normandy landings. I wondered if Normandy had been our first step into the unknown, the lion's den. Perhaps today's atmosphere was bolstered by a little confidence; since the D-Day landings on 6 June we had met the enemy and found him to be well-trained, battle-hardened and savage, but he could be beaten. We had begun to believe, and there was an eagerness to be at the enemy's throat.

A sergeant major called for quiet. The expectant din evaporating, he turned sharply to his left, remaining at attention, and crisply saluted General Urquhart as he strode onto the stage. Urquhart fetched a long thin stick from behind a stage curtain and removed his beret, stuffing it into his smock.

'Gentlemen, as you are part of my headquarters, you will be privy to information that is seldom distributed to other brigades in the division.' Although a large body of men was at Fulbeck Hall, elements of 1st Airborne Division were scattered throughout Lincolnshire. 'The entire Allied effort has been put on hold to ensure that what we are about to embark on is the highest priority in both firepower and logistics.' He paused to allow his opening statement to take effect, but he was also clearly hoping for a show of enthusiasm. However, the division had been stood down at a late stage so many times before. 'The plan is called Operation Market Garden. "Market" is the airborne element, "Garden" being the follow-up ground forces. The plan is for us and American airborne forces to seize key territory and bridges in order for ground forces to advance north, linking up with airborne elements as they proceed.'

Some had begun to scribble notes, so he paused to allow the scribblers the catch up, before pointing his stick at a cluster of American flags on the map. I found I still couldn't look at them without feeling angry. 'The American 101st Airborne Division,' Urquhart continued, 'will land around the city of Eindhoven, seizing key bridges nearby. Our XXX Corps will cross the bridges, and then be handed over to the American 82nd Airborne Division, who will land in the Nijmegen area.' Urquhart emphasized Nijmegen with a sharp tap of his stick on the map. 'Once XXX Corps have passed through the 82nd, they will push north, linking up with us here at Arnhem to use the bridges that cross the

Rhine – Arnhem's main road bridge and the railway bridge to the west.' He tapped the bridges with his stick.

I could hear a muffled hum of excitement coming from some sections of the audience, something that had been absent from previous mission briefings. The word 'Rhine' was doing the rounds. If we could get across the Rhine, we would be on the doorstep of Germany before you knew it. The hum became a din.

The general wasn't shy in calling for order. The room reluctantly fell quiet. 'Once XXX Corps pass through Arnhem, they will make a right turn and handrail the Rhine south into the industrial heart of Germany itself, the Ruhr Valley. A large percentage of Hitler's war production takes place in that region, and if we overwhelm that capability, his armies will only be able to fight on with what they carry. They will run out of fuel and ammunition before Christmas.'

The room filled with a roar, making me flinch. The senior officers were happy at the boisterous reaction of the men, Lieutenant Simmons nodding his approval. It was a chance to get the war done by Christmas. The general looked pleased with himself, allowing everyone to enjoy the moment, before calling for quiet again. 'There is however one factor which will affect our efforts at Arnhem. Both the 101st and 82nd will be dropping in one lift, to ensure the enemy doesn't hamper XXX Corps as they drive north. We are the poor relation in this respect, so we will be dropping into Arnhem in a series of lifts, over the course of three days. It's far from ideal, but the great majority of the aircraft and gliders used for Operation Overlord in Normandy were either lost or are beyond repair, and time and war wait for no man.

'Our first drop is scheduled for the 17th, and will consist of both parachute and air-landing glider battalions. Our drop zones are eight miles west of Arnhem, just north of Oosterbeek. Our American cousins have kindly offered us pilots to fly the parachutist aircraft and tow our gliders.' Along the side wall on the left the American pilots sat opposite our officers, their hair all neat and tidy, smoking cigarettes, chewing gum and taking notes.

'The air-landing battalions will establish security at the landing sites for the follow-on drops,' Urquhart continued, 'while the parachute battalions will move quickly on foot to secure both bridges at Arnhem.' One of the American pilots leaned forward and scratched his ankle. I was aware of Urquhart's voice continuing the briefing but I was no longer listening. Suddenly I was back in Richmond, back smelling sour breath, hearing that rasping voice and feeling the pain ripping through my stomach. The face was the same. My heart was beating like a bass drum in my chest to the point where it could burst at any moment. The pilot turned to say something to a friend. They both laughed, and my certainty wilted. Maybe I was wrong. It had been months after all, and how much had I really seen anyway?

'The majority of this headquarters contingent will arrive in the second drop on the 18th,' Urquhart went on as I tried to turn my attention back to the briefing, 'along with the remaining parachute and glider battalions. A few key people including myself will be landing with the first drop, meaning most of you boys will be kicking your heels for a day while we establish a headquarters over there, and wait for XXX Corps to arrive at the secured bridges.'

The general opened the floor for questions. A few hands went up. He chose one. 'What enemy forces are in the area, sir?' I didn't know the lad who asked the question, but from the flight wings on his smock it looked as though he was one of our glider pilots.

Urquhart nodded his approval of the question, then spun on his heels, attacking the map with his long stick. 'Little to none in the Arnhem area, you will be happy to know. Since we chased them out of France, the Germans are a smashed bag of all sorts. Fragmented units at best, with little armour and even fewer spares.'

'Is there any armour in Arnhem, sir?' shouted another lad.

The general shook his head. 'No. Our reconnaissance flights have not detected any armoured formations in the Arnhem area.'

The American pilot was looking around the room absently and for a second his gaze met mine. Just for a moment I thought a flash of recognition showed in his face, but then his eyes passed on and I was left wondering if I'd imagined it.

'General, how long do you anticipate we'll be waiting for XXX Corps to arrive?' Lieutenant Simmons' question drew me back to the present. It was a good question, since we could only fight with what we carried.

'Three days. American airborne will prevent any German units from disrupting XXX Corps' advance up the single highway.' I knew the Germans would move resources to the area as soon as they knew we had arrived. It sounded a long time to hold on without dedicated armour support of our own, but I thought we could probably manage it if the information about German armour currently in the area was accurate.

Urquhart made sure he answered every single question, before the briefing was brought to a close. We would be moving to RAF Barkston Heath that night, staying there until it was time to fly. We were instructed to pack up all personal possessions, since we would not be returning to England any time soon. Once XXX Corps had passed through Arnhem, we would be garrisoned in the area, awaiting further assignments. The last of our gear would then be brought over by ship.

We were dismissed, and I immediately stood peering over towards the Americans, but found myself being jostled by the throng trying to get outside into the fresh air. Someone said something to me but I wasn't listening. Instead I pushed my way over to where I'd last seen the Americans. I made them out, standing near the stage and lighting up. The crowd was thinning, and I wandered closer, joining a group looking at the map. The Americans were talking and laughing and I moved even closer, trying to tune in.

'I tell you, Jack, she gets worse every damn behaviour report I send,' said a tall pilot who looked like a film star. 'Damn it, she's got her mother picking out flowers.' They all laughed.

I risked a glance and got a closer look at my quarry. He was taking long drags at his cigarette before blowing the smoke up into the rafters. 'Ain't nothing to it, Bones. You just got to know how to treat 'em. You're giving her too much attention; no wonder she's got you snapping yer cap.'

My throat was dry. It wasn't just the words, it was the way he'd said it. Now I knew it was him, and I found myself joining their group without thinking. The Americans opened up as I walked forward.

'Help you?' I heard the film star say. I didn't reply, I just kept staring at the acne-pocked face of the pilot. His eyes locked on mine, and this time I saw the realization come into his face. His body went rigid.

'Everything all right, Stokes?' It was Simmons at my shoulder. I ignored him, keeping my eyes locked on the pilot's.

'You're fucking dead,' I said, my anger boiling over. I took a step closer and saw alarm come into his face, but then I felt a hand around my arm, restraining me.

'Stokes, for God's sake!' It was the voice of Sergeant Hilton. I felt his grip tighten.

The pilot looked at Hilton's hand, and his features relaxed. 'Is this how your soldiers talk to all officers, Mack?'

Bob Hilton pulled me back a pace, placing a hand on my shoulder. I shrugged it off and made to step in again.

Simmons was beside himself. 'Stokes, what the hell do you think you're playing at?'

'This piece of shit should be in jail, sir. He tried to rape my friend's wife in London a couple of months back.'

The group near the map had stopped talking and had turned our way.

The pilot shook his head and crushed his cigarette on the floor. 'Sergeant, I think you'd best get your boy out of here before he gets himself in a whole heap more trouble.'

'No, you don't, you bastard. I know it was you, and you're gonna fucking pay for what you did.' I tried to go for him, but Hilton had a firm grip and yanked me back. 'Stand down, Stokes. You're in enough trouble as it is.' Then turning to the pilot, 'Apologies, Captain Temple. Stokes here is a little hot-headed. He's just got back from Normandy.'

Temple nodded slightly, keeping his eyes focused on me. 'You got spirit, Mack, I'll give you that. Save your strength for the Germans – looks like you're gonna need it.' He gave me a lopsided grin and I felt the rage boil over. I went for him again. This time Hilton didn't mess about. He pulled my right arm up behind my back and frogmarched me away.

But I wasn't finished. 'I'm not done with you, you fucking tosser,' I bellowed over my shoulder. Officers and clerical staff clutching bundles of paperwork got out of our way as Bob shoved me outside, through the main door.

I knew Simmons would want his pound of flesh for embarrassing him and 1st Airborne. When he finally emerged, I was half-expecting an officer's tantrum, but he asked me to walk with him. In a very relaxed manner, he listened to my side of the story, inviting me to calm down every time I started to get a little upset.

'Whether you like it or not,' he eventually said, 'Captain Temple will be flying one of our Dakotas over the next few days. Do you honestly think anyone around here gives a toss about anything except Holland? You have no evidence. You've already played your ace and it's done no good. I'll tell you this much, Stokes. If you are as much as in the same room as Captain Temple between now and when we fly, I will have you on a charge and in the guardroom until the mission is over. Is that clear?'

Rank trumps all reason, I thought bitterly, but confined myself to saying, 'Yes, sir.'

'Good. I need you focused on the job at hand. I feel for your friend and his wife, I really do. In time you can pursue this through the proper channels, but for now there are much bigger fish to fry, and I need you to have your business head on until I tell you otherwise, understood?'

I nodded and he appeared content. 'I'm not saying you're wrong, Stokes, but you could have picked a bloody better time to bring it up.'

RAF Barkston Heath had become a vast city of canvas tents, sufficient to accommodate the entire 1st Airborne Division. General Urquhart joined his troops under canvas. It wasn't long before numbers of C-47 Dakota Skytrains arrived, their role to carry the parachutists and their equipment to Holland as well as tow the gliders. It sounded like the Dakotas had been used heavily of late, their engines coughing and spluttering like they were going to die at any moment.

We watched some of the lads leave for the first drop over Holland on the 17th. For the remainder of the day I felt sorry for Lieutenant Simmons. Everyone badgered him for information on the first drop. He often visited the yeoman of signals in attempts to find out anything from radio traffic but was as much in the dark as we all were. Apparently, nothing whatsoever was coming back from the first drop, not even general radio chatter. Radio antenna masts were moved and adjusted, but still nothing. It was worrying, given Holland was flat and therefore amenable to good radio reception. Some thought it was a good sign, but most thought they were all dead. It was typical army chat. Waiting men are nervous men, and nervous men tend to be pessimists. I wasn't so pessimistic, but the lack of news scared me, not least since without feedback from the first drop, we would be going in blind.

That night on my canvas cot bed I had no chance of getting any sleep. I knew it was pre-match nerves, although I hadn't experienced them going into Normandy. It was strange. This time I knew what was coming. The long uncomfortable flight. The horrific landing. The fighting. The mortars. God, I hated the mortars; you never heard them coming. I had encountered the Germans in my short career and had so far prevailed, but was that due to my soldiering skills or shortcomings in theirs?

'Psst.' I scanned the dark green canvas of the tent roof above me, looking for a shadow outside. 'Psst.' I propped myself up on my elbows, peering around. In the dimly lit tent I could just make out Tommy Kettles. He was also propped up, trying to get my attention. 'Sorry, Rob, I can't sleep. I saw you fidgeting.'

'Tommy, what's up?'

'Can we go outside for a chat? Don't want to wake the lads.'

'We are awake,' confirmed the unmistakable voice of Eddie Karlow. 'Piss off outside, will you?'

It was fresh outside with plenty of ambient light. While I waited for Tommy to find his tobacco, I watched the radio boys pratting around with their antennas.

'I'm worried about tomorrow, Rob,' Tommy began, 'really worried. The blokes over there should have radio contact with Arnhem. I made a few suggestions to the yeoman earlier, and he basically told me to piss off. Not good, mate.' He had a point, his Royal Signals background entitling him to offer suggestions. But my reservations were of a more serious nature: the German Army. He took drags of his cigarette in quick succession, not at all himself. His usual cheeky-chappie demeanour was nowhere to be seen. 'The Germans,' he continued, 'what are they like?'

'Come on, mate,' I responded. 'Why are you being like this? Thinking about this stuff won't do any good.'

His hand trembled as he put the cigarette to his lips once more.

His eyes fixed on mine. 'I'm scared, Rob. I don't care what anyone thinks of me, but I'm scared.'

'Me too.'

All of a sudden his sorrowful face beamed. 'You're scared?'

'Yeah, Tommy, I am.' I felt as if a weight had been lifted from me too. I knew what we were in for, which actually made my predicament worse than his.

But then his face changed to puzzlement. 'But you've already been to fight the Germans?'

'Tommy, I'm scared because we will be landing in a plane made of bloody wood, which has all the elegance and grace of a brick. If we survive the landing, we could be surrounded by German soldiers who won't give us a chance to scratch our arses let alone fight back. Let's just hope those who went today have got everything under control, because to top it all, we are going in broad daylight. So yes, Tommy, I am scared.'

'I've been bottling it up for days,' he admitted.

Eddie Karlow emerged from the tent, stripped to the waist, a lit cigarette hanging from his lips. He gave Tommy a jab in the arm. 'Nothing wrong with being scared, boy. It keeps you on your game.'

Tommy looked up at him, like a child talking to its parent. 'Are you scared, Eddie?'

Eddie took a drag from his cigarette. 'I hate the night before a job, Tom. Ask anyone. Robbie here was in Normandy, hours before I was, so you listen to this one – he doesn't talk shit like some will.' I had never heard anything remotely affectionate come from his lips before. I kept my trap shut and just savoured the moment.

'What do you think about the lack of radio traffic?' Tommy asked him.

'From the look of that big map they showed us, we could be landing in a kessel beside the Rhine.'

'Kessel?' I asked him.

'Like a cauldron, a fire pocket where you end up encircled.'

Tommy looked more worried than ever. But Eddie hadn't been the only one listening to my conversation with Tommy. Before long more boys were emerging from our tent, thanking us for being honest about our fears. Pride could kill most men, but not us, not on this night. Men who had not seen action listened to the exploits of those who had been in Normandy. Sometimes the listeners gave out a low whistle or shook their heads, and those of us who'd been in France felt eight feet tall. Sometimes they roared with laughter.

You could feel the tension lift. Yes, we were all scared, but we were a team. We were a team that had a job to do tomorrow: find and defend our division headquarters.

4
Crash Landing

18 September, 1944

The next morning was our time to fly. Aircraft were at a premium, so our second drop over Arnhem would consist of parachutists dropping from the Dakotas, and us landing in the gliders. We got our gear on, and before long I was sweating like a beast. I wasn't sure if it was better to be riding in one of the gliders or exiting the door of one of the Dakotas that towed them. Although flimsy and offering little protection against incoming ordnance, the gliders at least took you at speed all the way to the ground. After parachuting out of a Dakota at eight hundred feet, you floated down, possibly under fire. While the ground crew finished giving the gliders and Dakotas the once-over, we took our time applying camouflage cream.

The parachute boys were called forward. We'd never really had the chance to get to know our parachuting cousins. Technically, we were all airborne troops, but they tended to keep themselves apart. Some even glared at us, as if we were lesser men than them. Granted, they went through some tough training, but surely we were all on the same side. They cursed and grunted as they were shoved up into their planes while we soaked up a little more of the mid-September sunshine. It was nice weather, bright and fresh. A shame to go into battle on such a beautiful day. After our group confession last night, everyone suddenly had a spring in their step again. Those of us who had only recently joined 1st

Airborne Division now felt part of it, and maybe we'd even exorcized our personal Normandy demons.

We were called forward to our glider. Inside I shuffled down the side of our Jeep and trailer to my designated seating position, then tried to get comfortable. During earlier practice runs I had had no problem getting myself strapped in, but now I wore full combat gear. Somehow, I managed to fasten my seat harness. The equipment I was carrying didn't help. The Sten sub-machine gun was lighter and easier to handle than the Bren I'd had in Normandy, but the Sten came with eight magazines, including one fitted to the weapon. I was also carrying two hand grenades, two smoke grenades, a combat knife and two magazines for our Bren gunners. The Jeeps may have taken up a lot of room on the glider but at least they carried our Vickers machine gun kits.

Rammed in next to me was Si Walton. He ranted and cursed, unable to get his seat harness done up. After some time, he gave up. Next to him sat little Ernie Pullen. Crammed in opposite were Eddie Karlow, Mark Lavelle and Johnny Braithwaite. They were bigger men than our team, and therefore had even more difficulty getting comfortable. After struggling with their harnesses, they just shook their heads and stopped trying, although Tommy Kettles and Elliot Kemp managed to get strapped in either side of the trailer without much difficulty.

The pilots went through their cockpit checks. How they managed to hear each other over our cursing is anyone's guess, but they didn't complain. Before long, the glider lurched as we began to taxi. I peered forward between the pilots. The tow rope was one moment tight, then slack on the ground, then tight again. The tail of the Dakota was not too far from the nose of our wooden aircraft. The glider creaked and groaned as it was pulled along. I peered around and could see the nervous cam-creamed face of young Tommy. When he realized I was looking at him, he broke into a grin. He would be fine, I just knew.

When it was our turn to move onto the runway, I could do nothing more than brace myself for the huge lurch when the tow rope went taut as the Dakota struggled to take off. The whole experience was a little less frightening than my first time taking off for Normandy. Through a porthole between Eddie and Mark's heads, I could see the aircraft hangar floors and aprons covered in Dakotas and gliders. For the night-time Normandy drop there had been nothing but darkness. Suddenly, the lurch arrived. We were pulled at some speed down the runway, the incredible din growing louder as the air ripped past our glider. Road noise from our undercarriage added to the noise. As we lifted, the rumble of tyres on tarmac ceased instantly, but the rush of air remained. We were airborne, on our way to Holland and whatever the place had in store for us.

The noisy flight was uneventful. The glider bobbed and wove, creaked and groaned, but other than that not much else went on. Opposite me, Eddie and Mark were out for the count, their heads leaning towards each other, mouths wide open. The rest of the boys were trying to catch some shut-eye, which was just as well, since trying to talk over the whistling wind was near-on impossible. Our pilots had headsets on, making vital conversation between them possible.

I tilted my head back and managed to doze but nothing more. Sleep wouldn't come; instead I found myself thinking about my old unit: Dave Brettle, Al Grimes, Terry Thomson and Sean Wardle. I wondered where they were now. Somewhere below us, bogged down in Normandy still? Or had they fought their way free and were heading through France? It felt like a lifetime ago that I had been with them. Brave lads. Just like poor Kirby Green. I thought about him back in Mortlake, probably hating the Yanks, and I thought of Molly, and there the reel froze. Molly at the bar – that smile, that laugh. I silently cursed myself for running away and not saying goodbye to her. It might have been my last chance.

'Action stations!'

I stirred with a jolt. Everyone else was coming round and stretching. I could see white knuckles under cam cream, mine included, as everyone checked their gear over. In the cockpit the pilot on the left raised his right arm to a lever.

'Stand by!'

This was it, roller coaster time. Our glider suddenly jolted. There was a thud, then another, louder. I glanced around; there was a puzzled expression on everyone's face except Eddie's. He mouthed something as I caught his gaze: 'Flak.' I looked between the pilots, and sure enough puffs of smoke, dark as coal dust, were bursting all around the airborne formation ahead of us. Gliders suddenly detached from the formation and plummeted out of sight like stones; parachutists left the Dakotas. A flak burst caused the left-hand prop of our Dakota to catch fire, spraying fuel onto the front of our glider. Another thud caused the glider to jump a few feet upwards. I caught Eddie glaring at me tight-lipped.

Parachutists began to exit our burning Dakota, which was still pulling us along. The men were heavily laden, falling beyond view, their parachute bags flapping in the slipstream of the plane. I leaned as far forward as I could and screamed into the cockpit, 'Detach us, for fuck's sake!'

I thought the pilots wouldn't hear me, but one did. 'Not until the last man is out of the plane. We can't risk getting caught in the parachute rigging lines.' Men continued to exit the Dakota. As the last parachutists jumped, a pilot pushed the lever in our cockpit, the tow rope flicked away, and the glider then plunged with such force I thought my stomach was coming out of my mouth. We were going down fast.

Below us, gliders were packing onto an open plain. Some of them skidded in sideways, disintegrating as they rolled over. Some were smouldering, some blazing infernos before they even hit the ground.

Beyond the gliders lay a thick line of trees. We had no way of avoiding it. The pilots fought to keep our nose up. Their white knuckles and the sweat pouring off their faces told of their efforts.

The soundtrack to the landing became a high-pitched whine. Then there was an almighty thud and the cockpit caved in, the windows shattering and sending glass flying. As my vision swam back into focus, I could make out the bloody headless bodies of what had been our pilots. With dead men at the controls, all I could see was the treeline we were plummeting into at full speed.

5
The Drop Zone

Leaves and branches were the first thing to come into focus. Then I felt grass beneath my head. I tried to clear my vision, but I could only make out vague outlines, trees and some large birds moving between gaps in the leaves, their long bright tail feathers fluttering about. I shook my head again, and things started to come into focus. I could see the large birds were actually aircraft. The tail feathers became fire and smoke. It looked wonderful. Yet there was no sound.

A huge dark mass suddenly blocked my view of the sky. The dark mass became a black face, under what became a helmet. The face was moving its lips, but still no sound.

Sound slowly came from nothing, into a dull throb like a drumbeat, which became intermittent. The face disappeared but came back again, the throb becoming deeper and louder. I could hear the occasional crash of cymbals behind the throb, quiet at first, but gradually growing louder and sharper but with no real rhythm. The cymbals eventually sounded painfully in my ear. I felt an urge to raise my head. A very loud snapping began, the drumbeat not so deep now. I went to prop myself up on my elbows, but a locomotive came screaming through my head.

'Keep yer head down, you fucking idiot!' I winced as a rough hand shoved my head back onto the firm surface beneath. All around me the snapping became very sharp and acute. The face appeared again, screaming, 'Stay here! Don't fucking move, got it?' It disappeared once more.

I lay there looking up at the sky and the tree canopy that broke up the blue image. The snapping sounds felt very close. One of the branches above me splintered, scattering its pale innards. It came crashing down on top of me. I held my arms over my face instinctively, but the impact wasn't painful.

Amid the snaps I could now make out excited voices. Some shouting, some talking. I could also hear whimpering. I had no clue what was going on. I flinched as a dull thud rippled through, masking the snaps. The voices remained excited. I noticed one in particular. 'Stop! Stop. Hold your fire. Save your ammo. They'll be back.'

Grunting and heavy breathing approached the top of my head. I couldn't see who it was. All of a sudden the smashed branch was flipped off me and I was showered in leaf litter. I suddenly felt very exposed. The face appeared, but not quite so close. Then another face loomed next to it. I didn't recognize either of them. The second face spoke: 'How are you doing, big man?' I was at a loss, not quite sure if he was talking to me or someone else.

A careful hand was placed on my left shoulder. A bolt of pain shot through me, and I couldn't help but flinch. The hand was retracted straight away. The first face, the more familiar one, spoke: 'By the looks of it, he got bashed up pretty bad. At least he was strapped in, lucky bastard.'

Peering down at me, the second face nodded. 'Do you think you can sit up?'

I wasn't sure.

'Can you sit up?' the second face below the Dutch sky asked again.

I nodded; anything was worth a try.

But just as I got set to prop myself up on my elbows, the first face held me firm. 'The moment you feel pain in your neck or back, lie back down, OK?'

I slowly edged my way up. I felt stiff but was not in pain. It was kind of on a par with getting out of bed after a night on the tiles. I managed to sit up. My left shoulder was not feeling good at all. It really ached, and as I rolled my arm in its socket, it grinded like a bastard. My hips felt raw, almost burning. I winced as I rubbed them.

The first face nodded. 'Your seat harness did that. As for your shoulder, it took the brunt of keeping that fella in his seat. Shame he wasn't strapped in.'

I inched my aching frame round and saw Simon Walton. He was alive. Didn't look like it, but he was; I could see his chest rising and falling. I couldn't see any blood, but it was apparent how hurt he was. They had him strapped to a stretcher. It didn't look pretty: bandages, cargo straps, weapon slings, anything to keep him immobilized. 'He's broken his back,' advised the first face. 'Until the medics clear the drop zones, he's gonna have to stay here.'

The two faces made sure Si was comfortable. He managed to nod, and one of the faces waved me over. I carefully crawled the short distance along the ditch we were in. All around us I could make out rifle and machine-gun fire in the distance. We were in a wood, and just outside it was what could only be described as a glider breaker's yard: smashed aircraft everywhere, some on fire. Also on the ground, pale parachutes bobbed and weaved in the breeze, anchored down by their dead owners. Si fixed his gaze on me. 'You OK, Rob?'

'Yeah, I'm fine. You?' It was probably the most idiotic question I had ever asked, but you had to keep the chat going somehow.

He grinned. 'I'm good, mate, real good. No pain, so that's good for me.' I looked up at the faces. They almost imperceptibly shook their heads. They hadn't given him any pain relief. He was paralysed, hence no pain.

I peered down at him, grabbing his camouflage-creamed hands. 'We just need to wait for the medics. They'll get you to an aid post.

You'll be up and about in next to no time.' The faces glanced at each other. They knew there was more chance of him becoming Pope than coming back from his injuries. I knew it too, but you just have to find something to say.

'Here they come!' came a shout further into the wood. Instantly, the two soldiers were on their hands and knees, scrambling down the ditch towards the voice. I could just make out the profile of a Bren gun, a third soldier manning it. The faces kept low, pointing at something off to our left. I suddenly became conscious that I had no weapon. There didn't appear to be any nearby. I peered over my right shoulder, and my mouth gaped open.

We were in a shallow ditch with broken trees all around, and twenty metres away was the front portion of the glider with a Jeep hanging out of it. The aircraft was smashed almost beyond recognition; only the green and brown paint gave away what it was. It had clearly broken apart on landing. As my eyes adjusted to the scene I could see other pieces of it scattered in the undergrowth. There was wreckage everywhere, but no people. I turned back to Si. Could we be the only survivors?

I flinched as one of the faces appeared just a few feet away. I hadn't heard him coming. I noticed now the two chevrons sewn to his smock, indicating he was a corporal. 'Can you fight?' he hissed. I noticed for the first time he had a Welsh accent, having emphasized the 't'.

'What?' I blurted. I had no weapon and didn't even know if I could stand.

'Can you fight?' the Welsh corporal asked me again.

'Yeah.'

'Good. Follow me and keep low.' He took off on his haunches, flicking his head left as he went. I followed him, but my body was unforgiving, protesting at the activity so soon after the crash landing. I stole a glance back at Si. He was strapped to the stretcher, nothing but leaves, wreckage and clouds to keep him amused.

I arrived at a group gathered around the Bren gunner. A wave of relief washed over me. Tommy Kettles and Elliot Kemp looked rather roughed up but were alive. They managed a grin and a nod. I tried to smile back and pointed at their Stens. One of them understood and rummaged around, handing me a sandbag of Bren magazines, along with two grenades.

The corporal leaned in towards me and spoke in a hushed tone: 'We will sort you a weapon out in a minute. Had to get you out of that crate you arrived in. The Germans are all over the place.' He quickly peered over the top of the ditch. 'German infantry, just out front. They're after the glider. Help Ozzy with the gun,' he said, nodding to the Bren gunner, 'and when I call for grenades, you throw them at the bastards, got it?'

I nodded and he began tasking others in the group. I still felt dizzy and confused. I couldn't work out where the rest of the division were. As always, nothing bore any resemblance to the plan. I wanted to ask Tommy and Elliot, but I knew it wasn't the time. I tried to make sense of my surroundings. I could make out an undercarriage wheel and a fractured tail fin, but I couldn't be sure of the aircraft type.

I tucked in on Ozzy's left side, ensuring my grenades were readily available. Then I focused on ensuring the Bren magazines were ready to use.

'Behind the tyre,' Ozzy hissed. I refocused on the undercarriage, which was just over fifty metres away, but I couldn't see enemy around it. I moved away from Ozzy just a little, craning my neck to gaze over the top of the tyre. And there they were, beyond it at almost a hundred metres. The heavy foliage made everything seem closer than it was. Both German soldiers were hunched over slightly. One had what appeared to be a machine gun in his right hand, the legs of the gun splayed, ready to use. The other was draped in belt ammunition. Normandy had taught me that machine gunners don't venture out alone. I leaned back on my haunches, and whispered what I had observed along the line. 'Behind the tyre. Two enemy with MG 42.'

To my right, Ozzy gave me a thumbs up and hissed the information to the man next to him. I tucked back in next to Ozzy. 'When it goes loud,' he growled, 'we will focus on the MG 42. Watch where they take cover, OK?'

I nodded. As much as I should have kept my eyes on the MG 42, I couldn't help but pan right, searching for the rest of the German squad. I caught a glimpse of movement. Their comrades were moving up. They were not in the usual field-grey combat gear; they wore light-green and brown *Flecktarn* smocks and helmet covers. My blood ran cold. Waffen SS. I'd heard about them in Normandy. These fuckers were not your average German soldiers. Apparently they would literally spill their last drop of blood for Hitler and everything he stood for.

The corporal came crawling up the ditch, keeping low. He tapped on Ozzy's right boot. His instructions were hushed again, but urgent. 'Drop the bloke with the MG 42, understand?' Ozzy and I both nodded. I couldn't help but flick my eyes to the SS troopers closing in. The corporal snapped his fingers quietly. 'Be ready with the grenades. As soon as they go off, we're going to rush them. You two stay here. Keep firing and make sure the MG is knocked out. Clear?' I felt ashamed at the relief that swept through me. I hadn't fancied the idea of rushing the Germans. So much for veteran bravery.

The corporal crawled away. The enemy line was now level with the aircraft wheel. They paid some attention to it, bending down to pick up items I couldn't identify. Perhaps they didn't know where we were. It didn't matter much because right then Ozzy opened fire. The initial rounds that chugged from the Bren burst the two men forming the enemy machine-gun crew into a fine red mist. They dropped like liquid, just forward left of the undercarriage tyre.

Ozzy adjusted the gun in his shoulder, following up with two-to-three-round bursts into the undergrowth next to the wheel. He kept his bursts short and consistent, like the beating of a bass drum. I was transfixed as his fire rippled through the shrub and grass that now hid the enemy machine gun from view. He had seen where the crew had fallen, so kept the fire targeted there.

The Bren fire suddenly ended. 'Magazine!' roared Ozzy. Without hesitation I flipped the empty magazine off the top of the gun, a fresh one snapped on in a flash. He cocked the gun, then continued firing into the same area.

'Grenades!' came the order from our right. I scrambled into the depths of the ditch and prepared one, pulling the pin and counting the seconds. With the pin pulled and the fly-off lever wedged into the web of my hand, I knew I would have about a five-second delay. I squatted on my haunches, managing to identify SS troopers bobbing and dashing about in the undergrowth, taking pot shots at us. I lobbed the grenade into what seemed to be the centre of them and immediately sent my second in the same direction.

Just as I tucked myself back in next to Ozzy, the first grenade detonated with a loud, dull thud. It was the usual charcoal-grey eruption, leaf litter flying everywhere. The second grenade burst just right of the first. The corporal and his men jumped out of the ditch, firing as they went. Ozzy increased his rate of fire just in case one of the enemy had retrieved the MG 42.

The SS troops went back beyond the undercarriage wheel, then out of sight. Ozzy stopped firing and held out his left hand. 'Give me another mag, quick.' I slapped a fresh one in his hand. With a quick flick of his hand, the second empty magazine landed in my lap.

'Get ready to move,' Ozzy commanded. 'Al might need us.' Was Al the corporal? A few single shots rang out, then another grenade thudded, stripping a few branches of their leaves. It all fell quiet.

'Oz, move in!' came a shout from somewhere. Ozzy jumped up and out of the ditch. I had to get a gallop on just to keep up with him. My body still ached and protested, but I didn't have time to feel sorry for myself. As I caught up with him, it suddenly dawned on me how big he was. Even as paratroopers go, he was bloody massive. Not fat, just built like a Spartan. We jogged past the undercarriage wheel. I caught sight of the MG 42 team. They were a mess, both slumped on their fronts, smocks shredded from bullet impacts. Their helmets, stripped of their covers, were punctured in more than one place. Their heads were nothing but hairy pulp, dark clotting blood pooling beneath what had once been their faces. I knew Ozzy was looking at them. Our eyes met, and we exchanged nods.

'Over here.' We turned and saw the corporal and his four lads kneeling down in the shadow of another smashed glider. He asked Ozzy and me if we were all right, praising us for taking care of the MG 42.

Two dead SS troopers were lying nearby. They weren't as messed up as the machine-gun team, but I think one had taken the brunt of one of the grenades. His body was sitting upright against a badly splintered tree. Beneath the blood, you could see cheekbone and teeth, but his lower jaw was gone. One of the corporal's group walked over to the body and grabbed it by the sleeve, looking at an embroidered black band sewn around the sleeve. 'Landstorm Nederland,' the soldier read from the band. 'Are these fuckers Dutch?'

I didn't have a bloody clue. Neither did the corporal, who shrugged his shoulders. The soldier let go of the sleeve. The corporal called for order. 'Let's get out of here. They might be sending their men through all day, so we need to link up with another unit. Fetch our lad on the stretcher and let's push south onto the drop zone. We can leave him with some medics out there. Let's move.'

We backtracked to the ditch, following it until we found Si. 'You lot are a fucking noisy bunch,' he joked. 'Can't you see I'm trying to get some kip here?'

The corporal chuckled and knelt down next to him. 'We're going to move you now, get you to an aid station. I don't want to leave you here for the Germans to find.'

Si nodded with a grin. 'Glad you think that way. It was playing on my mind while you were messing around over there.'

The corporal put me and Elliot on stretcher duty, then led us all towards open ground. Just before we broke into the sunshine, I cast a glance back at the smashed wreck of our glider. I had a real issue with the prospect of going out onto the drop zone; no weapon still, my hands full with Si. I told the corporal, requesting permission to search the wreckage for a weapon. He nodded, and we put Si down.

I quickly approached the glider, swallowing hard as I saw a body lying crushed by a Jeep. I couldn't see who it was; perhaps it was one of the pilots. I picked my way carefully through what was left of the cockpit and into the gore-smeared innards. Eddie and Mark were slumped in their seats, the limp shattered body of John Braithwaite across their laps. I didn't want to look at their faces and fought to get a Sten unslung from John. I had to drag him onto the splintered floor to get the sling unravelled from his torso. His magazines and grenades were easy enough to get hold of. I unwrapped the face veil from around his bloody neck and draped it over his head.

I should have recovered the weapons and ammunition from the other lads, but I couldn't face it. I turned and scrambled out, fighting the burning bile that was climbing my throat. With Sten and magazines at my feet, I dry-retched, the burning inside me intense. Once finished, I wiped my chin and picked up the gun and ammo. I wanted to know what had become of the blokes I hadn't found, but there wasn't the opportunity. For now, 1st Division Defence Platoon was just Si, Tommy, Elliot and me.

Beyond the treeline, our drop zone was a mess, a real mess. Surrounded by trees, the open heathland made hell look tranquil. Dead men, mostly ours. Smashed gliders. A few burning Dakotas. Nearby, sporadic fighting could be heard. The dull echo of grenades indicated fighting in some woods to our left. As we picked our way across the drop zone, I braced myself to encounter German troops.

Off to our left, a very loud but distant thud made me flinch. My stomach tightened. Tank fire. I knew the sound of it all too well. The corporal got us all searching a nearby glider wreck. I hurried my search but located a shoulder-launched PIAT anti-tank gun with two bomb satchels, plus extra Sten gun magazines in the back of a Jeep.

When I rejoined the group, the corporal nodded and told me I was to be PIAT gunner once we had delivered Si to an aid station. He let me keep the extra Sten and ammunition, offering the PIAT to Ozzy's search partner. 'Young Matt Packham will carry the PIAT for you for the time being.'

Packham took it from him with mock enthusiasm. 'Why, thank you. You are just spoiling us today.'

The corporal, called Allan Peet, smiled as he gave the bomb satchels to another member of his group and Tommy. 'And my two beautiful assistants,' said Allan, 'young Ronnie Marsh and your boy Kettles, can carry these. We can move kit between people once we've got off this drop zone. Let's go.' It suddenly dawned on me that Marsh and Allan were the two who'd rescued me from the glider wreck.

We continued picking our way through the dead and the wreckage, in the vain hope of spotting medics who could take Si off our hands. We began climbing a gentle incline, approaching the treeline on the edge of the drop zone. At the top of the slope we found a stony railway embankment beneath the trees and, further along, an aid station.

I'm not sure how long it had been up and running but already it had its fair share of customers. Facing the treeline, all along the far side of the embankment, was a melee of misery. Dozens of wounded sat side by side, covered in bloody bandages and dressings. Some were on stretchers. Most appeared to be nursing broken limbs or sore heads. The medics moving about, taking care of them, didn't look much better; most were nursing injuries of their own, their dressings plain to see. Walking along the embankment, a corporal was taking notes, talking to one colleague after another. He looked to be in charge of the place. The dead were off to the left, face down in a neat row, their raincoats draped over them. Two medics carried someone over to the end of the row, placing him down gently, before taking water bottles and other useful resources from his kit.

The look on Tommy's face was one of horror. Elliot appeared to be taking it well. It was hard for Si to look anywhere other than up at the clouds. It was nothing worse than I had seen in Normandy.

The medic corporal caught sight of us and began to make his way over. Allan met him halfway, and they whispered out of Si's earshot. The medic nodded, waving to where he wanted our stretcher placed. As we laid Si down, a German medic came to tend to him. I noticed the collars of the medic's tunic. SS runes were sewn into the *Flecktarn* camo.

Ozzy spotted it moments after me, and I saw a furious look spread across his face. Allan stepped in front of him. 'Don't you lot fucking start,' warned the medic corporal. 'He works for me, so no funny business, understand?'

'Are you serious?' Ozzy gasped. He tried to get past, but Allan kept him at bay.

'Listen to me, you clown,' the medic corporal continued. 'I've got casualties all over the place, and I need all the medical staff I can get, Germans included.'

Ozzy glared at him, grinding his teeth, then looked across at Allan, who fixed his eyes sternly on him. 'They're medics; leave them be.'

The medic relaxed. 'You lot are not the first to get on their high horse about this, but look at us.' He pointed over to a small group of wounded soldiers who were being tended by British airborne medics. 'I've got that group to deal with as well, so don't be getting any ideas about them.' I realized the wounded group were SS troopers. Although slumped and receiving treatment, they were sharing cigarettes with their former adversaries. It was quite a bizarre scene.

The medic enquired if anyone else in Allan's group needed attention. He promised to look after Si and asked if we were leaving to find British units nearer Arnhem. He said that between us and the town there was nothing but rifle, machine-gun and tank fire. Getting into Arnhem sounded risky, but neither could we lounge around on the embankment all day. We followed the corporal to Si, who had managed to scrounge a cigarette from his new friend, the SS medic. I knelt down, taking the cigarette from the German and holding it to Si's lips. He took in some smoke. I put a hand on his shoulder and left him with the medic, who held the cigarette in place as Si took long drags.

As we sat resting at the railway line Allan took out a map and suggested that we should stay together as a group, seven of us in all. He thought we should then link up with the first formation we came across. 'If we follow this railway line, it will take us into Wolfheze, or whatever you call it.' I could recall Wolfheze from our briefing maps. North of the Rhine, it sat about four miles west of Arnhem and our objective. 'We can see who's about there,' continued Allan. 'There must be men scattered all over the place. I don't want us walking into a firefight and ending up with both sides shooting at us.' Judging by the variety of uniforms at the aid station, British and German, he was right about the scattering of forces. Everyone running about, trying to make sense of what was unfolding. One thing was clear: the drop hadn't gone according to plan, and our units were going to be heading towards Arnhem from all directions.

I observed a bloke approaching us from the treeline, grinning from ear to ear. Using a branch as a crutch, he didn't seem too bashed up apart from a limp. He appeared to be a Parachute Regiment captain. 'Corporal Peet,' he gushed. 'I thought it was you.'

'Hello, sir,' replied Allan. 'Good to see you're still in one piece.'

With a grunt and a curse, the captain eased himself down to sit with us. He pulled out a packet of cigarettes. Ozzy accepted one. The captain chuckled. 'What a surprise, eh, Burnett? Not got any of your own?'

Ozzy grinned. 'I've got plenty, sir, but when an officer is offering, you can't pass that up.'

The captain did the rounds with his cigarettes. Allan and his boys were very grateful. Only I refused. The captain looked at me, surprised. 'Not a smoker, lad?'

'No, sir. Those things are bad for you.' Everyone burst into laughter. Bad for you; the irony was overwhelming.

The captain introduced himself. 'Bob Wallace, B Company, 10 Para. Our drop went to shit this morning. My men were all over the sky. I came in pretty hard.'

'Private Robert Stokes,' I responded, 'Ox and Bucks, division HQ.'

'Ox and Bucks?' he said quizzically. 'You boys are a long way from home, aren't you? Thought you were in Normandy.'

I nodded. 'Most of them still are. Just a few of us were seconded to 1st Division, though God knows where they are now. Our glider came in hard as well, pilots killed on the way in.' I pointed at Tommy and Elliot. 'It looks as though these blokes and me are the only ones left.'

Captain Wallace went tight-lipped as he nodded. 'One hell of a morning, boys, that's all I can say. Anyway, Corporal Peet, are A Company here? I've not seen anyone else since landing.'

Allan shook his head. 'Not that I have seen, sir. Our situation was the same as yours. A Company took shitloads of fire on the drop. The boys are scattered all over the place.'

Wallace explained that the medic corporal had been upset to see our drop coming in. He'd practically shouted up at the sky, asking why we were still dropping troops in the area, given how hard the Germans had hit the drop yesterday. It had quickly been discovered that very few of the radios worked, and those that did weren't reliable.

We were dropping into hell, and no one in England knew anything about it.

6
The Railway Line

We made our gear ready to move out, a smiling Packham passing me the PIAT to add to my Sten gun. The PIAT was a bitch to lug about. You carried it strapped tight against your back, leaving your hands free to carry another weapon, in my case the Sten. I felt like a pack mule and was thankful that at least someone else had to carry the bombs for it. After bidding farewell to Captain Wallace, we headed alongside the railway line towards Wolfheze at a cautious pace, Ozzy in the lead as scout. Atop the embankment, stone sleepers held the rails in place. Trees now ran on both sides of the track. Up ahead of us we began to hear fighting. Although distant, it was a constant soundtrack: machine-gun fire, the crump of mortars, the thunder of tank fire rippling towards us. At the briefing Urquhart had said no tank formations had been spotted in the area, but it didn't sound like a stray panzer. So where the hell had the tanks come from? I felt exposed in the flat countryside, just a handful of us and a whole load of German tanks somewhere around. We wouldn't stand much chance if we stumbled across any armour now.

Up ahead Ozzy froze and then slowly raised his left hand. He went slowly down into a kneeling position, becoming motionless. Allan signalled over his shoulder for us to kneel, but we had already taken our cue from Ozzy. Allan moved up next to him. The pair of them crawled up the embankment and peered at something over to our right, which was out of sight to the remainder of us. Ozzy clicked his fingers for us to move up.

I stopped just short of Allan, who kept his voice down. 'There's something strange going on over there.' I was about to ask what it was when clapping and cheering erupted. It sounded utterly incongruous with a battle raging just down the road. Allan patted Ozzy on the right shoulder. Ozzy got to his feet, then dashed across the rails and out of sight. Allan followed. I raised my head, risking a look at where they were heading. I saw a number of tiled roofs beyond a thin screen of foliage.

'Over here.' I recognized Allan's voice. We scrambled over to find him with Ozzy, peering through the foliage. Allan turned his head, eyes full of surprise. 'You'd pay good money to see this at home. Take a look.'

Before me was the most bizarre spectacle I had ever seen. A young woman, probably not long out of her teens, was ballet dancing as naked as the day she was born. Beyond her, about half a dozen elderly men and women sat on a park bench in their nightclothes, cheering her. My eyes were firmly fixed on the naked girl. The German Army could have rounded the corner just then, and I doubt any of us would have taken our eyes off the show. Just when I thought the show couldn't get any better, she pulled one of her pale, smooth slender legs up to the side of her head, then pirouetted around, showing everything she had. The audience on the bench applauded, throwing in a few wolf whistles for good measure.

Suddenly she pranced over to the bush that sheltered us. My heart leaped into my mouth. She had seen Ozzy. Grabbing him by his smock, she pulled him into the open. He could handle himself when it came to the Germans, but this clearly terrified him. She wrapped her arms around his neck and gave him the sort of kiss you only saw in the movies, the lucky bastard. He stood there like a statue, Bren in one hand, his other hand floating randomly, as if he was scared to touch her. There was more applause from the bench, before she stepped away from him, blowing a kiss to the rest of us behind the bush. A few ballet moves took her to the bench, her audience standing to give her an ovation.

Ozzy walked slowly back to the bush, back to the war, looking rather pleased with himself. 'I think I'm going to like Holland.'

We all laughed. 'Right,' said Allan, 'the party's over. Let's go before you all fall in love and forget there's a war on. Ozzy, careful you don't get your hard-on caught on a branch.'

As we continued towards Wolfheze, the sporadic applause from the bench gradually faded, the battle ahead becoming louder. The PIAT was a real pain in the arse. We had to move in a kind of crouch in order to prevent our heads bobbing above the embankment, but the posture made the PIAT slip now and again, bashing against my knees. I tightened the straps of the weapon to try and solve the problem, but couldn't pull them in too much, since I had to keep the thing ready to fire sharpish, should we stumble on a panzer or two.

A little further on, the trees became sparser. Then to our left the treeline gave way to a vast open heath covered in abandoned parachutes and gliders. A second drop zone. Off in the distance there were a couple of smoke columns that could well have been associated with the drop, but I couldn't be sure.

'Not again! What the hell is going on around here?' Recognizing Allan's voice, I looked over to him. Above us, a naked woman was walking one of the railway lines like a tightrope.

She wasn't as young and svelte as the first girl, but Ozzy was nevertheless transfixed. 'Is someone taking the piss?' he mumbled.

'Come on,' sighed Allan. 'Just ignore her; we need to move on.' She blew us kisses as we shuffled away.

We were still moving through the various drop zones that I remembered seeing on the briefing map. On paper, they had been neat circles of red in the clear Dutch countryside; in reality the drop zones were anything but neat. Men walked, ran or lay scattered across a flat landscape littered with gliders in various states of damage, along with a fair number of parachutes dancing and drifting in the breeze. I caught the odd glimpse of soldiers battling their way out of their parachutes in the far distance, though the drop phase was supposed to be long since past and I could no longer hear the drone of aircraft. I tried to picture where we were on the map. If we'd come down in the right landing zone, west of Arnhem, then there should be paratroops behind us and to the south, but so far I'd only seen dribs and drabs. Where the hell was everyone?

Allan ordered us to rest, so we crossed the railway line, congregating around a couple of bushes beneath a tree. The remaining treeline was becoming thinner, and I knew we would have to make good use of the dwindling cover to avoid being seen from the rooftops. Up ahead a road ran parallel to the line, and some distance away to the east the line and road disappeared into a thinly planted treeline, which nevertheless blossomed with lush green leaves. Roads also led away to the north and south.

I suddenly realized that not all of the battle noise we were hearing was distant. Although sounding in fits and starts, some of the noise was more local. I wondered if this was coming from the woodland further along the track. As Allan consulted a map, I moved the PIAT to a more comfortable position, then had a quick drink from my water bottle. 'That's Wolfheze to our right,' he said. 'We'll give it a few minutes, see what's happening from here if we can, then venture in. We're bound to find someone.'

Vibration began grinding through the railway tracks. Way up ahead I spotted a grey mass on the line. I used my water bottle to point at it. 'What's that?'

Allan casually pulled binoculars from his smock. No sooner had he put them to his eyes than he snatched them away. 'Halftrack. Fuck! Get in cover!' He dived behind the bushes, then deeper into the sparse foliage. We scrabbled after him, but I quickly fell behind, the PIAT making me less nimble than the others. By the time I caught up with Allan, my lungs burned with effort, and I was glazed in sweat. He made sure we were all together before he spoke again. 'Right, sit tight. Packham and I are gonna go see what they've got and make a plan.'

'Are they definitely Germans?' asked Tommy.

'Yep,' Allan answered neutrally, 'we just need to find out how many. We've got the PIAT, which can do some damage, but we can probably only deal with a couple of vehicles; any more than that and we'll need to sit this one out.'

Packham and Allan scrambled back towards the railway line. Marsh handed me a projectile from a bomb satchel, and I began to make the PIAT ready to fire. The bloody thing seemed to take an age to load, and I kept swivelling my head round, fearing the Germans might appear before I was ready.

We were all at the end of our nerves, which wasn't good because mistakes could get you killed.

Packham and Allan returned, crawling back into view over the railway embankment. 'One halftrack,' confirmed Allan as he reached us, 'with a manned MG 42 machine gun on top, towing a panzer. There's a railway station up there.' He waved an arm away to our right. 'I saw three infantry this side of the halftrack, but they've got three panzer crew on the ground with them.' The numbers were about even, so I thought we might be able to take on the enemy group.

'OK, Al,' Ozzy said, 'what do you want to do?'

'We could lie low and let them go past, but someone else would only have to deal with them then. So I reckon it's up to us. We'll try and get as close as we can without being seen before opening fire. Ozzy, you, Kettles and young Kemp can provide fire support from where I will place you in a minute. I'll take Stokes, Marsh and Packham forward, and we'll hit the halftrack with the PIAT. Ozzy, you hose the thing with fire once we hit it. Make sure the machine gun is knocked out.' He pointed to Tommy and Elliot.

'And you two make sure you drop any enemy standing nearby. Any questions?'

There were none, and I swiftly moved out with Allan, Packham and Marsh, keeping ourselves hidden below the height of the embankment. As we got closer, we heard an engine cut out. Then we heard shouting in German and the sound of the engine trying to turn over.

We got a bit nearer before Allan waved us down. We flattened ourselves on the grassy embankment until his hand beckoned us forward again. We crawled up until we were hidden behind a hedge. Through the foliage, the halftrack came into view. The wheels at the back were tracked like a tank's, providing power, with conventional wheels at the front for steering. The enemy were preoccupied with trying to get it started again. Allan crawled forward a few more metres and carefully raised his head, trying to find the best position for the PIAT. He stayed there like a meerkat on lookout, probably for longer than was wise, before lowering his head and waving us forward.

Crawling with the PIAT was a complete pain in the arse; it was heavy and bulky. I fought hard to keep my Sten from clattering against it and giving us away. I was sweating like a beast, cam cream stinging my eyes. As I drew up on Allan's right side, he leaned in, his lips almost brushing my ear as he whispered. 'When I say so, slowly get to your knees and hit the halftrack, understand?' I nodded. The German voices now became animated as the halftrack engine started. Allan pulled on my smock sleeve. 'As soon as you've fired, get down and crawl backwards. We'll drop anyone running through here.'

My heart was pounding like mad. This was nothing I hadn't experienced before, but I just wanted to get the bloody fight over with. I checked the PIAT and its projectile again, ensuring the weapon was ready to fire. Allan raised himself quickly to scan the target. Its engine revved amid the screeching and squealing of wheels as it began to move the panzer.

'Now!' Allan half-shouted beneath the racket. With the PIAT across my right bicep, I pushed myself up with my left arm and slid the weapon into my shoulder, ensuring the shoulder pad was pulled in tight. I made sure the open sight was full of halftrack before I fired. My brief time on the range with the PIAT had been enough for me to know that it wasn't the most accurate weapon. The closer you were the better. And if you didn't want to dislocate your shoulder, then you pulled it in tight. I squeezed the trigger.

As the projectile left the launcher, I was rocked back and only just saw it hit the halftrack with an almighty thud. As the explosion faded, my ears filled with the chatter of Allan's Sten and the sharp crack of Packham's Lee-Enfield rifle. I got into better cover, temporarily ditching the PIAT, and grabbed my Sten in both hands, ready for action. To the rear and right of me, I began to hear the chugging drumbeat of Ozzy's Bren and the whizzing and plinking of rounds hitting armour plate. Two grenade thuds made my ears ring, then all gunfire ceased.

'Reorg, reorg!' came the cry. It signalled the end of the attack, and we broke out of the bushes. The panzer sat there with its turret hatches open. The halftrack was on fire, its MG 42 pointing skywards. Allan and Packham were standing beside its bonnet, waving me and Marsh in. At their feet lay two dead SS troopers. There was no sign of the other Germans. To my right, I saw Ozzy's group jogging up the railway line to join us.

'The rest got away,' said Packham, nodding towards the station. 'They won't be back any time soon, but best not hang around just in case. Stokes, you and–'

'10 Para!' a voice shouted, and we all swung round, pointing our weapons at a hedgerow. Two paratroopers emerged, limping heavily and wincing, their arms outstretched in a cruciform manner.

'What company are you?' enquired Allan, lowering his gun.

'C Company, sir,' one said. They hadn't worked out he wasn't an officer.

Allan looked concerned. 'What happened, boys?'

'We took fire,' said the same para, 'as we stood in the door of our plane, waiting to jump. We got out, but I couldn't tell you how anyone else managed.' He pointed to Wolfheze. 'We landed in the village. On concrete. Not fun.'

'What are your names?' Allan asked.

'Jimmy Hamilton and Billy Gardner, sir, er sorry, Corporal.'

Allan smiled at them. I think we were all happy to see some friendly faces. 'You can join us,' he offered. 'We're off to take a bridge . . . if we can find the bugger.'

7
The Woods

After a brief conference Allan decided to avoid Wolfheze and lead us up a ditch that ran north from the railway line. He wanted to link up with any troops still around the drop zones. As we moved off we could see the planes and parachutes indicating another drop had commenced a good few miles to the north. And we could also hear the sound of gunfire. I winced as I listened to it and thought of those poor buggers landing in a hail of bullets.

There was more gunfire closer ahead, coming from a thick wood that stood in our path. Allan signalled for us to proceed with caution, and as we entered the undergrowth a couple of mortar rounds landed close enough to shred the leaves from the upper branches above, showering us in leaf litter. I feared encountering an enemy unit; I didn't want to end up in a prison camp or dead. But I also feared approaching friendly units; running across one while it was in contact with the enemy was chancing your arm at the best of times. However, I was prepared to trust Allan's judgement.

We crept ever closer. Rounds snapped above us, shearing thin branches, splintering tree trunks. We began to hear screaming and shouting amid the gunfire. My heart was beating hard as we continued with what I believed was an ever more suicidal endeavour.

Allan waved us down again. We remained motionless for quite a while. I wasn't sure whether to face the direction of the fighting or to turn to ensure no one was following us. Another mortar round made me flinch. Allan ordered us to follow him, keeping very low. I became ever more nervous. The pace was very slow as we crept forward in short bursts. I guessed we were close to contact with whatever unit was nearest us. The rate of firing ahead increased, as did the concussion of grenades, but I was now able to distinguish British voices from German and was pleased to hear the British voices sounded much closer.

'Hey,' came a loud hiss. 'If you want to survive, I would suggest getting your arses in here.' I tried to find the source of the voice. Twenty metres to my right, a waving hand appeared from behind a pile of logs. Then I saw a helmeted British soldier looking straight at me. I alerted the boys up front to stop crawling. Only Ozzy didn't hear me, so I threw a large tree splinter at him.

We found a small group of soldiers behind the log pile. Like us, they seemed interested in the fighting up ahead. The group consisted of a major, a radio operator and two corporals, probably a company headquarters unit.

Allan was sweating like a maniac, breathing like a bull. The major found it rather entertaining. 'Corporal Peet, you are out of shape.'

Allan looked at him, then slumped to the ground. 'Thank fuck.' I knew we had found a significant presence from 10 Para. The major introduced himself as Nicholas Hartley, a company commander. He explained there was a platoon in reserve to our rear. I glanced round, for the first time noticing a good few men in a shallow ditch, although not enough to make up a full platoon. He added there were two further platoons nearby in the wood, forward on a broad front. The Germans were trying their hardest to push through the trees in order to get onto the drop zone, but the other companies that made up the battalion were holding a similar line further along.

Major Hartley took a cigarette from Allan. 'We can't allow these Germans to push through us and get a position overlooking the heath or they'll be able to pummel our boys in the drop zone,' he said solemnly. 'At present our blokes are out there scavenging whatever they can from the gliders and finding quite a few of our dead.'

Suddenly, all hell broke loose in the woods, two loud explosions sounding over the general noise of fighting. A lull followed accompanied by muffled screeching in the radio operator's headset. Major Hartley's radio must have been one of the few Allied radios working in the area. The major grabbed the headset and listened for a while, concluding with an approving nod. 'Well done, boys,' he said into the headset. 'Keep an eye out in case the enemy make another push. Once they have moved back, let me know, and I will launch the reserve. Out.'

He passed the headset back to his operator, then swivelled, directing his voice to the men in the ditch. '2 Platoon have managed to knock out a Panzer IV and a halftrack. Both crews bailed out; no sign of infantry.' There were restrained cheers and whistles from the boys in the ditch. The major focused on Allan. 'Sergeant Hardy is unaccounted for.' There was a brief but solemn pause. 'I need you to be platoon sergeant for 1 Platoon,' he told Allan, flicking his head in the direction of the ditch.

Allan nodded. 'Yes, sir.'

'As for the stowaways you have with you,' continued Hartley, 'they can become your group.' So Tommy, Elliot and I were effectively seconded to A Company, 10 Para for the time being.

A stream of loud gunfire suddenly sounded. Tracer whizzed and whined. Grenade thuds echoed, hysterical voices yelling. Some of the voices were German. They were close to us. There was another lull. Muffled chatter sounded in the operator's headset. I couldn't make out much but caught a mention of panzers. The major grabbed the headset again, a deep frown developing on his face as he scribbled on his map. 'Roger that,' he said into the headset. 'As we advance, keep an eye out for us moving through on your right. Out.'

The major flicked his finished cigarette away, passing the headset back to his operator. 'The battalion is making a move,' announced Hartley. 'German infantry has been spotted forming up five hundred metres to our front. We are going to make a bound forward so they don't get eyes on the drop zone. Our companies have still got blokes out there, recovering ammo and casualties. We are going to buy them some more time.'

Pre-battle nerves made my gut do somersaults. Promoted temporarily to platoon sergeant, Allan led the remnants of 1 Platoon out. Following our acquisition of Hamilton and Gardner, there were now eight in his group, and we followed the platoon in single file, fairly wide spaces between us. The PIAT didn't feel quite so heavy any more. Elliot was behind me with the projectiles when I needed them. Still limping, Hamilton and Gardner brought up our rear with their Lee-Enfields ready.

Fighting broke out to our right. Everyone knelt, fearing ricochets from the firefight. Allan signalled us to sit tight, then carefully made his way to the front of the platoon. Having left Major Hartley's headquarters group behind, we had no radio, so he needed to see what was going on. But from the darkness of the trees I could clearly hear the formidable clatter of metal tank tracks.

Allan came rushing back. 'PIAT with me, let's go.' He scampered away at a half-crouch. I led Elliot out, struggling to catch up. We veered away from 1 Platoon, and I started to feel very exposed and unprotected. Previously I had known the platoon was in front of me, with two further platoons ahead of them, but now only my newly assigned platoon sergeant was between me and the enemy.

We ran on for what felt like ages, the clatter of armour getting all the louder. I heard German troops shouting over the roar of gunning engines. I knew they must be close but couldn't see them. Allan slid to his knees, waving us down. 'Here, boys, set up here.'

We were behind a waist-high leaf-littered mound of earth. I didn't think it would stop incoming fire, but I made sure the PIAT was ready to go, a projectile in the launcher, another in Elliot's hands. Allan leaned in towards me. 'Tank destroyer with local camouflage on it. See?'

I strained to pick out the vehicle. I only saw it when its engine was gunned, dark exhaust smoke giving it away. It was operating within the treeline. They had done a pretty good job of camouflaging the vehicle with foliage, branches waving about like radio antennae. On top, even the soldier manning the MG 42 had foliage in his helmet lining. 'When our blokes fire on their infantry,' Allan instructed, 'you hit the tank destroyer. Got it?'

I now spotted the German infantry, advancing through the woods to the left of my target. I watched the tank destroyer approach to within fifty metres, wondering if the PIAT would be accurate enough at this distance. On a firing range it would be a piece of cake, but here there were trees in the way. And if I missed with my first shot then there was a good chance their elevated MG gunner would identify our position straight away and obliterate us.

The tank destroyer continued to creep forward, its diesel engine echoing the rapid beat of my pulse. Fire erupted from our platoons. Tracer screamed everywhere. I got up, putting all my weight on my left foot, my right foot further back. I ensured the mass of the armoured vehicle filled my sights, then pulled the trigger. The projectile left the launcher with an ear-popping thump, and the tank destroyer was immediately enveloped in a flurry of bright yellow sparks. My hit on it prompted rounds to snap through our position, earth, tree bark and leaf litter splintering and splashing up around us.

Hysterical shouting started, one screaming voice standing out: '*Achtung, Panzerschreck. Das richt, das richt!*' My heart leaped into my mouth as I saw a mass of German troops dash towards us, firing in our direction. Allan ran back, retreating at speed. I didn't need to be told, and was hot on his heels as rounds snapped past us. Knowing the enemy was right behind us made my fears of getting shot up by our own troops evaporate. My lungs burned like hell, but the PIAT felt like a toy in my hands as I sprinted to keep up with Allan.

We ran across a Bren gun team firing at the infantry around the smouldering tank destroyer and slid in beside them, Allan roaring at the top of his voice, 'Enemy infantry, switch left!' The Bren team looked confused. The infantry chasing us were no longer visible. Allan pointed in the direction from which we had come. 'Just fire the fucking gun.' I realized the Germans had gone down on their bellies and were probably crawling forward. The Bren chugged away at invisible targets in long, methodical bursts. Allan threw grenades in the same direction. They detonated with loud, dull thuds under the tree canopy. Tree splinters, leaf litter and bodies flailed in all directions. I ditched the PIAT, using my Sten to fire into the flickering undergrowth. The SS troopers were returning fire – popping up, darting around, never firing from the same position twice.

'Mortars!' came a roar above the din.

Allan got up on his knees. He pulled me up. His voice was muffled, my ears ringing. 'Look, they're falling back.'

I could see the burning tank destroyer. The German infantry were passing it, turning to fire in our direction but running. A mortar round almost landed on the vehicle, showering the retreating SS with debris, whose firing petered out under further mortar rounds.

The mortar fire ceased. I could hear people calling for medics. Sitting on the forest floor, I quickly checked myself over. A few German bullets had come past me, a little too close for comfort, but I was still in one piece. Allan knelt next to me. 'You all right?' He flicked his head at the PIAT. 'Nice shot with that thing.'

'Thanks. I was worried I would hit a bloody tree, not the vehicle.'

'Where's the other lad?' he asked me.

'What?'

'Kemp, or whatever his name is – the lad with your extra PIAT rounds.' I scrambled onto my knees, scanning the direction we had run from. Smoke from the burning tank destroyer obscured the more distant scene, some of the nearer undergrowth smouldering from tracer bullets and mortars. My heart sank. I couldn't see Elliot anywhere. I looked at Allan.

'My blokes, follow me,' he said quickly. 'We've got a man unaccounted for. Let's go.' As platoon sergeant he could have stayed back to look after the ammunition and wounded but, Sten in both hands, he went back out. I liked Allan, liked his style. He made it look easy, and I knew it was anything but. I followed him, Tommy Kettles falling in behind me, the others from the group quickly following. It struck me that until this morning we had been pretty much strangers. But now, while we weren't exactly friends, we were comrades, looking for one of our number who was missing.

As we reached the tank destroyer, it started to pop and fizz, its remaining ammunition combusting. In the undergrowth *Flecktarn* heaps of clothing and equipment marked where the SS had fallen. I didn't see any blood but I didn't care about them; I just wanted to find Elliot. Allan led us back towards the mound where we had set up the PIAT attack. I composed myself, expecting to see Elliot's body. Just short of the mound we encountered two dead SS. As Allan stepped around them, the undergrowth flickered and rustled. We all swung our weapons. If it was Elliot, he had better start talking quick.

Two bloody hands appeared, one brandishing what appeared to be a small digging tool. A hessian-covered parachutist's helmet followed. Elliot's blackened and blood-splattered face was a fright.

He looked shocked, terrified, his eyes wide and bloodshot. Allan calmly knelt, waving us all down. 'You OK, lad?' His tone was fatherly.

The last thing Elliot needed was a bollocking. He just nodded.

'Can you walk?' asked Allan.

'Yeah.'

'Are you wounded?'

'I don't know.'

'Come here, son,' invited Allan. 'Let's take a look at you.'

As Elliot emerged from the foliage and leaf litter, he began to sob. The digging tool turned out to be a little shovel, German Army issue. The flat spade end was glazed in dark blood. As he stood up fully, he dropped it, beginning to shiver. 'I didn't think I could do it. I thought they'd got me.' I looked down at the two dead Germans. Were they Elliot's handiwork? When I looked up, I could see he was trying to hold himself together, breaking into sobs as he continued. 'They grabbed me . . . I didn't want to be executed . . . I went mad . . . I didn't think I could do it . . . I just went mad . . .'

Allan put a hand up to stop him. 'Grab your gear, mate. We need to get out of here. Those bastards will probably be back soon.'

We found Elliot's rifle and PIAT rounds, and then helped him through the woods. Rejoining Major Hartley's headquarters group, we sat Elliot against a tree, a blanket draped over him, a mug of steaming tea in his hands. Company medics gave him the once-over. Just cuts and bruises for his troubles, nothing more. It turned out he had killed the two SS soldiers at the mound, their shovel his only weapon. If everyone in the division fought like he had, we might get to Arnhem yet.

8
Retreat to Wolfheze

As darkness fell, Major Hartley had us establish a frontage on the edge of the woods protecting the drop zone. The night passed uneventfully, but we could hear all hell breaking out towards Arnhem to our east. The relentless gunfire put everyone on edge. It was the third day for the lads from the first drop and no one seemed to be making much progress. Morale was pretty low by morning and it was a relief to get moving again. A patrol went forward to act as a screen against probes by the Germans, while we got to work reinforcing our trenches and cover. There was a lot of deadfall to our front. We dragged some of it back, stacking it on the left side of our position. We packed it in with earth, camouflaging ourselves as much as possible; it wouldn't stop bullets, but it might help against shell splinters. A Bren gun team dug in beside us, the idea being to guard our left flank, enabling us to focus the Vickers on any advancing SS.

Once we had finished establishing our position, we stood out in front to admire it drinking mugs of sweet tea. The tank destroyer I had hit still smouldered, and not all the dead Germans had been moved yet, but we enjoyed our drinks nevertheless.

'Only one battalion has managed to get to the road bridge at Arnhem,' Allan said, walking over to our position.

'Bloody hell,' I said. I thought back to General Urquhart's map: the ease with which the arrows showed British XXX Corps driving along the road into Holland, moving through the American 101st Airborne Division, then the American 82nd Airborne and then through us at the road bridge in Arnhem, in order to finally turn right to push through into Germany. It had all looked so simple, but if we couldn't push on and hold the bridge, then Operation Market Garden would fail.

'Yep,' continued Allan, taking a sip of his tea. 'Some clever dick felt we didn't need to know about the German armour.' There was an uncomfortable silence. 'The division plans to push on and regroup in Oosterbeek,' Allan eventually said, 'just the other side of Wolfheze, beyond where we took care of that halftrack on the railway line.' I thought of Urquhart's map at Fulbeck and pictured Oosterbeek as the next station on the railway line east of Wolfheze and the last stop before Arnhem.

'But we have people on the bridge, right?' Elliot attempted to clarify.

Allan nodded. 'For the time being. But they need to be reinforced, and there are a lot of Germans, with a lot of tanks, between Oosterbeek and Arnhem. The boys on the bridge have to sit tight while division comes up with a plan to get to them.'

I asked the million-dollar question: 'Are our lads on the bridge trapped, then?'

'Trapped is not a word I would like to use,' answered Allan, 'but you could say they are in a bit of a fix now, yes.'

We all fell silent and watched a stretcher party working around the smoking wreckage of the tank destroyer. It took me a while to realize they were removing the German wounded and dead. They had barely finished carrying away the last body before there was a whine in the air and the ground began exploding around us as mortar rounds rained down.

We hit the deck as rounds burst in the tree canopy, shredding branches above us, coating us in leaves and broken branches. I lay there realizing that the Germans must have been waiting for the stretcher bearers to do their job before opening up. It briefly occurred to me to wonder why the bastards hadn't cleaned up their own dead before my thoughts were interrupted by the company sergeant major shouting, 'Prepare to withdraw across the drop zone. We are heading back to Wolfheze. Get ready to move. Stokes, get your gun team ready to move straight across the drop zone. I want that gun set up in the railway station. Facing south, down the road, got it?' Before he'd even finished speaking, Elliot and Tommy had already begun stripping the Vickers down.

I lugged the gun on my right shoulder, the water can and hose on my weaker left. Tommy carried the tripod and gun cradle, plus a tin of ammo. Elliot hauled the ammo tin bracket, the water jacket for the gun and two full ammo tins. We also had our personal weapons, and as we moved across the drop zone heath I was sweating like a maniac. We ran, weaving between glider wrecks, parachutes and their rigging lines. Behind us, huge clumps of tree canopy were thrown skywards as our troops still in the woods continued to get hammered by mortars.

Wolfheze didn't seem to be getting any closer. My shoulders ached, my lungs burned, and I was soaked through with sweat. It felt like a furnace inside my smock, and my helmet was like a lid on a kettle. Behind me, Tommy and Elliot were puffing and panting as they jogged on. 'I tell you what, Rob,' Tommy gasped. 'The recruiting sergeant mentioned nothing about this malarkey.' Elliot sniggered as he struggled on. I was not unfit by any stretch of the imagination, but energy to crack jokes was beyond me. I just wanted the station to get bloody closer.

The burned-out halftrack on the railway line came into view, the crippled panzer it had been towing still there. I paused to catch my breath. Turning, I made out other groups on the heath making their way across, but no other Vickers crews. The woods were now getting absolutely hammered, trees falling left and right, and the remaining tree canopy getting sparser with every shell burst. Our blokes needed to get out of there fast, hopefully before panzers arrived.

Elliot and Tommy caught up with me, and we managed a last shuffle along the railway shingle up onto the station platform. I looked through the first window. Everything inside the picturesque building looked neat and orderly, as if the station master had just left for the day. We got to the waiting-room door, only to find the bloody thing locked. I set the Vickers down and took Tommy's rifle from him. I made short work of the window with the butt, then clambered through. I unlocked the door from the inside, and we wasted no time getting set up just inside the door. I planned on calling targets from a window to the left. We had good coverage of the road running away to the south and across the heath, but would be blind to an enemy approaching from behind the embankment.

It wasn't long before I spotted a large group on the heath moving in our direction. They weren't running, but weren't hanging about either. Major Hartley and his command group were in the lead, his radio operator puffing like a bull to keep up with him.

The major acknowledged us with a nod as he led his command group around the side of the building. More paras followed in a marching column. I heard the sound of breaking glass as they broke into the tea room. The station probably hadn't been vandalized since it was built. Not even the Germans had damaged the place.

No sooner had the crashing died away than a corporal arrived to tell us we were pulling back again. Fine by us. At least we wouldn't be the frontline against any Germans coming across the heath. Tommy and Elliot were already breaking the Vickers down again. They made the routine look effortless. Within seconds rather than minutes, we were ready to follow the rest of A Company to Wolfheze. Then the corporal returned and told us to leave the Vickers for those staying to defend the station position. I could sense Tommy and Elliot were as unhappy as I was about this. We all stared down at the Vickers like it was a pet we'd been asked to leave.

The corporal had brought me a spare rifle and I slung it over my shoulder, enjoying how light it felt compared to the Vickers.

The village wasn't in too bad a shape. It had a couple of burning buildings on its south side but appeared clear of Germans. There were a few parachutes draped about the place and some medical waste blowing about, but no other soldiers. It felt eerie. Like the station, there was a sense that everyone had just left in a hurry.

But it wasn't entirely deserted. In among the neat brown-brick buildings, along the immaculate brick-tiled roads, were more naked, giggling people. They were men and women of all ages. As we passed through, some sprang to attention, giving crisp salutes. Others blew kisses or even fondled themselves, chuckling. Things were getting more weird. We caught up with the major's command group, which was deciding where to set up. Some of the lunatics came over, trying to kiss them, but were shoved away. One naked man fell to the ground and began wailing like a baby.

'Something to tell the grandkids, eh, boys?' It was the company sergeant major, shaking his head.

'What?' I asked. 'Nude, weird Dutch people or fighting the Germans?'

'Both,' he replied. 'In fact, the story about them' – he pointed – 'will be more memorable, I reckon.'

'True, sir,' I agreed. 'It certainly is unique.'

'Poor fuckers. Apparently they're from a sanatorium. A bombing raid damaged the place a couple of nights back, and all the inmates just walked out. Doubt any of them have the slightest idea what's going on.'

'Not so different from us, then,' I said, and we both laughed. We were still chuckling when Allan came upon us.

'Bloody hell, two more inmates!' he said with a grin. 'Right, Stokes, you go get your head down. We've got some friends coming to join the party tomorrow, and if you reckon this lot are mad, wait till you meet our Polish comrades.'

'How are they coming in?' I asked.

'1st Polish Independent Parachute Brigade drop in tomorrow south of the Rhine.'

I couldn't believe what I was hearing, and forgot myself. 'Are they fucking serious? Didn't our landings tell them anything? The Polish drop will be a turkey shoot.'

Allan raised his hand. Although he wanted to stop me, he seemed unfazed by my outburst; I realized I was preaching to the converted. 'It's the other side of the river from us, but once they have got themselves sorted, they will advance on the southern approach to the road bridge at Arnhem. We will push to link up with 2 Para, who apparently hold the northern end of the bridge. If all goes according to plan, we'll have the bridge secured in a couple of days.'

I gave a rueful smile. Mad Poles and Englishmen.

9
Supply Drop

I woke to the drone of aircraft engines. The vibration rattled what was left of the windows and dislodged tiles from the roof.

We went outside to find the sky full of aircraft. My stomach turned. Were the Polish dropping early? I hoped not. The SS were as good as camped out on the drop zone in front of us, and were probably swarming all around the Rhine. I watched in horror as parachute canopies deployed from their static lines, descending towards the heath below.

I waited for the firing to start but it never came. Instead the parachutes continued to descend. And then I breathed a sigh of relief as it became clear they weren't paratroopers dangling beneath the chutes, but supply containers. The RAF was dropping supplies, presumably rations, ammunition and medical items. Unfortunately, it looked as though they were dropping it all on the Germans.

All we could do was watch the vast airborne armada drone away from us, many planes trailing oily smoke from ground fire. Some dropped out of formation, a few disappearing beyond the woods on the other side of the drop zone.

On the heath the containers fell to earth in various fashions. Some gently floated down among the glider wrecks. Some plummeted at speed to the ground, their parachute canopies fluttering uselessly above them like bags of laundry. Some containers were smouldering, hit by the odd stray German round. I knew we needed whatever was in the containers, but most were disappearing into the woods. My heart sank. The Germans would eat well tonight.

Suddenly there was a loud coughing and spluttering of engines close by, and we turned in time to see a Dakota screaming in from our right, flames pouring from its port-side engine, heading straight for the drop zone. We stood frozen to the spot as the pilot managed to lift its nose just as it hit the ground. It crunched heavily down on its belly, sliding sideways through the wrecked wooden gliders like a bull in a china shop, flipping them left and right and dragging parachute rigging and containers with it. A huge broadside skid brought the aircraft to a stop, with its nose facing us. All of its propellers were pressed flat around their cowlings, yet the engines still screamed at full power. The flames appeared to have gone out on the port engine, but dark black smoke billowed intensely.

'Corporal Peet,' bellowed the sergeant major, 'don't just look at the bloody thing, let's see what we can do for the crew.'

Allan led the way out across the heath. I felt horribly exposed on the open ground, knowing that the Germans were in the trees, but we knew we couldn't delay; the Dakota could explode at any time.

We slowed down just short of the badly scarred and crumpled nose of the plane, needing to ensure the Germans weren't trying to sneak up from the other side. Rigging lines and parachutes were draped over the wings of the burning aircraft, the smoke from the engine gradually turning from black to light grey. The sergeant major waved us down. With my rifle ready at my shoulder, I scanned to the left, peering past broken glider wings and parachutes, looking for any movement beyond. I couldn't see anything.

A tap on my right boot got my attention. I peered down my right side to see one of the Bren boys slowly opening the bipod legs of his gun and placing them gently on the ground. He then made a thumbs-down motion to indicate the presence of the enemy, pointing in the direction where he had detected them. I got on all fours and took a look: *Flecktarn* trouser legs and combat boots, lots of them, moving in slowly from the north. I tapped Allan's boot, and he alerted the sergeant major. The Germans were less than one hundred metres away. Some remained standing, while others knelt over our recently dropped containers. Over the din of the engines I could make out foreign orders being shouted.

The sergeant major confirmed a second group of enemy moving directly towards the Dakota, using a clenched-fist gesture, which indicated the presence of a machine gun. Folding up the legs of his Bren, Toby crawled forward to join the sergeant major, who gave a slow sweeping-arm motion. We responded by crawling out to the left to establish a hasty ambush position. Allan leaned over to me and, loud enough to hear over the Dakota engines, said, 'Fire when the Bren starts. Pass it down.'

Elliot Kemp was to my immediate left, and passed the message on. I pulled my rifle into my shoulder and lined up my sights on the legs moving about directly in front of me, no more than about seventy metres from us now. I blinked the sweat from my eyes and controlled my breathing.

The Bren erupted, instantly creating pink mist amid the Germans patrolling towards us. As they began to fall, I fired. In my sights I had nothing but *Flecktarn* uniform, and in an instant it had gone. As I fed the next .303 round into the breech, I was presented with a grubby face wearing a helmet, looking over the bodies of his comrades. I squeezed the trigger. The face burst like a tomato, the helmet flicking back as the chin strap broke with the impact of my shot. And then it was over, and the gunfire died, replaced by groaning of the Dakota engines, the aroma of cordite and hot metal. No Germans remained standing.

'Corporal Peet,' the sergeant major ordered, 'get some lads into the aircraft. I'll have the remainder provide security. Move now.'

We followed Allan down the port side of the Dakota. Its door was open, the static lines from dropped parachute containers draped out of it. He was shouting something, but the engines wouldn't let me know what. Allan gingerly moved close enough to look in the doorway, Sten at his shoulder. He then relaxed his posture and waved us forward, clambering in as I got to the door.

As my eyes adjusted to the dimly lit interior I could make out Allan tending to one of the crew, who didn't look like a pilot. The injured man's parachute was still attached via a static line. He must have been the jump master, the crewman who ensured paratroopers managed to get out of the door, with or without their blessing. I remembered hearing about men being court-martialled for refusing to jump. 'Get up to the cockpit,' bellowed Allan, 'and just pull all the bloody levers until the engines cut out.'

I clambered over canisters of supplies. When I got to the cockpit, I could see the windows were peppered with flak splinters and blood, and the forward left side was open to the elements. The Dakota must have taken a direct hit to cause that kind of damage. Before me were blood-speckled dials, switches and levers all over the place. I didn't have a clue as to what did what. I began flicking, pressing, pushing. After what felt like an age, the dreadful theme tune coming from the engines petered out to a deathly rattle and hissing, before cutting out completely. The silence was wonderful.

'Check on the pilots while you're there, will you?' Allan asked. I looked back. He was busy applying a dressing to the bloody head of the jump master. Elliot clambered forward to join me.

The pilot sitting port side was a goner. His face was caved in, his helmet tilted forward into the cavity. I didn't see any point trying to deal with him. The one on the starboard side was messed up but conscious and groaning. His face and neck were badly bloodied, with numerous puncture marks. I reached a hand out to his shoulder. 'Hey, mate. You still with us?'

All I got out of him was a nod. I fumbled with his harness release, which was tight against his sternum, causing the pilot to groan some more. Maybe he shouldn't be moved. As I turned to inform Allan, I saw the sergeant major peering in through the door. 'I think this bloke is going to need medics to get him out of his seat,' I told them.

An almighty thud shook the aircraft, causing the pilot to wince. The sergeant major looked straight at me. 'We are now getting mortared, son, so forget about medics and get that pilot out.'

I tried my hardest not to cause him any more pain as I released the harness. The pilot grunted as I draped the straps over his shoulders, and Elliot helped me pull him from his seat. As we heaved him out, a mortar round slammed down nearby. He let out a yelp. 'Legs, my legs,' he gargled in an American accent, blood frothing from his mouth. I peered down; his feet weren't caught in the tail rudder pedals but may have been broken. But we didn't have the time to be gentle; we needed to get the hell out of there. Another mortar round thudded into a nearby glider, cartwheeling what was left of it across the nose cone of the Dakota.

'Look, mate,' I told him, 'we need to get you out of here, so it's gonna hurt, OK?' Before he had the chance to protest, Elliot and I had a bicep and armpit each, and we dragged him to the rear of the aircraft. He wailed and begged us to stop, but once outside he enjoyed a brief respite while some medics came jogging in with a stretcher. The medics cut open his quilted flying trousers, exposing a pale thigh, and injected him with morphine before strapping him down for the move back off the drop zone.

The sergeant major stepped forward as a mortar round finished off another glider close by. 'Good effort. Stokes, Kemp, help the medics with the stretcher. Corporal Peet, we'll fall back to the railway station. We just haven't got the manpower to collect all this equipment, but any ammo containers we find on the way back, let's have them.'

We heaved the stretcher up and began the trek back to the station. The mortars falling felt close. The jump master was bashed up but capable of walking. He came alongside the stretcher and peered down at the bloody-faced pilot. 'God damn, Captain Temple,' chuckled the jump master, 'how many lives have you got?'

10
Advance to Oosterbeek

'Don't waste too much on his looks; the Germans have cut the water off in the area.' At Wolfheze station the sergeant major was getting a little animated about how much water the medics were using to clean Temple's face. I, on the other hand, would have happily run down to the Rhine with a bucket, if it would have helped. I just wanted to see the pilot properly, in order to be sure it was Temple. Morphine was taking him to another place, so he would not be conscious for a while. As they finally removed the last of the filth from his face, my stomach turned. It *was* him. Captain Troy Temple.

My stomach gave a jump and my heart thumped heavily in my chest. Everything seemed unreal. Home always seemed a million miles away when you were in a war zone. And yet here was Temple, an unwanted reminder of it. My anger, which had dissipated, returned with a vengeance. I stood there for minutes, just trying to process things.

'What are you hanging about for, Stokes?' snapped the sergeant major. 'Do you fancy him or something?'

'Sorry, sir?'

'What are you doing here?'

'I just wanted to see if the pilot was OK. Took one hell of a landing earlier.'

He looked at me, not sure if I was taking the mickey. 'Well, piss off back to your platoon and rest. This lad isn't going anywhere for a while. There's every chance we'll be moving to

Oosterbeek soon. There's an aid station there, so we'll take the wounded with us.'

'I'll help carry him,' I said rather too enthusiastically. I didn't know what I was planning, but I knew I wanted to stay close to Temple.

The sudden frown on the sergeant major's face spoke volumes. He was now suspicious; when did soldiers ever volunteer for anything? 'Thanks for the offer. I'll bear it in mind.'

The intention to move to Oosterbeek was confirmed. Unless we were on watch, we were ordered to rest at the station prior to the move, a welcome prospect. But I kept on wanting to go and have a look at Temple. I wanted him to open his eyes and to see me standing there, an avenging presence, a reminder of his sins.

The day wore on and as darkness fell the Germans hit Wolfheze with mortars. It wasn't a heavy bombardment, but sporadic and annoyingly persistent. I flinched as every round crumped into a rooftop, street or garden. I heard cries for medics, but from where I couldn't be certain. I wondered if our own mortars were being fired at us, the Germans having liberated them from our supply containers. I drifted in and out of sleep, not knowing whether the explosions were in my dreams or not. One thing I was sure of: if a mortar round took Temple, it would be bittersweet but some kind of justice.

I was woken by the grumbling of my own stomach. I couldn't recall the last time I had eaten. Allan nudged me. It was becoming light. I knew it would be my turn to take watch at some point, since the company was so undermanned now. As he gave another two lads a shove, I began to get my gear on. 'Are we going somewhere?' one of them asked groggily.

Allan knelt, replying in a low voice, 'Battalion is moving out towards Oosterbeek.'

I looked outside to see daylight flooding over the heath. The beginning of what promised to be another long day. Everyone was on edge. We knew we were falling behind schedule, and you didn't have to be a senior officer to sense that the whole operation was hanging in the balance. I flinched as shells began to thud into Wolfheze once more. Did the Germans know we were moving, or was this just another attempt to dig us out of our positions? I caught Tommy's expression. He bit his lip and slowly shook his head. Elliot's face haunted me. He had the look of someone who didn't want to die in Holland. I tried to calm them with a smile and a wink, but it felt unconvincing.

It was late morning before Allan finally sent word down the line to advance. We collected the wounded from behind the train station, including the still strapped-up and unconscious Temple. No one objected when I took up a post walking next to the pilot's stretcher. He was looking pale and feverish, and I asked the medic if he was worse. He just shrugged and said he'd know more when we got him to a proper facility. I found myself hoping Temple wouldn't die. I wanted to get my revenge, and for that he had to live.

The company column hugged the southern boundary of Wolfheze for as long as it could, trying to stay out of contact with the Germans. Finally though we peeled off east and began making our way slowly uphill through fairly sparse woods. Firefights broke out to our left as other Allied troops encountered resistance in the push to Oosterbeek. The stretcher party stopped, crouching, resting aching hands and swapping places. A few rounds shot high through the trees – stray bullets, not intended for us – but the sudden thunder of tank fire echoing through the woods put the fear of God into me. I wasn't sure if we had any PIAT rounds left in the company. I hadn't noticed anyone carrying a launcher, so if German armour detected us, we would be slaughtered.

As we crouched there, I suddenly knew I was being watched. I turned to find Temple's eyes boring into mine. He looked worse than ever, and I wondered if he wanted to confess, to perhaps ask for forgiveness before meeting his maker. But then there was the slightest quiver in the corners of his mouth and he was wearing that lopsided smirk I'd seen before. If Allan's voice hadn't ordered us on at the moment, I think I might have taken my rifle butt to his head then and there, and damned the consequences. As it was, I could only nurse my fury and bide my time. Somewhere, some time, there would be the opportunity to get the bastard alone, I told myself. And he wouldn't be smirking then.

More gunfire nearby. I tired to refocus, aware that tiredness and anger were making my attention drift. The pace was painfully slow. Eventually we approached a row of buildings and an area surrounded by a high chain-link fence. Inside it I could see people walking around or sitting on the ground. As we drew nearer, I realized they were German prisoners being kept on a tennis court. Close by, Allied troops were digging a network of trenches. Apparently, we had found Oosterbeek.

Allan called a halt while the sergeant major made off in the direction of a large off-white mansion, waving for the wounded to follow him. As the stretcher team moved off, I joined them as inconspicuously as I could. The mansion was magnificent, even with all the damage it had sustained. As we trudged into its shadow, I could make out the bold dark letters of its name over the main door. HARTENSTEIN.

I recognized the dishevelled profile of Lieutenant Simmons, the Defence Platoon commander, emerging from the mansion and skipping down the steps towards us. It dawned on me that we had finally found Divisional Headquarters, our objective since landing. Simmons looked tired under his helmet and filthy smock. The sergeant major went over to speak with him. Remembering Simmons' role in my altercation with Temple at Fulbeck Hall, I tried to fade into the background. The sergeant major would no doubt tell Simmons the names of the casualties and the nature of their injuries. And indeed Simmons shot me a glare as the sergeant major read out the details from a notebook,

Simmons clearly recognizing the significance of Temple on a stretcher and my presence close by.

His conversation with Simmons finished, the sergeant major waved us forward. I managed to grab a handle of Temple's stretcher, and we all lifted our loads, crunching our way over a shingle path to some external stairs leading down. Simmons had perched himself on the main stairs leading up to the mansion, and acknowledged both Elliot and me as we shuffled past with Temple.

The sergeant major indicated that we should take the stairs to the cellar, which was serving as an impromptu aid station. I was overwhelmed by the stench of unwashed bodies, cigarette smoke and the coppery tang of blood. A tired-looking medic pointed to a space for us to put down our casualties. As we backed away I looked at Temple's face, but he was too far gone to even look at me this time. The journey had clearly taken a lot out of him, and I wondered again if he was going to rob me of my revenge. Looking around the squalid cellar, I certainly didn't rate his chances.

As we emerged into the daylight, I heard the sergeant major address Mr Simmons: 'I understand they are from your platoon, sir, but my company could do with the manpower.'

'Sergeant Major,' Simmons replied, 'we have units scattered to hell and back. These chaps are but a few of my original number. They have divisional work to do. I assure you, if we can spare them, I will have them returned to the 10th Battalion. Lord knows, you guys need the men.'

I heard the words, but my mind was still on Temple and the significance of them didn't sink in until they turned to me. The sergeant major nodded to me and Elliot. 'Thanks for all you've done, boys. If I can spare the lad, I will have your man Kettles sent over too. But I'll have to run it past Major Hartley first.'

He led the remaining stretcher party away and we were left with Simmons. 'Good to see you, lads. We need to talk.'

He led us up the main steps into the grand house. You could see it had been magnificent but the troops had made short work of it: furniture was piled up against the windows and there was kit everywhere. Radio operators were shouting into mouthpieces, trying to contact units in the field. Those troops not talking on radios or bent over tables gawping at maps were looking out of the windows in fire positions, like knights defending a castle. Simmons took us over to a table while extracting a folded map from his smock. Pulling it open, he laid it flat. 'Before I give you the really good news, have you heard from any of the platoon?'

I thought back to what I had witnessed inside the glider. 'Corporal Braithwaite, Karlow and Lavelle are dead. They died in the landing.'

Simmons remained deadpan. 'Anyone else?'

'Corporal Walton broke his back. We had to leave him at an aid station next to the landing zone, and we can't account for anyone else, sir. We've been fighting with 10 Para ever since.'

'I can't account for anyone else,' admitted Simmons. 'I don't think any of our gliders landed in one piece.' There was silence as we processed the scale of the losses. He adjusted his smock and webbing before addressing the map, a filthy trigger finger pointing at relevant features. 'We are here in Oosterbeek at the Hotel Hartenstein. We have the division forming a defensive perimeter east, north and west, with the Rhine as the base to the south of us. The 2nd Parachute Battalion are here at the northern end of Arnhem's main road bridge. When they landed on the first day, they attempted to seize the railway bridge on their move into the city, but the Germans destroyed it just as they got there. We haven't been able to radio 2 Para since they got to the bridge, so we have no idea what shape they are in now. We can only judge from the battle noise you can hear in the distance that the Germans are knocking the hell out of them. There are SS units on the south side of the bridge, along with panzer units in the town, so we can conclude that 2 Para could well be surrounded.' The distant thunder of tank fire emphasized their plight. 'But we require proof of life. We need someone to go into Arnhem and find out what shape they're in. If they are already finished, there's no point in wasting effort by fighting into Arnhem and reinforcing them. Already there's word of an evacuation back south across the Rhine.'

I was shocked to hear such talk. 'Evacuation?'

'By its very nature, an airborne operation is only temporary. We can only fight with what we arrived with. Those supplies you saw being pillaged by the Germans were an essential component of Market Garden's success. Without them we're running out of ammunition and have nothing to knock out their panzers. Meanwhile German strength continues to increase and, last I heard, XXX Corp weren't getting it all their own way on the road either. So relief will be late, if it comes at all.'

Elliot and I looked at each other. I was lost for words. But after just a few seconds, Simmons hit us with the ultimate bombshell. 'We need intelligence if we're going to make the right decisions, and you and Kemp are going to get it for us. Find out what has become of 2 Para.'

'What?' I half-shouted, forgetting myself. It sounded like a suicide mission.

'You heard me, Stokes,' he barked. 'Now both of you go and get some rest. You'll be going in tonight. We're still working out the best route in, and you'll get a full briefing later.' He turned to Elliot. 'Kemp, feel free to grab a brew for both of you from the kitchen. Our radios are no good, and we have next to no ammunition, but the tea did get through. The water will be a little ropey; we have had to drain the radiators since the Germans have cut off the water.'

Elliot, stunned about the task we had been given, left the room. Simmons wasted no time getting in my face. 'Now then, Stokes, what's going on with that American? Last time I saw the two of you, there was talk of bloodshed. Now I find the two of you again, and there's blood and broken bones. What's going on? Come on, out with it, I don't have time for this shit.'

'His plane crashed, sir,' I said simply.

He looked thoughtful. 'Well, that explains his injuries but not what you're doing hanging around his stretcher.'

Suddenly, I couldn't think of anything to say. I was tired, emotional and confused. I just shook my head. He relaxed and stepped back a pace. 'Listen, Stokes. What we spoke about in England . . . There are channels for pursuing this sort of thing, even for an officer. If there's evidence, I will back you to the hilt, but now is not the time. Understand?'

I could feel my eyes glazing over. What the hell was becoming of me? I was stuck in the arse end of Holland, surrounded and exhausted but still trying to right a wrong from home. He put a gentle hand on my shoulder. 'Let it go, Stokes. There are bigger fish to fry, and I need your help to do it.'

Simmons was talking sense. I could feel the dams break, as tears cut paths down my filthy cheeks. He patted me on the shoulder and began to fold up his map. I turned and leaned into the table, making a bad effort at trying to hold back my tears. He was right: we had a job to do here. Justice for Kate and Kirby would have to wait. 'Sit tight with young Kemp,' concluded Simmons.

As he left the room, Elliot appeared with two tin cups, their contents steaming. I cuffed away the tear streaks and walked over to Elliot, taking one of the cups.

His face was full of worry. 'Why on earth are we going into Arnhem? Just the two of us?'

I wondered for a moment if I had the heart to tell him what I'd just realized – that Simmons hadn't chosen us at random. 'Sorry, mate, I think it's my fault. Simmons is trying to keep me out of trouble.'

'He's got a funny idea about how to do that, then, hasn't he?'

11
The Bridge Too Far

'So Temple raped your friend?' Elliot asked as we sat drinking another cup of tea and looking out of the window at the tennis court.

'Yeah, while I was on leave in London.'

'Are you sure it's him? I mean, are you certain?'

'It's him, no question. I challenged him in England, when we got the briefing for this mission. He denied it, so I took a swing at him, and Bob Hilton turfed me out of the room.'

'Bloody hell. What are you going to do?'

'I haven't got a clue. Do things the correct way, I suppose. I need him to confess, and I need a witness. I can't go near him here; Simmons will have my nuts on a plate. I just need to think about it.'

We decided to go outside and find ourselves a place in the trenches. A mortar round hit the hotel. Somewhere to the north we could hear someone getting a pasting from a heavy-calibre weapon, probably a flak gun. Its rounds then began to scream through not far from us. We could see the prisoners on the tennis court dropping on their bellies.

After some time the fire from the flak gun petered out, and people began running about with stretchers. Elliot tried to get a cigarette lit with the useless matches issued in our ration packs.

'*Kamerad, kamerad.*' One of the SS prisoners was waving Elliot towards the fence. The German had lit a match for him. After a few drags, Elliot had the cigarette well and truly lit. He rewarded the favour by handing over two cigarettes, before heading back to our trench. '*Danke, danke*,' said the SS man, backing away from the fence. He handed one cigarette to a friend, who smiled, nodding his appreciation.

Over the course of the next two hours the sound of gun battles erupted from various directions. Some lasted a few minutes, others dragging on. We heard the odd stray round ping and whizz, one clipping the top of the fence.

Simmons joined us. 'Bloody Germans keep hitting the hotel. I think you blokes have the right idea.' Another mortar round landed in the gardens, making us flinch. Simmons tapped me on the knee. 'Got a route sorted into Arnhem for you. I'll take you out to the eastern perimeter at last light. The Germans have been hammering the north and west sides all day, so we're banking on their forces being light on the east for the time being. But we can't guarantee that'll be the case when you get back.'

'If we get back, more like,' said Elliot, looking worried.

Simmons gave him a warm smile. 'You'll be fine. The Germans will not be expecting two British soldiers to be walking about. Just keep your wits about you. They're probably just as knackered as we are.' It was a lie and we all knew it, but it was good to hear none the less.

For a September day, it felt like it took for ever to get dark. The odd mortar round landed in our perimeter, but other than that, the Germans had pretty much called it a day.

Finally Simmons arrived to lead us to the easternmost positions marking the perimeter boundary. We moved gingerly down the main street of Oosterbeek, hugging the right side, tracking slowly through gardens and ducking into shop doorways. This part of Oosterbeek didn't look too bad, considering the recent fighting. Simmons waved us into a stairwell that led to cellars under a parade of shops and a bakery, and from his smock he fished out a piece of paper. He handed it to me and in hushed tones said, 'You are to give this to the commanding officer of 2 Para. We have already radioed the message, but we cannot be certain they have received it. Read it so you know it word for word. You will not be taking this paper with you.'

Under red-filtered torchlight, I read the handwritten text. 'Division in Oosterbeek, making good progress. Hold on as long as you can. *Utrinque Paratus*.'

'What does that mean?' I whispered.

'It's the Parachute Regiment's motto,' Simmons replied. 'It means "Ready for anything".'

Nice touch. I would just give them the English version. Latin was never my strong point. I handed back the paper and shook Mr Simmons' hand. 'See you soon, sir. Stay lucky.'

'And you, Stokes, and you.'

Elliot and I climbed out of the stairwell and began our long walk to Arnhem. Every corner, every alleyway felt like it could host a potential ambush. The main road from Oosterbeek into Arnhem was a wide avenue paved in brick, just like the pavement, often making it difficult to distinguish where one started and the other finished. Large bushy trees lined the entire route, some badly splintered from shelling. Beneath them sat the smouldering remains of cars, trams and trucks. We kept our distance from German armoured vehicles on the road, picking our way through gardens and back alleys.

Every few hundred metres or so, we would rest to catch our breath and tune in to the sounds and smells. In one side street we watched German troops carrying their wounded into homes. It was odd to see the Germans in these circumstances, away from the firing line: looking after wounded, having a smoke, a chat and a brew. It could have been Hartenstein, just different uniforms.

We could see the dark profiles of German infantrymen, slumped, their helmets off, dragging large rustling ponchos over their heads for a nap. We jumped the fence into a park, feeling surreal as we crept through a children's play area, trying to avoid a number of panzers. We could make out cigarettes hanging from their crews' lips as they unloaded tank shells from trucks.

Finally the unmistakable silhouette of Arnhem road bridge appeared ahead. In the gloom it still looked a long way away. Dodging German infantry and tank crewmen all night had taken its toll on our nerves. But I knew the real challenge was not getting shot by 2 Para.

One street at a time, we got closer to the bridge, the buildings showing more shell damage the closer we got. The roads were covered with a sea of smashed masonry and smouldering vehicles. We tried to make ourselves appear friendly, while at the same time not offering a clear shot to any trigger-happy British sentry. We were both on edge, waiting for the crack of a shot and the ripping pain as the bullets tore through us.

'Halt, who goes there?' a hushed but commanding voice sounded from somewhere.

I remembered having to go through the link-up routine numerous times in Normandy. Get it wrong, God help you. 'Private Stokes, Divisional Headquarters,' I hissed back, not too sure in what direction I should be talking.

'Keep walking forward,' came the hushed command. We did as we were told. The crunch of masonry under our boots sounded deafeningly loud in what had become a very scary Arnhem street.

'Hold it there,' a whisper instructed us. 'How many in your patrol?'

'Two,' I whispered back. 'We're messengers from Divisional Headquarters.'

'Keep coming,' said the voice. 'Be careful. German snipers everywhere.'

'As if we weren't bricking it enough already,' whispered Elliot.

'And not a fat lot we can do about it now anyway,' I replied. We continued forward, knowing we couldn't do anything else for risk of alarming our own side. We approached a row of badly damaged buildings. A shattered road led off to our right, down to the moonlit expanse of the Rhine, the dark profile of Arnhem bridge leading over it. As my eyes focused on the buildings, I could pick out helmets and grubby faces in the ground-floor windows. We had reached the 2 Para perimeter. All the way into their position they kept their weapons pointing at us. They looked a sorry state, most sporting at least one bandage that had long since given up trying to stop the blood seeping through. But as we finally reached them, they all cracked into smiles. 'Morning, lads.' One of them rose to greet us. 'And what can we do for you?'

'We have a message from Divisional Headquarters,' I answered, trying to sound official, 'to deliver to the commanding officer.'

He grunted and waved us to follow him. 'Well, then,' he said, hushed and deadpan, 'let's just hope it's good news.' He led us through the shattered ground floor. Everywhere troops were in fighting positions, most sleeping, but at least one soldier in every room was ready for action. There was evidence of the place having been hit with all sorts of weapons. We moved through a large hole in a wall and up a rickety staircase. A radio operator manned a set on a large table. I wondered if he was trying to call Divisional Headquarters. Some of the walls of the upper floor were missing, giving us a view of the highway that ran across the bridge. We couldn't see the bridge itself, just its approach ramp to our front left. 'Wait here,' the sentry told us. 'Keep away from the windows. It's getting light, and the Germans are early risers.'

I heard the sound of boots on a wooden landing. A small stocky soldier entered the room, along with two others, both taller and slimmer. The stocky man held out his hand and shook both mine and Elliot's enthusiastically. 'You have a message for me, gentlemen?'

'Yes, sir,' I replied. 'Division in Oosterbeek, making good progress. Hold on as long as you can. Ready for anything.'

We stood as he regarded us in stony silence. I became uncomfortably aware of how underwhelming the message sounded. I felt Elliot shifting in the awkward silence. 'Didn't they make you learn the Latin?' he said finally.

I looked at him, confused, and he broke into a smile. I grinned back. 'Yes, sir, but I just couldn't remember it.'

He grunted. 'Bloody Divisional Headquarters, sending only two men. Congratulations on getting here in one piece, however. The Germans are reinforcing their units by the truckload. Fresh troops keep coming at us. We know this, since their dead are clean shaven and freshly laundered. I'm sure they cannot say the same for ours.' He was intense, which was not surprising. And now Elliot and I had delivered some poxy message he probably already knew.

I didn't know what to say. 'Yes, sir,' I blurted. 'I only regret not bringing better news.'

'Oh, but you have brought good news, young man,' he enthused. 'We've been completely in the dark, only able to communicate with other 2 Para companies, but your message lets us know that Divisional Headquarters haven't forgotten about us and that means a lot. Now then, since I doubt you will be trying to get out of here in daylight, make yourselves comfortable, and Captain Scrase here will tell you what's going on.'

One of the taller soldiers pointed at some chairs piled up behind the door. We took seats at the table with the captain and the CO. As tired as I was, I knew I needed to take in what I was about to be told. The radio operator moved to a fighting position at a window, leaving his set on the table. With a map opened flat on the table, Captain Scrase used a pencil to point out locations. 'We are occupying this area, either side of the bridge approach ramp. Our companies occupy these buildings – here, here and here.' He indicated several squares on the maps at the north end of the bridge. 'Up until yesterday we also had the buildings on either side along the riverbank, but German tanks on the south bank made continuing to occupy them untenable – they would just shell the hell out of us. We have men situated either side of the bridge ramp at street level, preventing German infantry from getting into the buildings we abandoned, something that would enable them to push us further from the river. Since we've been here the Germans have been fighting very hard to drive us away.' The situation didn't look good.

'The Germans north of us,' he continued, 'across this large open plaza here, are not having it all their own way.' So Lieutenant Simmons' guess had been right: 2 Para were indeed surrounded, the bridge being to the south of them. 'Their armour to the north has been reluctant to approach us,' he went on. 'We have been fortunate to get some good PIAT strikes on their less powerful assault guns, but they hit us with rounds from their Tigers now and then.' Things were sounding even worse. PIATs were capable of stopping the Germans' less formidable panzers – their older tanks and assault guns and flak guns mounted on tank chassis – but were largely ineffective against the heavily armoured and legendary Tigers.

As the improving light seeped into the room, I could see he was exhausted, under considerable strain. I dared not think when he last had the chance to sleep. But he wasn't done. 'The Waffen SS are learning the hard way, but our main issue is ammunition. The Germans are a lot of things, but stupid they are not. They know all they need to do when facing an airborne force is to just keep fighting us. They're pouring fresh men and material into this bloody place, and we're losing men and ammo. We know the Poles have landed south of the river, but that's no bloody good to us right now, since the panzers still remain on the south bank. Lord knows what the bloody Poles are up to. And as for XXX Corps and their 50,000 men . . .'

The CO noticed that the captain was getting irate. 'Charlie. How about you go grab a tea off young Darwin; the water's just boiled.'

'Yes, Colonel. Gentlemen.' The captain got to his feet and left the room.

The colonel smiled. 'Apologies for our lack of manners; it's all been rather busy around here of late. I never got your names.'

'I'm Private Stokes and this is Private Kemp. We're members of 1st Division Defence Platoon. We got tasked to come and get . . . erm, proof of life.'

The colonel looked surprised. 'Proof of life? What kind of mission have they sent you on? Bloody clowns. You don't need to be a genius to know that if you can hear fighting, we're still alive.' He looked at the map. 'I wonder where the hell XXX Corps are? If they can't break through, then all your boys at Divisional Headquarters can do is buy us a bit more time.'

'Yes, sir. I'm afraid I did hear the XXX Corps weren't having it all their own way. And it's been pretty tough for the paras at HQ too, sir.'

The colonel nodded. 'Aye, we're all going to earn our pay before this operation's done, that's for sure.' He looked out of the window. 'Anything else for us, boys?'

'Sir?' Elliot piped up.

'You just walked through their lines, lad; you must have seen something!'

I answered for Elliot. 'Infantry resting. Quite a few in the residential areas. Tanks getting resupplied on the green spaces on the outskirts. But they do have a lot of casualties. We passed one of their aid stations.'

'I would mortar the pitches,' replied the colonel, 'just to harass those panzers, but I have no bloody mortar ammunition left, so we will just have to deal with them when they come and play later.'

Right on cue, the grind and squeal of armoured vehicles echoed through the house. It was coming from the north – the resupplied Tigers, I thought.

The colonel clearly had the same thought. 'Pity you boys didn't take care of them when you passed through,' he said with a grin as he pulled his smock straight, adjusted his webbing and ensured his chinstrap was correctly done up. 'You two chaps will stay up here, and assist Briggs with covering the bridge. They couldn't get any more vehicles across it if they tried, but their infantry aren't so shy. Keep your ears to the ground for any orders shouted up to you, do you understand?'

'Yes, sir,' I assured him.

He gave us a nod and a wink. 'Good. See you soon, and don't let Briggs pinch all your cigarettes.' He led the captain from the room. Elliot and I grabbed our weapons and tucked in on the left side of Briggs. I peered down the road towards the approach ramp of the bridge. The colonel had been right about no more German vehicles coming across. It was crammed with smouldering wrecked vehicles: assault guns, halftracks, even a motorbike and sidecar. What madman had thought he could get through on a bike? I had plenty of dead German soldiers to choose from. They littered the tarmac between the wrecks, some smouldering like the vehicles. Their blood had pooled beneath them, appearing like splashes of dark sticky paint running to the kerbside. Their personal weapons were missing, so I guessed the 2 Para lads had gone out and collected them.

The din of engines and tank tracks from the north continued to get louder. It was almost impossible to ignore it. 'Hold up,' said Briggs. 'We've got movement on the bridge. Let them know downstairs.'

I went to relay the warning, but Elliot was already scrambling over to the doorway. He hissed the warning as loudly as he could before resuming his fighting position. Movement caught my attention on the bridge. I saw German troops hugging the side of the structure. They shuffled along, hunched over, fearful of being fired on.

Briggs let fly with short, sharp bursts of his Sten. Tarmac and sparks flicked up around the feet of the lead SS trooper, causing him to flinch and sprawl to the ground for cover. The soldier behind him took off in a full-on sprint across the approach ramp towards us, followed quickly by a large cluster of others. Elliot and I fired our Lee-Enfield rifles into the field-grey mass. Another group of SS dashed forward along the right-hand pedestrian path and began to disappear down a flight of steps leading to the street; they were too quick for any of us to get a decent shot on them. But as I fed my rifle as fast as I could, some crumpled to the ground, fire pouring into them from other positions.

Some of the Germans took cover amid the vehicle wrecks on the bridge, taking snap shots at us. Most were well wide of their mark, but then a burst of pink and green mist exploded just in front of me, and I heard an almighty whack. I thought Elliot had been hit, but it was Briggs, who roared angrily, staggering back from the window and dropping his Sten. Above the cracks of incoming and outgoing fire, he cursed and growled through his teeth, his broken right forearm swinging limply as he fought to stop the bleeding.

Moving towards him, Elliot fought through his smock pockets for a field dressing, but Briggs waved him back to the window. 'Deal with them first.' Elliot rejoined me. Having fed an ammunition clip into my rifle, I popped up and took a few shots but knew I hadn't hit anything useful. Behind me I could hear cursing and groaning. I turned, expecting to see Briggs in a mess on the floor, but instead what I saw took my breath away and made me proud to be British.

He stood with one boot firm across the fly-off lever side of a grenade, grunting as he used his good hand to pull the pin. With the pin removed, he grabbed the grenade before taking his boot off it, then side-stepped to the window, lobbing it among the SS men below. They yelled hysterically and dashed in all directions; some were cut down by our fire, others making it out of sight. The rolling grenade eventually detonated among the vehicles and the cadavers of the dead on the bridge approach ramp.

It was then that I saw the flak panzer and yelled a warning. The vehicle had muscled its way onto the approach ramp, its crew working like madmen to slew the turret towards us. Although its multiple guns were designed for anti-aircraft fire, the Germans had learned the value of angling the barrels down for use against ground troops.

I instinctively grabbed Elliot's smock and dived away from the window as the room erupted in a series of ear-popping thuds. Books on shelves burst like confetti, masonry dust and room fittings showering us. The tracer rounds even set fire to the long curtains that flanked the windows. The firing continued for what felt like a lifetime. Briggs was rolling about, trying to pull the radio set off the table. As it hit the floor, my ringing ears only allowed me to register a dull thud.

I was distracted by movement in the open doorway. Captain Scrase was kneeling at the threshold, waving at us. 'We're moving next door. We can't stay here. Let's go.' As Elliot and I got to our feet, Scrase dashed into the room and grabbed the radio from Briggs, pulling him to his feet by the collar of his smock with his other hand.

We followed Scrase out onto the landing. I noticed a beautiful chandelier. It could well have been crystal; I wasn't in a position to inspect it closely.

I was moving rapidly down the staircase following the wounded Briggs when I fell. One moment I had hold of Briggs, then next moment I was falling against the bannister and into a crumpled heap in the corner. As I hit the deck with a jarring impact, there was a flash and a high-pitched scream. Dust enveloped us and I heard the dull crash of something heavy. I could see people milling all over the ground floor below. I heard both English and German being shouted somewhere close by. My vision was swimming, but I could just make out Briggs and Scrase lying in a bloody pile at the bottom of the stairs.

Two green- and grey-clad SS troopers jumped over them and charged up the staircase towards me. As the lead soldier reached me, there were two sharp cracks from above which sent both of them flying backwards down the stairs. I looked up; Elliot's smoking rifle muzzle was not far from my face. He helped me to my feet, and we made our way gingerly to the bottom of the stairs. We dragged the dead Germans from on top of Scrase and Briggs. They were both conscious and looked like they could do with a stiff drink.

A sergeant appeared at my elbow, helping us to get Scrase and Briggs to their feet. 'How you doing, boy?' he yelled in my ear. He had a German MP 40 sub-machine gun in his hand, and once we'd got the men to their feet, he was immediately off rummaging through the dead Germans' pouches, searching for extra ammunition for it.

'I'm OK, Sergeant,' I replied, not certain he was listening any more. My response was so muffled to my ears, it sounded like it came from someone else. Another grenade thud thundered through the house. As the dust settled again, the sergeant charged through a door. Briggs jumped up and chased after him, despite his shattered arm. Elliot followed, plus a couple of other guys who appeared from nowhere. I dashed after them, to find two smashed rooms like a butcher's shop. Smouldering British and German bodies littered the floors, pulverized by grenades.

I was breathing hard, sweat flowing freely down my face. The sergeant ordered Elliot to strip the bodies of ammo and weapons.

I think it was the first time Elliot had ever been given that kind of order. It was clear each bullet was precious and we were going to have to make every one count. My throat was raw with thirst. I hoped Elliot might find a few full water bottles. Looking out at the street, I realized we had been quite fortunate. One of the enemy dead outside was equipped with a flamethrower. The small fuel tank strapped to his back was draped in what looked like a dark brown hessian cover. At the end of a hose, a long thin cylinder dangled from his hand, a small pilot flame flickering from it. Thankfully someone had got him before he finished setting up.

Elliot had just finished collecting his booty when the place erupted around us again, incoming fire splashing all over the interior. From the houses across the street, German troops were giving us everything they had. I hunkered down beneath a blown-out window as books and keepsakes on shelves burst like exploding pillows. I chanced a glance outside. About a dozen enemy soldiers were advancing across the street. I pointed my rifle towards them, but before I could pull the trigger there was an almighty roar, and all the air was pulled from the room. My face tingled with the intense heat that washed through the building as a huge fireball engulfed the oncoming Germans. We coughed and spluttered, gasping for breath. As I returned to my senses, I became aware of the screaming in the street.

I peered outside and wished I hadn't. The German infantry were rolling about on the ground, screaming as they attempted to put out the flames that were consuming them. One was staggering about horribly, screaming for his mother. I thought about ending his pain, but we couldn't spare the ammo.

'Jesus! Sorry about that,' the sergeant gasped. 'I shot at that flamethrower, and . . .' He didn't need to go on; we all got the picture. It was gruesome, and I reckon if he'd known what the result would have been he might not have done it. But he'd probably saved our lives. War is hell, and maybe all soldiers end up there.

A strange sort of calm then descended on the street. Ash floated down like snow, and for a moment there was no sound of firing. Then someone shouted that the roof was on fire and the hiatus was over. We had to get out, quick. With Captain Scrase unsteady on his feet like a punch-drunk fighter, I decided to take the lead. I carefully peered into the street, then took a cautious half-step outside. The firing had started again, and through the shell of the three-storey building next door I could see some paras blazing away. Meanwhile it looked like the Germans across the street were regrouping. I went for it, and what was left of our group followed me. No sooner had Elliot made it out than the house collapsed behind us.

Discouraged by the failure of their attack, the SS in the buildings opposite moved back from the windows, and the fighting petered out. I could hear Briggs cursing the medic as he put his shattered arm in a sling of sorts.

I slumped down on a pile of rubble, wondering how the hell Elliot and I had got ourselves into this. Bloody Temple! I kicked at an empty shell case as I thought of that bastard safe in his cellar, while my quest for revenge had landed me in this hell. I'd be lucky to be carried out in one piece.

Captain Scrase was now more steady on his feet. He grabbed my arm and nodded to Elliot. 'No time to rest, lads. After me.' We followed him into a room on the next floor up. The windows give excellent coverage of the street, and we set up shop, moving the furniture around to give cover.

There was a squeal of tracks, and a Tiger appeared a few hundred metres away, creeping down the street from the north. Its commander was leaning out of his turret, talking to the two columns of infantry flanking his tank as they dashed in and out of the rubble of the buildings. When they got just short of two hundred metres from us, the Tiger commander disappeared into the beast, closing his hatch.

As it moved ever closer, the tank caused our building to start shaking. Glass shattered, furniture crashed, and then suddenly an entire house immediately beside the tank collapsed, consuming the Tiger and the men immediately surrounding it.

A cloud of dust enveloped the street. There was a shout from below us, and about a dozen grenades were thrown into the dust cloud, detonating almost as one. As the dust lifted, Bren gunners poured their fire into half-buried SS men. The Tiger, overwhelmed with building debris, fired its main gun in defiance, the shell thundering down the street to hit the approach ramp of the bridge. 'Let's take care of that Tiger,' shouted someone. 'It's still in this fight.' A small group of our lads dashed out and clambered up onto the rubble-strewn tank, carrying what I was sure were wine bottles.

'What are they doing?' Elliot asked.

'Molotovs – petrol bombs,' answered Scrase. 'We ran out of PIAT rounds days ago.' The paras pulled masonry off to expose the top of the turret. A shot snapped, and one of them burst in a green and red mist. Tracer bullets began clattering into the tank, the paras completely exposed. All of us winced as they fell flailing and screaming, coming to rest among the SS troopers in the rubble. 'Fuck's sake,' Scrase murmured. 'We're dying by inches here. Where the hell is XXX Corps?'

Before anyone could think of an answer, a colossal explosion ripped through our building. The concussion knocked me across the room. I couldn't move. I just lay on the bare floorboards, my head ringing, masonry dust stinging my eyes. The world around me slowed with my heartbeat. Gunfire and German voices came from the floor above, but I realized I must be imagining things as they couldn't have got up there.

But then I looked over and saw Scrase firing up through the

ceiling. 'How did that happen?' he was screaming. The chattering of Stens and the snap of rifle rounds dominated the floor above.

'They blew a hole in the wall from next door,' someone shouted.

Clever buggers, I thought in my dreamlike state.

A stick grenade tumbled down the open wooden staircase to our rear. My eyes followed it as it came to rest at the bottom. Briggs dashed over, picked it up and went to heave it back where it had come from. The detonation blew past me, carrying what was left of Briggs with it. It felt like his entire body had sand-blasted me in one giant shot.

Whether it was the horror of the situation or the blast, it roused me. I rolled over and looked around for my rifle. 'You OK?' Elliot asked, handing me my weapon. I nodded, wondering if I looked as awful as he did – covered in blood and dust. The loud chugging beat of a Bren sounded from behind us, and we looked over to see a para at the bottom of the stairs, Bren in both hands, firing long deliberate bursts up the stairs. SS troopers crashed and slumped around him as their lives expired in violent bursts of green and pink. It reminded me of Escoville in Normandy, another lifetime ago.

The Bren gunner changed magazines. The chevrons on his smock sleeve gave away the fact he was a corporal. 'OK, boys, let's go,' he said. 'They're falling back.' He charged up the stairs, firing short bursts as he went. Other paras scrambled up behind him as Elliot helped me to my feet. I followed everyone upstairs, still a little dazed.

It was one hell of a mess. Paras, dead and dying, lay among SS dead and dying. The large jagged hole the Germans had blown in the wall was piled about thigh-high with their dead. They had tried to rush the room en masse. Evidence of hand-to-hand fighting was everywhere: bloodied knives, bayonets and small German Army shovels littered the floor.

Scrase pointed to the pile of SS dead. 'Stokes, grab those

Panzerfausts.' He meant German shoulder-launched anti-tank weapons, far more advanced than our PIATs. Elliot helped me turn over the dead Germans and remove two Panzerfausts, both covered in wet, clotting blood. Fighting raged in the street below and on the ground floor, where chaos reigned. Grenades were being exchanged. Scrase scanned the street. 'Get them ready to fire; we need to hit that fucking panzer. It's not here yet, but I can hear it.' I was glad he could; my ears were still ringing from the last explosion.

Elliot and I carefully prepared the Panzerfausts for firing. I could hear the gunning of an engine, and the building began to vibrate. Scrase waved us forward, pulling us down as we drew near the window. 'Hit the bloody thing before it can turn towards us. Its gun will be pointing right at us, so don't miss.' The pressure was immense, although we had two chances to kill the panzer. As the engine noise grew louder, the panzer clearly struggling to surmount the rubble, I was thankful the SS troopers in the buildings opposite hadn't detected us. 'You, young man, are first,' Scrase said to Elliot. 'Stand by.' Elliot looked at me for inspiration. I gave him a reassuring nod – at least I hoped it was reassuring. 'Here we go,' said Scrase. 'Get ready.'

Elliot bounced on his haunches, ready to spring up. I hoped he wouldn't miss.

'Now,' roared Scrase. Elliot was up, aiming down the street. With a loud thud, the bulbous projectile shot away from the Panzerfaust launcher. The detonation rocked the entire street. 'Hit it again, now,' Scrase screamed. I moved to the window. Below, the street was swarming with German troops scrambling past the panzer, which was screeching and rattling in reverse, its right track broken in the road.

I filled the sights of the Panzerfaust with the tank and squeezed the firing lever. The projectile lurched from the launcher, hitting the back engine deck of the panzer in a flurry of sparks. With black smoke billowing from it, the vehicle slewed off to the side of the road. I knew that with one track remaining, it would now be nigh on impossible to reverse it out or steer it. The infantry accompanying the panzer were falling back, throwing grenades and firing as they went. Some fell dead to British fire, some were limping and crawling behind whatever cover they could find. The tank crew bailed out, fleeing with bullets splashing and screaming about them.

After a few minutes the street became quiet. 'Good effort, men.' Scrase was beaming. 'Bloody good shooting.' I slumped back onto the floor, lying on the dead and feeling like one of them.

Later that afternoon, Elliot and I were summoned to see the colonel. We scampered through the rubble, aware of the sound of more fighting on the bridge. Eventually we reached the CO, who was sitting with a bandaged leg propped up in front of him. As we entered he held up a hand, and we waited as he dictated a message to a radio operator sitting next to him. Judging by the looks on their faces, it wasn't an optimistic message. He waved us forward. 'You fought well, lads. Captain Scrase is full of praise for you.'

'Thank you, sir,' we replied in unison.

'How long have you two been in the Parachute Regiment?' he asked.

Elliot and I looked at each other briefly; it was Elliot who spoke first: 'Begging your pardon, sir, but I'm in the Royal Signals.'

The colonel frowned and then glanced at me. 'I'm from the Ox and Bucks, sir.'

He grinned. 'I'll be damned. Well, you fight like paras, I'll say that for you.'

'Thank you, sir,' I said and meant it. I knew how proud the paras were of their own.

He put on a more serious face. 'Lads, I need to get a last message to Divisional Headquarters, so I need you two to run the gauntlet again tonight.'

Elliot and I looked at each other again. I nodded. 'Yes, sir. And don't worry, sir. We'll get through and guide the reinforcements in.'

The colonel swallowed hard and I could sense the radio operator trying to hold himself together. The colonel's eyes glazed before he spoke once more. 'When you get back, tell them what my boys have done here. Please. They deserve that much.'

He leaned forward and handed me a small folded piece of notebook paper. 'I'm sure you won't need to bother with the Latin for this one. Please read and digest.'

I opened the paper, and what was written on it broke my heart. 'Out of ammo. God save the King.'

12
The River

'The river,' said the sergeant major cheerfully, 'that's the ticket. Keep the water on your left and you can't go wrong.' Fishing out a torch and map, he partially covered the torch to reduce the glare. He used a grubby forefinger as a pointer. 'We're sitting about here,' he pointed to the north side of the road bridge on the map. 'A few hundred metres west is the railway bridge. Take care as you move past it. There could well be Germans knocking about underneath, resting and regrouping. Past the bridge there's a lot of open ground between the river and the residential areas, so ensure you don't get caught in the open. Our guys, and by that I mean the guys from Oosterbeek, could have patrols out there, but the Germans might too, so take your time.'

Elliot and I nodded, not trusting ourselves to speak. We were both nervous as hell.

We made our way out of the 2 Para perimeter. At the edge of the shattered buildings I tried to ensure everything ahead looked quiet, but sporadic fighting all around made it difficult to gauge where noises were coming from. Then I heard voices nearby. I waved Elliot down behind me and slowly picked my way through the loose bricks and rubble of what must have once been an industrial unit. Even in the dark, you couldn't miss the twisted steel that had held the place up, all now exposed to the sky.

The noise was indeed talking. I peered over a low broken wall. Just beyond it were some German troops. A nearby group were just sitting about, some smoking. Beyond them I could make out the dim profile of at least a dozen others carrying ammunition to their mortars, which were set up ready to fire. One soldier was directing the rest with the beam of his torch. Was this the assault that would finally finish 10 Para? I wondered. I contemplated throwing a grenade in, but I knew the colonel would want the message to get through.

We managed to sneak away, and as we made our way west along the northern bank of the Rhine the buildings gradually appeared in a better state of repair. Eventually, the collapsed railway bridge loomed above us, its frame slumped, buckled and twisted where it jutted out over the dark, wide river. Carefully we picked our way underneath. An engine coughed and spluttered into life, almost causing me heart failure. As a second engine started, we hugged the darkness offered by the slimy, moss-covered broken brickwork of the bridge. I inched forward. Beyond about a hundred metres of open field, more buildings appeared, a children's play park over to the left. In front of the park a dozen panzers or more were crammed in together, their crews illuminated by the glow of their cigarettes. I guessed these were the same units we had observed on the way into Arnhem from Oosterbeek. Two ammunition supply trucks then pulled up next to the panzers, and the tank crews began to transfer the shells.

A tap on the shoulder startled me. I flicked my head around. 'What are we gonna do?' Elliot whispered. I wasn't entirely sure but knew we had to keep moving; once daylight arrived, we would be very exposed. However, I didn't think we could just stroll past a load of panzers either.

Elliot followed me into a wide expanse of waterlogged reeds at the water's edge. It sucked at our boots, but at least it afforded us cover. It was hard going, but we passed the panzers, their crews passing tank shells along a human chain, and before long we were on firmer ground. The riverbank flattened out to our right, and we found ourselves trudging across an open flood plain. I felt horribly exposed, just waiting for the shout of alarm and the flash of a torch beam. My throat felt dry, and I paused to fill my bottle in the reeds. I crouched for a moment gulping it down and feeling revived.

'Rob, Rob,' Elliot whispered urgently.

'What?'

'Near the destroyed bridge, on the riverbank.' I peered back over his right shoulder as he pointed towards the bridge. I tried to focus on anything there. Nothing. But then I noticed movement, much closer. When you see something in the dark, your vision distorts the image; you have to look slightly around the object for the eye to focus better. People were slowly moving about. Then we saw more movement, further along the riverbank back towards Arnhem.

'What the hell . . .' I began.

'I reckon 10 Para are following us out,' Elliot suggested.

'Maybe,' I agreed, wondering why no one would have mentioned it.

We watched both groups slowly coming our way for some time, the second catching up with the first. Then suddenly the riverbank was illuminated by a fireball, and the aroma of burning petrol wafted through our position. There was a scream from the first group as two human torches flailed and flapped in the reeds, then shouts and splashes as the two groups clashed. Some of the second group continued to advance along the riverbank, coming our way fast.

'Well, one of those lots is on our side,' I said, 'but I don't think I want to wait to find out which.' I started to strip off.

Elliot was undressing but not as quickly. 'Rob,' he whispered, 'I'm not all that great at swimming.'

The flamethrower let out another long, roaring lick, and I suddenly remembered Kirby Green, the landlord of the Jolly Gardeners in Mortlake. He had horrendous scars from a flamethrower attack on the Western Front in 1915. 'Neither am I, mate,'

I whispered. 'Just swim as hard as you can. Let the current take you. We can't stay here.'

He knew I was right and showed a new sense of urgency. I pushed out into the water in just my boots and underwear. The cold Rhine water enveloped my bollocks, taking my breath away. The flamethrower roared again. Already the current was pulling me away. I trod water, just able to make out Elliot's head and shoulders following me. I struck out using breaststroke. The current became stronger and faster, keeping my head above water a challenge. I began to swallow more than I breathed. I had a horrible feeling I wasn't making any progress. My arms felt like they weighed a ton.

The current pulled me under a couple of times, and as I fought to stay up my arms began to tire. I looked up and was surprised to see the reeds of the south bank rushing past me. I fought to get closer, not having much left in me. I lunged, trying to grab them. Any notion of swimming style had now gone; I was now thrashing like a maniac. My first contact with the reeds was brief. They stroked my left hand. A second clump scraped across my face, poking me in the eye, which caused me to gasp and inhale a load of water. I hugged a third clump, coughing and spluttering like an old man. The Rhine was still trying to drag me away, and I was losing the fight to hold on.

I heard boots squelch in the water. A large shadow leaned over me, grabbing me by the scruff, then by my right armpit and then my pants, pulling them right up the crack of my arse. I realized there were two people carrying me, slipping in the reeds and cursing. I felt firm ground as they laid me down. Burning bile erupted from my insides, and I had to lean over to allow the Rhine to escape my soaked, exhausted frame. I slumped on my back, a wonderful sensation of sleep beginning to overwhelm me.

I didn't care whether my helpers were German or English; I was finished. I just needed to leave this hell behind.

13
Dante's Envoy

Voices and the smell of cooking were the first things I registered. I lay for a while just enjoying the sense of warmth. Then I began to listen to the voices and I realized they were British. I opened my eyes. I was in a large barn. There were troops milling about: some were British, others had foreign-sounding voices. A Sherman tank was in the barn, one of its tracks in pieces. Oily, grubby men were working on it, cigarettes hanging from their lips.

'Where the bloody hell have you been?' At first I didn't register the question but then I turned to find Sergeant Bob Hilton of the Defence Platoon, 1st Airborne Division, the man I had been supposed to report to after landing in Holland. I was confused, still not understanding where the hell I was. I tried to respond, but a voice interrupted me.

'Give those a try, matey,' said one of the tank mechanics, throwing a sets of overalls at me. I looked down at my naked torso and remembered the swim. I must be on the south side of the river, but what the bloody hell was Hilton doing here? I'd ask Elliot . . . I stopped, realizing I'd completely forgotten about him. I turned and surveyed the room but couldn't see him.

I suddenly felt very alone again. I wondered where Elliot was, hoping he had made it across the river, perhaps a little further downstream. After all he had been through, he deserved that at least. I donned the overalls feeling like a tramp: a week's worth of growth on my face, my hair matted, and now some oily overalls to top it all off. The tank repair crew didn't look much better, but I realized they had plenty of water and rations. The aroma of cooked food became all the more acute, and I remembered I had not eaten properly in a week. I decided to take a look. Behind the tank one of the crew was playing chef on a little stove. He announced breakfast was ready. His crewmates downed tools to eat. I also got an invite. Fried Spam and eggs, and bars of chocolate.

A captain approached us, IRISH GUARDS sewn onto his shoulder. I looked at the emblem for a moment and then gave a short laugh. He looked down at me. 'Something funny, lad?'

I shook my head. 'No, sir.' It wasn't funny, it was bloody tragic. The uniform told me I'd found XXX Corps; I'd found the colonel's reinforcements a day late.

The captain was all smiles as he squatted next to me. 'Good to see you're still with us anyway. You looked a right mess when they brought you in.' He gave me a hot drink, which I took gratefully. 'Here. It's not the best tea in the world, but better than sod all.' I glanced at the sorry-looking brown liquid, but given the circumstances I wasn't going to complain. I carefully took a sip. It was a gift from the gods, plenty of sugar in it.

I cupped the warm nectar in both hands as he led me back to the foot of my makeshift bed on the barn floor. 'My name is Captain Burns-Campbell, Irish Guards. My boys fished you out of the river last night.'

'Thank you, sir. I'm very grateful.'

He grinned and patted my thigh. 'The company commander and the intelligence officer would like to have a chat with you. We've encountered very few airborne chaps, save the Polish. A few of them are over there. They're a prickly bunch to get on with.' He pointed over to a corner where a group of soldiers were hunkered down. I noticed some of them were wounded, wondering if they'd been injured during their drop.

I remembered Elliot. 'Did your boys pull anyone else out of the river last night, sir?'

He shook his head. 'Just you. Come on.' We walked out of the barn in silence, my mind unwilling to process what his answer meant. I'd led Elliot into the water when he said he couldn't swim. I'd led him to his death.

He led me to another large barn, which served as a headquarters building; radios crackling, officers poring over maps, crockery chinking and clattering. We went through the barn to a little outbuilding wallpapered with maps and photos taken from the air, symbols all over everything. A short, stocky, red-cheeked captain rose from a folding canvas chair. Burns-Campbell introduced us. 'Johnny, this is the chap my guys pulled from the river.' He looked back at me. 'I'm sorry; I never did get your name.'

'Stokes, sir. Private Robert Stokes, Ox and Bucks Light Infantry.'

The stocky captain offered me a huge hand. 'Captain Warner, intelligence officer, Irish Guards. I'm afraid the major is having a meeting with the Polish. He'll join us when he can. Please, take a seat.' As Burns-Campbell left, I found another folding chair and sat down. 'Stokes, you are one of the first real-time intelligence sources we've had since we got here the other night. So I hope you're not in a hurry to go anywhere. We need to have all you know about the other side of the river.'

'Yes, sir. Whatever I can do to help.' He threw question after question at me, explaining the terrain using the photos and maps. No stone was unturned, and rightly so. I went through everything I had encountered in Oosterbeek and Arnhem itself. He wanted to know everything about the Germans: their equipment, average age, morale, weapons. Did they look well fed? Were their vehicles in good condition? And so on. We paused for tea at one point, and he told me to focus on what I knew, not what I thought. He only appeared satisfied after asking me some questions to which I didn't know the answers. I heard the gunning of an engine and the rattling squeal of tank tracks outside. Then the sound of a voice that sent a prickle down my spine. I knew that voice.

'Get that damn thing in the barn! And sort that fucking radio out!' The owner of the voice stepped into the room, and I smiled. Bloody Dave Brettle, who I'd last seen on Gold Beach going off to join the Irish Guards.

'Captain Warner!' Brettle roared. Warner sprang to his feet, meeting Brettle at the door. I couldn't see Brettle but felt his presence. 'Johnny, have a word with that Polish prick. If he tries to use one of my call signs as bait again so he can spot where that fucking 88 is firing from, I will drown the fucker in the river, get me?'

'Of course, sir,' said Warner. 'We have fresh information from north of the river. Young Private Stokes here has swum the Rhine.'

Brettle peered over Warner's shoulder and looked straight at me. I felt it only right to get to my feet. Brettle was clearly not in a good mood, but his menacing glare broke into a smile as he swept inside, thrusting out a hand. 'Fucking hell, Robbie Stokes. Well I never. How're you doing, kid?'

I accepted his iron grip. 'I'm OK, sir. I'm OK.'

'Well, you don't look it. What corpse did you find them overalls on?'

'Private Stokes arrived in his underwear, sir,' Warner said with a smirk.

'Bloody hell.' Brettle turned back to Warner. 'Sort that Polish clown out, Johnny. And have Paget bring this soldier some battledress and a shaving kit.'

Warner left, leaving me with Brettle. We spent a while catching up on everything between Normandy and Arnhem. A private dropped off some battledress, which looked a little too big for me. He also left a small tatty towel, a razor and a bar of soap. I thanked the bloke, who nodded to Brettle as he left.

'You look like hell, Stokes,' observed Brettle. 'But before you make yourself presentable, tell me how things are going on the other side of the river?'

'May I speak freely, sir?' He nodded. 'We've been getting the shit kicked out of us,' I began. 'The drop went all to hell; the resupplies went to the Germans, and we didn't have the muscle to keep their armour at bay. We've been pinned down everywhere waiting for . . .' I tailed off. 'Well, sir, the sooner your tanks can help the paras out, the better.'

He nodded. 'Nothing I'd like more, Stokes, but all along, despite original intelligence to the contrary, we've encountered serious German armour on the southern approaches to the road bridge in Arnhem, heavily supported by infantry. I've been with the Polish all morning, trying to work out how we can hit them hard enough to force a crossing.'

'And 2 Para on the bridge?'

He looked down. 'Our reconnaissance boys, along with the Poles, have been watching the north side of the bridge since the day before yesterday. And I'm afraid I think we'll be too late to change the outcome for 2 Para, even if we went for it now. German strength keeps on increasing, and their anti-tank screen on the bridge's southern approach is well concealed and deadly. I've lost two tanks this morning.'

I dropped my head into my hands and spoke without thinking. 'What a bloody mess.'

Brettle was quiet for a moment. 'It's been a challenge every step of the way. We were delayed by the destruction of a key bridge at Son, down near Eindhoven. We had a hell of a job getting through Nijmegen. The 82nd have taken a battering too.'

He sighed and beckoned me out of the room into the bright light of a beautiful September morning. It seemed so peaceful. I couldn't hear any fighting. The large cluster of barns and farm buildings looked like they hadn't been touched. He lit a cigarette, looking around. 'We're on the outskirts of Driel, by the way.' Then he hung his head. 'I'm sorry, lad.' He looked me right in the eye. 'Truly, I am.'

I was taken aback. 'Why's that, sir?'

'Sorry we didn't get here sooner. We haven't reached the road bridge in Arnhem, so Operation Market Garden has in all probability failed. Sorry we couldn't get to you.' I didn't know what to say. He wasn't generally in the business of apologizing. I wasn't going to milk the moment, though. 'We can only hope that we've done some good here: every enemy killed is one less to face next time.' He paused, looking out over the countryside. 'How are the other boys from D Company, by the way? Have you seen any of them?' I shook my head. 'A fucking mess, eh?'

I nodded, at a loss what to add.

'Listen, Stokes,' he continued. 'I'm kind of stuck as to what to do with you for the time being. What about being my runner until we can get you back to England?'

'Really?' It was the last thing I was expecting.

'Sure. Besides, the regimental sergeant major would have kittens, if he saw the state you're in. Best you keep a low profile until we can get you sorted and hopefully re-equipped. He doesn't find the airborne look all that appealing.'

The next couple of days felt a little surreal. I ran errands for Brettle, but he wouldn't let me go near forward positions. He must have felt I had seen my fair share of action for the time being and that a breather would do me the world of good. Medics took care of the minor cuts and bruises I sustained when Briggs was killed by the grenade. My ears continued to throb. The medics couldn't see if they were permanently damaged, so when it was possible I would go to a field hospital in Nijmegen. Brettle continued to have arguments with the Polish on how he should best employ his men and his Sherman tanks. Sometimes the tank repair barn emptied as the arguments built to a climax. I chose to sit them out safely in the headquarters barn.

The atmosphere was pretty subdued. We never received official confirmation, but everyone knew the operation had failed, a view confirmed when what was left of 1st Airborne Division was evacuated across the river to join us. Having said a fond farewell to Dave Brettle, I joined them near Driel, feeling Elliot's absence keenly. We'd left a lot of friends on the fields and streets of Holland, and we didn't have a lot to show for it.

14
Nijmegen

The field hospital facility just south of Nijmegen was a vast city of canvas tents. In the end it wasn't my ears that took me to hospital, it was my bellyful of Rhine water. As a non-urgent case, my wait to see a doctor was delayed as the battered and broken men of XXX Corps arrived along with a steady stream of wounded and dying from the 82nd Airborne Division.

I found myself watching groups of patients in various states: broken legs in plaster, on crutches, bandages all over their heads. They were waiting patiently: smoking, chatting, never complaining. I wandered around, occasionally saying hello to a familiar face. There were Polish, British and American accents all mixed in a cacophony of noise, with men crammed into tents trying to escape the rain.

I squeezed into one tent and stepped out of the way of a lad in a wheelchair and knocked into another man on crutches. I turned to apologize and found myself looking at the profile of Captain Temple. He moved on, ignoring me. My stomach and heart leaped up to meet each other in my throat.

Outside the rain had stopped. I followed him, casually keeping my distance. I had to be conscious of my own pace. He wasn't moving very fast, and I didn't want him spooked. A pretty female nurse in American fatigues smiled at him. 'Hey, Captain Temple,' she said, 'how are you doing?'

'I'm swell, thank you, Sergeant,' he replied. 'Back to England shortly, then Stateside once I get this goddamn cast off.'

England's fine, I thought, but we'd have to see about him making it back to the United States.

She smiled warmly at him and continued on past both of us, on her rounds. Temple carried on and then disappeared inside a large tent. I made my way over to the tent and peered inside. It was lined with hospital beds. Temple shuffled over to the far left corner, to a bed enclosed by olive-drab privacy screens. He stepped between the screens, stopping only to awkwardly close them.

I made my way slowly into the ward. Most of the beds were full. A couple were pulled closer together so their occupants could play cards. A radio played tunes in the background. Cigarette smoke hung heavily in the air.

I stopped in front of Temple's screens. I could hear him whistling along to the tune on the radio. I took a deep breath and shoved my way in. He was sitting, leaning over the far side of the bed, tending to something out of my sight. 'If you want to bathe me, Sergeant,' he chuckled, 'you're gonna have to . . .' He sat bolt upright, realizing I wasn't the attractive nurse. 'What the hell is this?' he demanded, face like thunder. 'Do all you asshole Brits like causing trouble with American officers?'

'Only the ones who attack my friends.' I wasn't giving him the satisfaction of calling him 'sir'.

'I told you last time,' he protested. 'You have the wrong man. I didn't rape that broad.'

'So you remember it was rape, then.'

'Don't get wise with me, Private,' he bellowed. 'I'm just about sick of your shit. I didn't get shot down resupplying your lame asses just so I could end up getting heat for a goddamn rape in Sheen. Do you understand, Private?'

'I know it was you, you lying bastard.'

I could hear tittering and a few gasps from the other side of the screens. The other patients were getting some juicy entertainment. Temple glared straight at me. 'You don't know anything,

Private, and you're going to get busted so hard for harassing me that–'

'I never mentioned Sheen, you cocky fucker,' I interrupted, stepping closer and jabbing him in the stomach.

He kept his poker face. 'I'm gonna give you three fucking seconds to take your stinking Limey hands off me, before I have you arrested and thrown in the brig for the rest of your days, you fucking asshole.'

I was out of ammo and I knew it. I didn't have the evidence, and he wasn't about to give me any. He saw the resignation in my face and a smile split his.

'You're going to like jail, kid. Lots of your sort there. Now let me just go and find one of your superiors.'

I took a step back, cursing myself inwardly.

His smile broadened. 'You played and you lost, son. Seems you ain't got the balls for this either.' He winked. 'How are they, by the way? Still ache, do they?'

'What?'

'How're your balls, kid?'

I couldn't keep the contempt from my voice. 'So it *was* you.' My teeth ached as I spoke; I was grinding them together.

He stifled a chuckle, holding his arms out. 'Look around you, man. Nothing but death and destruction. All men want to do is fight and fuck, man. Who around here is gonna give a fuck what you tell 'em?'

I was about to finish him once and for all and damn the consequences, when the screens were pulled abruptly apart. Dave Brettle glared menacingly at him. 'How about a major, Captain?'

If Temple looked a little confused, I was just stunned.

I was trying to put the words in the right order when Brettle put me out of my misery. 'Thought I'd come and see my boys. Those ugly sods over there are from my company.' He drew an Colt automatic pistol from a holster and pointed it at the American. 'Private Stokes,

I want you to find a couple of Royal Military Police and bring them here.'

Temple rolled his eyes at Brettle. 'And what will you do with that thing, if I get up and walk out of here? You have nothing on me.'

Brettle raised his eyebrows and chin slightly. 'Captain Temple, you are under guard at gunpoint by a commissioned British officer, and as you pointed out just a moment ago, with all this death and destruction, who's gonna give a fuck what you tell 'em?'

As Temple slumped back on his bed, Brettle gave me a wink. He flicked his head. 'Haven't got all day, Rob.'

As I jogged away, all I could think about was getting home and getting word to Kate, Molly and Kirby as quickly as possible. We got him. By the love of God, we got the bastard.

EPILOGUE
The Jolly Gardeners

The train squealed and scraped its way out of Mortlake station, leaving me engulfed in its steam. As the last of the carriages passed me and the steam lifted, I was presented with a magnificent sight, one I thought I would never get to see again: Watney's brewery.

I took my time crossing the green to the Jolly Gardeners, for I needed to get all my thoughts in order before barrelling in there. I was dreading facing Kirby and Kate, not to mention Molly, after slipping away to Lincolnshire. Despite all the action I had seen, I still felt a coward.

Only two days before I had flown back to England with what was left of the British 1st Airborne Division. The parade at Fulbeck Hall had had a funereal atmosphere about it. It was truly heartbreaking to see battalions represented by maybe double figures at best. The 10th Parachute Battalion, which had taken me under its wing on the drop zone, had no officers left at all, just a handful of NCOs and private soldiers.

Major Hartley hadn't made it. His sergeant major had apparently drowned while trying to swim the Rhine, swept downstream, never to be seen again. Allan Peet and Ozzy were killed while holding their position on Oosterbeek's eastern perimeter. Matt Packham and Ronnie Marsh made it back, but only just. Their faces bore the scars of bitter close-quarters fighting, but they would live to fight another day. It was while chatting with some of the guys that I found out about the death of Tommy

Kettles – killed during shelling while I was in Arnhem. I missed Elliot too; he had been through so much, and what got to me most was that he had perished so near the end, having gone through the worst of it. Good men wasted on a futile operation. Although perhaps some good might come of their deaths. I thought back to what Dave Brettle had said: 'Every enemy killed is one less to face next time.' And there would be a next time, I was sure of that.

As I reached the Jolly Gardeners I could hear the sound of crates being shunted about in the cellar below. I tried the pub door, hoping it would be locked; I would then have time to muster the courage to come back later. It wasn't to be; the door was unlocked. I pushed my way in. Sitting in their usual corner were Wally and Bernie. They looked up from their dominoes, full of smiles. 'Hey, it's Robbie Stokes,' Wally piped up, 'back from his adventures.'

I kind of wished Wally didn't talk so bloody loud. No sooner had I put a finger to my lips for him to be quiet, than the crate-moving below stopped. Instantly, the telltale click-clack of heels began to gather momentum up the stairs. I had had moments when I was scared stiff in France and Holland, but the thought of facing Molly Gardner put the fear of God into me. She came striding into the bar, ignored me and spoke to Bernie and Wally. 'Same again, gentlemen?' She pulled two fresh pint glasses from the shelves and began to fill one with mild from a pump.

'Yes, please, Molly,' Bernie responded, standing to pull change from his pocket.

Molly waved him down, then looked at me. 'Don't you fret, Bernie. This gentleman is buying; in fact, he'll be buying for the rest of the day, for whoever is in.'

I opened my mouth to speak as she turned on me. 'Don't say a word, Robbie Stokes. When I needed you, when Kate needed you, you just fucked off into the night without a word. At first I thought something had happened, but then your mum said you'd just upped and gone. How fucking dare you, Robbie, how fucking dare you.'

'But I–'

'But what?' she ranted. 'But what? Please dazzle me with why you felt you should just vanish, thinking it would all go away and be back to normal when you come home the fucking hero. Well, guess what, Rob? It isn't. Every day I have to look at Kirby, trying not to cry. Every day I listen to that man on the phone, begging his wife to come home. Kate has been at her mum's since she got out of hospital. She can't face coming back here. It's breaking Kirby's heart . . .' Her eyes and nose ran, ruining her make-up and that gorgeous face. 'It breaks my heart.' She advanced on me. I flinched as she shoved her face into my chest. She sobbed without caring that Bernie and Wally were packing up their dominoes, making their excuses to leave. Both cut me a look that wished me luck. I closed my arms around Molly's bouncing shoulders and held her tight.

'I got him, Molly.' It was all I could think of saying. 'I got him.'

She pulled her tear-swollen face out of my chest, looking up at me. 'What? Who?'

'Troy Temple, Kate's attacker. I got him. It's over.'

Molly looked up at me, a smile appearing on her wet face. I cupped her cheeks, kissed her forehead and pulled her in tight again.

'Well, that's a start, Robbie Stokes, that's a start.'

Well Past Trouble

1
The Ardennes Forest

Cold.

It was all I could think about. It made me want to stop breathing. Each intake seemed to draw the cold down inside me, chilling my core. I was shivering despite being in full fighting gear topped off with a greatcoat. We huddled together in the back of the truck as it bumped and weaved through the darkness of the Ardennes forest. I drifted off. As we approached our destination, a small village called Tellin, a spine-shattering jolt from a pothole pulled me from my miserable slumber. The lorry ground to a halt, not for the first time. Everyone groaned. We were all dreading having to get out in the open again. My hands were still stinging with the cold from previous efforts to push the trucks out of the ditches into which they had sunk. Each time one of the vehicles got stuck, Serjeant Major Jackson organized a team for pushing duty. Jackson was no respecter of rank, everyone being expected to help out. And this time was no different, since above the howling wind, I heard shouting, cab doors being opened and slammed, then boots crunching on the frozen, snow-packed road, as they made their way to the rear of our lorry.

The back door opened. 'Serjeant Wardle?' yelled Jackson above the din of the blizzard.

'Yes, sir?' Sean responded.

'The lead truck is also stuck now, blocking the way. Get your blokes out. We march from here.'

This announcement was greeted with a mixture of groans and

ironic cheers. 'That's enough,' said Sean. 'Out. Corporal Stokes, I need them ready to march in three minutes, and if anyone's left any kit, then I'm holding you responsible.'

We clambered from our frozen mobile tomb like old men. There was general grumbling which I knew I ought to put a stop to, but I didn't. The stripes still rested strangely on my arm, and part of me still thought like a private. I turned to Private Dougie Chambers beside me. 'Fancy giving the truck a sweep for anything left, mate?' He nodded and I climbed down over the tailboard, grateful that despite my promotion we had managed to remain mates.

It hadn't been so easy with all the others. I looked over at a group casually passing cigarettes around and sighed inwardly. Another battle, another test. Part of me felt too bloody tired and cold for it, but I knew I had to confront them. Their insolence was aimed at me. 'Private Richards!' I called over at the group and they broke open, the bulky figure of Bob Richards emerging from the centre. 'Put that tab out and help Chambers sweep the truck. I don't want any equipment left behind. The rest of you, load up and get ready to move out.'

For a moment no one reacted, the scene like a movie that had stopped, and then Sean Wardle came round the side of the truck and everyone started moving at once. Bob Richards smiled as he passed me and I cursed under my breath, wishing Sean hadn't arrived. It was only going to make things harder next time.

It was January 1945 and we'd been back on the continent for a month trying to catch up with the rest of our battalion, which was being hammered by a German counteroffensive. The Germans had been retreating pretty steadily for months. Operation Market Garden around Arnhem in the Netherlands may not have succeeded, but the sheer numbers of Allied troops in France had taken their toll and forced the Germans back. But in December the Nazis had struck back through the dense Ardennes forest and fought the Allies to a standstill. And C Company of the 2nd Battalion of the Oxfordshire and Buckinghamshire Light Infantry had been called forward to help break the deadlock.

I hadn't been enthusiastic. It wasn't so much the thought of going back to the front that bothered me; it was that I wasn't going back with my old company. The battalion, with the exception of our headquarter elements consisted of four companies, A to D. I'd fought with D in Normandy and had been looking forward to being reunited with them, seeing some old friends and hearing the news. However, I'd barely had time to get my bearings after coming back from the Netherlands before Al Grimes, my old colour serjeant from Normandy, had taken me aside and explained that C Company was being sent into action and would need to be reinforced from the other companies. I was going in with them, and with a promotion to corporal. He'd said it so quickly, I hadn't time to take it in before I'd been marched off to meet my new comrades.

I don't know whether I was still sick from Arnhem, or whether it was all just too new, but I made a mess of it. I hadn't acted like a corporal, and there'd been a bad feeling from the start. Looking back, I wonder if anything I'd said would have made a difference. Some of them hadn't wanted an outsider, and they'd made that very clear from the start. After forty-eight hours of being ignored and battling for respect, I was ready to hand my stripes back, and then Serjeant Sean Wardle and Private Dougie Chambers had walked in, fresh off the train to join C Company, come to join the party and save my sanity. Suddenly, I wasn't the only new boy in a company of strangers.

2
The Fires of Bure

I tried my best to pull the collar of my greatcoat up high enough to shield my face, but the cold still stung my skin. I smiled ruefully to myself as I realized I'd take a glider drop over this any day. Visibility on the road was severely reduced. I could just make out Sean's group about twenty metres ahead as I began to hear the thunder of tank fire. I couldn't tell whether the tanks were ours.

Someone made a joke about Napoleon's retreat from Moscow, and a few of the section laughed. It sounded good, and I wished I could be a part of it, but I wasn't. Instead I growled at them to be quiet as we arrived at the outskirts of Tellin. I knew from my map that the village lay a few kilometres east of our target, Bure. The wind dropped, though the snow still fell heavy and constant. The flakes muffled sounds and there was a sense of calm about the place. We followed the main road into the centre of the village and gradually became aware of the night sky to the east glowing orange. Tracer from tank rounds and machine guns flicked skyward. It was coming from Bure and sounded like hell. The loud thuds and crumps of artillery rolled through. I could only dread what awaited us, not envying the paras there.

As we arrived in the dimly lit village square of Tellin, my stomach turned. In the semi-darkness I could just make out small groups of troops with walking wounded and carrying stretcher casualties. Dimmed by red filters, their torches guided them towards what I could only imagine was an aid station in some small shops, crude lighting set up inside. We continued on through the square, keeping to what we thought was the road, but ankle-deep slush and snow was everywhere, so it was hard to see what we were walking on.

Sean called a halt on the eastern outskirts of the village. Jeeps and universal carriers approached, bringing more wounded, and we moved into a long ditch to the left of the road, which mirrored a second ditch on the right. I flinched as tanks on open high ground began firing shell after shell into Bure. On the other side of the road, steep wooded slopes were getting hammered with artillery, but was it enemy artillery or ours?

On the road I could just make out the dark profile of two Sherman tanks. They crept forward, their tracks making one hell of a racket. One tank suddenly rocked back on its suspension in a flurry of sparks, and the deafening impact of a projectile made my ears ring. The tank began to smoulder instantly; I could see its crew bailing out. The other tank rattled back in reverse as fast as the conditions allowed. A projectile screamed in from the direction of Bure, just missing the reversing tank, before whizzing off into the unknown.

The crew of the stricken tank slid into the ditch we were shivering in. They were puffing and panting, their grimy faces gleaming with sweat. Their thick parkas and tank overalls looked a damn sight warmer than our smocks and greatcoats. They calmed their nerves with cigarettes, and we all just sat there, watching the flames take hold of their dead mount. The flames looked rather welcoming in the cold, but no one was going to approach the tank to take advantage of their warmth.

Serjeant Major Jackson appeared close to us, in the middle of the road. 'Let's get moving, C Company, we've got work to do.' He wasn't even wearing a greatcoat or gloves, just a smock over his battledress. With both hands on his Sten sub-machine gun, he didn't give as much as a shiver. I'm not sure if he was immune to the cold or just putting on a brave face for the boys, but it impressed me either way. We scrambled up from the ditch, some having to be pulled out. I slipped and a gloved hand reached down to drag me up. I couldn't see who it was, but I knew Dougie was ahead, and I wondered if perhaps I had made more friends than I thought.

The fires of Bure drew closer. Among the sound of mortar rounds smashing into the woods above us, I could now make out occasional bursts of MG 42 machine-gun fire. Ditches still ran down both sides of the road. A Sherman tank was stuck in the left-hand ditch, nose deep in sludge and snow. A further Sherman appeared on the road and both crews started to attach tow ropes to drag out the beleaguered tank. As we passed the tank crews, I could just make out the first of the outbuildings and cottages that marked the edge of Bure. The buildings didn't look in such bad shape, and I could make out red torch filters bobbing and weaving all over the place. Sean brought the column to a halt, and we instinctively sought the protection of the left-hand ditch once more.

The snow was falling even thicker, more heavily than I had ever seen before. The wind dropped to almost nothing. I could hear flames crackling and popping as they consumed a roof. The crunch of mortars still sounded in the tree canopy above us. I still had no idea who was shelling the higher ground, but there had to be someone up there. Somewhere in the village a flak gun spluttered into action. Shattering glass and the crunch of disintegrating roof tiles and masonry announced its impacting rounds. A tank shell hit, the vibration of its detonation rippling through us. So much for the rumour of the Germans being as good as finished. I heard tank tracks, slowly getting louder, but couldn't see the source of the sound.

Another universal carrier appeared, moving almost at a crawl, carrying more stretcher casualties. They were wrapped in blankets, curtains and whatever else the medics could salvage to keep them warm. Medics clung to the vehicle, each with one hand holding a plasma bottle aloft connected to a patient by a thin rubber hose. Walking wounded followed the carrier in two columns, wrapped in whatever they could find to keep the cold night out of their broken frames. Some of the wounded were German. Blood-soaked bandages were evidence we had treated them, but none had the luxury of a blanket or other covering. Berlin seemed a million miles away. I wondered if the war would ever end. Some C Company boys made their way over to the wounded, lighting cigarettes for them, often wedging the smokes between bloodied lips. None of the Germans were given cigarettes. It was a change I'd noticed since Normandy. Back then a wounded German was a fellow soldier; now he was the enemy. We'd all seen too many horrors in this war.

'Section commanders up front,' someone said, a hushed message passed from the front of the column. I scrambled out of the ditch, watching other section commanders follow suit. We followed the snow-covered road to one of the first dwellings. It appeared intact. A red glow showed from within. Around low steps on the west side of the building, facing away from the centre of Bure, I could see a small group forming. Cigarettes hung from lips, cherry glows showing in the night as long greedy pulls were taken. They constantly stamped their feet. I reflected that although our hobnail-soled combat boots weren't designed to keep out the cold, they wouldn't be heard in the snow, no matter what you did.

We joined the group. In the dim light I recognized Major Joshua High. I had learned he hailed from Eastbourne. Goodness knows how he had ended up with the Ox and Bucks, but that's war for you. The previous company commander was wounded in Normandy, so High had been shipped in from an army staff college or similar. I didn't know him all that well, but he appeared a decent sort. Despite his lack of combat experience, he seemed to go down the road of using common sense, which was fine by me. I also recognized section commanders Ray Clifton and Karlton Hill, Serjeant Major Jackson, Serjeant Wardle and Lieutenant Filler, my platoon commander, who seemed a nice enough bloke. Everyone in the platoon affectionately called him Boss. Most of the more senior men were new to C Company, most fresh from training rather than combat operations. Like D Company, C Company had taken a battering in Normandy and been pretty much recreated from scratch.

Garry Jackson waved us all in close, so Major High didn't have to shout. 'Welcome to Bure, gentlemen. We are on the German Army's western limit of exploitation. We are here to help them change direction.

'We are reinforcing 13 Para, who have been here for two days now and are starting to really feel the pinch. They are trying to dislodge some German infantry, who are supported by mobile assault guns, flak panzers and, as far as we can determine, one Tiger tank.' A low groan sounded. The company had PIAT anti-tank guns, but they were only really effective on lower-grade enemy armour. PIATs could disable assault guns and flak guns mounted on tank chassis – the flak panzers were able to angle their anti-aircraft guns down to use as devastating ground weapons – but couldn't knock out Tigers, although the concussion of a hit might be enough to encourage a Tiger crew to bail out and leg it.

Major High raised a hand for quiet. 'We are however supported by artillery, mortars and a squadron of yeomanry. At first light tanks will help us clear out Bure.' Yeomanry units were reservists. I wondered about the tank assistance, thinking he was referring to the four Sherman tanks I had seen. Although they were capable of taking on Tigers, one Sherman was burning, one was stuck in a ditch, one was engaged trying to unstick it, and the other had been in retreat. But I thought better of telling High about them. 'Mr Filler's platoon will cross the road,' he continued, 'and will move through the houses on the right. You will encounter a para platoon, which you will be relieving. They need a breather.

'The remainder of the company will stay this side of the road, moving up to just short of the S-bend in the centre of the village. The flak panzers and possibly the Tiger are really making progress difficult, so we are going to relieve the paras held up there. When first light comes, we will then push on with the tanks. Any questions?'

There were none. On the way back to the ditch, Jackson told us to have our PIATs loaded in case of a chance engagement. I heard engines roaring and tracks squealing from deep into Bure and knew he was right to warn us. I jogged back to where I'd left my section, to find only Dougie and the PIAT lads, Jack Lillie and Matt Ingall, crouched and waiting.

'Where the hell are the others?' I hissed at Dougie. He nodded over at a barn fifty yards away across a frozen field. I could just see the glowing ends of cigarettes in the doorway. 'Fuckers,' I said under my breath. Then to the two lads in the ditch, 'You boys wait here. Dougie, come with me.'

He jumped out of the ditch and we made our way across the furrows of the field.

'Maybe I'm not cut out for this, Dougie,' I said, catching my boot on a frozen clod.

He spat loudly. 'Rubbish, Robbie. You've seen more action than most of the officers around here. You've more than earned the right to your promotion.'

'These blokes don't see it that way.'

'Then make them see it, Robbie.'

'It's not that easy,' I said, thinking about my first meeting with them back in England. 'They resent us because we're outsiders and there's something else too . . .'

'Bob Richards?'

'Yeah, something's not right there.'

'He's a prick, you mean.'

I laughed. 'For sure, but he's also got their respect. They do what he says, and I've never been in a section where one private carries such weight.'

'Well, he's a good rifleman, a bit of an old hand. He wasn't always a private, of course.'

I stopped in my tracks. 'What?'

'Sure. He used to be a corporal.'

'No one told me that. What did he get busted down for?'

He shrugged. 'No one seems to know.'

'Shit,' I said. 'My job just got a whole lot harder.'

We were almost at the barn and I braced myself for another battle of wills, but as we approached, there was the high-pitched whine of incoming rounds. We hit the deck just as the shells started dropping in the field around us. I looked up just as one hit the barn square on the roof, exploding in a flash of white light. When the smoke cleared, the roof had collapsed, and the five missing men from my section were tumbling out of the door.

I ran up and grabbed two of them, yanking them outside and throwing them to the ground. 'Down!' I roared. The rest hit the deck next to Dougie and me, coughing and spluttering.

After a couple of minutes the bombardment ceased. 'Everyone all right?' I said. They all nodded. I could see they were shaken and I couldn't bring myself to give them a dressing-down. 'Right, let's get back to where we should be.'

We jogged back across the frozen ground to the ditch, where two anxious faces were waiting. I felt as though the temperature had dropped again. I squatted down close to the edge of the ditch, and my section huddled together beneath me. I relayed Major High's plan to them, signalling to Matt and Jack that their PIAT should be ready. They looked back at me sheepish and nervous. 'What?' I prompted.

Jack spoke first. 'It's seized. We can't load the thing.'

My chest tightened. 'What do you mean, seized?' I hissed. 'When was the last time you cleaned and checked it?'

'Last night,' answered Jack. 'The cold makes the oil thick and hard to work.' My anger evaporated. I knew it wasn't their fault. Oiling weapons was a problem in the cold. But I had to think fast. We didn't have time to strip and clean the PIAT. It would have to wait until we occupied our new position. But what if we had to deal with German armour before then? With no PIAT, it might not end well for us.

I looked up to see Sean crouching in the road ahead, accompanied by Lieutenant Filler. Sean gave me a wave and we moved forward, following the right-hand ditch until we reached the first cottages and outbuildings. Tracer and white-phosphorus rounds from panzers had resulted in a number of buildings catching fire. I hadn't a clue where the civilians were, but as we crept through the gardens the fires felt wonderful. It was selfish to derive comfort at the expense of someone's home, but I couldn't remember the last time I had been warm.

We came to a stop, kneeling in the snow, flames dancing all around us, our shadows looking devilish against the shattered cottage brickwork. Filler and Sean had gone on ahead, and word came down the line that we had linked up with the para platoon, who would soon be passing through us. Sean and Filler might have already discovered what we would be facing, reminding me of my section's PIAT problem. I wasn't looking forward to telling Sean about it. Following his return from hospital after being seriously injured in action, his fuse had become even shorter, so I would have to take it on the chin.

Sure enough, Sean appeared nearby with a para who was probably his opposite number, a sergeant. The para had really been through the mill. A pile of blankets loomed in a nearby garden. I realized they covered his dead. He and Sean pored over a map, discussing enemy positions; dim red torchlight highlighted their fingers pointing to features on the map. It was as good a time as any to throw my PIAT problem into the mix, so I introduced myself to the para and explained my predicament. Sean glared at me, trying his hardest not to bite my head off. 'Swap yours with ours, mate,' said the para. 'We had the same issue. The cold makes cocking the bastard even more difficult. We managed to work ours loose.'

PIATs were swapped as the para platoon moved through us. I wondered if I'd be alive to explain to our quartermaster why the serial number of the PIAT we'd taken out didn't match the number of the one coming back.

The platoon occupied the nearby dwellings. My section was positioned furthest forward, in a smashed cottage which thankfully still had its roof. Evidence of battle was all about us. Just off the front porch were a couple of German dead, covered in blankets. The section to our left overlooked the road. We had no clear view of the road; just gardens, chicken coops and outbuildings. To our immediate right a steep earth bank supported spindle-like naked trees, bowed under the weight of snow. We tried to close the window shutters to keep the wind and snow out, but they had taken some punishment and were on the verge of falling from their hinges. There were no blankets to keep us warm; they'd already been used to cover the dead.

Two of the boys kept watch while the others in the section tried to sleep. Some managed to doze; it always amazed me how some soldiers could nod off even in the most uncomfortable places. We heard a single tank round. I had no chance of getting kip in any event, having to stay awake to take messages from Lieutenant Filler's runner. The platoon had radios, but we had to save the batteries, stuffed down our smocks to keep them warm and working.

One message confirmed the Tiger tank was lurking at the far, eastern, end of the village. The tank was supported by a considerable number of infantry. A flak panzer was also spotted. There were snipers too, which had already produced casualties among the portion of the company moving up to the village centre. They also had dead and wounded from the tank round which we had heard. It wasn't a good start.

In the early hours, when the cold was at its worst, an order was passed round for a tank-stalk patrol to knock out the Tiger. I thought the Tiger was going to wait until first light, but I suppose losing some of our lads to it changed everything. The reserve section from our platoon, led by Corporal Ray Clifton, got the short straw, but they would need extra PIATs to bolster their hitting power, so I had to loan them my team.

Jack and Matt weren't impressed, grumbling and blowing warm air into their gloved hands, but they eventually appeared beyond the front porch among Ray's men. Matt and Jack had their PIAT and satchels containing projectiles for the anti-tank gun but still managed to keep both hands on their Sten guns. It would have been better if I'd been told the team for the patrol would form up within our line of fire, but war could be chaotic. We watched the patrol move away through the gardens, heading towards some smouldering houses. The rumble of an engine sounded, together with the clatter of heavy tank tracks. The tank sounded like it was very close, but distance could be deceptive at night. The patrol knelt until the sounds drifted away. As their dark profiles disappeared into the darkness, I wished them luck, hoping they'd all come back safe. Matt and Jack were the only two in my section who didn't seem to be under Richards' spell.

Time dragged. I thought I would get tired, but when you are expecting all hell to break loose, you'd be surprised how alert you stay. My Bren gun team, Andy Blackmore and Charlie Wyld, took a turn on sentry duty. Before long, they clicked their fingers, waving me over to their window. Charlie held out his hand to hush me. 'Look,' he whispered.

I couldn't see or hear anything. Then, through the darkness, I just made out a lone figure outside. My stomach tightened. Andy pulled the Bren into his shoulder. The figure had its arms outstretched in a cross, a rifle in its left hand. The snow had stopped falling. The figure moved slowly towards us, and I gradually recognized the profile of a British helmet. 'Hold it there,' warned Charlie. 'State your name.'

'Clifton, corporal, C Company.'

'How many in your group?' pushed Charlie. It was just possible Ray had bought it, an enemy assuming his identity to gain entry to the cottage.

'Twelve.' I quickly ran the numbers through my cold, sleep-deprived brain. His section made eight, and he had two extra PIAT teams, which made twelve.

'Advance,' Charlie confirmed.

As the soldier below moved forward, I was able to recognize him as Ray. Joining us, he patted me on the shoulder, the patrol beginning to follow him in. 'No kill then, Ray?' I asked, just able to hear the sound of a distant tank.

He shook his head. 'Couldn't get anywhere near it without taking a big risk. Besides, we couldn't locate their infantry. Just wasn't worth taking a chance.'

At first light a message from Major High confirmed that, as originally planned, yeomanry Sherman tanks would support a C Company advance through the village. We got some tea on the go – good to keep warm, even better for settling pre-battle nerves.

Shermans began to sound from our rear, engines throbbing, waiting for us to begin the advance. Filler briefed everyone. Our platoon was to clear all the houses and outbuildings on the right-hand side of the road. The Shermans would be a short distance behind, and would only be called forward if we came up against a problem, such as German armour or a strongpoint. We needed to clear the buildings quickly, since we had to keep up with another platoon, which would be clearing the buildings on the left-hand side of the road. A whistle blast would signal the start of the advance.

After Filler left, no one talked. We sat there, shivering and waiting. I heard the tank engines gunning. The whistle blew. We clambered to our feet, groaning like old men, but moved into the gardens with purpose. I didn't think the first cottage, just beyond ours, would be occupied, doubting the Germans would have been able to sneak in during the night. Strands of wire and fences made keeping any formation difficult, my section more or less in single file. I noticed Karl Hill's section was also struggling. Despite the cold, I was already starting to perspire. Matt and Jack actually vaulted a fence with their PIAT, puffing and cursing as they went. It was no easier for Andy, lugging the Bren.

Chris Lenor, one of my riflemen, slipped arse over tit on a sheet of ice and got himself caught on a rickety fence. I helped free him of it and, having navigated the first set of fences and wire, we fanned out. But we had lost pace with Karl's section. Filler became animated, urging us along. Karl's section reached a building. I was within thirty metres of the first cottage. Andy and Charlie scampered ahead of me, mounting the Bren on top of a log pile. We were going to do things properly, even though I thought the place was empty.

We reached the cottage. I waved the rest of my section to stack up one behind the other along the back wall; Chris and my other rifleman Peter May in front of me, my lance corporal Stephen Cooper accompanied by Charlie and Andy immediately behind me, with Jack and Matt bringing up the rear, since the PIAT more than likely wouldn't be needed inside. I followed Chris and Peter along the wall, everyone keeping their head beneath the window ledge, below the view of any Germans that might be inside.

I gave Chris a thumbs up. He carefully leaned across the hinge side of the small back door and grasped its handle. With a twist, there was a loud click, and the door creaked open. He gingerly stepped across the threshold – no nonsense about kicking the door in, since there was no indication it had been locked or chained, and the noise might give away our position.

I followed Chris into a kitchen, fighting to adjust my eyes from the bright snow-covered gardens to the dark interior. No Germans. Peter swept past me and an exposed wooden staircase, peering carefully around a door connecting to the next room. He disappeared from view; obviously no Germans in there. I returned to the back door and waved the others to join us inside. Chris was poised, ready to climb the stairs. Hoping my initial instinct about the place being empty was correct, I gave him a nod. Each stair creaked and cracked, sounding almost unnaturally loud. With every step I expected the walls around us to burst with rounds from German weapons.

Nearby, I could hear breaking glass and shouting. In contrast to my section, Karl's men were evidently smashing their way through the place next door. Ahead of me, Chris reached the top of the stairs, peered into a room on the right, then disappeared into it. Following Chris upstairs, I saw two further closed doors on the left of a short landing. My stomach turned over. Chris rejoined me. I thought he had pushed his luck far enough, so called Peter up to open the next door. We all breathed a sigh of relief as we looked in on another empty room. I hadn't felt this nervous since the Arnhem operation. It didn't seem to get any easier. I wondered if I should have joined the navy, not the infantry. There was just one door left to go.

Machine-gun fire suddenly rippled, fast and constant. Ricochets flicked off roof tiles above us. 'Contact!' yelled an excited voice downstairs. Bren bursts began to chug. I lurched straight through the last door, all thoughts of the room being occupied by Germans pushed to the back of my mind. The room was empty. I rushed to a small net-curtained window, crouching before peering outside. Below, I saw Karl's section had been caught in the open and some of his men were now pinned down behind an outbuilding. Two were lying motionless in the snow, crimson stains spreading below them. There was a burst of machine-gun fire from a two-storey house opposite and I looked over to see the flash of a MG 42 muzzle. The enemy rounds splashed and flicked around Karl's section. I realized at least one of those lying out in the snow was wounded, still alive. He struggled to move, but a burst of pink mist indicated a hit to his buttock. Above the din of the MG 42, I heard his mates screaming at him to stay still.

From downstairs, members of my section engaged the enemy with Sten and rifle fire. I heard Chris and Peter firing from the next room. But the MG 42 kept going. I knew I had to do something quick to stop it. 'Andy, get up here, now,' I roared. I just heard an acknowledgement above the gunfire. Andy and Charlie came bounding up the stairs, the legs of the Bren splayed, ready for action. I swept trinkets from a table beneath the window. 'Top right window opposite,' I boomed.

Without hesitation, Andy positioned the Bren on the table, crouching to fire short controlled bursts at the window sheltering the German machine gun. The right edge of the frame surrounding the window burst and splintered, but the MG 42 continued to spray Karl's section with long greedy licks. 'Got the bastard!' bellowed Andy as the MG 42 stopped firing. But then it started up again and he swore.

I decided to call up my PIAT team to put an anti-tank round through the window, but Lieutenant Filler's voice called out from downstairs. 'Corporal Stokes?'

'Yes, sir?' I shouted.

'Come here, I need your help.'

I found him at the front door. About fifty metres away a Sherman tank sat throbbing, its crew squinting at me, cigarettes hanging from their lips. 'Put these boys to work, will you?' asked Filler, patting my shoulder. 'You know what needs to be done.'

A tank was just the ticket. I legged it to the tank and got a thumbs up from its commander to climb aboard. His chevrons told me that he was a sergeant. As I reached the turret, he pulled off his headset, then offered me a cigarette. I declined, since I didn't smoke. 'MG 42, top right window opposite,' I explained loudly over the engine rumble, pointing at the shattered window frame.

Wire fences and outbuildings lay between us and the house. The commander shook his head. 'You're gonna have to cut the wire.'

I couldn't understand why. It was just wire, we had a tank, and surely he could engage the MG 42 from where we were. 'Are you taking the piss?' I ranted, losing it. 'We've got wounded in the open.'

'We need to get closer. And you'll have a tank stuck in the open if we get wire caught in our running gear.' I could feel rage boiling up inside me, but before I could explode, he flipped open one of his storage bins and handed me some sorry-looking wire cutters. I snatched them, deciding to have words with him later.

I ran forward at a crouch, waiting for the sound of the MG 42 opening up. My jaw was tensed so tight that it ached by the time I reached the wire and began snipping. After a few snips, the commander waved me out of the way. He powered through the outbuildings, firing his machine gun as he went. I stuffed the wire cutters down my smock and ran back to my section.

Andy had stopped firing, content to watch the tank commander finish off the MG 42. Hopefully, it was dead. Below us, smoke grenades covered Karl's section as they dragged their wounded back to the house they had taken. Through the smoke, long smears of blood appeared in the snow. My ears popped. A high-pitched whine announced the Sherman following its machine-gun fire with a tank round. The back of the room housing the MG 42 burst, its contents falling into a garden. The MG 42 was definitely toast now, the thatched roof of the house on fire. The Sherman put a shell through the ground floor for good measure, easing my anger towards the tank commander, but then I noticed two white-clad German infantry, a Panzerschreck team. The Panzerschreck was a shoulder-launched anti-tank gun, much more powerful than our PIAT.

'Panzerschreck left,' I screamed as I pulled my Lee-Enfield rifle quickly and clumsily into my right shoulder, squeezing off a round, the first I'd shot since I arrived in the Ardennes. Pink mist registered a shoulder hit. The man supporting the soldier with the Panzerschreck spun down into the snow. The man with the anti-tank gun dropped to one knee, taking aim at the Sherman. I couldn't work my rifle bolt quickly enough, and his rocket zoomed away. There was an almighty thud as the projectile hit its mark, a huge flurry of sparks raining across the gardens. I heard the scraping and grinding of metal on metal as the tank ground its way back in reverse, smoke already billowing from its hatches.

Before I could establish if the crew had got out of the Sherman, or think about assisting them, my attention was caught by German infantry scurrying out of the house hit by the tank. 'Enemy front!' came an excited scream from downstairs. I fed and fired my rifle as fast as I could, aiming at the white-clad Germans as they sought fighting positions. The rest of my section opened up. Some of the enemy who were hit stayed down; others managed to scramble into cover. Grenades were lobbed outside, detonating huge plumes of snow, turf and split timber.

A sharp crack sounded behind me. I spun. A bullet had whizzed past my head to smash a framed picture on the wall. 'We've been spotted,' said Charlie, stating the bloody obvious. We crouched a little lower, halting our fire for now and hoping the rest of the section would take care of the remaining enemy.

'Rob? Robbie?' The voice had come from downstairs.

'Hang on, I'm coming,' I yelled back. I gave Andy and Charlie a pat on the shoulders and headed out of the room, keeping as low as I could. German rounds were penetrating the upper floor, coating me in brick dust, masonry and wallpaper. I peered down, seeing Ray Clifton crouching at the bottom of the stairs.

Ray gave me a thumbs up. 'Boss wants me to clear that house in front of you, the one that's been giving us all the trouble.' I nodded, beginning to make my way down the stairs. Enemy rounds shot through the ground floor, shattering the banister above his head. He flinched, holding his face. I held my breath, fearing he'd been hit, but he removed his hand, revealing no blood. 'Stay here,' he said. 'You and Coops help us clear the gardens.' I'd forgotten all about Stephen Cooper, my second-in-command, but judging by the fire support we'd had from downstairs, he must have kept everything in order. I wondered if he should be leading the section, not me.

I scrambled back to Andy and Charlie. The Germans outside were now shooting at someone else. I heard them scream orders at each other. The two-man Panzerschreck team were now a bloody heap, face down in the snow. The odd grenade thudded in the gardens. Andy got the Bren back up and firing, Charlie snapping off rounds with his Lee-Enfield. An enemy soldier dashed from cover in an attempt to retrieve the Panzerschreck, but was cut down. Around the gardens others were hit: some limping away to cover, some sprawling in the snow, turning it red as their lives faded away.

A volley of grenades arced across the gardens. As they detonated, Ray's section came sprinting out. The enemy infantry dashed back to their house, but most were felled. A few stood up, trying to surrender, but were also cut down in the hail of fire coming from Ray's section and my boys. Ray's boys then used grenades to clear the enemy from the building.

All things considered, Ray's section hadn't fared too badly. Two of them had been bashed up in the house, one wounded by grenade splinters, the other catching a round in his left thigh. Karl's two lads hit outside were shot up pretty bad, but were stable; they wouldn't be playing football any time soon.

Sean appeared with Major High, Lieutenant Filler and Serjeant Major Jackson. We were to take a breather while our artillery hammered the Germans at the other end of the village. My section could have done with some more ammunition, but the reserve platoon couldn't risk trying to cross the road to resupply us. Jackson advised us to husband our ammo and use any German weapons we found. Lieutenant Filler was all for using enemy weapons, but Sean wasn't keen. Although we had used German weapons a lot in Normandy, the distinctive sound of some enemy guns, particularly the MG 42, risked attracting friendly fire.

Once our artillery stopped, Filler ordered my section forward to continue the clearance of the village. We would work the right-hand side of the road, Ray's section assisting us. Given its mauling in the gardens, Karl's section would now be in reserve.

In the first house my section entered we found a full coffee pot deserted by the Germans. The coffee tasted awful but was better than nothing. Only afterwards did it occur to me that they might have poisoned it. One window overlooked the road running through the village. Many of the cottages were smouldering. Beyond an intersection with a minor street, the road veered off to the right and out of sight. Some dead Germans lay on the road, some covered in white sheets. A smouldering Sherman sat at the intersection. It looked like the tank had been there a little while, perhaps since before we arrived. One of its crew members lay on the rear engine deck as if asleep. No one had risked going out there to retrieve him. It began to snow, fat flakes soon resting on his body. I realized he was the only British soldier I could see outside. The view of the road made me rather sad, so peaceful yet violent in equal measure. The sadness was compounded by the loneliness of the body on the tank. I wondered again when the madness of the war would end.

'Corporal Stokes?' The voice snapped me out of it. I spun round to find Lieutenant Filler kneeling with his radio operator in the doorway. Keeping low, I made my way over to them. Filler glanced out of the window. 'Just beyond those forward houses,' he began, 'we have reports of a broken-down panzer supported by another. Company Headquarters also reports infantry in the road. We are to push forward and make sure their infantry don't get established. Prepare to move, but wait for my whistle, as we have another Sherman moving up the road to support you. The platoon across the road won't stay level with you because the left-hand side of the road will soon be visible to the panzers round the corner up ahead. We need to hit the panzers hard, understood?'

I heard the clatter of tank tracks behind us, together with the rumble of an engine. The supporting Sherman came to a halt on the road. I ordered my section to get ready to advance, instructing Jack and Matt to stay close to me so I could get them to work as soon as we saw the panzers. Not that they'd be able to do too much if one of the panzers turned out to be a Tiger. 'We've got Germans moving about in the houses out front,' advised Stephen. I looked through the window. He was right. I could see movement inside more than one house. My stomach turned once more. Filler's radio operator reported the movement.

Suddenly Ray's section opened fire from a nearby house. There would be no need for Filler's whistle, but I thought we should sit tight until he ordered us to move. The Sherman rumbled forward, spraying machine-gun fire. The tank commander took no chances, following up with tank rounds. The Germans in the buildings were taking a hiding. I thought most would have retreated, since to stay would mean certain death. The Sherman stopped firing.

Filler ordered us forward. We legged it through gardens, trying to close the distance to the buildings hit by the Sherman quickly, in order to prevent any enemy survivors escaping.

The house we arrived at had no front wall. Part of the upper floor had collapsed into the kitchen. We found a couple of German dead. A third was rolling around on the hall floor, groaning and cursing. We roughly searched him, ensuring he was unarmed. He didn't appear badly injured; the concussion of the tank rounds had probably taken it out of him. We decided to leave him to it. I took a few blokes upstairs to ensure the place was clear. As I darted back downstairs, I cursed myself for not checking whether it was possible to see around the corner beyond the intersection. Lieutenant Filler and his radio operator caught up with us. Filler decided that Karl's reserve section would take care of the injured German until medics from Serjeant Major Jackson's group arrived and directed his radio operator to make the necessary call.

The Sherman rumbled forward again, its machine gun firing, rounds hitting houses on the other side of the road. The area was crawling with German infantry, some in white, some in field grey. Then I heard a high-pitched whine and barely had time to duck before a huge bright yellow flash exploded around me. As my vision swam back into focus, I made out muffled shouting and the faint popping of weapons firing. There was a God-awful engine roar and the squealing and grinding of metal on metal. My stomach turned at the thought that we'd lost another Sherman, but as the dust cleared it was still in one piece, but a white-hot gouge smouldered across its front armour. The Germans had bloodied its nose good and proper. The turret crew were busy trying to pull the driver out of his seat.

I became aware of PIAT anti-tank gun fire, but I had no idea who was responsible. The whole operation had become a mess. I knew I needed to get on top of things, so I ran back upstairs and peered out of the window at the unfolding scene. What I saw gave me a hell of a fright. Beyond the intersection I saw two Tiger tanks, not one. Both were almost stationary. The nearer tank was smouldering slightly, a large black scar on the side of its turret. The further tank was just beginning to pull the stricken one backwards using tow ropes. But, even more concerning, a mass of German infantry, probably many more than a company, was swarming all over the road, many firing bursts at Ray's section.

I jogged back downstairs to report to Filler. His face fell as he heard what was coming down the road. 'Well, that changes things, doesn't it?' he said, sucking air through his teeth. 'We're going to be outnumbered pretty quickly at this rate. Right, Corporal Stokes, prepare to withdraw. Back to our previous positions.'

Messages were sent out to Ray's section to withdraw and to Karl's reserve section to cover us. We left as we'd arrived, evacuating the houses one by one. It was a bitter blow, giving up what we'd fought so hard for, but by the time we'd got back to the cottages everyone was dead on their feet and glad of the respite.

The next morning we fell back on Tellin and in the town centre we ran into our paras coming the other way. Major High was there as well and climbed up on a trough to congratulate us on a job well done. 'Lads, it may feel like you're back where you started, but you've given the Germans a damn bloody nose and what's more you've given these para boys a chance to regroup. The enemy will think twice before coming on, and that's enough for now. Furthermore, I think I'm permitted to tell you that, if what I've been hearing is right, there's a major operation being planned back home and you boys could be a part of it. I can't say more now, but for the moment your front-line duties here are done and you will be retiring to the Netherlands.'

The relief was instantaneous. There were some cheers and laughter as the stress of the last thirty-six hours ebbed away. People formed into groups, sharing cigarettes and chatting, and I suddenly felt the loneliness of my position. I turned and walked away from the square. There was an old church up on the hill and I wandered towards it. I kicked a stone along the road, considering the stupidity of my situation. Here I was, a veteran of three campaigns and confident in my abilities to take on the German Army, yet completely at a loss to know how to deal with my own side. I was lost in thought as I turned a corner and found myself face to face with Bob Richards. The encounter was so unexpected I just froze, and he grinned. 'Out walking on your own? Best watch out for yourself. Lots of enemy about, you know.'

I shook my head. 'Why do you seem to hate me so much, Private? Is it because you wanted these stripes for yourself?' I tapped my upper arm.

His smirk disappeared. 'Our previous section commander had his head blown off in Normandy. He was one of us. A man we respected and a leader we could follow. Respect's important, wouldn't you say? Some earn it and some don't.'

I looked him up and down. 'And, let me guess, you think you've earned it, Private?'

He didn't answer but stepped closer, towering over me.

I tried to keep my voice level as I continued. 'Perhaps you had it, Private, back when you wore these stripes, but you don't have them anymore, which means I don't give a fuck what you think. I'm commander of this section now, and if you don't like it, then tough. You may not think I can lead, but I tell you what: we're at war and I know how to fight. And when we're next facing a Tiger, you'll find that's worth a lot more than respect. Either you follow me and learn how to kill Germans or you'll die. Your choice.'

'Fine words, but you're forgetting one thing: according to the major, we ain't facing any more Tigers nor anything else for a while, so we'll see where your famous fighting skills get you in the meantime, hey?' And with that he sidled away, a smug lop-sided grin on his face.

3
Hamminkeln Glider Landing

The men of C Company of the 2nd Battalion of the Oxfordshire and Buckinghamshire Light Infantry were crammed into an aircraft hangar, much like when we were briefed for our first glider assault into Normandy – which felt like a lifetime ago. An operational name was written on a large wooden board: Varsity. On the floor bedsheets hid what I knew were clay models of the terrain we were about to be tasked to attack.

The company commander, Major Joshua High, appeared behind the models in the hangar, flanked by his second-in-command and serjeant major. The bedsheets were carefully lifted. A buzz of excitement and speculation swept around the hangar. I was impressed with the magnificent models – the fine detail of the terrain, its features and contours. Indeed, you could be forgiven for thinking you were looking down at the real landscape from a lofty position in the clouds.

One model showed the area of the operation in general; the other was a more detailed representation of the smaller zone containing the opening objectives for C Company. The first showed part of Nazi Germany; to the north was the town of Rees, to the south the city of Wesel. A broad length of blue fabric represented the river Rhine, with the town of Xanten on its south bank, and on the north bank the village of Diersfordt along with its large forest. Our focus would be Hamminkeln and Ringenberg, judging by the level of detail modelled around them: bridges, road junctions, a train station on the outskirts of Hamminkeln, and even a long broad piece of grey fabric indicating an autobahn under construction bisecting the two towns.

'Gentlemen,' Major High began, 'you are about to receive orders for Operation Varsity, an assault beyond the Rhine deep into Nazi Germany. We are going all in, and hell is coming with us.'

I heard plenty of mutterings about the war definitely being over by Christmas. I couldn't help but chuckle to myself. That's what they said last Christmas.

Operation Varsity was under way. I was sweating buckets in my fighting gear. The glider was packed with my section and a forward observation party from the Royal Artillery. The job of the observers would be to call in fire from Allied guns sited west of the Rhine. The primary objective of the 2nd Battalion of the Oxfordshire and Buckinghamshire Light Infantry was to secure the northern flank of a German town called Hamminkeln, just north-east of the Rhine, the flank being defined by the river Issel. Hamminkeln was almost forty kilometres from the Dutch border. The battalion was to secure vital links on or close to the Issel: a road bridge, a railway bridge, the local station and a key road junction. Its second objective was to protect units belonging to our parent 6th Airborne Division, as they used these links to pass into the town, by preventing enemy forces moving along the riverbanks. Once the Hamminkeln area was secure, the links would be used by elements of the main Allied force coming across the Rhine and commencing a final push east to Berlin, some five hundred kilometres to the east.

The mission of C Company was to capture and hold the railway bridge. Worryingly, the whole thing reminded me of Arnhem. We were to hold until relieved by units of the main force. Deep in enemy territory, there was a risk of us becoming trapped in a *kessel*, a fire pocket, our perimeter becoming ever smaller until we were pushed back into the Rhine.

Our glider drifted quietly and sedately behind our towing aircraft, a Dakota. The flight had been uneventful. My section had managed to keep airsickness at bay, but the Royal Artillery hadn't been so lucky, the aircraft reeking of cigarette smoke and vomit. The glider pilots were not sympathetic, shouting back that the artillery weren't of the same calibre as airborne forces.

'Get ready, boys,' yelled one of the pilots. 'We've got flak.' Many had been too nervous or ill to sleep, but those who had managed it were nudged awake.

The officer in charge of the artillery boys clambered over bundles of ammunition to reach the cockpit. He shook his head. Whatever he saw through the daylight outside, it didn't look good, and he cursed. I caught his attention. He spoke into my ear: 'The landing zones are covered in smoke. I couldn't see the ground properly.' He found his seat, slumped into it and secured his harness.

'Flak,' cried a pilot. The wooden glider airframe flinched and creaked, bobbed and weaved. I hated this part. The tow rope to the Dakota had been released, and we were about to swoop down to the landing zone. The looks on some of the boys' faces gave away their fear.

'Stand by.' Another warning from the cockpit. We lost altitude. My stomach lurched up into my chest, a sensation I doubted I would ever get used to. We banked violently right, almost to the point where the blokes sitting opposite were above me. I prayed the pilots wouldn't let the thing flip over. I had been through so much and didn't want to go out like this.

The glider levelled out and began a shallow dive to the left. I craned to look through the cockpit windows, but all I could see was smoke. 'Brace!' A scream from the cockpit. The nose lifted. *Please don't break up on landing, please.* I felt the wheels touch down but lose contact with the ground straight away. The glider then hit the ground a little harder. The nose came down, but just when

I thought we had landed safely, there were awful grinding and tearing sounds beneath me. The aircraft lurched to the right, then violently to the left, suddenly dropping a few feet. We had lost our undercarriage. Now belly down, we ground to a sudden stop, perhaps in less than two lengths of the glider. The stop winded me, and a few of the boys gasped.

The landing was over. It had been relatively good, as they go, but my relief was short-lived as tracer ripped through the fuselage. Jesus, I thought, here we go again! Nobody was hit, but a mad scramble to get out of the glider began, the artillery officer getting rough with the rear door.

In a mad rush we all piled out into dazzling sunshine. To our horror, we were in the middle of a flat open field, with no real cover. The area was criss-crossed with wire-strand fences and dead cattle. The bass drumbeat of anti-aircraft fire dominated the landing zone. More tracer rounds sliced through the glider. Everyone dived to the ground. The glider began to smoulder. I tried to get my bearings, but any landmarks were blocked by the wreckage of the other gliders around us.

The tracer intensified. We had to get away from the area. I knew all my section and the artillery lads had got out of the glider but couldn't account for the pilots. I stood, managing to get a view of the cockpit. Close to me, through the windows, I saw one pilot helping the other out of his harness. They noticed me, waving me away.

The windows burst inward with a massive thud. I dropped to the ground, ears ringing. Just above me, the nose of the glider disintegrated as round after round smashed into it. I couldn't be sure the pilots were dead but assumed they had not survived. Smoke began billowing from the glider. I remembered the ammunition bundles strapped to the floor. We had to move away, now.

'Follow me.' It was the artillery officer. He was crawling towards a distant series of low-lying buildings, smoke rising from all of them. With not much else on, I motioned everyone to follow him.

On our bellies, we couldn't return fire. To stand up was suicide, bullets whizzing over our heads. The odd dips in the ground weren't deep enough to take cover in. I watched numerous gliders swoop in on their final approach. Incoming fire turned one to matchwood. It cartwheeled away, out of sight. Others landed, smouldering from the impact of high-explosive cannon fire. The night-time glider landings in Normandy hadn't been without losses, but to land in broad daylight without support at the drop zone was pure madness.

We approached three dead cows. 'Get behind the cattle,' I shouted. 'Now!' They offered a semblance of protection; you could use them to hide even if they wouldn't stop a bullet. I crawled behind them with a few blokes, but we didn't even know which direction the enemy fire was coming from. Sweating, my chest heaving, I took greedy gulps from my water bottle. I realized my section were all with me. They all drank, some even lighting cigarettes. In the circumstances I wasn't going to chastise them for smoking while under fire. I felt sorry for Matt Ingall and Jack Lillie, who had lugged the PIAT anti-tank gun while crawling. Similarly, Andy Blackmore and Charlie Wyld had hauled the Bren.

Peter May held up a hand. 'I can hear a motorbike.' I could just make out its engine. I knew certain units in 6th Airborne Division used motorcycles, but when the rippling of an MG 42 reached my ears, I guessed the bike wasn't a British vehicle.

I carefully got up on my knees, peering over the top of a cow. Amid the ruined gliders, I could make out two motorbikes, both fitted with sidecars. The crews were skidding and weaving through the glider wrecks, shooting our boys with mounted MG 42s. Both bikes came closer. We didn't have time for precise orders. I got to my feet and aimed my Lee-Enfield at the centre of mass of the lead bike. I saw my round hit its rider behind the handlebars, already working the bolt for the next shot. I had given away our position behind the cows, but before the bikes could retaliate, a hail of Sten, Bren and rifle fire from my section and the artillery stopped them in their tracks, riders and gunners exploding in a burst of red and grey mist. My second shot had hit the rider of the rear bike. Both bikes rolled to a stop, engines coughing and spluttering for the last time. One of the artillery lads ran out and fired short controlled bursts into the lifeless crews. The riders jerked as they fell behind their handlebars, machine gunners flinching in the sidecars. The artilleryman quickly searched the bodies, coming up with binoculars and two maps.

As he passed his prizes to his officer, I tried to work out where we were on my map. I thought a distant church spire was in Hamminkeln, meaning the town was south-east of us. Three hundred metres to the north, the burning buildings were the train station. We were in the wrong area – D Company's landing zone, not ours – but I couldn't see anyone from D Company moving about. I tried to compose myself. In the distance I noticed an anti-aircraft gun stop firing, grenades exploding at its base, small-arms fire crackling and rattling.

I shouted my findings regarding our location to the artillery officer. He had come to the same conclusion. We agreed to make our way to the station and then follow the railway line to the C Company landing zone. I knew the move to the station would be a nut-buster. There was no real cover, our only option being to move from glider to glider, but the first glider was seventy metres away. I could see some dead among its wreckage.

We moved at a rushed crouch to the wrecked glider. Incoming fire had all but ceased, the odd round snapping through. The glider was a mess. It had broken up on landing, raked by flak or machine-gun fire. The dead were from our battalion. I tried to keep my curiosity from getting the better of me. I wanted to see if I knew any of them, but now wasn't the time. It was a real horror show, some of the boys still strapped inside the glider. One had taken a direct hit from a shell burst. I could see the pulverized pilots in what was left of the cockpit. I didn't think anyone had got out.

The next wreck was another fifty to seventy metres away. It looked in better shape, but an artillery radio operator vomited when he saw the dead. I waved everyone on to the next glider. It had been hit by ground fire, but there was no trace of any dead, trapped troops or crew. Blood was evident, but I could tell they had evacuated their casualties.

'Boys, over here,' someone shouted. My head swivelling, I tried to identify who it was. I saw a hand waving from what I could only assume was a ditch. The hand became a head and torso. I could tell the soldier wasn't German, so I waved everyone over to him. The ditch was shallow but easily good enough to shelter everyone from the glider we had just checked. My section and the artillery blokes joined them. They were from the Royal Ulster Rifles. Although they were part of 6th Airborne Division, the soldier explained their landing had been messed up.

I found Dougie next to me and he handed me his water bottle. 'Welcome to Germany,' I joked, taking a swig gratefully. 'Just once I'd like to land among friendlies.' He laughed, and I turned to look around. The Ulster lads were in the process of getting a wounded man ready to move. I offered medical assistance, but he refused the offer. He had copped a fragment of flak in the arse, and when they got home they were going to tell all the Belfast girls that he got a splinter up his bum. It created a chuckle. All the wounded man could do was soak up the banter and give us all the middle finger. My section got another cigarette on the go, and to be fair I didn't blame them.

I wished the Ulster boys all the best and said I'd look forward to a beer in Berlin with them. My section and the artillery lads moved towards the train station. Each glider we encountered was more heart-breaking than the last. Already, it seemed, the landing forces had taken heavy losses all round.

As we neared the station buildings, I made out gunfire and shouting. Tracer snapped past us, high right. I waved everyone onto their bellies. There was fighting in the station, and I didn't want us walking into a crossfire. The artillery officer crawled up next to me, fishing his binoculars from his smock. He put them to his eyes, beginning a running commentary. 'Friendlies moving about. Grenades being thrown.' The thuds of their detonations reached our ears. 'Friendlies carrying casualty out of the main building. Shooting, plenty of shooting.'

If we were to support our men in the station, hooking up with them where they were taking their casualties would be a good start. I spun away from the artillery officer, rolling back to my section. 'Listen up, boys,' I began. 'We've got friendlies in contact at the train station. Follow me. No shooting unless you can be certain it's enemy. We've got men all over the place at the moment. Any questions?'

There were none. I clambered to my feet and shuffled towards the station. It wasn't long before I saw a casualty being placed on the ground among the others. Those around the casualties waved me in with a real sense of urgency. My section must have been watching because they soon skidded in beside me, sweating like bulls. 'Who are you people?' the harsh southern accent of a serjeant demanded.

'Corporal Stokes, C Company, Ox and Bucks.'

He held out his hand. 'Hello, mate, and thanks for lending us a hand. I'm Bob Castle, D Company.' I took his hand. 'We've got a glider crash-landed in the middle of the bloody station platforms,' he explained. 'Many dead in the glider wreckage, but there are also wounded. The Germans are in the main building, trying to stop us taking it, but have men on the far platform too. Serjeant Major Grimes and his lads are in the middle, trying to sort out the wounded from the glider and get them evacuated. I heard more shouts, German voices. They sounded close. 'There's a lumber yard behind the far platform,' continued Bob. 'I've got some men off to the left, so the enemy don't try and sweep round behind us. I need you lot to clear the main building. The whole station is a mess. There are two wrecked engines and smashed-up carriages in there as well.'

'Who do you have in the main building?'

'One section of six. Their wounded are out here with me. I need you to reinforce them. They have no commander, I'm afraid.'

I knew it was going to end up in a messy fight, having experienced my fair share of them. I warned my section to expect close combat and have grenades ready to use. I wanted Matt and Jack behind me, with the PIAT ready to fire, since I planned to fire an anti-tank round at the Germans in the main building. Andy and Charlie would be on our right flank, so their Bren could take care of any Germans trying to reinforce the building from the far platform. After the PIAT strike, the Bren could also kill any enemy falling back towards the lumber yard.

We cautiously approached the main building of the train station. We made it to the doorway then heard all hell break loose inside. Rounds burst through interior walls, the concussion of a grenade blowing out the last of the windows, making my ears ring. We heard rifle and Sten fire, along with shouting in English and German.

After what sounded like a short but savage fight, English profanity prevailed, followed by silence. 'Friendlies,' I chanced. 'We are coming to you.'

'OK, stay low,' replied a voice. 'Have you got a Bren or something with you?'

'Yeah. Do you want my Bren team first?'

'Yeah. I need them covering across the rail line; enemy keep reinforcing themselves.'

I sent Andy and Charlie forward. A couple of D Company soldiers met them, gesturing them into position before disappearing.

I led the rest of my section inside. The two soldiers reappeared, taking us towards what appeared to be the station tea room. A space behind it might have been a large larder or a small waiting room. The coffee machine in the tea room looked a little sorry for itself, punctured many times during the fighting. The furniture was all but destroyed. The main counter looked like a sieve, but a glass vase of flowers on top remained unscathed. Such simple beauty.

'The enemy keep reinforcing,' one of the soldiers explained, 'trying to clear us out. There are blokes out there in the wreckage of a glider. If the Germans clear us out, they'll be trapped, along with Serjeant Major Grimes and his boys, who are trying to rescue them.'

I found Andy and Charlie overlooking a maze of twisted rails. Among the rails I could see Grimes and his men, slowly getting the wounded out of a glider. Train wreckage surrounded them. A steam locomotive was jack-knifed across the rails, carriages piled all around it. The rear coaches were crushed under the smashed carcass of another engine, which had clearly been travelling on another line. It looked as though a crash had been caused by the station being bombed some time ago. Landing on the wreckage had done the glider no favours, but the debris was actually providing it with cover from most directions.

A commotion in the direction of the tea room caught my attention. I briefly glimpsed the profile of a German soldier behind the counter. I had no idea where the non-PIAT members of my section were, or the two soldiers from D Company who had guided us in, but they weren't nearby so I wasn't about to wait for the enemy to kick off. I lobbed a grenade over the counter. As it clattered and rolled into the space, I heard hysterical German voices. Loud grunts echoed with the concussion of the explosion. 'PIAT, now!' I roared over my shoulder, my voice muffled in my ringing ears.

Matt Ingall stood up. He fired an anti-tank projectile through the tea room and into the room beyond. An almighty bang followed, the concussion of the detonation rippling through the shattered building, making me feel like I had been kicked in the nuts and knocking me over. The vase of flowers shattered. Hearing what sounded like Bren-gun fire, I was on my feet straight away, Lee-Enfield in my shoulder. I moved into the tea room, picking my way through the debris strewn across the floor, before kicking down the remains of the wooden partition that had separated it from the room behind. This was wrecked: scorched wallpaper, furniture shattered and smouldering, framed pictures burst.

I encountered two Germans. They were still alive, but looked really banged up. Their filthy hands were palms uppermost, signalling they were no longer a threat. My blood was up, and if the boys in my section hadn't appeared, I would have shot them out of hand. Even though we had lost so many men on the landing ground, I had to control my temper now I was in command. I knew at least one German had escaped the room, because a blood trail led outside. I moved cautiously to the back of the room and carefully peered through a broken window frame. Three German soldiers were lying on the tracks, victims of Andy and his Bren. 'Andy, Charlie,' I shouted, 'get in here now!' The two D Company soldiers reappeared and searched the two Germans, who sobbed and muttered until they realized they weren't going to be executed. The search came up with nothing.

'Corporal Stokes?' came a shout. The shout had come from the tea room, so I made my way there.

Al Grimes stood in front of me, his boys bringing in the wounded from the glider. They looked a real mess. He held out his hand, and as I took it, the big ginger sod gave me a hug. 'Fucking hell, Robbie kid, you are one of a kind. Great job.'

But I was about to give him another headache. 'You've now got two wounded Germans to look after as well, sir.'

He bit his lip. 'Can they walk?'

'I don't know. I hit them with a grenade and a PIAT round, so they won't be giving you any trouble.'

He gripped my right shoulder. 'Well done. I need your help for a little while longer. I'll sort this lot out here, but I need the lumber sheds on the other side of the station cleared. I can't have the enemy sneaking up on us.'

I contemplated taking my section to clear the lumber yard, but got a reprieve. 'We've got friendlies on our right side, sir,' Bob Castle shouted. 'Platoon strength, maybe more.' I followed Al outside. A load of blokes from our battalion were kneeling or lying around, a mixed bag of reconnaissance and Company Headquarters men. Al briefed the serjeant who was looking after them as the wounded were brought outside. The two German wounded were laid among ours. One of our more badly wounded put a cigarette between the lips of a former adversary and lit it for him. My recently acquired bitterness towards enemy wounded evaporated instantly. I had been brought down a peg or two. Who was I to get on my high horse about who lived and died? How could I think of shooting wounded out of hand?

The headquarters and reconnaissance sections took the lumber yard. A few enemy were killed, two wounded captured, but most legged it towards the autobahn being built between the river Issel and Ringenberg. We had taken the train station, one of the four vital links in Hamminkeln.

4
Hamminkeln Road Bridge

Although unintentionally, it appeared I was back with my former company. An ad hoc force occupied the station, but the majority were D Company, this being their objective, on the edge of their landing zone.

After a couple of lads found yard brooms, the station tea room was swept out and used to house the wounded. Non-injured German prisoners helped place the dead in a single location. The bodies were covered with sheets and blankets, before being stripped of rations, water and cigarettes, all of which were distributed among the wounded of both sides.

It was established that the Royal Artillery officer, Captain Gidalla, was the senior ranking officer in the station. He gathered all the infantry commanders, including junior commanders like me, for an impromptu meeting. He was particularly interested in one of the maps taken from the German motorcycle crews, and spread it out. It was crudely marked up with the anti-aircraft defences in the area. It was no wonder our airborne forces had been shot up so badly. The map also showed scribbled symbols and German handwriting around the nearby town of Ringenberg.

Meanwhile Al Grimes and Bob Castle's radio operators had been working the frequencies in an attempt to establish where everyone was. Across the four companies making up the battalion, many commanders had failed to respond to repeated calls. My heart sank. It was obvious the battalion had taken horrendous losses, but enough contacts were made to establish the other companies were in the vicinity of their objectives, even if they hadn't taken them yet. So the centre of mass of B Company was at the road bridge to the north, the core of C Company was further north at the railway bridge, and A Company were in force at the key road junction to the west. That said, it was obvious the original plan for Operation Varsity had gone out of the window. It was bloody Market Garden all over again, I thought. We could only sit it out at Hamminkeln station and await further developments, and Hamminkeln didn't feel like a safe place to sit and wait, but my section couldn't link up with the main body of C Company at the railway bridge because we'd risk becoming embroiled in B Company's fight at the road bridge en route.

Later that afternoon, Captain Gidalla's radio operator reported that B Company had heard panzers out near Ringenberg, and had consequently requested assistance. Gidalla decided my section would reinforce them, offering us extra PIAT projectiles. His radio operator would confirm we were coming to the road bridge, which would incidentally get us closer to our own company at the railway bridge.

I didn't like Gidalla's plan, since it was largely open country between the station and the road bridge, but I was more worried about approaching B Company than running into the Germans since, like all our boys, B Company had already taken a beating and might therefore be more inclined to shoot first and ask questions later. However, I managed to find a drainage ditch leading off to the east. It wasn't ideal but was better than making our way across open farmland.

I set off, leading my section along the ditch towards the river Issel, with the PIAT lads struggling along with their extra loads. Beyond the river the partly built autobahn ran parallel to it. In the far distance smouldering buildings amid a large cluster of tall trees marked Ringenberg. Our artillery was already pummelling the place, the concussions rippling in our direction.

After a fair while we stopped, kneeling in the ditch so I could consult my map. As I fished it from my smock, I could feel it was damp. Turf suddenly flicked up around us, rounds snapping through our position. We all hit the deck and stayed face down in the ditch, waiting for the firing to let up. Behind me, I heard groaning, gurgling and cursing. I tried to turn but the ditch wasn't wide enough and I wasn't about to stand up. I looked back under my armpit. 'What's happened?' I called out.

More rounds zoomed over our position. 'Coops is hit,' a sobbing voice called back. 'Fucking hell, he's hit bad.'

My stomach turned. 'Can you look after him? Have you got enough dressings? Pass along what dressings you have.' I rummaged through my pockets, passing a field dressing back to Chris Lenor. The groaning and gurgling grew louder and more desperate.

'Can you patch him up?' I asked.

'I'm not sure. I don't know where to start,' replied Andy Blackmore.

I was struggling to bring the situation under control, so I suddenly lost my cool. 'What do you mean, you're not fucking sure?'

'He's got no fucking jaw, and he's been shot through the fucking throat.'

I swallowed hard, getting myself back under control. 'Do what you can, mate. We're stuck tight in here.'

The gurgling faded away, to be replaced by sobbing from a few of the boys. I had never felt so useless. Lance Corporal Stephen Cooper was dying in pain in a drainage ditch. I wondered again when the war would end. The temptation to just lie there and be absorbed by it all was overwhelming, but I had the section to take care of. I had to make decisions. 'Stay low, boys, and follow me.' Difficult though it was, I began crawling along the ditch, knowing I had to show the way and we had to leave Stephen there. The sobbing behind me continued for a few metres, but was soon interrupted by grunting and cursing about equipment.

After what felt like a sweat-soaked age, we had to stop for a breather. We had crawled what felt like hundreds of metres, but I knew it hadn't been that far at all. I heard Andy groaning and grinding his teeth. 'Andy, what's up, mate?'

'When Stephen got hit, I caught one in the hand. Burns like a bastard.'

I managed to swivel a little and got a fright when he held up his damaged hand. He had lost at least one finger, another hanging by the skin. 'Jesus, Andy,' I moaned, 'why didn't you say?'

He shrugged his shoulders, looking crestfallen. 'With Stephen and everything, I didn't want to give you any more problems.' I nodded, grateful for the show of support. 'Silly sod,' I said kindly. 'Can someone dress that hand before it starts giving us all nightmares?' Charlie Wyld started on the shattered hand.

Squatting on my haunches, I risked a peek over the lip of the ditch. I was knackered and knew we couldn't carry on along it much longer. Smoke billowed out of Ringenberg. Then, among some sparse bushes and hedges, movement caught my eye. I caught sight of what I was certain was a Bren gun. Its owner jumped over a low hedge, holding the gun by the carrying handle, its curved magazine clear to see. I saw other soldiers moving about in a crouched fashion, before realizing there were gliders nearby. Two gliders looked untouched, others not too great. At the base of one wreck I saw something white flicker. I was tired and struggling to concentrate but realized it was a medic's armband. Soldiers were milling around the medic. They were filthy, soaked, but one sported a brilliant white bandage.

I was fairly confident we had found B Company. 'Not too far now,' I told the section. 'I think we've found friendlies. I'll take young Lenor and May. The rest of you sit tight and keep an eye on us. If it all goes tits up and they happen to be Germans, you'll see us running back here.' That raised a few chuckles, from Richards in particular, but Peter May and Chris Lenor didn't find it amusing. I told Chris and Peter to leave their PIAT satchels behind. I needed hares not donkeys if we had to get out of there quickly.

I moved up onto the open ground and began a very lonely walk, until with grunts and a few curses Peter and Chris clambered out of the ditch. No one seemed to notice us, everyone looking in the direction of the river. But we were close enough to recognize the uniforms were not German. The wrecked glider was being used as an impromptu aid station, dead, dying and exhausted men all around. A wounded man looked in my direction, and I gave him a wave. Three soldiers walked out to meet us. I told Peter to go back to the ditch and get the others to join us, before Chris and I knelt down with the soldiers: a serjeant major accompanied by a radio operator and a soldier with a Sten. 'Good morning, sir,' I began. 'Corporal Stokes, C Company. I've been told you need some PIAT men?'

The serjeant major nodded. 'Yes, mate. Happy to have you with us.' He held out his hand. 'Serjeant Major Jules King, B Company.' He jerked the thumb of his free hand north, towards the railway bridge. 'Your lads are over there somewhere.'

I took his hand. 'My section are on their way in. We've got a PIAT and plenty of projectiles.'

'Good man,' he replied. 'We could do with those. The enemy are behind the river and the autobahn. My men are trying to get up on the road bridge, to see what's what on the other side. An RAF observer is forward with our officer commanding, trying to get some planes to hit Ringenberg.'

I heard the puffing and panting of my section jogging up behind me. They knelt around me, hastily fishing for their water bottles. 'What happened to your hand, lad?' King enquired of Andy, who still carried our Bren.

Andy looked at the bandage on his hand as if he had just noticed it. 'Got hit in the hand while on the way over from the station. It's OK, though, sir. I've got another one.'

King grinned and nodded, acknowledging Andy's toughness before turning to me. 'Not much of a Bren gunner with one hand, Corporal Stokes. He needs to sit this one out.'

I bit my bottom lip and looked at Andy. The expression on his face spoke volumes. He wasn't ready to sit things out. I could never understand why wounded soldiers felt they were letting the side down. I had known in the ditch that he wouldn't be able to continue with the Bren, and probably wouldn't be able to continue the war with any gun, leaving the section another man short, but I hadn't found the heart to tell him. 'Andy, make your way over to the glider, see what the medic can do for you.' He nodded reluctantly and swapped the Bren for Charlie's Sten, before trudging towards the aid station. 'If they can't fix it,' I called after him, 'don't give them any stick, OK?'

'Yeah, yeah.' He waved his good hand dismissively.

King smiled and wandered over to the rest of my section, offering cigarettes. 'Rest of you all OK?'

'Those of us who are here, sir.' It was Richards, and his tone immediately put me on alert. Sure enough he continued: 'Corporal Stokes left one of our lads behind; too heavy to carry, apparently.'

I was so stunned I just looked at him open-mouthed. King meanwhile pursed his lips and looked from Richards to me. Then he nodded and walked over to me, taking my elbow and leading me away from the group. 'Something I should know about, Corporal?'

'Yes, sir. I have a dead man in the ditch back there.'

'Not that, Stokes. This private, speaking up like that. I don't like it.'

I flushed red. 'It's nothing. Private Richards is just a little overwrought by the loss of a comrade. Could someone collect the body when they get a moment?'

'I can't see it being a problem, but B Company is in a shit state right now. We lost just short of two platoons on the way in. The Germans waited until we landed before pulverizing us with flak guns and MG 42. We've got just about enough unscathed men to form a platoon, including our headquarters lads based here. It was a mess.' He looked at his soldier with the Sten. 'Young Boyd is going to take you forward to link up with our company commander. If the panzers we heard materialize, Major Wells will put you to work, taking care of them. We've had contact with German infantry in the last hour or so, but managed to beat them back. By the sound of it, they've got some heavy gear beyond the autobahn, maybe Tiger tanks, and we need to be ready.'

I looked at Matt Ingall carrying our PIAT anti-tank gun, knowing it wasn't capable of knocking out Tigers.

'Your PIAT is just cover,' said King quickly, 'until our six-pounders are in the right place. The whole operation has gone to pot. No surprises there, eh?' Six-pounders were artillery pieces which fired projectiles weighing roughly six pounds. They were our only effective counter to the Tiger menace.

As Boyd led us away, I caught Richards' eye and held it until he turned away. I smiled, my first victory.

The terrain was open and I ordered my section to fan out, Matt closest to me with the PIAT. I realized I had failed to nominate a second-in-command to replace Stephen and reflected that King's men were already probably making plans to collect him. My heart sank again. Someone would have to tell his new wife that he wouldn't be coming home. I would have rather faced the SS every day than have to explain how I left her broken husband in a ditch.

Our progress was understandably cautious, but the west side of the road bridge soon appeared in the near distance. I could hear panzers further away, but it was difficult to establish even an approximate location. The rough earthworks of the autobahn looked a little intimidating. Ringenberg continued to get hammered by our artillery. Then, out of nowhere, a pair of Typhoon fighter-bombers swooped in, firing their air-tearing rockets into the town before banking away from the inferno. I was impressed at the closeness of our fire support. With the planes, and our artillery established on the west bank of the Rhine, we could pretty much smash anything that came our way.

Our journey became more disjointed, with plenty of stopping and starting. We gradually began to encounter soldiers, Boyd asking where Major Wells and the tactical air controller were. Eventually Boyd began to crawl. I waved my section down, going forward with him.

Just a hundred metres short of the road bridge we came across two kneeling soldiers deep in conversation over a map. One occasionally talked into a headset. The soldier without the headset acknowledged Boyd. I realized the other was probably talking to the Typhoons. 'Major Wells, sir,' Boyd began, 'this is Corporal Stokes, C Company. He's our PIAT man, courtesy of the serjeant major.'

'Thank you, Boyd. Good work.' He turned to me. 'Corporal Stokes, good to see you. Please tell me it's not just you.'

'No, sir. I've got a section with one PIAT and plenty of projectiles.' The relief on his face was a picture. Clearly he had become used to assigning heavily depleted units.

Boyd nudged my arm. 'I'll guide the rest of your boys here. OK, Corporal?'

'Cheers, mate, thanks.'

As Boyd crawled away, I joined the major. He glared at me with the look of a man out to get some revenge on the enemy. 'Stokes, I lost two thirds of my company getting to this fucking shithole. I have no intention of giving this bridge up. I need you and your men off to the left of the bridge. You hit the first panzer that tries to cross it. Stop the first one, then you have a sixty-ton roadblock in the middle of it, and that will suit me fine. They can shoot at us all day after that, but they cannot be allowed to cross to this bank. Do you understand, Corporal?

'You're big and ugly enough to site your own men. I'm not going to do it for you. Captain Gorman here is doing a sterling job with his Typhoons, but they only have fuel and rockets for so long, and the enemy behind the autobahn aren't taking the hint, so get ready to fight. Is that clear?'

I already liked him; to the point, no airs or graces, just business. 'Yes, sir.'

He turned back to the tactical air controller. I didn't need any more prompting so moved away. I knew I couldn't site Jack and Matt too far left of the bridge. For a start, Matt would need a clear shot up the length of the bridge. We also couldn't risk getting too close to C Company at the railway bridge, just three hundred metres away. Close to the road bridge there was cover for Matt and Jack in the form of a low grass bank they dug into. But Matt would have to break cover briefly to get a decent angle for a shot up the bridge.

The rest of the section were digging in around them when I told Peter May that he now had Stephen Cooper's job. Bob Richards briefly glared at me; the fact Peter was so young didn't help. I told Peter there would be no debate about it, and he merely nodded, going back to finish digging his foxhole.

I checked we were dug in properly, not that the boys needed much encouragement. Our holes needed to be good ones, since infantry support would certainly follow panzers, particularly in this terrain.

For the remainder of the day the area of the bridge got hit by mortars now and again. Part of me wished the Germans would wreck the bridge by accident, which would make our job less nerve-racking. At one point rifle and machine-gun fire broke out on the other side of the bridge. Some B Company boys were dug in over there, but we couldn't see what was going on, and no one supplied us with updates. B Company was really strapped for manpower, of course, but our isolation made us feel a bit lonely. Our artillery bombardment of Ringenberg continued throughout the day. We often heard C Company battling for the railway bridge, not knowing if they were getting the upper hand. When the Typhoon raids on Ringenberg stopped just before last light, our artillery turned its attention to the ground beyond the road bridge.

After dark the sounds of battle around us became sporadic. Generally we heard just the odd pot shot, machine-gun burst or artillery round, but occasionally an engagement would erupt somewhere, lasting for a few minutes. Darkness gave us the opportunity to stretch our legs, which was welcome, but I guessed the Germans would eventually use the darkness to sneak their infantry up to the bridge. Perhaps the infantry would be supported by tanks, so I hoped the six-pound guns Major Wells talked about were lying in wait somewhere.

Movement to our rear caught me unawares. It was Major Wells with his radio operator, along with Serjeant Major King. 'We've got some of A Company digging in behind us,' Wells began, 'so they can reinforce us if required tonight. Given all the panzer movement this evening, I would put money on them having a shot at the bridge soon.'

Wells's mention of panzer movement was well timed. Beyond the river and the autobahn earthworks, the gunning of engines began. It sounded creepier in the darkness. Our artillery started up, star shells streaking over our heads, before bathing the Ringenberg area in white light. 'If we light up their concentration areas,' explained Wells, 'their forces will be more inclined to stay put, which will hopefully make tonight a little more comfortable.' As we watched, the sound of panzers indeed lessened while the star shells fizzled and drifted in the cloud-laden sky. But no sooner had the light faded out, the tank engines began to roar and grind again. 'I've got a section on the far bank,' Wells quickly continued, changing the subject, 'acting as early warning of an attack on the bridge. Engineers will be under the bridge shortly, to prepare it for demolition. If we can't stop the enemy, the commanding officer has given me carte blanche to blow it sky high.' I liked the demolition plan, not having much faith in the PIAT, even against the less powerful panzers.

I asked King if he could help me out with a set of binoculars. Without hesitation, he pulled his own binoculars from his smock and handed them to me. 'Here you go, kid. You'll probably need them before I will.' Wells and his radio operator left with him, to continue their rounds of nearby positions.

As the night progressed, star shells continued to illuminate the landscape, but despite the continued noise of engines, I couldn't observe any German movement beyond the bridge, even with the binoculars. As I sat and waited, Dougie next to me, I couldn't help thinking of France. 'Normandy seems like a lifetime ago,' I quietly remarked, 'but this place reminds me of it.'

'Whatever the cost,' agreed Dougie, copying my whisper, 'capture and hold a bridge until relieved.'

'Be prepared to blow it up, if you can't hold it,' I expanded. 'But this operation has spilt much more battalion blood.' Even without the star shells, I noticed how Ringenberg glowed on the horizon, its fires cracking and popping. 'I wonder if the local population moved away before the fighting started.'

'I don't care.'

I realized I didn't care either, a sure sign of how our attitude towards German civilians had hardened. 'Yeah, we're in Germany now, not France, Belgium or the Netherlands. Am I wrong not to care about the German people?'

'Nope. They allowed the Nazis to come to power, rallied to their cause. And the world has paid for it.' The conversation was on the verge of getting a little deep, especially for Dougie, but he was on a roll. 'Because of the ambitions of one man and his delusional followers, the world is now smashing itself to pieces.'

'I don't think Hitler's done it alone, Dougie.'

'I know, but what I mean is that it's the soldiers who are

fighting the war, not the men who started it. Look at us. Look at what we have resorted to doing. We are fighting because of a fucking bridge. I mean, look at it. How many people have died today because of a couple of bloody bridges? Why would people do that?'

Although the battle sounds had more or less died out around us, his words made me wonder again how C Company were managing at the railway bridge. 'I don't know the answer, mate.' I wasn't saying it to calm him; I was actually lost for an answer to his questions.

'Do you mean to tell me that those fuckers over the other side don't want to just jack it all in and go home?' He was getting more worked up. 'Of course they do. I'm sure the last thing they want is to be fighting for this place, no more than we do. I bet they're having the same conversation we are right now.'

I shook my head, trying to keep my voice low, worried that in his excitement he might advertise our position to the enemy. 'I think they have the fight in their hearts, more than ever now.'

'Why's that?'

'Because we're on their home soil. If they were on the outskirts of your home town, what would you do?'

We fell into silence as gunfire erupted in the area of the railway bridge, tracer flicking skywards. A star shell burst above the end of the road bridge, flooding the far bank in light. Small groups of Germans made dashes towards the far approach ramp. Tracer from B Company screamed at them, making them dart back into cover. I told my section to save their fire, putting the binoculars to my eyes. I followed a group of our troops coming across the bridge from the far bank. Two carried a wounded man. The others turned back, kneeling as they fired. As the star shell faded out, German infantry dashed for the bridge again. In the darkness tracer ricocheted screaming off the bridge structure. Small bursts of light began on the far bank, accompanied by the din of explosions; B Company were exchanging grenades with the enemy.

Another star shell erupted above the far bank. I lowered the binoculars. Light from the shell illuminated two halftracks rushing towards the bridge. Their rear wheels were tracked like a tank's, providing power, the conventional wheels at the front providing steering. The light surprised their drivers, the vehicles rocking to a sudden halt, their camouflage foliage of leaves and branches swinging wildly. 'Can we have a go at them, Rob?' Charlie called out.

Although the PIAT was capable of knocking out halftracks, I wanted to save the rounds for tanks, even if they did turn out to be Tigers. 'Just the Bren. Everyone else stay in cover. Keep an eye out for tanks.'

Having taken over the Bren gun from Andy, Charlie let off short controlled bursts. To begin with his tracer fell low and right of the halftracks, but then a burst landed in the area of the front vehicle. Sparks flicking off the engine cover confirmed he was on target. 'That's it,' I encouraged him. 'Have another go, Charlie.' He scored more hits on the front halftrack, but its crew were undeterred as the vehicle drove onto the bridge ramp. I wondered if the bridge was about to be lost, the fight moving to our side of the river. But then the halftrack erupted in a flurry of sparks, the soldier manning its mounted MG 42 bursting like a tomato.

The smouldering vehicle reversed as fast along the road as it could, covering a fair distance, but was hit hard again, flames beginning to lick from it. As the star shell faded out, a grim pantomime began, hysterical screaming human torches emerging from the stricken vehicle. The descent of darkness only contributed to the ghastly spectacle. They flailed, flapped and rolled about, screams and hysteria reaching a climax as they cooked on the road. My stomach turned. It reminded me of an occasion at Arnhem Bridge when a German flamethrower team had been engulfed by their own exploding petrol tank.

The men around the halftrack stopped moving, flames consuming them, their vehicle an inferno. As another star shell flooded the area with light, I realized the Germans had withdrawn, the second halftrack gone. I knew they'd be back before the night was over.

Midnight passed without incident. The knocked-out halftrack glowed, popping and fizzing as its ammunition succumbed to the flames. Our artillery fired star shells at irregular intervals, preventing the enemy from taking advantage of a routine. Then German infantry tried to sneak up to the bridge again, using the halftrack as cover. Rifle and machine-gun fire drove them away, but they kept coming back, even though their casualties mounted.

At about three in the morning we began to hear panzers growling beyond the glow of the halftrack, yet our star shells didn't reveal them. I wondered why we could hear tanks but not see them. My question was answered by an almighty thud as a tank shell screamed across the bridge, detonating down the road behind us. I knew the shell had come from a panzer lurking among trees on the far bank. Tracer followed the shell, then the tank fired another round from the same position.

Another cluster of star shells lit up the far bank. The sight revealed was truly terrifying. Three tanks had sneaked up on us. The tank firing was accompanied by another. The third had craftily made its way up to the burning halftrack, firing its machine gun at B Company. 'Get ready, Matt,' I screamed.

He looked at me before clambering from his trench with the PIAT. 'There's no way I can make the distance from here, Rob.'

Before reaching its final position, the destroyed halftrack had reversed away from the bridge, and like the panzers in the trees, the one beside the halftrack was over two hundred metres away. There wasn't a snowball's chance in hell of the PIAT propelling a projectile that far, let alone hitting a target. But there wasn't any cover close enough to the bridge – nowhere I could safely ask Matt to fire the PIAT from. 'Look, Matt, just aim high, distract it, do whatever it takes to put it off its aim.' There was nothing else we could do for now.

Matt fired a projectile at the panzer next to the halftrack. I had no idea where it went, but didn't think it could reach the tank. However, the panzer rocked back on its tracks, sparks billowing high and wide as it took a full-frontal hit. I was transfixed, shocked, but most of all impressed. Matt dropped onto his front, crawling like a maniac back to his hole. The panzer began to reverse away along the road, its tracks grinding horribly. I saw Matt smile, but then the same panzer was hit again, a similar frontal impact. Matt looked crestfallen, his claim to fame evaporating. I realized that, as had been the case with the destroyed halftrack, something big was firing from behind us. Major Wells had told us A Company were setting up. Perhaps they had been supplied with a six-pounder.

The panzer that had fired from the trees moved up, advancing towards the bridge. I raised my binoculars, realizing for the first time we were facing Panther tanks, lighter but more manoeuvrable than Tigers. I observed the rear exhausts of the advancing Panther pass the halftrack, then there was a tremendous explosion. Steel, timber and charred bodies shot skyward, before the explosion rippled over us. My ears screamed and rang.

I hadn't noticed engineers in the vicinity of the bridge, but they must have finished wiring it for detonation, Major Wells exercising his prerogative to prevent it falling into enemy hands. What little remained of the bridge collapsed into the river. High-explosive artillery shells then began thundering into the far bank, ripping up huge chunks of earth, turf and trees. A star shell burst, illuminating the bombardment. I watched in awe and horror as German infantry sprang from various pieces of cover, attempting to retreat. Not many made it back to the autobahn earthworks, the spread of our artillery shells moving back with them as they fled, denying any opportunity to regroup. Some enemy infantry were mown down by their own panzers, which were also retreating through the confusion.

Eventually darkness and quiet descended. We settled down, trying to rest as best we could. I kept watch for a while. The star shells became less frequent. At 5 a.m. an immense din erupted at the railway bridge. The sounds told me that German tanks and infantry were trying to cross it. Star shells illuminated the area. Up along the far bank I could just make out panzers darting back and forward, tracer screaming after them. I made out distant screaming and shouting, but no words were recognizable.

The battle raged for the best part of an hour. In the half-light just before dawn I watched panzers heading for the autobahn earthworks. They were dashing for cover, knowing our Typhoons would be in the air after dawn, hunting them. I hadn't heard an explosion large enough to signal the demolition of the railway bridge, so I breathed a sigh of relief, since the German retreat meant C Company had managed to hold on.

After dawn, Major Wells and his entourage came to visit us. He congratulated us on a job well done. I didn't have the heart or courage to tell him we had fired just a few bursts from the Bren and an awry PIAT round. He passed around a hip flask of single-malt whisky. I took a polite sip, which burned the back of my throat. He sniggered as some of my section coughed and spluttered like schoolkids trying their first crafty fag behind the cricket screens.

'Friendly armour has arrived at Brigade Headquarters,' he advised, smiling. 'A troop of four tanks will be assigned to B Company, so we have a more effective anti-armour screen.' But then his smile disappeared. 'C Company took a hiding last night, and had to withdraw. Only daylight saved the railway bridge from the enemy. When the time is right, our brigade will take the lead, using the bridge to cross the Issel. The Royal Ulster Rifles and the 12th Battalion of the Devonshire Regiment will bypass Ringenberg, clearing the high ground beyond. Our battalion will clear the town and will then remain in reserve.'

It was an honour that our parent unit, the 6th Airlanding Brigade, which formed the lion's share of 6th Airborne Division, had been chosen to lead the Allied force out of the bridgehead we had created east of the Rhine. Once Operation Varsity was complete, I had half-expected to go home to England, but now I found I was excited by the prospect of finishing the job.

5
Ringenberg

As daylight took hold, our artillery opened up again on Ringenberg, and Typhoons appeared in the skies. We were trying everything to stop the Germans getting their act together, but they still managed to mortar our positions and mount a ferocious assault on the Devons' 12th Battalion as they moved forward.

It was late morning before the Typhoon offensive afforded some relief by destroying the enemy or driving them back into cover. But all day one stubborn panzer remained on open ground between us and Ringenberg. The tank kept firing at our positions, but somehow neither the artillery nor the RAF could get it. Eventually, the panzer withdrew, probably out of ammo. It made a long afternoon for us – no one visiting our positions, everyone fearing attention from the fearless panzer commander.

It was just after dark when Serjeant Major King paid us a visit. 'Get your shit together. The Jocks are going to take over our positions, so we can move to Ringenberg.'

It didn't take us long to get ready, because we had little in the way of equipment. While the section prepared to move, King tugged my smock sleeve and led me to one side. 'We've recovered your man,' he whispered. 'He's with our dead. The padre has already done the documentation, so you don't need to fret about him being left here. But tomorrow, before you go to Ringenberg, I could do with some help regarding our boys who are still in the gliders.'

My stomach turned. Clearing glider wrecks was a grim task,

but I was in no position to refuse so just nodded. After King had left, I told my section about Stephen. They acknowledged the news but avoided eye contact with me, fiddling with their kit. I sighed inwardly, aware that the death of Cooper had driven a further wedge between me and some of the men. I wondered if I should say something but couldn't find the words. War was hell, it was as simple as that.

The rumbling and rattling of armoured vehicles began behind us. Before too long, a large platoon of Scottish infantrymen, complete with Churchill tanks, arrived to relieve B Company. The tanks were huge lumbering beasts, heavily armoured. I shook hands with many of the infantrymen, but they soon began to grumble when they realized they would have to dig trenches. My section's foxholes were usable, but B Company had taken so many losses on landing, they hadn't required as many trenches as the larger Scottish force would.

I led my section to the makeshift B Company Headquarters among the gliders, finding Major Wells and his entourage poring over a map, red filters on their torches. King pointed us to an intact glider, telling us to settle behind it to get food and rest. There could be no white light, since A Company, patrolling our perimeter, were still occasionally encountering German stragglers.

Indeed, throughout the night, we occasionally heard small firefights break out to the north. I hoped A Company were killing the probing Germans, not each other with friendly fire. It was March, and despite the fact we had no sleeping bags or blankets, some of my section managed to sleep. I was exhausted but could only mainly doze; it seemed that every time I dropped into a wonderful slumber, the cold would jolt me awake, making me shiver like crazy for a few minutes.

First light was a sobering sight, slowly revealing what remained of B Company. They were all armed, but most were wounded. Some dozed, sprawled out on the leaf-littered grass. Others sat smoking or eating their rations cold. Two even managed a game of cards. But despite it all, I was overwhelmed by a deep sense of pride. It wasn't too long ago that I would have rolled my eyes at the cliché, but they had fended off infantry and panzer attacks using only what they could scavenge from their destroyed gliders.

A soldier approached me. It was Andy Blackmore. His injured hand displayed a fresh bandage, a trail of cigarette smoke drifting from his lips. He plonked himself down, looking around at the section. A few were awake. 'All right, boys?' he enquired.

'Yeah,' I answered. 'You?'

'Good, actually. I think I'm on my way home soon. There's talk about the wounded being moved behind the Rhine. Nijmegen was mentioned. Can't complain.'

Nijmegen was familiar to me. I had been looked after in hospital there, after the Arnhem operation. 'Good for you, mate.'

'I helped to collect Stephen,' said Andy. 'It was horrible. They took care of him, though. C Company know about our unofficial secondment to B Company. I don't think Serjeant Major Jackson is expecting us back any time soon, given the lack of manpower around here.'

We weren't in an ideal situation, but I was glad our company knew where we were. I guessed they had probably been told about Stephen.

As the light grew brighter, I watched B Company get to their feet. Serjeant Major King walked among them, giving many a pat on the shoulder, accepting the odd swig of brew or helping them to light cigarettes.

Eventually, King approached us. I knew what was coming. 'We are ready to recover our dead from the gliders, along with any equipment we can salvage. The Jocks might have taken over from us, but don't let your guard down while you inspect the gliders, because enemy troops might still be lurking about. I'll tick the gliders off as you check them. You might find some surprises out there – just a chance you might find wounded men. Move off when you're ready.'

The section unhappily got to their feet. I was preparing to lead them for the glider clearance when Major Wells caught my eye. Sipping on a cup of tea, he looked exhausted. Looking around, I became very conscious of the lack of officers. 'Corporal Stokes, don't rush off; the officer commanding needs a word.'

'Yes, sir.' My stomach slowly turned. Why would Wells want to speak to me again? Acting as my new second-in-command without fuss, Peter May led the section towards the nearest group of gliders. He was a good lad, and they seemed willing to follow him. Richards however couldn't help but comment on the task. I couldn't make out what he was saying, but at that moment I didn't care.

King stood with me while Major Wells conjured a second brew from somewhere. I accepted it gratefully. Wells waited until my section was out of earshot, before addressing me. 'Cracking job you did at the bridge.'

'Sir?' I responded uncertainly.

'You held your position,' he enthused. 'I was observing you when the Panthers tried to rush the bridge. Your man with the PIAT, I thought he hit it too.'

He chuckled. This instantly lifted the tension I was feeling. He confirmed a six-pounder had knocked out the halftrack and had hit the Panther twice, although the tank had apparently rolled away, living to fight another day. He complimented me on keeping my boys upbeat and aware of what was going on. I smiled. Was he really talking about me? He dismissed my modesty with a wave of his hand.

'Corporal Stokes, I have seen some fine NCOs clam up when the shit hits the fan. I've seen others flourish and excel in battle, and I would put you in the latter category.' Under my grime and camouflage cream, I could feel myself beginning to blush. My section had contributed next to nothing to the battle for the road bridge, which had ended in its loss. 'I've had to move things about in this company,' continued Wells, 'to keep us a fighting unit. Until we get reinforcements from England, and having discussed it with Serjeant Major King, you are to be acting platoon serjeant until further notice.'

I stood in stupefied silence for a few moments and then garbled, 'Thank you, sir. I won't let you down.' I thought I'd thanked him with confidence but felt very much out of my depth. It all felt rather bizarre, and I suddenly decided to put my cards on the table. 'Sir, may I speak freely?'

'Go on,' Wells said deadpan.

'I hardly know my own company, let alone yours. I'm having some issues with my own section, as it appears outsiders are not too welcome from other companies. Are you sure I'm the man for the job?'

The major opened his mouth to speak, but King beat him to it. 'Stokes, you've got the job until you get killed, or until I find somebody better, so you are just gonna have to deal with that shit in your own time, understand?' His face was stern, and he was clearly in no mood for a diplomatic debate over promotion on the battlefield. 'You're a good soldier. We know it and the boys know it. They talk about you and Arnhem, as well as the fact you fought in Normandy. You have their respect as a soldier; you don't need them to be your mates. They don't want to be on your Christmas card list, they just want you to say two things to them, when it's all going to shit: "Follow me." Your promotion will be effective when we reach Ringenberg.'

I didn't think it was the speech Wells would have given me, but he had stayed relaxed while King talked.

I nodded. 'Thank you, sir.'

They turned away and I looked out over the countryside. I was going to be a platoon serjeant in B Company. A bloody platoon serjeant! I let the rank roll around my mind. It felt ridiculous. Sean Wardle had been my platoon serjeant back in Normandy and he'd been a giant. I couldn't be a platoon serjeant! And yet, here I was, promoted twice in quick succession and now responsible for four sections. Could I be a giant? I wondered. I found myself standing taller. It did feel different. I felt different. I don't know whether it was King's backing or the thought of Sean Wardle but I felt a swell of confidence suddenly surge through me. I'd never seriously thought about promotion. The army had never seemed like a career; it was just a job that needed doing. But as I stood there, I suddenly knew I wanted to be more than a soldier. I wanted to be a leader. I was still lost in thought when the boys started drifting back from the burned-out gliders. They looked pretty shaken up and I wandered over. It was then that I noticed that Richards was missing.

'Where's Private Richards?' I asked Dougie. He looked around and shrugged.

'All right lads, well done. Take a break and boil up a brew.' When they'd trudged past me, I marched off in the direction of the gliders. Their broken skeletons stood scattered across the flat ground, surrounded by an array of army detritus and the occasional body. It felt surreal to walk between them, as though I was in an alien landscape.

I found Richards in the furthest glider. He was sitting with his head in his hands beside a body lying on the floor of the glider. His posture made me swallow the rebuke that had been on my lips. He didn't look up as I stepped inside and took a seat on an upturned crate next to him. We sat in silence for a few moments. 'He saved my life,' he finally said.

I looked down at the body on the floor, taking in the private's uniform and the middle-aged face. 'You served together?' I asked.

'No, back home, in Whitechapel. My father had turned up

drunk again and was giving me a hell of a beating with a spanner. I remember thinking the bugger was never going to stop. He was going to kill me that time for sure. I think he would have too if Tommy hadn't stepped in.'

'He was your brother?'

'Cousin.'

'I'm sorry,' I said, feeling the inadequacy of the words.

'He was always a scrapper, Tommy was. I thought if anyone was going to survive this war, it would be him.'

I picked up a discarded jacket and carried it over to cover Tommy's face. 'One thing I've learned in this war is that staying alive is mostly about luck. You've either got it or you haven't.'

He looked round at me, remembering the words from Tellin. 'And you think you've got it?'

I shrugged. 'I don't know, Bob. I've certainly had some luck so far. Maybe it'll run out soon. What I do know is that I want this war to end before it does, and for that to happen we need to scrap like Tommy. I want to win this bloody war, but we can only do that if we fight together. I can teach you to fight and hopefully you'll be lucky – luckier than poor Tommy here. But you need to trust me. I'm done playing.' I nodded at Tommy. 'People are dying. Friends are dying. Either you get behind me or you can stay here with Tommy. Your choice.'

I stood and stepped out of the glider.

The tea was boiling by the time I got back to my section. The mood was still sombre but gradually lightened as the tea was passed round. We were getting refills when a voice pitched in from behind me. 'Any left for me?' I smiled and passed Bob Richards a mug.

Half an hour later we joined A Company, crossing the railway bridge in single file. We traversed the deserted autobahn roadworks, dead Germans, smouldering vehicles and equipment lying all around. The closer we got to Ringenberg, the more violently it seemed to smoulder, devastated by our firepower. The small town reeked of sewage. Dead German soldiers and horses littered the streets. I found it bizarre that the mighty Nazi war machine was mainly horse-drawn.

Our lead units ensured no ambush awaited, others checking the shattered buildings for booby traps. As we walked through, pitiful-looking civilians, pathetic wretches, emerged from the ruins. Elderly men and women approached us. We viewed them with suspicion, but their hands were exposed to show they were no threat. They repeated the same few words over and over. Someone told me that they were simply saying the German Army had moved out, so there was no need to fight any more. They just wanted the war to pass over them as quickly as possible, probably worrying that if we stuck around, German soldiers might come back to engage us.

The column occupied some buildings that hadn't been hit too badly. More civilians emerged from cellars. I felt rather sad, beginning to notice toddlers, infants, older children and a few teenagers. There didn't seem to be any men of fighting age. I supposed they had all been conscripted. We continued to monitor the adults cautiously. I hoped we wouldn't be in Ringenberg for long. If the enemy showed up, I didn't want kids running around during the fight.

During the afternoon we heard fighting off to the east. I wondered if the Devons were engaging the enemy again, possibly the same enemy units that had evacuated Ringenberg. The odd shell landed close to the town.

Without being prompted, the locals began to clear the dead horses and German soldiers from the streets. We gave them a hand because the women among them had children to look after. It was my bet that horsemeat would become the staple diet in the town long after we moved on. I had nothing against the frightened children; they were just caught in the middle of it all. It was their elders that needed to be held to account.

Fighting to the east continued into the evening, and massive quantities of armoured vehicles arrived in Ringenberg, units from 7th Armoured Division. The town soon became a giant traffic jam, and we were told we had to sit tight until they had passed through.

I talked to Major Wells and Serjeant Major King, who were keen to finalize a revised structure for B Company. In addition to Peter May, King nominated three other private soldiers to become my section commanders: Kenny Hills, Benny Piper and Connor Clout. He assured me they were good solid lads, and before I knew it, Wells had wheeled them in. I was no judge, but they seemed decent enough.

I bedded down in a cellar for the night. Opportunities to rest were fitful at best. Orders were shouted. Tank engines rumbled and roared. Noisy mechanical repairs were undertaken. At dawn I was still knackered, craving sleep, fatigue fogging my head. I knew that as platoon serjeant I would have to see Wells again to hear his plans for the day. With no platoon commander to help me, I would have to distribute rations and ammunition to my four sections. But suddenly I was shaken alert by a crash in the street. I scrambled up the cellar stairs and shoved open the heavy wooden trapdoor at the top.

Daylight revealed a grey overcast sky. Below it, a Sherman tank was covered in brick, masonry and timber debris from a collapsed building and accompanying chimney stack. The driver and radio operator were all right – they had slept inside the tank – but the other three crew members had slept outside beside it. I called my section up and we joined random troops, clawing away at the rubble. We could hear groaning beneath it.

Before long, we reached the three crew, huddled in sleeping bags. One of them complained about his legs, which were crushed. His two colleagues had pulled their bags over their heads to guard against the cold. They were motionless, killed by the collapsing house. At least we were spared the looks on their faces. Medics lifted the injured soldier out, complete with sleeping bag. His sobs and groans shuddered through me. We were picking away at the debris around the bodies when we heard a baby crying from the ruins of the house. Finding renewed energy, we began to fight our way through what had once been the ground floor, ignoring the cries of the radio operator and driver to open the tank hatches.

Much of the building had collapsed into the cellar. As we rummaged through tons of rubble, we could hear shouts for help from women and children, drowning out the shrill of the crying baby. Sweat was pouring from me, my hands bloodied. As help arrived from all over the town, the soldier next to me told us to adopt a more methodical approach. I wasn't sure what rank he was, but very quickly everyone was organized into a line. A medic passed a piece of masonry to me. I passed it to a German teenager, who passed it to an elderly man, who passed it to Richards. The war was forgotten during the rescue effort, the cries below becoming more hysterical.

The teenager behind me started sobbing, snatched a brick from me and slung it away. I wondered if his family were trapped somewhere underneath. He made me feel useless and unwelcome. I couldn't speak German but helped him the best way I could, by continuing to move rubble. A bloodied dusty hand suddenly shot from beneath the wreckage, grabbing him by the ankle. He yelped, then fell backwards. I helped him up. Grasping the small hand with both of his, he jabbered away in German. He became hysterical, interfering with the rescue rather than helping. One of our medics and an elderly German man pulled him away, but he fought them, tears and snot streaming down his face. Peter joined me, and we carefully removed the rubble around the hand, creating a hole. The elderly German returned. He held the hand, talking calmly to those below. We worked like maniacs to make the hole bigger, brick by brick, curse by curse. We saw the bloodied face of a little girl, hysterical but alive.

After what felt like an age, the girl was free. She was covered in cuts and grazes but overall didn't look too bad. As she was carried away, she cried back to someone. Peter stuck his head in the hole. 'I can see legs. Quick, help me.' He lowered himself feet first into the hole. Peering after him, I could make out that timber frames from the roof had created a void. He disappeared from view. I could hear him grunting, breathing heavily in the dusty darkness. As more of the surrounding rubble was removed, he re-emerged, face ashen, tears scarring his face. He struggled to speak, waving at us to stop digging. 'Rob, help me out.' He looked at the bloodied little girl we had rescued, now sitting on the German teenager's lap across the street. He was obviously her brother.

I helped Peter pull the body of their mother from the hole in as dignified a manner as possible. She had been heavily pregnant, not much time before her child would have been due. Our medics put her on a stretcher, covering her with a blanket. As they took her away, we slumped high amid the pile of ruins, taking a breather.

The trapped baby was rescued, along with its mother, but when it came to the pregnant woman, I told myself we had been too slow, should have worked faster. The teenage boy glared in my direction, his sister still on his lap. His eyes cut deep into my soul. He addressed his sister, who glared in my direction too. I had no idea what to do.

But then the girl climbed off his lap and made her way across the road. She approached Kenny Hills, her eyes welling up with fresh tears, her bottom lip trembling. She hugged him, then moved to Bob Richards, clasping him too. As, one by one, she hugged her exhausted rescuers, her brother pulled himself together and joined her. But instead of staying at her side, he made a beeline straight for me. He cuffed away his tears, snot running from his nose, and held out his hand. I carefully took it. He clambered higher up and hugged me. His embrace broke me in half, as I fought back the tears. He didn't speak, he just held me tight. Down on the street the Allied advance to Berlin had come to a halt. Infantryman, tank crewman, dispatch rider, truck driver, medic and civilian: they all just stood there, watching us in silence, the distant sound of fighting rippling away, so at least for a few moments there was peace.

6
Gun Battery

It took the rest of the day for our armour to move out of Ringenberg, so we stayed in the town overnight. The next morning we sat out in the open air, watching the locals begin rebuilding their town. There was something very efficient about how they worked. No one stood about; each adult and child had a purpose. Bricks that could be used again were stacked neatly, as was timber that could be recycled. Broken timber was also piled up, probably for use as fuel against the cold nights. In the sky clouds gave way under their burdens, but the light drizzle wasn't enough to prompt the locals to seek shelter; they just carried on.

I watched as they sifted through the rubble from the caved-in house where we had rescued the little girl. Family furniture and possessions were stacked away from reusable timber and bricks. I thought of the little girl's dead mother. Her husband would almost certainly be of fighting age. I wondered if he was serving in Germany or was already dead. I kind of hoped he was dead, not because there would be one less German to fight, but because dying would spare him from coming home only to discover his wife had been killed, his house destroyed. But then I remembered he still had two children, so hastily changed my mind, hoping he would survive the war after all.

D Company had been relieved at the train station so led us out of Ringenberg towards Rhede, some ten kilometres to the north-east. As we marched out, the locals stopped their reconstruction work to watch us leave. Most looked at us without so much as a flicker of emotion on their faces, but some of the more elderly men gave us nods of courtesy. I supposed they knew we were off to kill more of their boys, but on the other hand, given the toll taken on their town, it was clear they wanted the war over as quickly as possible.

As we crested the high ground north of Ringenberg, fighting could be heard in the distance. The Devons and Ulsters were ahead of us, but we heard it was the 3rd and 5th Parachute Brigades, also part of 6th Airborne Division, encountering a stubborn rearguard. We couldn't get a real pace going in any event, since D Company was advancing with caution, fearful German troops might have let the Devons and Ulsters pass through, to see if easier Allied pickings would follow.

The road into Rhede was littered with vehicle debris; wrecks of cars, trucks and horse carts smouldered, victims of RAF Typhoons. Their occupants lay bloated and putrefying surrounded by bluebottles in the remains of the vehicles, on the flanks of the road or in the fields. Small clusters of civilians held their hands up as we moved through. I knew they were looting the vehicles for food. Indeed, I observed a heavily pregnant woman searching a truck riddled with cannon fire, full of dead German soldiers. She kept her dignity until we passed, but, looking back, I spotted her eating a bar of chocolate while passing other food items to her three children.

We arrived in Rhede by mid-afternoon. It had drizzled all day, so it was nice to see the town was intact, since it would be our home for the night. My platoon settled in a large house for the night. There was a family in residence already but we had orders to take over the house so an elderly couple and a teenage boy had to move into the cellar. They didn't look happy about it but I told the boys to treat their house with respect. Most only had eyes for the house kettle anyway, making endless cups of tea and soothing their feet in front of the open fire. The edge of the town would be patrolled all night, but my platoon wasn't expected to contribute to the patrols, or to the guards for the surrendering enemy soldiers until someone picked them up.

Serjeant Major King arrived, along with Major Wells. The teenage boy was up with us, boiling water for his family. The major glared at him. The boy became jittery. The elderly man, perhaps his grandfather, came up through the cellar door. He held his arms out, palms uppermost. The major spoke to him, pointing to the boy: '*Soldat?*'

The boy's hands shot up in the air. The sudden movement caused all of the soldiers present to reach for their weapons. I knew I quickly needed to put a lid on things. 'Take it easy, boys. Put your weapons down.' The lads slowly complied, but I wondered if I was being naive. Had Wells seen something I hadn't?

The old man moved over to the boy, shaking his head and jabbering to Wells in German. I had no idea what he was saying but guessed he was trying to convince him that the boy wasn't a soldier.

Wells gestured to the boy. King moved forward. 'Lift his shirt. Lift.' It was bizarre. The boy looked petrified. The old man slowly lifted the boy's shirt up to the armpits. Was Wells looking for weapons?

Wells bounded over, roughly inspecting the boy's armpits. My men all looked at me with raised eyebrows. I had no idea what was going on. What was I missing? After what felt like an age Wells appeared satisfied. 'OK, OK. *Bitte schön.*' The old man lowered the shirt. 'Any male of fighting age,' Wells explained, 'check their armpits. SS soldiers have their blood group tattooed in their armpit. So check them.'

'What if we encounter a blood group tattoo, sir?' asked Jack Lillie.

Wells nodded. 'Just separate them from other troops. We don't want the SS trying to organize any trouble. As a rule, SS and

Wehrmacht don't get on, so you should be able to spot a natural separation among prisoners. SS can be arrogant arseholes. They often think they're better than regular forces, hence the two groups don't mix.' I had no idea there was such a rivalry, a divide in the German forces. The old man and the boy had flinched when Wells mentioned the SS, probably knowing why the boy's armpits were of interest. The old man collected the hot water and guided the boy down the cellar stairs.

The following morning King did the rounds. One of my platoon quipped that Wells was obsessed with armpits. King stopped dead in his tracks. 'Major Wells served with a platoon of the Royal Norfolk Regiment in 1940. In France his platoon was taken prisoner by SS troops. They were murdered in a barn the fuckers set fire to, after throwing grenades in. Wells managed to escape, the only survivor. So keep your fucking wisecracks to yourself.' He eyed me with a look that demanded I keep my platoon in order.

We were ordered to march to Coesfeld, about forty kilometres nearer Berlin. The brisk pace and the distance weren't a problem, as we had done more than our fair share of forced marches on Salisbury Plain, but the constant rain made things miserable. Before long I was soaked, but the pace kept the cold at bay. I hoped the lodgings at Coesfeld would match those in Rhede. We skirted the towns of Borken and Velen. They didn't appear too badly affected by the war, just some light damage on the outskirts. White sheets hung in abundance from the windows. You could be forgiven for thinking it was laundry day in Germany, but it was a signal the locals didn't want fighting in their streets. We heard local German units had not long departed eastwards, so the pace of our advance increased, rest breaks becoming less frequent, because the powers that be worried if we got too far behind, it would allow the enemy time to reorganize.

We halted about four kilometres west of Coesfeld, moving off the road and south into woods. While we rested, our reconnaissance blokes moved forward into the town. I checked around my platoon. Everyone was OK, bar a few blisters and a turned ankle. Many had tea and cigarettes on the go. Initially, it looked as though we would need an attack plan for Coesfeld, but further feedback from reconnaissance via locals indicated only wounded German soldiers remained in the cellars, waiting for the Allies to take them prisoner. We moved into the town and settled down for the night.

By first light, it had stopped raining. We were all damp and filthy. Ambulances arrived to take the German wounded away, who thanked us for looking after them overnight, some giving us cigarettes. Some had tears running down their cheeks, happy their war was over. Most weren't much older than children. In the half-light the ambulance journey back behind our lines would be perilous without headlamps.

We marched on to the small town of Greven, another forty-two kilometres north-east. I stopped and listened.

'Still nothing.' I looked around to find Richards at my elbow. I nodded. Unusually, we'd heard no sounds of battle all day.

'The sound of victory?' he said with a half-smile. I wondered for a moment if he was mocking me, but before I could make up my mind he'd moved off. It did feel like the end was approaching. White sheets hung from windows welcoming us into the town.

We were not settled long in Greven before we received orders to move overnight to the Dortmund-Ems Canal, about five kilometres to the east. By first light, we needed to be secure on the nearside western bank of the canal. There was potential for trouble, as we would be passing close to a German airbase, just west of the canal, and it hadn't been established whether the base was occupied.

Our A and D Companies led out towards the canal, and it wasn't too long before they encountered resistance. We moved off the road, sitting tight in the darkness, watching star shells illuminate the airfield, tracer flying all over the place. Half-expecting to be called forward in support, we were relieved when a barrage from our artillery caused the Germans at the airbase to retreat, enabling us to move on again.

A large number of Luftwaffe ground personnel faced us at the Dortmund-Ems Canal, but they all wanted to surrender. Retreating from the airbase, they had planned to escape across the canal, but our engineers had already blown the bridge, reducing it to a series of stepping stones. A platoon of Ulsters arrived, relieved from front-line duty some while ago, their war over, but they got landed with the final job of escorting our latest prisoners away. Throughout the remainder of that day surrendering Germans appeared on the other side of the canal, retreating from the fighting ahead. Group after group of them used the stepping stones to reach us.

Engineers arrived to build a new bridge over the canal. We stayed in our trenches that night, watching them work on the construction by torchlight. Major Wells issued orders for us to move forward to Ladbergen at dawn, just a couple of kilometres to the north-east. I was given my own radio operator, Alfred Cox from the battalion's Signals Platoon. I had the nagging feeling that I'd seen him somewhere before but couldn't place him. He'd been wounded in Normandy, returned for the operation in the Ardennes, but hadn't seen any action there. I liked him straight away; upbeat and fit, he followed me everywhere, his radio squawking away.

The replacement bridge wasn't ready at first light, so we were ordered to cross via the stepping stones but delayed when a caravan of supply trucks and other vehicles arrived to support our march forward. Thankfully, by the time it was agreed what the transport would carry, the engineers had declared the new bridge open, so 2nd Ox and Bucks moved across the canal, D Company in the lead, with B Company last. We found the Devons and Ulsters dug in to the east, so we pushed through them, our battalion in the lead now.

Reconnaissance had spotted a column of German units leaving Ladbergen, heading north-east to Lengerich, eight kilometres further on. The recce boys wasted no time calling in artillery to break up the enemy column. Our artillery shells streaked over our heads at a furious rate; the Germans responded by shelling the engineers at the new canal bridge behind us. We were ordered to speed up our march into Ladbergen, fanning out on the approach into town. D Company led along the road, but our route through fields and hedgerows was much more difficult. D Company had received the unwelcome attention of what appeared to be panzers, shooting them up badly.

By the time we had moved into some houses in the town, we were soaked in sweat and knackered. Alfred took off his heavy radio rucksack, then pulled a sorry-looking cigarette from his damp smock. He found a kettle. 'Here, Corporal, it's still hot.' The Germans must have left in a hurry, but it was music to my ears, since I could murder a brew. Taking it on himself to make the tea, Alfred reached into my backpack, grabbing my cup.

Despite the plentiful supply of water in the kettle, he only made a mug for me. I looked at him curiously. He pulled a battered army-issue mug out of his rucksack. It showed two bullet holes, entry and exit holes from a single round. 'Why don't you get it exchanged?' I asked. 'It's free, you know.'

He grinned, dismissing my suggestion with a casual wave. 'Pah. I don't drink brews any more. They're not good for me.'

'Well, you won't be able to drink much from that bloody cup.'

For the first time I noticed scarring on his cheeks and lower jaw. 'A German sniper took offence at my constant tea drinking,' he half-joked, 'and put a round through my cup.' He waved the mug in front of his face to indicate the angle from which he had been drinking at the time. 'Trouble was, the cup was full of hot brew, and I was trying to take a sip. The tea burned my face, and the round broke my jaw.'

'Bloody hell.' I winced.

'Yeah. Certainly stung a bit, and my ears were ringing for days. And on my way to an aid post on a stretcher I got hit by mortar splinters. Bad day all round.'

'Where did you get hit?'

'Er, in the face.'

'No, smart arse, where was the battalion at the time?'

'Herouvillette.'

'Bloody hell, that's where I've seen you before.' It had been the last place we defended in Normandy before being shipped back to England a lifetime ago. The Germans had given us a hard time in the area.

'Surprised you recognized me,' he said with a smile. 'They had to rewire my jaw when I got home.'

We were interrupted by the arrival of Major Wells. 'Follow me. Leave your radio man here.' We advanced for about a kilometre beyond the village, before stopping behind a bank. He waved me to the ground and then we moved up together to peer over the top. Wells pointed at something in the distance. 'Recce have some explaining to do. We've got two flak panzers out there. You've seen how they chewed up D Company. The panzers keep moving, so we need to get close enough to take care of them. I need you to stalk the bastards. What do you need?'

I thought back to a similar task I'd had in Oosterbeek near Arnhem. 'Two PIAT and two Bren, two support, sir.'

'Fine, let's do it.' We scrambled back down the bank and he used his own radio to call up the section. I chanced a crawl up the bank to take another look in the direction Wells had pointed. I spotted one of the flak panzers. It moved behind a small ridge lined thickly with spindly trees, reappearing at the far end to fire. I couldn't see the other panzer anywhere. Puffing and panting announced the arrival of the tank-stalking team. I crawled back down the bank. Major Wells had guided them forward. He looked fresh as a daisy, but Matt Ingall and Jack Lillie stood gasping before me. A second PIAT team from B Company accompanied them; their names escaped me. Charlie Wyld and Peter May both carried Bren guns. They had no support men.

I looked over at the other boys. 'Alfred, we're going to need the radio, so you're going to be in support.' I caught Richards' eye. Time for a test. 'Richards, you'll be the other support.' I could feel my heartbeat quicken, anticipating a confrontation, but he just nodded and picked up his weapon. Wells gave me a thumbs up and nodded his approval. 'Go to it.'

I quickly briefed the team. 'We've been tasked with taking out two flak panzers that have D Company fixed. We need to skirt round the panzers, hit them with PIATs, and then hose the gun crews as they try to leg it, understand?' Nods surrounded me. We made our way forward to the end of the bank. There was a low hedgerow to the right about thirty metres away. I couldn't see the panzers, so they couldn't see me. Taking a deep breath, I dashed like a maniac towards the hedgerow, sliding in behind it. Alfred was never more than a few steps behind me.

Forward right was the ridge I had seen. It looked as though a copse sloped away behind it. The flak panzers had churned up a track of sorts across the front of the ridge. The second flak panzer appeared, pulling up alongside the other at the far end. The crews began shouting at each other, exchanging ammunition. They were too far away to engage with a PIAT. We had to get closer. From a decent position among the trees at the top of the ridge or from the copse down the other side, we had a chance of hitting both before they realized what was going on. It was worth a go.

The crews were still arguing over ammo, which as well as giving D Company a chance to clear their dead and wounded also kept their attention from us. The near side of the ridge was just thirty metres away, so I dashed out from behind the hedgerow, the others in hot pursuit. The cover wasn't great: open ground with a little sparse heather, short for the time of year. It felt like the longest dash in the world. As I crested the ridge, I noticed the spindly trees grew taller on the other side. And I noticed something else: the ground dropped away into an almost sheer drop. I leaned away from the drop, trying to keep a foothold on what was a very narrow crest, but the soil gave way, and I went tumbling down, landing with an almighty thud in a ditch. The impact winded me, and I fought to get air back in my lungs. A small landslide followed me. Then a solid mass landed on me, all oxygen punched out of my lungs once more. The mass flailed and then rolled off. I looked over to see Alfred struggling like an upturned beetle next to me. I put a finger to my lips.

I heard the crackling of a radio close by. It seemed I was in a trench system of some sort. I rubbed my hand along the wall of the trench, feeling a strange kind of wicker-basket effect, wooden strands woven into the soil.

I noticed movement to my left. It was Richards slithering down the slope. He held a forefinger to his lips, indicating for me to be quiet. I frowned, irritated at his insolence, but he pointed beyond me. I slowly turned my head and got an almighty fright. About twenty metres away a dugout was cut into the wicker-latticed trench. A bare-headed German soldier was talking into a radio headset. Another soldier, also wearing a headset, was too busy smoking to give us a glance. I assumed their headsets had stopped them from hearing us, saving us from being discovered. My stomach flipped. I looked back at Richards. He was looking up the ridge we had tumbled down. The remainder of my team was perched close to the top of the ridge, using the trees as cover. They had horrified looks on their faces.

Excited radio voices crackled from the dugout. The bare-headed German soldier removed his headset, then pressed it to one ear, using his free hand to write something. He turned to his companion, stealing the cigarette from his lips, and then took a greedy drag, before returning it. Paper in hand, he dashed out of the dugout. Running away from us along the trench, he began shouting at the top of his voice. So they had at least one other comrade nearby.

Carefully, I pulled myself up to a sitting position. I realized I didn't have my rifle. Alfie pointed down. It was almost covered by the loose soil. I fumbled for the rifle, my eyes locked on the smoking German. I slowly pulled it towards me. It would need a bloody good shake to get all the soil off, but I couldn't risk doing that now. The bare-headed German was still shouting his head off. A distant voice answered him. Then a second voice responded, followed by a third, even closer.

I realized the opposite side of the trench faced down into the copse. Keeping my eye on the smoking German, I carefully got onto my haunches, then stood. The trench was only waist-high, and being fully exposed wasn't good, so I quickly glanced into the copse before sitting down in the trench again. My stomach churned. What I had seen was unreal. Enemy troops, lots of them, in huddles and walking around. And heavy artillery guns, probably the ones that had bombarded our engineers at the new canal bridge. I counted at least four big guns with crews, camouflage netting over the top of each gun. It was a battery, the wooden wicker trench system running down to it. I understood now why my team had looked so worried. We had bitten off more than we could chew; there was no way we could take them all on with just seven men. I felt like an idiot for falling into the trench, putting the rest of my team in real danger.

Behind us, I heard the flak panzers screeching and squealing as they manoeuvred again. They stopped, then started firing. I heard movement in the copse. An artillery gun was loaded, then fired. I was transfixed by the sheer power of the sound. The concussion felt like a jab in the face and guts. I realized the bare-headed German had probably relayed target coordinates. My hearing returned in time to hear him bellowing out more orders.

It dawned on me that he could walk back to the dugout at any time, and approaching it from the other direction would put us in his direct line of sight. Now was the time for us to leave, especially as all the enemy's focus would be on the guns firing.

A second artillery round sounded. There was a low whistle nearby and I saw that Richards had scrambled back up the side of the trench and was beckoning to Alfred and me. We took his hand and he hoisted us out of the trench one by one. Then I looked round and saw the smoking German staring at us wide-eyed. He started out of the dugout, but the four grenades that rained down from the top of the ridge made him dash back inside. A third artillery round sounded, masking the sound of the grenades exploding. As Richards, Alfred and I legged it up the ridge to the others, I doubted if even the bare-headed German would have heard the grenades going off.

My lungs were heaving and burning as I led the team down off the ridge, and back to the hedgerow. As the enemy artillery barrage continued, I wondered if we should still try to knock out the flak panzers. But then Richards grabbed my arm, 'The radio. Get Major Wells to shell them, quick.'

Why hadn't I thought of that? I told the rest of the team to watch out for the flak panzers while I worked out the grid reference of the gun battery on my map. Alfred helped me with call-sign information, before patching the radio through to Wells. I put the radio headset to my ear. 'Hello, Bravo Zero Bravo, this is Bravo One Zero Bravo. Fire mission. Over.' Alfred nodded his approval.

'Zero Bravo, send,' Wells's voice crackled through the headset.

'Fire mission,' I repeated. 'Grid five four two, zero seven five. Direction one five zero zero. Enemy artillery position. Dug in. Over.' I hoped it was good enough. But a long silence followed. I wondered if he was bemused that a gun battery could be so close to his position on the bank. But the headset eventually crackled again, and Wells read back my information verbatim, no differences for me to correct.

A short while later Wells was back in touch again. 'One Zero Bravo, friendly eyes cannot identify the target area. Mark position with smoke if you can. Over.' Our artillery couldn't spot the battery with their binoculars. It was behind a ridge, and was superbly camouflaged. We hadn't seen the battery until we were right on top of it. I took a smoke grenade from my webbing, pulled the pin and then threw it as hard as I could at the ridge. While still in flight, close to the top of the ridge, the grenade popped, brilliant white phosphorus smoke billowing up. Smoke continued to pour out as it bounced back down the ridge.

I wondered if the flak panzers might notice the smoke but had no plans to stick around and find out. We all started to leg it back to the bank, but Alfred then knelt down behind a clump of heather, calling me over. 'Corporal,' he gasped, lowering the headset, 'Wells says we've got one minute to get out of the area before the shooting starts.'

I didn't need to be told twice, so we rushed after the others. Wells was in the same position on the bank. He nudged my arm. 'What artillery?' I managed to control my breathing and described how we had stumbled on the gun battery. 'Fucking hell' was all he could manage.

A voice crackled over his radio. 'Shot. Over.'

'Shot out,' answered Wells immediately. Friendly artillery shells streaked over our heads. With a cluster of mighty thuds the treeline at the top of the ridge was shredded. Other shells rumbled into the copse. Our guns continued to thunder away, producing geysers of timber and turf. As the echo of our artillery faded away, it became clear the enemy barrage had stopped, their battery effective no more. Wells put his radio headset to his ear. 'Bravo Zero Bravo. Good shooting. Record as X-ray one one. End of mission. Over.'

7
Advance to Kutenhausen

Heavy rain greeted us the next morning, some of the heaviest I had seen in a while. Serjeant Major King did the rounds. 'No move before midday,' he reported, which I thought might be enough time for the rain to stop. 'We've got trucks taking us on to a town called Hasbergen,' he continued, 'about ten kilometres away. The para brigades are taking the lead until further notice. The Devons have taken a load of prisoners up on the ridge. Their officer wanted them all to make a last stand in a quarry up there, but they ignored him and came out with their hands up.'

Our transport arrived just after noon, but morale plummeted straight away. It was still raining, but the trucks had no canvas covers. Nevertheless, King ordered us to move. We were all soaked to the skin before the trucks even set off, even King and Wells. The distance to Hasbergen was short but the journey seemed to take an age as we crawled along behind a jam of para vehicles. There were cheers and broad smiles when we arrived to be told we were to have a few days of rest. No sooner were we allocated houses than soldiers were stringing up wet clothes and lighting fires.

Boyd woke me in the early hours, saying Major Wells needed to see me. I had a feeling the promise of a few days' rest was about to be broken. Boyd led me to the house Wells was using as his headquarters. Under low light he was poring over a map with Serjeant Major King and some other officers I didn't recognize. Wells broke away to speak to me.

'Stokes, I've got some good news and some not-so-good news.

Which do you want first?' I shrugged, too tired for games. 'Good news is,' continued Wells, 'after the Devons cleared the ridge above Hasbergen, it enabled the Ulsters to move on. The Ulsters have made a rapid advance east, clearing a lot of towns and villages between us and the river Weser. In doing so, they have discovered a prisoner-of-war camp. Plenty of our boys there. Many of them have been prisoners since '40 and have never seen a British soldier in a maroon beret. The bad news is that we're moving out again at first light. We're aiming to catch up with the Ulsters at a little village called Stemmer. Another long wet truck ride, I'm afraid, but at least we shouldn't run into any Germans.'

He wasn't joking about the length of the journey. Stemmer was about eighty kilometres to the east and I wasn't relishing telling my boys. 'Yes, sir. I'll wake the men and get them ready.'

'Good man, carry on.'

My platoon took the news better than I expected. We were on the trucks once more just before the sun broke the eastern horizon. Its orange glow was short-lived and it soon started raining again.

It rained all day. Each time we ran into one of the numerous little villages and hamlets the Ulsters had cleared, we encountered a huge traffic jam of military vehicles. Our military police had caught up with the advance, units bickering over who had priority. Also, the nearer we got to Stemmer, the bigger became the clusters of German prisoners on the roadsides. They were guarded by fewer and fewer MPs, and I'm sure they could have escaped if they'd wanted to, but none showed any inclination, content to wait to be picked up.

We pulled into Stemmer at last light. The place was overwhelmed with most of 6th Airlanding Brigade, along with tanks of various descriptions and a few large engineer vehicles carrying bridging equipment. You didn't need to be a general to guess we had a big job coming. I was summoned with my section commanders to see Wells, leaving Alfred Cox and Peter May to dish out ammunition to the platoon.

In the warm cosy cellar of an undamaged house Wells had assembled me, Kenny Hills, Ben Piper and Connor Clout, along with an armoured troop leader and a captain from an artillery regiment. I was expected to brief Peter later. The next objective was the village of Kutenhausen. It was just two and a half kilometres to the east and was important to the Germans. The remnants of D and C Companies were back up with the advance. B Company would be forward right in Kutenhausen, C Company forward left. A and D Companies would be in reserve.

'Recce spotted a large number of German infantry moving into Kutenhausen,' explained Wells, 'with Panzerschreck and Panzerfaust. We've got a squadron of tanks with us, so we need to make sure the anti-tank weapons don't knock them out. We must clear Kutenhausen in order to secure the western bank of the Weser, so our engineers can move their bridging equipment up. Enemy strength is unknown on the far bank. Any questions so far?' There were none, so Wells continued. 'Corporal Stokes, I need you behind our lead sections tomorrow – that's Hills' and Piper's. Leave the PIATs with the company quartermaster. You may need extra Bren magazines and grenades. Serjeant Major King will set up a Company Aid Post, so make sure any casualties are backloaded to him.

'We've come too far to take unnecessary risks. Whatever you see in Kutenhausen, I want the tanks to hammer it before we push on. Is that clear? Ensure you mark enemy strongpoints with smoke grenades, but don't use the grenades to cover your movement, so the tanks have unobstructed views of enemy positions and ours. Let the tanks keep German heads down for you.'

No PIATs meant there were no panzers in Kutenhausen. No one wanted to say it out loud but you could sense the questions on everyone's mind. Was this it, the last stand by the Germans? Were they about to throw in the towel? Was just one big effort required to convince them fighting on was futile? I hoped so.

Back with my platoon, I was relieved to see them getting all their weapons and equipment together. Serjeant Major King was ahead of the game, already dishing out grenades, plus additional Bren and Sten magazines. I traded my Lee-Enfield for a Sten. The PIATs had already gone, the PIAT teams carrying rifles or Stens now. Matt Ingall was rolling his shoulders. 'Feels weird not having a PIAT launcher around my neck. I feel so light on my feet – it's like I've just given birth.'

Jack Lillie grunted. 'Bloody ugly baby. I'm not sorry to see the back of it. Those bomb satchels get right on my tits.'

As darkness fell, adrenalin was pumping and no one was even bothering to try and sleep. Most were playing cards or just chatting.

'I wonder what we'll do once the war is over,' said Alfred next to me. No one answered for a while. I thought about London and Molly, but I kept the thoughts to myself, almost fearful of jinxing my survival.

'I've been dreaming about a beef and onion pie. You know, with loads of gravy and good spuds,' Dougie Chambers answered.

'Nice,' responded Peter May. 'With a sponge pud for afters.'

'Yeah, my girl makes a fantastic sponge,' Dougie cooed. They fell into silence at the mention of girls, each lost in his memories. I pictured Molly serving behind the bar of the Jolly Gardeners in Mortlake. We'd not had time to develop our relationship as much as I'd have liked on my last leave.

'There's a girl at home I've been meaning to ask out,' reflected Peter. 'That's what I'm going to do when I get home.'

'Good for you, lad,' Chris Lenor said. 'No point waiting. Look what happened to Stephen Cooper. You make it to the end of this bloody war, then you make the most of it.'

The mood changed at the mention of Coops. 'Was he married?' Charlie Wyld asked.

'Aye,' Chris informed, 'on his last leave.'

They fell into silence and I felt myself welling up at the thought of Cooper. I got up, heading out for some air, but only got a couple of steps before Boyd arrived with a piece of paper for me to read. It was from Major Wells, who wanted to update his orders without the need for a meeting. 'Enemy forces likely to be Waffen SS. Possible Hitler Youth. Increase in anti-tank weapons in Kutenhausen. Tanks to lead and suppress likely firing positions prior to break-in by infantry.'

My stomach tightened. I glanced at Boyd, who looked like he wasn't a fan of the message. No one liked fighting the SS. I decided to keep their possible involvement as quiet as possible. The last thing we needed was to lose our nerve or our reason if we happened to capture some SS. Sometimes ignorance was bliss, a lesson I had learned in Arnhem. I resolved not to relay the SS element of the message to Peter, but decided to allow my other section commanders to make their own decisions.

Early morning found the heavens opening once again, making everyone feel cold and unmotivated. C Company were already competing for spots on the Churchill tanks that would accompany them into Kutenhausen. Those who couldn't find a space on the engine decks would be walking. C Company rolled out of town, their tanks screeching and clattering as they slowly accelerated away. Our Churchills then crunched and ground up alongside us. I realized how depleted B Company had become, everyone fitting on the tanks, no one having to walk. I wondered how well I'd kept track of my new company's losses, wondering when we might be reinforced or placed in reserve again. The engine decks were slippery with grease and rainwater, but it was a warmer for those lucky enough to be sitting near the exhaust louvres.

As we moved out of Stemmer, I thought about the prospect of fighting the SS. We crept along behind C Company into the little hamlet of Westerort, about a kilometre and a half down the road.

The hamlet seemed remarkably undamaged by the war. Ahead, we began to hear the chatter of machine guns and the thud of tank fire. Our column vibrated to a standstill. Holding on to the two rear turret periscopes, I got to my feet. I made out the rocking profiles of the Churchills up front as they fired at something ahead of us. I noticed C Company weren't mounted on their tanks any more. Muffled chatter in Alfred's headset caught my attention. Eventually, he pulled it to one side. 'The tanks up front are shooting up likely enemy positions in Kutenhausen. C Company are now on foot and advancing.'

I watched the C Company tanks firing for a while, before our convoy very slowly lurched forward again. I fought hard to keep my grip on the turret. Just forward of me, the tank commander sat atop it, his soaked beret squashed under his headset. Every so often he put binoculars to his eyes and then talked into his radio. The din of the roaring engine made it impossible for me to listen in to him.

As we reached the outskirts of Westerort, I saw Kutenhausen for the first time, smouldering in the near distance. The C Company tanks were off the road to our left, infantry on their bellies around them. Steam rose from the tanks and the prone soldiers, a prize sight for any German artillery spotter. But if the enemy had no tanks in the area, then they probably had no artillery support either. In the distance, flanked by infantry, two C Company tanks were moving towards some wooden outbuildings that marked the outer boundary of Kutenhausen. I made out C Company Serjeant Major Garry Jackson with their headquarters contingent in a drainage ditch to the left. The ditches ran down both sides of the road into the village. Jackson was talking into a radio headset while waving someone over to him.

Our tanks crossed the drainage ditch on the right-hand side of the road, heading into the fields. Ahead, C Company's tanks stopped firing, the infantry getting to their feet. Then their lead

Churchill rocked back in a flurry of sparks as a smoke trail from an enemy anti-tank weapon found its mark. The explosion gave off an almighty thud, the tank's front plate fittings flicking skyward.

'Get off, get off,' our tank commander roared, waving frantically. 'Get in the ditch.' We jumped or tumbled off the tank to comply. C Company's other forward tank was hit. I couldn't identify where the enemy were firing from. By the look of it, neither could our tank commanders, since with no real direction of shot, they began to pour machine-gun fire into the treelines and hedgerows leading south away from Kutenhausen. The other C Company tanks were directing serious firepower into the village, but every now and then a rocket trail would streak out to meet them. But they were further away than their two smouldering lead tanks, and the Germans' aim wasn't so good at longer range, their rockets streaking skyward, or thudding into the ground with loud crumps. I doubted the enemy anti-tank gun crew were experienced but knew we needed to close with them to eliminate the threat.

Alfred handed me the headset, but I struggled to pick anything useful out of the radio chatter. B Company was beginning to move down the right-hand drainage ditch. I blindly followed those in front of me, uncertain where anyone was, but I spotted Major Wells and his headquarters contingent. He noticed me too, giving me a thumbs up.

About two hundred metres along the ditch, everyone became bunched up. Ahead I could see white phosphorus grenades being thrown at a house, although a clear view of the village was becoming difficult, rain pushing the cloud down to street level, the sudden lack of wind allowing mist to hang heavy in the gardens. The house shrouded in white smoke suddenly burst in a flurry of roof tiles, bricks and masonry, showering the lead C Company troops in debris. More tank rounds thundered into the already wrecked house. Fire was then concentrated on the house to its right, shattering it in quick order. I suddenly felt confident in our ability to take care of the enemy in the village and neutralize their anti-tank capability. The C Company tanks stopped firing. 'Let's go, boys,' I shouted, hoping to connect with my platoon in the ditch. 'Let's get in them houses. Two-section frontage, let's go, let's go.'

I saw Kenny and Ben climb out of the ditch, their sections clambering after them and then advancing through the lingering white phosphorus smoke, heading for the houses. Connor's boys began checking the outbuildings. It seemed a fair plan to me.

With Peter, I led my old section towards the two smashed houses. Tracer erupted out of a Churchill, long streams zipping down the right-hand side of the village. A rocket smoke trail screamed across the front of my section, the rocket thudding into one of the outbuildings. As had become their policy of late, the enemy were using anti-tank guns against targets other than tanks. Connor's section was caught in the open, crawling about on their bellies, looking for cover. They soon crawled out of sight, but their damp steaming uniforms gave away their hiding places. A hornets' nest of MG 42 machine-gun fire then snapped across our front, splashing among the outbuildings and Connor's men. Quickly leading my section back to the ditch, I could make out the faint splutter of machine-gun muzzle flash in the village, as the enemy firing continued. I considered ordering Connor's section to sprint back to the ditch, which would have needed smoke grenades to cover their lengthier retreat, but ruled out the idea, since any confusion created by more smoke could result in them getting shot up by our own tanks.

But I decided to use a smoke grenade to try and mark the position of the enemy muzzle flash I'd seen, hoping our tanks could then home in on it. I pulled a grenade off the side of Alfred's backpack, one of two clipped to it. A long throw was required, so I pulled the pin, launching the grenade high in the air. It fell well short, but I hoped if our Churchills fired through its smoke, they might just take out the machine-gun position.

The air suddenly became thick with projectiles, large and small. The din was incredible. The repeated concussion made my ears ring. I realized I had given away our position in the ditch. Major Wells caught my eye, looking like he wanted to kill me, but the Churchills began firing, and the MG 42 fire soon petered out. Connor's section got to their feet, rushing after Ben and Kenny's sections. I decided to rush forward with my section to join them.

As I clutched handfuls of wet grass and mud to climb out of the ditch, I heard the thud of grenades – C Company fighting their way into the houses. As we reached Connor's section, I noticed the two lead C Company tanks had their barrels down. They had been knocked out. I smelt the unique chemical fragrance of smoke from phosphorus grenades and suddenly heard the hysterical shouting and crying of German children. It looked like Connor hadn't lost any men. We dashed into one of the front two smashed houses that had been hit by C Company's tanks, Major Wells's group soon joining us inside to find cover.

Another anti-tank rocket streaked past us, finding no target. Ben and Kenny's sections had entered the other smashed house. I decided to dash across to check on them, stumbling and tripping over debris en route.

I couldn't find Kenny or Ben. I heard shooting upstairs, followed by Kenny's shouting voice. I fought my way to the shattered staircase. 'Kenny?' I yelled.

'Yeah?' he roared.

'How you getting on?'

'German troops in the gardens, watch out.'

I crouched down, picking my way closer to the back end of the house. I heard English voices in a back room. 'Friendly incoming,' I shouted.

'OK, keep low,' came the reply. I realized Alfred was right

behind me. We entered the room, encountering two of Kenny's boys. One had a Bren mounted on a wooden table, pointing through a smashed window into a garden. The other stood against the back wall, observing.

He pointed at something outside, then threw a grenade at it. Rifle fire erupted upstairs, hysterical children's voices crying out. Downstairs, the Bren gunner let off short, sharp, chugging bursts. 'There they go,' he shouted. The man standing against the back wall moved forward, Sten in his shoulder, also firing short bursts. Outside, his grenade exploded, its concussion rippling inside, slapping me in the face. Both Bren and Sten gunners changed their magazines as the firing upstairs petered out.

'That's enough,' Kenny ordered upstairs. 'They're down; leave them alone.'

I felt we had the house under control, but found his words puzzling. I returned to the staircase. 'What's the matter, Kenny?'

I heard boots clumping along the landing above me. Kenny appeared, rifle in hand, looking like he could do with a hug. He flicked his head, signalling me to ascend. Alfred and I carefully ascended the busted stairs.

Kenny said nothing as he led me into what must have been a child's bedroom. Two of his lads were sitting on a bed, looking stunned, tears running down their filthy faces. Bedding was stripped, cupboards cleared of possessions, a few toys littered about the place. Kenny carefully took up a position at the open window shutters. 'I've seen it all now. Take a look.' I cautiously moved forward, peering over the window ledge. The German soldiers piled up in the garden were a sorry sight: a dozen or so of them, soaked and blood-splattered. A cluster of houses and cottages lay beyond them. The soldiers' twisted faces told a horrid tale of a bullet-ridden, grenade-mangled death. A few looked like they were just sleeping. But 'soldiers' was pushing it. They were just children, not even old enough to be out of school, stuffed into military uniforms far too big for them, thrown at us to be killed. 'There are three more in the kitchen downstairs,' added Kenny. 'Grenades took care of them.' I could see his eyes were glazed, dams ready to burst. 'They now have their children fighting us,' he said. 'What kind of a fucking place is this?'

I couldn't think of a reply so just made my way back downstairs. The Bren gunner opened fire again, shouting about movement in the buildings beyond the garden. 'Stop firing, you fucking idiots,' screamed Kenny from upstairs. 'I can see white sheets being waved about in there.' The Bren stopped firing, crying children and the distant thud of grenades the only sounds. I wondered how many kids were in the village fighting us.

'From now on, only shoot when you're sure they're bloody armed!' I shouted.

Major Wells arrived with his headquarters contingent and Serjeant Major King, demanding an update. I explained we had encountered what appeared to be Hitler Youth. King made his way upstairs. 'Here we go, fellas,' he soon called out. 'They're coming out from the places opposite.'

We scrambled to the windows, weapons at the ready. Waving a bedsheet, one of Hitler's uniformed children emerged from a battered cottage across the garden, his hands high in the air. The rain made the sheet wrap around him, as he screeched out something in German over and over again. He couldn't have been more than thirteen. More uniformed children began to emerge, hands up, all calling the same thing.

By the pile of bodies in the garden another dozen or so of Hitler's master race gathered. They stood soaked and shivering, some caked in blood with recently applied field dressings. Their faces told a story of loss and fear. We looked at them curiously, not entirely sure what to do with them. Out on the road a Churchill ground to a halt. King reappeared. 'Let's get them searched. Peter May has got the job.'

I called Peter across from his position in the other smashed house. Before long, his section arrived to help him with the task. Some of the kids dropped to the ground, fearing reprisals. Distant firing started again, C Company engaging more enemy. I wondered if the enemy were more Hitler Youth, or whether the *Wehrmacht* had found the guts to stick around. The Churchill outside gunned its engine, moving forward in support. It could have only moved fifty metres, before I heard its machine gun spraying. Kutenhausen was far from ours, and the day had only just begun. I tasked Connor's section to check the cottages and houses from which the Hitler Youth had emerged.

Their search of the kids completed, Peter's section got the task of marching them back to Westerort. Wells said his headquarters contingent would accompany them, deciding to temporarily base himself there. While Peter's section were away, we got orders to rest, A Company moving forward to relieve us.

As A Company moved through our position, I joined Richards in one of the cottages opposite. Some of the lads had minor injuries, mostly from splinters. In that cottage alone the Hitler Youth had been given enough anti-tank ammunition to knock out all our tanks. Projectiles were stacked under the kitchen table and across the living-room floor, where we found two more dead kids, messed up really bad. Blood pooled on rugs underneath the bodies. Evidence of their fight for life was littered all around: field dressings and their wrappers. One of the boys had a trouser leg ripped off, a tourniquet fitted. It was such a waste of life.

'They've seen too much already,' I said sadly.

'Just when you think this fucking war can't throw up any more surprises.'

I nodded. We'd all seen too much.

8
Advance to Wietersheim

Major Wells organized a meeting of my platoon in the kitchen of an undamaged house in Kutenhausen. He spread out a map, covering the whole surface of a kitchen table. We could still hear the German artillery barrage hitting the eastern end of town, as he began. 'As soon as it gets dark, our engineers will head towards the Weser riverbank, with C Company as protection. The engineers will build a raft system of sorts. As soon as it's ready, B Company will be first to cross the river. Our mission is to get up into this village here, Wietersheim.'

We all craned in closer to see the place he was pointing at with his pencil. It was just three kilometres away, on the other side of the Weser.

'It's in this bloody place that their spotters are holed up, advising their gunners and giving us problems. We are to clear the place and stop the shelling. As we go about our business in Wietersheim, D and A Companies will cross the river and move as quickly as possible into Frille, here.' He had shifted his pencil to the next village, another three kilometres east. 'Because of our lack of numbers we will have priority on artillery support. It will be dark when we cross, so we are to use caution when we advance on Wietersheim. Our tanks and artillery have been hitting it all afternoon. Chances are, we have persuaded them that to remain there is not good for their health. I have spoken with the artillery battery commander. We will primarily be asking for star shells and should have our observation officer back from A Company tonight, so shouldn't have to call in fire ourselves. Any questions so far?'

'What if we find an entire German regiment in Wietersheim, sir?' asked Kenny Hills.

'We return to the river crossing point and have the artillery reduce the place to dust, then move in and take care of the survivors in the morning.' Everyone nodded. The plan was simple, and simple made it seem far more achievable.

As we started to lose daylight, an engineer column moved up from behind Westerort, waiting for the imminent order to move out with C Company. I didn't envy them; the shelling of the eastern end of Kutenhausen had become sporadic but was intense while in progress. And airburst shells had a nasty habit of tearing up everything underneath them.

Once darkness consumed us, my platoon led B Company across Kutenhausen. I hoped the raft system was already in place. Even from the town, I could see frequent star shells from the German artillery illuminating the area between us and the river, particularly the crossing point, where the light display was sometimes followed up with airburst shells. But their aim wasn't good and didn't improve with practice, leaving me to wonder if the enemy artillery was being fired by boys as well.

We arrived at the eastern edge of town, which A and C Companies had cleared earlier. Only A Company remained there now, based in a single building. They had encountered their fair share of Hitler Youth. The corpses of dead German child soldiers were strewn among the gardens and outbuildings, periodically illuminated by their own star shells.

We rendezvoused with a few of the engineers and made our way towards the river. They led the way, making sure that undergrowth, trees and hedgerows protected most of our route. But once out beyond the town, we froze like rabbits caught in headlights the first time a German star shell popped above the river.

I felt horribly exposed. One of the engineers waved us on. 'Ignore those bloody things. They know we're coming; no point trying to sneak about now. Keep moving.' As another flare drifted off to our left, I heard a rumble behind us. Our artillery had begun returning fire. Ahead in the glare I could spot C Company in crude untidy trenches, helmets bobbing about.

The river rafts put in place by the engineers were pontoons, moved using a bizarre two-way rope-and-pulley system. Each pontoon had its own engineer pilot. We were hustled onto the pontoons with no ceremony. I realized teams of engineers on the far bank were pulling the pontoons across. At least one team must have swum the river to set it all up, and the current was rough and fast, downright bloody dangerous. As my platoon crossed the river, airburst shells ripped up a nearby piece of riverbank, punching holes in the water. I knew if one exploded above us, it would be over.

We made the far bank, quickly forming up to move on Wietersheim. It was decided A Company would move on Frille alone, with D Company in reserve, in case the enemy in either village proved troublesome. It was a simple enough change to the original plan. On the eastern side of the river the openness of the farmland was unnerving, but just two hundred metres on, star shells revealed a thick treeline at the edge of some woods, the rooftops of Wietersheim jutting over the trees.

Friendly tank fire and machine-gun tracer screamed in past our left side as our fire support strafed the treeline. It made me feel a little more secure on the open ground, but as enemy airburst salvoes began to follow us from the river, I worried about our fire support mistaking us for enemy troops.

The airburst shells became more frequent and moved a little closer, probably prompting Major Wells to blast on his whistle, signalling the B Company charge into Wietersheim. My platoon took the lead. I was starting to get nervous looks from a few of the lads as our own fire continued to pummel the ever-closing treeline. I looked around, trying to find Wells, but instead noticed A Company moving away at a tangent, on their way to Frille. 'Rob,' gasped Alfred, holding the radio headset to one ear, 'Major Wells says keep moving.'

Our fire support ceased just before we reached the treeline, but as our lead sections moved into the woods, enemy tracer shot through the trees, snapping out towards the river. His section furthest forward, I recognized Connor Clout's excited voice crackle over Alfred's radio. 'Contact, infantry. Wait. Out.' My first reaction was to go to ground and find cover, but Peter and Connor's sections had other ideas. They zoomed into the woods, soon out of sight. I dashed after them as the trees in front of me erupted in tracer and grenade detonations. Behind me, an almighty thwack sounded, and something solid hit the ground.

'Man down.' I spun round to see Ben Piper rolling on the ground next to a rock. I approached and in the low light saw that it wasn't a rock at all; it was another body. Alfred. I sprinted over. A lad was tending to Ben and I crouched down next to Alfred. He was groaning and flailing, the shock of being hit finally sinking in. I tried to fight through Alfred's waving arms. Someone flicked on a torch. In the dull red glow I could see Alfred was in a really bad way. He had a small entry wound in the middle of his throat. I began packing the wound with a dressing, dark fluid already spoiling my efforts. Alfred's groaning became more of a gurgle as he struggled to breathe, fighting for his life.

I felt a firm hand on my shoulder. I looked up at the dark profile of Serjeant Major King. 'Corporal Stokes, you have two sections in contact. They are your priority. Take Corporal Hills and his section. Go now.'

Shuffling back, I got to my feet. I briefly looked at the harrowing scene below me, but fresh grenade detonations and gunfire in the woods grabbed my attention. King was right. I stepped away from the red glow, my night vision returning. 'Kenny,' I shouted, realizing there was no point in being quiet now, 'bring your lot to me.'

Kenny was nearby. 'Roger that. Follow me. Let's go!' In the gloom I could just see him jogging towards me.

A star shell burst above us. Kenny's lads were directly behind him. They all stopped, seeing Alfred's plight. 'Let's go, boys. Follow me,' I shouted, knowing I had to capture their focus. I spun on my heel, heading off into the woods. Tracer spat through the trees, more grenade detonations thundering. I slowed to a walk, trying to identify the members of my platoon already in the woods. Partially obscured by heads and shoulders, muzzle flashes showed me where a few of the boys were, but I couldn't tell who was who, as they dashed about changing fire positions, shouting at each other.

The tempo of the fighting briefly slowed enough for me to recognize the cry of a child. More Hitler Youth. I waved Kenny and his boys down behind me, thinking to use them as reserve for Peter and Connor's forward sections.

Ahead in the woods, sporadic rifle fire petered out. 'Get your hands up,' I heard Peter roar above the whimper of Hitler's children, 'or you will end up like the others. Hands up now.' The whimpering got louder.

I carefully approached the chaos. 'May?' I shouted, admitting to myself that I felt pumped up.

'Yeah?'

I wasn't the only one who was pumped up, judging by the sound of his voice. 'What have you got there, mate?'

'Three prisoners, one MG 42 and a load of Panzerfausts. The rest are dead.'

'Sit tight, mate. I'm coming to you with another section.' I waved Kenny and his boys forward. We linked up with Peter's section, who were searching our snivelling new prisoners, Connor's section ahead in the village. Thinking of Alfred, I wasn't in the mood to deal with Hitler Youth. My stomach began to rise in my throat.

I carefully put a hand on Peter's shoulder. His head flicked round, his eyes looking wild. He was lusting for blood. I decided not to mention Alfred and Ben. 'How are you doing, mate?' I asked softly, trying to soothe him. His shoulders instantly dropped, as if I had released a valve. In the glare of someone's red torchlight I could see three scared faces. They thought we were going to shoot them. And why not? I thought. We were in pitch-black woods.

Up ahead there was more gunfire and I snapped back to reality. I wasn't going to have the prisoners killed. Judging by the heavy gunfire up ahead, Connor's section was already killing enough children. I just wanted to get the night over with. 'Everyone accounted for?'

'Yeah, looks like everyone is OK. Just lucky on this one. We killed their commander. They didn't want to fight after that.'

I knew we had to advance to Wietersheim. We no longer had a radio but couldn't afford to wait for Major Wells to move up. I took Kenny and Connor's sections towards the village, leaving Peter's men in reserve, looking after the prisoners. But whatever German forces were originally in Wietersheim had gone. I wondered where the recent sound of heavy gunfire had come from. The enemy in the village had either lost their nerve and fled, or felt the place wasn't worth holding. We found evidence of their occupation in various buildings and at road junctions, including two anti-tank guns, so they were expecting to oppose armour. Just-boiled water sat in coffee pots. Someone had recently shaved, leaving his whiskers floating in a bowl beside a smouldering fireplace. We were closing on the adults who were sending the kids out to battle.

9
Consolidation

On arrival in Wietersheim, Major Wells called a halt to our clearance activities. Accompanied by Serjeant Major King, he called a meeting with me and my section commanders in a kitchen. We were told A Company had taken a battering before even reaching Frille. From a room above the kitchen, I'd already laid eyes on the village, realizing it was the source of the heavy firing I'd heard from the woods. The place looked like the end of the world, bathed in the glare of flares, tracer screaming skywards, grenade detonations flashing in the houses. The fighting looked so bad, I'd decided not to tell the platoon about it.

'Corporal Piper and Private Alfie Cox are dead,' King said quickly and quietly. No one spoke for a while. King didn't seem his usual brash self, the losses appearing to knock him sideways. I thought about the brief time I'd known Alfie. Always upbeat and happy-go-lucky. But his luck had run out, I thought glumly. He'd survived Normandy and a bullet through the jaw, only to die here with the finish line in sight. Luck – the difference between life and death in war. Would mine hold out? I wondered. Suddenly I wasn't so sure.

With a loud clunk, King hauled Alfie's radio onto the kitchen table. Major Wells got everyone's attention. 'We need a new section commander and a new radio operator. Serjeant Stokes, I'll leave it up to you to assign these positions, but do it quickly. We move out in a couple of hours.'

King walked out, concerned with other duties, leaving us and the major circled around Alfie's blood-smeared radio backpack. No one spoke. Finally, I stepped forward and picked up the radio set. I turned, taking in the faces. 'Lads, I will assign this to someone if I have to, but first I'm going to ask for a volunteer. Anyone?'

No one spoke. Heads were bent, eyes avoiding mine. The silence stretched until it was broken by someone clearing their throat. I turned to find Richards stepping forward. 'I'll take it.' He held my gaze, sure and steady.

After a minute, I was about to give the set to him, when the major shook his head. 'Not you.'

I saw Richards' jaw harden, his face a picture of determination and disappointment. 'You . . .' he started, clearly gunning for me, but it was the major who cut him off quickly before he could say something he'd regret.

'A corporal can't carry a radio as well, Richards.'

He stood frozen, shocked into immobility. I stood, impassive, enjoying his confusion.

'What do you mean, sir?'

'Private Richards, I am promoting you to corporal. You understand now?'

He stuttered some more, but finally his face split with a grin, something I doubt anyone had seen before. A few of the boys came forward and patted him on the back. He acknowledged their congratulations before turning back to the major and me. 'Thank you. I won't let you down.'

Wells nodded. 'You just make sure you get it right this time, Richards. You owe your pal Tommy that.'

'I do,' he said simply. 'Second time lucky.'

In the end, Chris Lenor volunteered to be my new radio man. I was glad and said I'd clean the pack up before he had to use it.

Alone upstairs, I kept my promise, using the opportunity to

crackle the radio back to life. I listened to the frantic voice of A Company's radio operator, almost drowned out by shouting and gunfire. Reports were of heavy resistance and casualties. I tracked D Company being summoned from reserve, but even after they arrived in Frille, reports continued of the enemy putting up a hell of a fight. There was confused talk of PIAT anti-tank guns being used against enemy MG 42 positions, but everyone had surrendered their PIATs before Kutenhausen, when it became clear there were no enemy tanks nearby, and I hadn't heard anything about the anti-tank guns being handed out again.

Wells had warned us that B Company might be required in Frille, but A and D eventually won the day, occupying the village, from which they spotted enemy armour in the distance and launched a patrol to knock out a rail gun. C Company arrived in Wietersheim at first light, along with our supply vehicles. The report of enemy armour was enough to prompt the resupply of PIATs to the companies. We rested, replenishing our supplies of food, water and ammunition.

We then marched on towards Winzlar, some thirty kilometres to the north-east, meeting no opposition. En route, it became obvious that, as we approached, the Germans were hurriedly abandoning their positions and retreating. The villages became more and more untouched by the war, dead German soldiers fewer and further between. Major Wells learned that our 3rd and 5th Parachute Brigades were encountering resistance to the north – not *Wehrmacht*, but Hitler Youth and Luftwaffe drafted in as infantry. To the south, the Americans were advancing rapidly. As we increased the pace of our march, it seemed the Germans were on the ropes.

We finally reached Winzlar in the early hours. It had been a long trudge, and my feet hurt. The enemy had once again fled before us. I was surprised that some on our side were bitter about this, clearly spoiling for a fight. First light revealed a lovely little

German town with no battle scars. Our supply vehicles caught up with us again. They were carrying fresh troops. Many of us were unshaven, dirty, and in various conditions of undress, but by contrast the troops in the trucks looked clean, fresh, rather nervous and out of place, not a lick of mud on their boots.

It dawned on me that we were being reinforced. Immaculate officers stepped down from the trucks, shepherding their troops into ranks. It seemed odd to drill in the middle of a town in war-torn Nazi Germany. Distant battle noise caused some of the replacements to flinch, others deliberately standing tall and straight-faced. Some of my platoon let out a little chuckle. This soon became quiet mickey-taking. I knew I should have quelled it straight away, but I had to admit I was smirking myself. It struck me how old we all looked, compared to them. I decided to let my lads carry on, although it wasn't long before some of them got bored with it all, returning to cleaning weapons and shaving..

The following morning, complete with reinforcements, we were crammed into trucks and moved east to a town called Heitlingen, another thirty kilometres closer to Berlin. Cleared by our para brigades, it sat to the west of an abandoned Luftwaffe airbase.

I was called to see Major Wells and Serjeant Major King. 'Come on in, Serjeant,' greeted Wells. 'By the way, I can confirm your promotion has been made permanent.' It still felt a little strange to be addressed as a serjeant. I hoped I would live long enough to get used to it.

I was surprised when C Company Serjeant Major Garry Jackson joined us. He shook my hand. 'Congratulations, Rob. Well done, mate.'

'I'm rather pissed off I can't keep hold of you, Serjeant Stokes,' said Wells. 'You're a good soldier and one hell of a fighter, by all accounts.'

'I get about a bit,' I replied modestly. 'Thank you for the compliment, sir.'

'And this greedy man,' Wells waved at Jackson, 'wants your section to return to C Company too. I can't pretend I'm happy with that. I've a lot of fresh, green blokes in my company, and the experience offered by you and your men will be sorely missed.'

'I am but the messenger, sir.' Jackson smirked.

I was asked to fetch Peter and his boys. As Wells shook their hands, King pulled me quietly to one side. 'Can't believe you're going, Rob. I won't lie to you; there are some right ones among the reinforcements. Some look like they want to cry, others want to hunt Nazi skirt. I think I'm gonna have problems.' I agreed but wondered how the new C Company recruits would stack up. Although I had originally served in D Company, I supposed it was good to return to the company with which I started Operation Varsity. Hamminkeln felt like a lifetime ago. We had all come so far. Some people coped with sudden change rather well, but others, like me, were often knocked sideways. I prayed I would see out the war without any more surprises.

Jackson took me to see Major Joshua High, who held out a large hand. 'Good to see you again, Serjeant,' High gushed. 'Congratulations on your promotion.'

'Thank you, sir,' I acknowledged. 'It's good to be back. Never thought I'd return after Hamminkeln.'

High nodded. 'Hamminkeln was a mess. But, given the losses sustained by the battalion, we didn't fare too badly in the landings, which is why B Company had you lot on loan, so to speak, until we got fresh troops in.'

'Do we have any of the new boys, sir?' I ventured.

He looked at Jackson, who answered for him. 'Twenty-five. They have already been distributed among our platoons. You will have 7 Platoon. They have a fresh section of eight, who look OK. Their gear looks in good enough order. You will have May in command of your old section. The others will be led by Ray Clifton and Pete Newland, who's just been promoted to section commander. May will get his stripes today.'

I was pleased to hear official confirmation of Peter May's promotion. He had certainly earned it. 'What of Corporal Hill,' I asked, 'Karlton Hill?'

'Took grenade fragments in the legs at Kutenhausen,' reported Jackson. 'He's alive but won't be back any time soon.'

'Oh . . .' I trailed off. I suddenly felt deflated. No one was safe from the war.

Jackson strolled away, going about his rounds, leaving me alone with Major High. 'Our advance across Germany has gone well,' began High. 'We've bought ourselves some breathing space – 15th Scottish Division is moving through us, taking the lead. We're going to be here for some time. What I want is to keep the new blokes busy. I'm afraid idle hands make the Devil's work, if you get my meaning. We need in particular to keep on top of any issues involving the local women. Captain Filler is on hand to help you out.'

'Yes, sir.' High's wishes were nothing I hadn't heard before, but I hadn't seen Filler since the Belgian Ardennes, noting his promotion from lieutenant.

'Don't worry, Stokes,' reassured High. 'You'll do just fine. If we didn't think that, you'd still be a Bren gunner.'

Normandy seemed a long time ago, a faded memory until now. 'Leave it with me, sir. Is Serjeant Wardle about? I could get some pointers from him.'

'He's in command of 8 Platoon. Officers are a little hard to come by at the moment. As it stands, it's just Captain Filler and myself.'

10
Women Trouble

My platoon settled into some decent houses in Winzlar. Four new recruits joined Peter May's section. They looked like solid blokes. Mark Dale hailed from St Albans; he would be the section's new Bren gunner, with Nathan Seeds from Windsor supporting him. They had already trained together as a Bren team. Nathan Tructer was a Twickenham lad, just up the road from Mortlake, but keen to avoid over-familiarity with a new man, I resisted the temptation to talk about home with him. Tructer would be a rifleman, along with Darren Lane from Kingston upon Thames.

It rained for the next few days, the town a constant melee of traffic. By all reports, the advance of 15th Scottish Division was excruciatingly slow, hardly the pace we had maintained. Life became boring, and despite a good start our efforts to keep the new recruits occupied evaporated. Those of us who had been around since Operation Varsity needed to recharge our batteries, rather than spend all our time keeping the new lads busy. Nevertheless, the replacements were pretty much licked into shape. A small group felt they were invincible, but the more seasoned blokes soon knocked it out of them.

I eventually caught up with Serjeant Sean Wardle. He looked refreshed, sipping a mug of something hot in a kitchen. 'How you doing, Rob? Take a seat.' He offered a congratulatory hand. 'Well done, mate. By all accounts, you've certainly earned them stripes.'

Blushing, I glanced at the chevrons I had sewn on my upper right smock sleeve. I felt a bit of a fraud, since when I was serving with Sean as a private soldier in Normandy, he was already a serjeant. 'Thanks, Sean. Not too sure if I'm the right man for the job.'

He waved a dismissive hand. 'Nonsense, mate. You've proved you have the nerve and the clout to lead, when it all goes to shit. No one can ask any more than that.'

I made us both tea. His tea leaves had certainly done the miles, since I had to really give the water a good long stir in order to darken it. So with a splash of condensed milk that looked like it was about to turn, I made sure to apply a good helping of sugar.

As I handed him his mug a slightly built young man knocked on the open kitchen door, standing apologetically at the threshold. Sean stood. 'What's up, Corporal Lynch?'

Lynch looked embarrassed. 'Ah, Serjeant Stokes, I'm glad you're here too. We've got a bit of a problem with some men from our sections.'

Sean beckoned him in, gesturing to a seat. Lynch declined to sit, and with both hands clutching his maroon beret to his chest, he appeared to struggle to find the right words. Back in Normandy Sean would have told the man to just spit it out, but this didn't feel right. Sean tried to reassure him. 'What's happened, son?'

Lynch became even more anxious. 'Two of my section have absconded, Serjeant, and, well, I'm afraid they're with one of your men, Serjeant Stokes.'

Sean and I looked at each other, frowned, and then looked back at Lynch. 'Absconded?' I piped up. 'You mean done a runner?'

'Not exactly, Serjeant,' said Lynch. 'What I mean is they have taken matters into their own hands. With German women.'

Trouble with the locals over their women was the first thing Major High wanted to avoid, and images of a broken and bloody Kate Green presented themselves to me, images of her lying in an alleyway in Sheen, rape victim of American Captain Troy Temple. It flashed into my mind that I hadn't caught up with the latest on

Temple for some while, such had been the pace of our advance across Germany.

Sean got to his feet. Leaning forward with both hands on the table, he glared menacingly at Lynch. 'Where are they? No fucking about. Where do you think they are?'

After fumbling inside his smock, Lynch pulled out a map and unfolded it just enough to point out where he thought they were. 'I took the section on patrol on the south side of town. We passed a house. Two women were breaking up logs in their garden. The boys took the normal interest but I moved them on. It was only later that I realized two of mine were missing. I then bumped into one of your corporals, Hills, who told me that one of your platoon was missing as well, a chap called Richards.'

'Richards?' I almost stammered.

'Yes, Bob Richards, I believe.'

I nearly fell off my chair, while Sean shoved himself away from the table and spun to face the kitchen sink, head bowed. I could hear him cursing under his breath. His raised shoulders relaxed as he composed himself, turning slowly to address Lynch once more. 'Which of our lot are gone?'

'Newbury and Brennan, new boys.'

I wanted to berate him for not getting to grips with things, but I guessed he had been picked from his peers to lead as a section commander and was still a bit green. Not that I was one to talk, when it came to dealing with Richards. How could I have trusted him? My shock turned to anger. 'Take us there now. Rob, come with me. Richards is your man, and I might need some help with this one.'

Weapons slung across our backs, we followed Lynch out of the house. The town was considered secure, and a patrol programme of sorts was running, but it wasn't quite out of the question that we might encounter stray enemy troops. We walked at a brisk pace to the southern side of town, stopping outside a beautiful house, worthy of any chocolate-box lid. Despite the war washing around the house, it appeared untouched. Light grey smoke drifted from its chimney, a fire on the go.

Sean pushed through the front gate, and we scaled three steps leading to a large wooden front door. With one swift motion, Sean turned the door handle and barged his way in.

Someone in a British uniform sprang up from a large sofa in the hall, leaving a naked girl on the cushions. The young soldier had made the mistake of grabbing his Lee-Enfield, so Sean felled him with a shattering headbutt. The young man let out a girlish yelp as his nose broke, before sliding down the wall, cupping his face. Lynch mouthed that this was Brennan. I felt this was old-school justice: one down, two to go.

Sean moved on, leaving Lynch with Brennan, trying to keep his hobnailed boots silent on the tiled floor. Following him, I peered around a corner into a room. The man of the house was clearly a Nazi in every sense of the word. I saw pennants on a wall, SS runes adorning a highly polished plaque. Large framed portraits of Hitler and Himmler appeared. Other pictures showed what must be the house occupier shaking hands with men in SS uniforms, all true members of the so-called master race. Suddenly there was a crash from upstairs and we all charged up the single flight. At the top of the stairs Sean burst through a door on the right and I followed close behind.

We froze in shock at the wriggling mass of bodies on the floor: limbs, hands and hair coming out of everywhere. It took me a moment to work out that a naked girl was clawing at the back of the head of a man, who in turn had his hands round the throat of a shirtless man between them. The man on the top was Richards. The blood roared in my ears at the sight of him and I elbowed past Sean, reaching down to grab him round the neck. The girl screamed, suddenly aware of more men in the room. Sean came to my side and helped me separate the men.

'What the fuck is this?' he roared, lifting the half-naked man to his feet. I had hold of Richards' collar, and he was coughing and spluttering, unable to speak.

'Why don't you all fuck off,' said the half-naked man, his breath stinking of alcohol. Sean slammed him against the wall. 'Corporal Lynch, get in here.'

Lynch appeared at the door. Sean didn't even bother turning to face him. 'Is this your man?'

'Yes, sir, that's Newbury.'

'Right, fetch a medic for the girl and call the military police to arrest these buggers – their luck has just run out.'

11
Belsen

'The OC should never have promoted you. A leopard can't change its spots, and a bastard like you can't stop fucking up.'

Bob Richards was sitting at a table between two military policemen. I was so angry I couldn't bring myself to look at him. I'd been reluctant even to see him but he'd sent repeated messages and eventually I'd gone to see him with Wardle.

'It wasn't what it looked like.'

'And you expect me to believe that? You were there with Newbury and Brennan, stinking of booze and with a half-naked girl in the room.'

'Serjeant.'

Finally I looked at him. His eye was swollen and his lip cut. He held my gaze. 'Serjeant, I didn't do it.'

My resolve softened slightly. 'Jesus, Bob, what the hell were you thinking? I gave you a chance. I risked my neck for you.'

'I know, and I'm telling you, I haven't let you down.'

'Really? We may have different ideas of what's expected of a soldier then.'

He shook his head. 'It wasn't what it looked like,' he repeated again.

I sighed loudly. 'OK then, Bob, why don't you tell me what it was like then?'

He ran a hand through his hair. 'Everyone knows Newbury and Brennan are a bad pair; they've got charge sheets as long as your arm and reputations that stretch further. So when I saw them go into this house on their own I decided to take a look. The scream from inside told me everything I needed to know. I tried to get in, but the front door was locked, so I went round the back and found an open window. I crawled through and found myself at the foot of the stairs. I heard a scream from upstairs and so I ran up and opened the door. There was Newbury, swigging from a bottle of brandy and slapping the girl.' Richards stopped, looking down at his hands as he fidgeted with a cigarette packet on the table. 'I grew up with drunks, and I know them. I know how they pollute and destroy everything they touch.' He sighed. 'I saw Newbury there and, well, I lost it. Next thing I knew you were hauling on my collar.'

He finished and the room fell silent. Richards was looking down at the table. One of the MPs cleared his throat. It sounded loud in the confined space. I thought back to what I'd actually seen when I entered the room: the mass of limbs and bodies. Could he be telling the truth?

I stepped forward and stood directly in front of the table. He looked up. 'Is that the truth, Bob?'

He nodded, holding my gaze, steady and level.

'I believe him, Sean.'

Sean Wardle gave a bark of laughter. 'Well, you've changed your tune.'

'His story makes sense. He wasn't undressed like Newbury and, while I'd be the first to believe the worst of him if it was a case of insubordination, well, he's never shown any sign of anything like this before.'

'Whereas Newbury and Brennen have.' It was a statement rather than a question. 'Yes, I've been told they have form. Well, you may be right, Rob. I'm not sure I believe he's guilty either, but we can't just let him off. It's a matter for a senior officer and they've got bigger fish to fry right now. No, I reckon his war is over. He'll stay in irons until after this final push is done. Then you can come back and speak for him if you want. For now, you've lost yourself another corporal, and we've got to move.'

I nodded. We already had our orders, so I knew I'd be leaving Richards behind, but I wanted to do my best for him – partly out of guilt for having doubted him in the first place. The trucks were leaving immediately so I asked Sean to explain the situation to Richards and assure him that I'd be back to speak for him. And to tell him his luck hadn't run out. But as the trucks drove off I couldn't help feeling I'd left another good man behind.

There were the usual traffic jams en route, before we gathered in a large, densely wooded area just to the north of the town. There weren't enough tents to go round, so some dug trenches, including us. We were told the woods hadn't quite been cleared of German troops, so a defensive trench system was required. At least we wouldn't have to join in night patrols; our reconnaissance platoon would be covering that.

As darkness fell, we settled in our trenches and I became aware of a foul odour drifting on the breeze. It smelled like meat gone bad, mixed with a kind of mustard and off-milk scent. It clung to the back of your throat. No matter how much you swallowed or coughed, nothing would shift it. 'What the hell is that stink?' Sean Wardle was holding a piece of cloth to his nose. 'It's like something's turned in the larder.'

'An abattoir, I reckon,' said Chris Lenor. 'There was one in the town where I grew up.'

'Jesus, how did you stand it?'

'I don't know. We just got used to it, I suppose.'

'Well, I'm not getting used to this,' Sean replied and trudged off into the darkness.

I must have got used to it though as next thing I knew there was a tug on my sleeping bag. It was dawn, but the dense trees kept most of the light out. Major Joshua High stood over me. 'Serjeant Stokes. Serjeant, wake up.'

'What's up, sir?' I managed.

'I have a job for you, lad. Come and have some tea while I explain.'

I followed him to his trench. He spread his map out above the trench, needing a torch because of the gloom. 'We are here, just inside this wood line. Over the course of the night we've had some developments that are rather difficult to explain.' After an awkward silence, he looked at me strangely. It wasn't like him to struggle for words. He looked down at the map, jabbing it with his finger. 'Here . . . there is a camp, if that's the best way to describe it. 11th Armoured Division came across it. It's full of people who need a lot of medical attention.' There was another long pause. '6th Airborne Division have been asked to send all medical facilities and expertise to the camp, as well as our laundry and shower unit.' He looked up, blushing, almost embarrassed. 'I don't feel this task needs all of us, but I'm sending your platoon to escort the laundry and shower unit.'

It sounded an unusual task, but simple enough. 'I see, sir. Why do they need an escort, though?'

My simple question seemed to give him renewed focus. I followed his finger, as it traced a route across the map. 'The woods still aren't properly cleared. Medical personnel will meet you at a railhead by the camp.' His finger lingered over the camp.

A caravan of trucks headed off towards the railhead, my vehicle in the lead. After about a kilometre, we began to see military police on motorbikes. At a junction a crude sign had been constructed. It read, 'Belsen'. We were waved down by a military policeman. 'What have you got in your column, Serjeant, if you please?' he asked me.

'Laundry and shower unit. Been told to take it to the railhead.'

I noticed his face was pale and drawn. He shook his head and mumbled, 'Poor buggers need a lot more than that.'

He waved us on, and as we pulled away I was struck by how much stronger the vile stench seemed to be getting.

After another five minutes or so we passed a railway level crossing and two more military policemen. One had a handkerchief over his nose and mouth. The other was bent double, throwing up. The MP with the handkerchief waved us to the left. As we turned I saw a wrecked train behind a lengthy open platform. Steam drifted from the train's smashed innards. All along the length of the platform, battered wooden rail carriages were backed up behind the train. On the platform a sizeable crowd of people were covering their mouths or being sick. Some wore military uniforms, some were dressed in civilian clothes.

As we approached, the scent of burned coal and oil added to the ghastly smell that had become so familiar. The crowd was a mixture of British armed personnel and civilians with cameras. I clambered down from the truck. 'Wait here,' I instructed the driver. 'I'll try and find out where we need to take the laundry and shower, lads.' But some of them had already begun climbing from their vehicles, as had some of my platoon.

My weapon slung behind me, I made my way onto the platform, picking my way through the locomotive debris. The foul odour became a little stronger. A coal bin stood on the platform, the only one I could see. Pieces of roof from the carriages were strewn around the bin. A few carriages had intact roofs, but some looked as though a huge hand had ripped the tops away.

I carefully eased my way into the crowd, going onto tiptoe to try to see what was beyond them. Then, bizarrely, the crowd parted, as though Moses had commanded it himself and everything seemed to go quiet.

I was suddenly exposed to a horror more appalling than I'd seen on any battlefield. Men, women and children were stacked up like firewood, faces frozen in wide-eyed horror as their lives had expired. I wanted to look away but my eyes continued to take in the hellish scene: the blood-clotted hair, the neat bullet holes through their foreheads. My stomach churned. I fought to keep down the burning bile in the back of my throat. Finally, I turned from the scene, looking down, trying to compose myself. There were puddles of vomit on the platform.

I forced myself to turn back, this time looking beyond the pile of bodies on the platform, and into a carriage. Shafts of daylight from the splintered roof lit a ghostly interior. It was horrific: people crammed in so tight, they had died standing up. Some of the dead were dismembered. Lifeless mothers cradled headless infants. I felt the presence of someone beside me and the click of a camera. I turned to face a journalist. He held his hands up, open-palmed, camera wedged under his armpit. 'Sorry, my friend, but we need to record this.'

I turned again to the carriage. 'What the fuck happened here?'

'By the look of it,' the reporter speculated, 'our fighters strafed the train and the Germans finished off those who survived the attack as they retreated.'

'Finished off?' I was struggling to find words through my rage. 'Why? Why would they do such a thing? These are civilians. Why would they shoot their own people?'

'Not their people: Jews.'

'They were being brought to the camp,' said a second photographer who had appeared from behind the train.

'What fucking camp?' I said, trying to get my head round what I was seeing.

'That one.' He pointed across the open ground to a fence in the treeline. I looked back along the line of carriages. They were all the same: the same heart-breaking cargo, inside and out.

I walked back to my platoon, which had gathered by the final carriage. Their faces looked as white as the MP's had.

'Why would they do this, Sarge?' asked one of the drivers, tears dripping from his chin. 'In God's name, why?'

I didn't have an answer for him. The journalist had told me how it had happened – those who had survived an air attack had been executed on the platform – but could anyone really tell us why?

'What do we do, Rob?' Peter asked, his eyes glazed and bloodshot. He was past trying to hide his tears.

I realized the entire platoon was staring at me, looking for a lead. I swallowed hard, trying to keep myself from breaking down. My voice shook as I issued orders. 'We have a job to do. Peter, take the lads and fetch the vehicles, please. Park them in front of the treeline, unless you can find a way into the camp.' They all nodded, returning to the trucks.

Knowing my section commanders would organize things, I followed the crowd of journalists and British soldiers towards the trees. I noticed bodies strewn at the roadside. Most were clothed in normal civilian attire, but some wore filthy blue and white striped suits, resembling prison clothes. They looked almost skeletal. I walked over to one corpse wearing a striped suit. A faded yellow star of cloth was crudely sewn onto it. The sign of Judaism. The Star of David. Their death warrant.

I heard my trucks rumble into life but kept walking towards the treeline. The trees were quite sparse in places. Beyond them stood a barbed-wire fence. A number of bodies hung from the fence. On the ground below them, inside the camp on the other side of the fence, were row upon row of semi-naked people – living people, although living skeletons would have been a better description. Some were sitting, some standing weakly. As I walked slowly between the fence and the trees, a sea of dark sunken eyes fixed on me. It felt like the inhabitants of a cemetery had clambered out of their graves to watch me.

The rows of living dead continued unbroken all the way to a gate, where my convoy of trucks was waiting. The camp had all the markings of an establishment designed by architects of the

Reich. Excellent timber barracks overlooked by well-built watch-towers, all seemingly now devoid of the bastards that had guarded the place. I made my way over to the British troops guarding the entrance. Journalists were queuing up, showing their passes, the soldiers waving them through. I realized I had no documentation on me, apart from my pay book, notebook and map. 'Sergeant.' One of the soldiers greeted me with a nod.

I scratched my chin and then waved at the trucks pulled up behind me. 'Good morning. I'm from 2nd Ox and Bucks. I've been told to deliver a laundry and shower unit to this facility.'

He looked at the trucks, then went into a sentry box. I saw him pick up a phone. 'Don't suppose you know what this place is, do you?' asked a second soldier.

I shook my head.

'Nazi concentration camp,' he replied deadpan. 'Belsen, should hell ever have a name.'

'Nazi what?'

'Concentration camp.'

'They brought people here to murder them?'

He looked me square in the eye and said something I would never forget. 'In here murder was an escape from the madness. If you were unlucky, you were just left to perish.'

Unlucky, I repeated to myself grimly. That was one word for it.

The other soldier returned from his phone call. 'Right then, Sergeant. They're expecting you. They'll send someone down to collect you and your men, but I must brief you on what you must and must not do in here. Could you please call your men in? I need to brief everyone.'

It took a while to gather my entire platoon around the soldier who had made the phone call, who began reading verbatim from a clipboard. '"Please ensure your weapons are unloaded. Only Royal Army Medical Corps personnel are allowed to be in possession of loaded weapons . . ."'

'Why is that?' I interrupted, curious. I couldn't remember the last time my Sten had been unloaded, apart from when I cleaned the thing.

'We have SS soldiers and medics working here,' explained the soldier with the clipboard, 'helping clean up the mess they made. The last thing we need is people taking it out on them. They will be dealt with in due course.' He continued reading. ' "Do not feed, touch or approach the patients. You are at extremely high risk of killing them with food, and in return catching lice, typhus and dysentery . . ." '

'Feed them?' Jack Lillie wondered.

'They're starving,' answered the soldier. 'The doctors in the camp are slowly trying to get food into them. Please don't feed them, no matter how much they beg, and whatever you do, don't go in the huts.' He resumed reading: ' "There are German civilians assisting us with removal of the dead. Do not fraternize with them. They have been pressed to clear up the mess they initiated. More are arriving from the nearby town today, and they too are not to be fraternized with." '

'So the Germans sent Jewish people here to die?' Chris Lenor asked.

'Not just Jews,' answered the soldier with the clipboard. 'Gypsies. Homosexuals, Jehovah's Witnesses, anyone they didn't like.'

'Here they come,' his mate announced.

Two captains approached. They returned the sentries' salutes, then mine. One captain shook my hand, his cap badge Royal Army Medical Corps. 'Thank you, Sergeant. Lord knows we need you. We can start getting these poor souls cleaned up.'

'No problem, sir,' I replied. 'Never seen anything like this before.'

He grunted, casting an eye along the rows of skeletal people lining the fence. 'None of us has. Reports say this camp is tiny compared to a huge one the Russians discovered in the east, which is about the size of a small city, so I'm told.'

'There are more camps?' I said in disbelief.

He nodded. 'The Americans are coming across a few in the south. The Nazis have a lot to answer for. No point getting twisted up by it all, though. We're here to try and save these people.' Not far along the fence one of the living dead collapsed. The captain shook his head. 'We're losing thousands per day. Some are just too far gone. I'm sure some are just letting go because the nightmare is over for them. Can we get your vehicles inside? And whatever you do, don't get in the faces of any SS. Among other things, they're guarding some of the compounds we have yet to unlock. If we open those compounds, the patients in them will get out before we're ready, and the threat of typhus is very real.' I was numbed by it all. We were surrounded by cruelty, starvation and disease.

The convoy moved inside the camp gates. The laundry and shower unit was taken off our hands, and I went off alone again. The camp was a real horror show. Dead and barely living were slumped side by side in the open, the majority naked. Some of the skeletal living were sitting up, but others looked past the point where they cared if they lived or died, and many were already past help. Fire licked out of old oil drums, which were being fed with filthy camp uniforms.

Rows of wooden barracks, half-sunk into the ground, sat in neat rows. A pile of bodies lay outside each hut. British medics moved in and out, every now and again adding another body to the ever-growing piles of human tragedy.

I thought I heard the screech and rattle of a tank beyond the huts. But as I picked my way through towards the sound, I realized it was a bulldozer. It sat stationary beside another, which was excavating a long, wide trench. The trench was being filled with bodies. Remembering that the captain had mentioned there were compounds yet to be opened, I realized there must be thousands, perhaps tens of thousands of murdered people in the camp. I struggled to believe there could be camps similar to this one, or even bigger. British soldiers supervised civilians and German soldiers working in pairs next to the bulldozer. Each pair was carrying a body to the edge of the trench and throwing the pathetic bundle in. Some of the civilians were women. I heard movement behind me, only now realizing some members of my platoon had followed me. They instinctively raised their weapons towards the Germans, even though our guns had all been unloaded.

I soon realized the futility of the captain's words about not getting twisted up. If the pairs of German soldiers and civilians let up their pace for a moment, the British troops stepped forward to give them a little push or shove. I remembered the words of the man with the clipboard: the SS, German medics and civilians were being used to clear up the mess they had made. I knew how efficient the Germans were. The camp must have necessitated a lot of administration, and I'd heard the Nazis often gave civilians supporting roles. And now those civilians were here working in pairs to bury their crime.

A British soldier nudged a civilian woman to speed her up. Dressed as though she was going to a dance, she challenged him. He slapped her hard in the face. She staggered back to the edge of the trench, still looking up at him. A few nearby German soldiers froze. She composed herself and spun round, hands clasping her face. Then holding out a hand, she began sobbing in German to the sea of dead in the trench. The British soldier moved forward, kicking her up the arse, sending her head first into the trench.

A few boys in my platoon stepped forward, soon followed by others. Before I knew it, we were walking towards the trench. What was I to do? She had clearly worked at the camp and must have known what was going on all around her. But the inhumanity shown by the British soldier was also far from right. She was retching, wailing, screaming and ranting. Around her a group of sightless, skeletal children stared back at her. We gathered around the trench, other British and German soldiers also watching her. A couple of SS leaned forward, offering their hands, but she was out of reach. A few of the supervising British soldiers raised their weapons, prompting the SS to step back from the edge. I realized the British were Royal Army Medical Corps, the only soldiers permitted to wield loaded weapons in the camp. The woman stood, awkwardly balancing on the bodies. She took a step towards the edge of the trench, but fell, ending up on her back. An RAMC sergeant stepped forward. 'Get back to whatever you were doing, everyone,' he bellowed. 'Let her get herself out of there.'

She looked straight at me. I suddenly realized I felt no sympathy for her nor for any German, civilian or otherwise. They had all backed the Nazi regime, and the camp, the ultimate statement of what that regime stood for, had pushed me beyond caring. Now I wanted revenge even more. I turned away, my platoon beginning to do the same.

Time to finish it.

12
Countdown to Victory

Everything felt different after Belsen. Even those who hadn't been there heard about it and there was a collective urgency, a desire to win quickly and wipe out the evil we'd witnessed. We still met pockets of opposition as we advanced – the Luftwaffe unexpectedly strafed us on the road to Nettelkamp – but the resistance felt weaker as we progressed deeper into Germany, through Emern, Kahlstorf and Roche.

And then one afternoon we got orders to clear a village called Polau, just about twenty-five kilometres short of the Elbe. Reconnaissance reported German forces in the village. Orders came to us thick and fast: the Russians were advancing from the east and we were told not to hang around. Such was the speed of our march towards Polau, I worried we were sacrificing tactical caution for speed.

Over a kilometre of open ground lay between us and the village, with only sparse hedgerows for cover. Major High decided the advance would be safest if the village was shelled, so our tanks stayed back, firing with artillery support. He also believed the woods beyond Polau were tactically important; we needed to keep enemy heads down in the village to prevent them from escaping, as well as keeping reinforcements from reaching them.

As the bombardment from the tanks and artillery ceased, Serjeant Sean Wardle's platoon accompanied mine into Polau, everyone advancing cautiously. The dwellings on the edge of the village were clear of Germans, but we unexpectedly ran into fire from a 20-millimetre flak gun sited in a house. Corporal Ray Clifton's section tried to silence the gun, but were driven back, suffering a few minor injuries. Supported by smoke grenades, Sean's steely-eyed platoon were then sent forward to destroy the gun, only to discover it was supported by two MG 42 positions and a large group of infantry.

Sean's platoon engaged the enemy. Grenade detonations, crashing glass and loud shouts in English and German indicated fighting in and around the house, the childish sound of German voices signifying they were Hitler Youth. One of the MG 42s was eliminated, but despite the poor calibre of the opposition, Sean's men were forced to retreat, suffering a few wounded. Major High called two of the Churchill tanks forward, but one was rendered useless by a Panzerfaust anti-tank gun. Under a hail of automatic fire, the smouldering tank crew needed help from Sean's platoon to bail out. The other Churchill fired a tank round at the house where the 20-millimetre was set up.

The flak gun fell silent, so I dashed forward into the house. The gunner sat dead in his firing seat, coated in brick dust, blood already drying across his face. His three colleagues had been blown into the garden; two were dead, one rolling around groaning. I realized the house opposite contained the remaining MG 42 position and waved Peter May's section forward. The MG 42 position was hit hard with Bren, Sten and Lee-Enfield fire, but we couldn't flush it out. Then, undoubtedly enraged by the Panzerfaust attack and probably by what he'd heard about Belsen, the commander of the second tank ordered it into the gardens, his Churchill crushing fences and sheds, before putting white phosphorus rounds into the house shielding the MG 42.

Germans started pouring out of the house and its wooden outbuildings in an attempt to escape, prompting the tank commander to fire long scything bursts with his machine gun. What was left of a window burst, revealing the gyrating bodies of the MG 42 crew being mashed to a pulp. The commander didn't discriminate: civilians, outhouses and soldiers, probably including the Panzerfaust crew, were blown to smithereens without remorse until only the quiet throbbing of the tank engine could be heard over the crackling, burning mess.

As the guns fell silent, no one realized that we'd just fought our last action.

It was confirmed the following morning. Major High stood in front of what was left of the Ox and Bucks and issued the order most of us would remember for the rest of our lives: '6th Airborne Division are to make safe their weapons and remain in current positions until further notice.' There was a cheer and he held up his hands for silence. 'All division vehicles are to be off main transit routes, as British and American follow-on units will be moving through to take the lead.'

The war had to be almost over.

Over the next few days British and American units poured through Polau. We heard lead units were pursuing what remained of the once mighty German Army. For us the days were filled with sleeping and washing. Then we advanced again, from Ebstorf, then thirty kilometres north-east to Suttorf, where we caught up with our 3rd and 5th Parachute Brigades, before using a Bailey bridge to cross the Elbe and settling down for the night in the small hamlet of Buchhorst. Finally we reached a place called Nostorf, and there we met the enemy again.

Their weapons were neatly organized in piles on the main square, where groups of them sat around drinking and smoking, singing German Army songs. They were *Wehrmacht*, not SS. One German soldier wobbled up the street with a bottle of champagne in each hand, his tunic undone. He did a double-take of me in the glare of headlights from a halftrack, and snapped to attention. 'Breet-ish Tom-mee.' He belched. 'I surrender.' He fell through some bushes, his comrades rolling around in fits of laughter.

Falling straight to sleep, only his legs protruded. It reminded me of a Saturday night in Richmond, never mind Nazi Germany.

By late morning we had gathered up the drunks for transition to PoW camps in trucks. Most were still singing, but the jollity was muted by hangovers. Most shook hands with us, tears in their eyes, glad they had survived the war.

We camped in Nostorf for a few days. Setting up patrols, we imposed a night curfew on the locals. We searched every cellar, finding some weapons and ammunition but not enough for an uprising. The town was pretty much untouched by the war, and by day the locals went about their business as though nothing had happened. Some went to church. They even challenged us to a game of football. It was with a little sadness that we got orders to march through the night to a place called Schwartow, just over five kilometres to the east. Leaving under cover of darkness, we left our ball and all our chocolate on the doorsteps of the young footballers.

At Schwartow we encountered thousands of civilians on the roads, laden with all they could carry. The road often became jammed, our progress painfully slow. As we moved on, German soldiers appeared more and more often among the civilians, everyone heading west. Some of the enemy soldiers even gave us friendly waves. A few grinding hours closer to Wismar I heard cheering coming from the front of our column. We stopped. Leaving the trucks, we poured onto the fields. Everyone craned their necks to see what was going on.

Hundreds of British personnel straggled along the roadside. They appeared a little underweight, but were dancing, shouting and cheering. It suddenly dawned on me that our parachute brigades had freed them from a PoW camp. Questioning established why German civilians and soldiers were packing the roads: they were fleeing from the Russian advance, which was closing on Berlin from the east. The Russians were on the march and out for revenge.

I wanted revenge too, particularly after Belsen, and part of me hoped the Russians would slaughter everyone in Germany, but then I found myself remembering the towns and villages we'd passed through on our advance: the girl buried in the rubble, the footballing youths of Nostorf, those ordinary people who had fallen victim to the concentration camps, even the German soldiers who had so openly welcomed the end of the war. Perhaps revenge could wait. It deserved to be meted out on those who were responsible for the horrors of Belsen and they weren't on the front line.

13
The Greatest Day

We never made Wismar. The roads were too busy, so we ended up stopping for the night in a town called Lutterstorf, a few kilometres short. The next day, after a short truck journey from Wismar to the south-east, we stopped at Bad Kleinen, a town on the shores of Lake Schwerin. We were greeted by what looked like a nightmare: a large force of fresh, fit-looking and very well-supplied German troops assembled in the town centre. However, after salutes and handshakes between senior officers, it transpired the troops wanted to surrender, and to us rather than the Russians.

On 8 May 1945 the 2nd Battalion of the Oxfordshire and Buckinghamshire Light Infantry was ordered to form up in the town square. The weather was good. The lake spread out to the south and east. Most of us had taken at least one gorgeous swim in it. The commanding officer of the regiment, a colonel, was introduced. 'Relax, gentlemen. Please stand at ease.' We complied as he cleared his throat. 'Gentlemen, the armed forces of Nazi Germany have surrendered.'

There were loud gasps and sighs of relief. In front of me, some of the lads of C Company lowered their heads, their bouncing shoulders giving away their sobs. No one mocked them. They were hard men, but they were also human. Some broke ranks. Arms were put around shoulders. I looked at Sean Wardle. He too was struggling to hold himself together.

'According to German and Russian authorities,' continued the colonel, 'Hitler has escaped capture and justice by taking his own life. The very man that promised his people world domination has now left his shattered Reich dominated by foreign armies, something I find quite ironic.' That complemented a thought that had been with me for some time: it wasn't lost on me that the German people had responded to Hitler's promise by supporting his regime.

'We must now take time to reflect,' philosophized the colonel, 'but more importantly we must take the time to learn. Most of you standing here have been through some trying and challenging times in the last year or so. Some of you were tested at the beginning of all this madness in 1940. Some of you have not been with us as long. But we are as one, regardless of pedigree and prestige. You can be proud of what you've achieved and the battle we've won here today.'

I thought of Arnhem and Normandy, which all seemed a very long time ago. The colonel was right: we had come a long way. I tried to picture myself during my first deployment into Normandy, a green and untried private. Almost all of the people I had fought with in the Netherlands and France were dead, but somehow I had got through it all, a veteran soldier now. A lucky soldier. I wondered when my luck would run out. Would I be called upon to fight again? Would Molly still be waiting for me? Would she marry me and would we live in Mortlake near my folks? My dreams floated before me like a mist: Molly and I walking along the Thames, a baby in a pram . . . I smiled to myself. I liked the picture. It was the picture I'd fought for. It was the picture I'd not dared to think about until it was over. And now it was. Finally the war was over. We'd fought from the beaches of Normandy via the bridges of the Netherlands to the villages of Germany. We'd left friends and enemies dead. We'd fought and we'd won. And now we were going home.